TRIONRISING

Other books by Robert Elmer

The Wall series:
Candy Bombers (Book One)
Beetle Bunker (Book Two)
Smuggler's Treasure (Book Three)

Visit Robert Elmer's website at *www.RobertElmerbooks.com*

To my son, Kai Elmer –
An eagle-eyed editor and creative advisor

ZONDERVAN®

Trion Rising
Copyright © 2008 by Robert Elmer

Requests for information should be addressed to:

Zondervan, *Grand Rapids, Michigan 49530*

Library of Congress Cataloging-in-Publication Data: Applied for
ISBN 978-0-310-71421-7

Published in association with the literary agency of Alive Communications, Inc., 7680 Goddard Street #200, Colorado Springs, CO 80920. www.alivecommunications.com

All Scripture quotations, unless otherwise indicated, are taken from the *Holy Bible: New International Version®. NIV®.* Copyright © 1973, 1978, 1984 by International Bible Society. Used by permission of Zondervan. All rights reserved.

Interior design by Michelle Espinoza

Printed in the United States of America

08 09 10 11 12 13 • 22 21 20 19 18 17 16 15 14 13 12 11 10 9 8 7 6 5 4 3 2 1

TRION RISING

ROBERT ELMER

ZONDERVAN®

ZONDERVAN.com/
AUTHORTRACKER
follow your favorite authors

When the Trion sets below the Plains of Izula,
you will know the end of the age is near.
~ Codex 47:9

BENEATH
TRION'S SHADOW

I thought you said you knew how to fly this thing!"

"I did. I do. Trust me."

Easy for him to say. Oriannon could only grip her stiff bucket seat with both hands and count down the final seconds of her young life. She cringed at the buzz of a high-pitched warning.

"On present course, nine seconds to impact," came the metallic warning voice. "Eight seconds ..."

Ori wondered how she had let Margus Leek talk her into sneaking aboard the little two-seat interplanetary pod. It was fast, but built for speed and certainly not comfort. If she stretched her arms even a little she would elbow the pilot.

"Relax, Orion." Margus Leek yanked the joystick to starboard, and their pod brushed by the antenna of a rather large telecommunications satellite. "I grew up flying these little things."

"Tell me why I don't feel any better." Oriannon tried not to scream as they buzzed by another piece of space debris—an old fuel tank—leaving it spinning in their wake. "And my name isn't—"

"I know, I know. Sorry. You don't have to tell me. It's Or-i-ANN-on." When he smiled, she could almost see his eyes twinkling through his scratched sun visor. "Oriannon, Oriannon. Don't know how I can forget a VIP passenger like the esteemed and honorable Oriannon Hightower of the Nyssa clan."

"It's just Oriannon, okay?" she told him. "Forget all the other names."

He laughed as they dipped below an orbiting solar collector, close enough to read the warning label on the underside. She closed her eyes and wondered what it would be like to grow up without all the baggage that came with being an elder's daughter. If her father wasn't an elite member of Corista's ruling Assembly —

But the impact buzzer sounded again, and she snapped her eyes back open.

"Whatever you say, Just Oriannon." Margus smiled again. "And don't worry. I'm watching where we're going."

Could have fooled me, Ori thought.

Now Margus readjusted his nav-system by passing his index finger across a colored grid screen and tapping in several coordinates from memory. The move doubled their speed and set them on a direct course to Regev, the largest of their world's three suns. Anything not strapped down, including Ori's lunch sack, crashed into the back of the small cargo area behind their seats.

"So how about a tour of the Trion?" asked Margus, sounding like a tour guide.

As they picked up even more speed, Ori frowned and twisted the family ring on her finger — the ring with the tiny, brilliant blue corundum stone set in the distinct diamond shape of Saius. As the second largest but most intense of their suns, the real Saius now filled her eyesight even more than it had back on the planet's surface.

Unfortunately, she could also smell overheating deflectors, like burning rubber. Did he really have to jerk them around so much? This time the impact alarm insisted they veer away from a restricted zone.

"Immediately!" screeched the buzzer voice.

"What's that all about?" asked Oriannon. Margus silenced it with a tap to the flashing amber screen.

"No problem, Your Highness," he told her just before they flew straight into a blinding white light and every alarm in the pod went off at once.

"Margus!" Oriannon held a forearm to her face, but that did not help her as they tumbled out of control in a maelstrom of warning lights and screeching alarms. So this was how her life would end? She broke out in a sweat and gagged at the nose-burning smell of fried electronics.

"Do something!" Oriannon cried. She coughed and held on as the inside of the pod warmed to sizzling. In the blinding light she couldn't even make out Margus sitting next to her.

"Just a sec," mumbled Margus. And as quickly as the light had overpowered them, it suddenly blinked out, leaving them spinning slowly, silently, and in the dark. A lone alarm buzzed once then died to a pitiful whimper.

"Are you going to tell me what just happened?" Ori slowly lowered her arm and blinked her eyes, but the horrible flash of light and heat still echoed in her eyesight. It would take several moments to get used to normal space light once more. Margus shook his head and tapped at the control panel in front of him, as if he were trying to wake it back up. A few of the dials flickered, but not all.

"Weirdest thing I've ever seen." He looked around and behind them. "I think we got caught between two of those big solar reflectors, and—"

"And what?"

"And, uh, it's probably a good thing we didn't stay back there." He jerked his thumb and tapped the instrument panel once more. "Looks like it cooked us a little."

A little? Ori swallowed hard, wishing she could just stop this ride and get out right there.

"Look, Margus," she finally whispered, choking back the bitterness that curled her tongue. "I don't know what we're doing here, and my dad's really going to be upset with us when we land. *If* we land. We've got to turn around right now."

"That's the one thing we can't do." Margus was sweating under his silver flight helmet visor too. "We can't go back that way. Better just enjoy the view. There's the Trion, see?"

The Trion — which meant "three lights" in the ancient Coristan tongue — was made up of three suns. Regev, a red giant, never blinked as it cast a perpetual rosy glow over the brightside of Corista. This rosy glow was offset by the white-blue of Saius, a much brighter and more intense flame. Between the two suns, the Brightside of Corista never saw darkness. Heliaan — the smallest, distant yellow sun some people missed — stayed in the background. Together the three suns joined to create the flickering violet hue of the pretty Coristan sky, though it had turned darker the higher they climbed.

But right now Oriannon wasn't impressed. She peered up through the clear plexi bubble over their heads, the only barrier between them and the cold vacuum of space and the searing light of one of those space mirrors.

"You sure we can't just go back?" she asked, shaking off her jitters.

"I'll get us back, Your Highness." By this time he'd removed a panel and was yanking out circuits. "Just have to override a couple systems, and we'll be good to go. My dad showed me how to do this once."

"While you were up here?"

He paused a moment before answering.

"Uh, no. Back in his shop. But it should work."

So he wrestled with the controls as they bounced from one space mirror to the next, ducking behind them to avoid being fried all over again. Margus touched one wire to another, showering sparks in his lap but firing the ship's thrusters as they glided — the long way — between the orbits of their home world and eleven other distant moons, all circling the big planet.

"I never knew there were this many of these mirror things up here." Ori braced for the next deflector bump.

"Must be hundreds of them," Margus said as he nodded. "I just don't get what they're for. There's something strange about all this."

Strange wasn't quite the right word. But all Oriannon could do was look out the window as they dodged the curved mirrors, each one many times bigger than their little pod. She couldn't pretend to care about the stunning view Margus had promised before they took off on this horrible ride. But if she cared to look, Oriannon would have seen the lush green landscape of Corista below, bathed in the trebly bright light of their three suns.

In fact, if she had cared to, she could recite every detail of the landscape. Sometimes her eidich's memory came in handy, if she could just put aside all the mental baggage that crowded her brain with bits and details, faces and names, trivia and conversations that would never go away.

The Plains of Izula reminded her of a quilt her grandmother Merta had once showed her, decorated by patchwork fields of grain and orchards of every colored fruit a person could imagine: trees loaded with golden aplon, deep purple pluq, and her favorite, the lip-puckering orange simquats. And when she finally looked down, she couldn't help catching her breath at the forest green, myrtle green, emerald green, fern and sea green, lime green, moss green, deep cobalt green, viridian-that-matched-her-eyes green, olive, and everything-in-between green. Here it stretched all the way to the horizon, which wasn't far in this tiny, well-watered garden planet, Corista.

And there! In the Highlands, not far from the boundary between light and dark, was Seramine, perched like a jewel in the jade crown. Seramine, the capital city, her city. Were they finally getting closer? Even at this height she could imagine how the bright windows of grand whitewashed palaces and halls seemed to catch blue and red rays of sun, winking back at her. Did they know she was up here watching?

Once more, they bumped off the back side of another orbiting mirror, sending them spinning into the clear. Oriannon instinctively gripped the handle next to her seat, ready for anything.

"Sorry." Margus pointed ahead. "But see? I think we're all clear now."

"Wonderful." Maybe she didn't sound as enthused as he would have liked. "I'm still thinking about what my dad's going to say."

"I thought you said he was always too worried about Assembly stuff to pay much attention to you. Is he really going to worry about one little borrowed pod?"

"You don't know my dad. And the pod—are you sure you can land this thing now?"

She adjusted the headset of her comm and went back to peering out through the hard-shell bubble—just before a new screech of warning alarms pierced the tiny cockpit.

"So it needs a little maintenance." Margus shrugged and replaced a circuit panel, bringing back the lights while spewing a plume of smoke at her feet. Oriannon could only hold her hands over her head and close her eyes. She hoped it would all just go away, and soon.

But once more the pod jolted and lurched to the side. And as Margus grappled with the controls, they once more spun out of control, falling like a delicate cerulean flower petal through the edge of the atmosphere. Even without looking she could feel the heat radiating from the bubble above their heads, but this time the fabric of her silver coveralls kicked in with coolant that flowed through its built-in blue tubing. If they were going to die in this little pod, at least they would die comfortably.

"I think," she moaned, trying to ignore the butterflies in her stomach. "I think I'm going to be sick."

"You might want to hold off on that a few minutes, Your Highness." Besides that infuriating grin of his, he could also sound infuriatingly cocky. Maybe that's why she liked him, though she'd never admit it. After a few minutes the shuttle spun a final time, then rocked from side to side like a hammock, before the scream of wind around the cockpit told Oriannon they'd dropped back down into Corista's violet atmosphere.

"Forty-eight thousand klicks," announced Margus, as they swooped ever lower, leaning dangerously to the side. And now he could have almost passed for a Coristan shuttle pilot, instead of a fifteen-year-old impostor who had hijacked the little pod for a silly joyride. "Forty ... no, wait."

He tapped on a dial with the palm of his hand. That dial wasn't working, either.

"Margus—"

"No worries." Didn't he ever worry about anything? "We don't really need that thing. It's just for show."

"I don't believe you, but listen—"

He looked over at her with his eyebrows arched, waiting for her to finish.

"Thanks." She finally got the word out.

"What, for getting you into trouble or for almost killing you?"

"No." She shook her head. "For not giving up."

He shrugged. "No wor—"

"Don't say it." She interrupted him. But it didn't matter now as they finally slipped into a landing pattern, a lineup of incoming shuttles and pods—each separated by only a few meters and held in place by point-to-point tractor beams. Oriannon wished she could slump just a little lower in her seat so the pilot in the larger shuttle behind them wouldn't recognize her. But she could hear every word that now crackled over the comm line, which seemed to work.

"You're out of order, Bravo One-Nine," came the voice over the comm. That would be the guy in the shuttle. And it sounded just like someone complaining that Margus cut into the lunch line at school.

"Sorry," Margus responded through his own headset. "We've got mechanical problems. Need to touch down right away."

"Stand by," came the voice again, and a moment later the shadow of the much-larger ship hovered over them, and they felt the lurch of a grappling pad pulling them up.

"Hey, ah ..." Margus got back on the comm line. "We don't really need a tow."

We could have used one a long time ago, thought Oriannon.

"Relax," the voice told them. "We'll have you back to port in just a minute."

Or ten. Either way, Oriannon held her breath until landing thrusters screamed and she felt a comforting *thump* as they finally landed, upside-down, in the midst of Spaceport Corista. While the engines wound down, a beehive of workers in blue coveralls bustled around the ships, attaching power cables and fluid exchangers, rolling up with floating lev-carts full of tools.

"So how do we get out of here without anybody seeing us?" she wondered aloud, raising her voice to be heard over the scream of still more engines.

"Too late for that." Margus hit the canopy control so it lifted clear with a whoosh of air. "Follow my lead."

"That's what got us into trouble in the first place," Ori mumbled, but she climbed out after Margus, and they hopped down to the tarmac. Her knees buckled for a moment as she readjusted to the planet's light gravity.

"Coming?" Margus already had a step or two on her as they hustled past dozens of parked shuttles, pods, and cargo ships. They nearly made it to the hangar exit when one of the workers caught up with them.

"You! We didn't get your flight plan download." A tall Coristan with typical olive-colored skin and typical sunshades tapped his clipboard. "In fact, looks like you were flying through a restricted area, and I don't even have an original flight plan for your unit. It's still in the maintenance pool."

"I know." Margus had to crane his neck to look up at the worker. He inched toward the exit as they spoke. "We just had it out to test the systems."

"You know that's not how we do things. But, hey—" The worker crossed his arms and looked them over a little more closely. "Aren't you Supervisor Leek's kid?"

By this time Oriannon was ready to melt through a crack in the concrete floor.

"Uh . . ." Margus had to be looking for a way out too. "We were on assignment from the Assembly."

Oh, Margus, she thought, *anything but that.*

And sure enough, the worker threw his head back and laughed, long and hard.

"Nice try." He finally stopped laughing long enough to notice Oriannon, and it probably didn't do any good that she tried to look away. "You'll come with me to the office, and we'll . . ."

His voice trailed off, and he stared at Oriannon's hand. Her ring, actually.

"Like I was saying . . ." Margus tried to explain once more, but this time the wide-eyed worker waved him off.

"I didn't realize," he muttered, backing up a step. "Sorry to bother you. You know the way out?"

Margus looked at the guy with an expression that said *Huh?* But Oriannon knew exactly what had just happened. She answered for the both of them.

"We know the way. Thanks." And she didn't waste any more time chatting. But a quick glance up at the corner of the huge hangar area told her what she was afraid of: A small, grapefruit-sized security probe hovered like an eye in the sky, its red light telling her that it had not missed a thing. In fact, the small silver sphere had probably recorded every word of their conversation with the maintenance guy.

"That was cool!" whispered Margus as the double doors slid open for them. "What did you do, some kind of mind control?"

She fingered the ring. "Something like that."

Only problem was, she knew that what had spooked the hangar worker wasn't going to impress her father.

And the trouble, she told herself, *hasn't even begun.*

17

2

Oriannon woke from her daily two-hour sleep cycle with a jerk, holding her hands up, gasping for air, and whimpering like a baby. All her sheets had been tossed to the floor in a heap.

"Aren't you going to school today?" Her father knocked gently on the sliding door to her room. It would have opened if Oriannon had set it to automatic. "I've been hearing a lot of noise in there."

"Up in a second." She was, and instantly her window's tint lightened to let in more Coristan sunlight. Two hours for a daily sleep cycle, then up again for twenty, and that was it. Nobody really needed three hours, the way her father always told her. Who wanted to waste more time sleeping than she had to?

She checked her handheld for any messages—nothing interesting except a couple of gossipy notes from her girlfriend Brinnin Flyer—before quickly rubbing her face under the spigot of a sonic cleanser, running her hands through her tousled black hair, and shuffling out to the great room. This time, she thought, maybe it was better to leave her ring back on her dresser.

"Hey there, sleeping beauty." Her dad was already dressed and eating his third-hour meal: aploncakes garnished with pungent green parse. And he wore his usual go-to-meeting clothes: freshly pressed white linen slacks and a pullover robe the color of the sky, edged with the silver trim of his high office. So the Assembly would be meeting again today. They'd been meeting a lot lately. He studied her over a mug of steaming clemsonroot tea.

Did he know?

"Must have been dreaming this last cycle," she mumbled, pouring herself some tea. Sweetened up and with several teaspoons of cream, it wasn't so bitter really. Her hand shook, and she poured a big puddle right onto the polished pluqwood table.

"Careful there!" Her father scooted out of his chair to keep from being spilled on, while a biomouse instantly flitted out to suction up the spill.

For a moment Ori thought she actually remembered a dream, though of course she never did. She imagined that she saw herself falling out of the sky with Margus Leek, screaming, hitting way markers, and crashing through satellite mirrors that burned her skin with a horrible hissing sound. They both tumbled down into the dark night of Shadowside, landing hard on their backs. They landed so hard that biomice came to pick up the pieces.

"Ori?"

She cleared her head and looked over at her father. She checked her arm to make sure it wasn't burned, set down the teakettle, and tried to ignore the pesky little biomouse as best she could. She had never cared for the little creatures—half mouse and half kitchen appliance—but they did the job well.

"Sorry."

"I thought we lost you there for a minute. You still look a thousand klicks away."

If he only knew. He looked at her, as if waiting for something.

"I'm okay. Just a little tired." She considered telling him everything about what happened yesterday. He should hear it from her, no matter what would happen to her if she did. She even started to open her mouth, and then changed her mind when their housekeeper, Mrs. Eraz, hurried into the kitchen, leather case in hand.

"Now you two be sure to grab some lunch out of the—Oh!" The small wiry woman looked at the mess on the table. "Someone had a little accident here?"

"It's nothing." Oriannon's father dropped his napkin on top of the stain. "You go ahead to your next house. We're both about to leave."

Mrs. Eraz stopped for a moment, long enough to frown at both of them, but shrugged before heading out the door with a wave.

"I'm late!" She glanced at her bracelet, which had already begun to glow pink-red, a different color for each hour of the daily cycle. Oriannon still didn't know how the older woman managed to tell the time with that old thing. Much easier with the contact lenses people wore now, with time and temperature readouts in the corner of the field of view.

But never mind. The wood-paneled door slipped closed behind their housekeeper, sealing off the rest of the home from the day's heat, already hot enough to make Ori sweat. Oriannon's father stood as well, but turned to face his daughter.

"Ori," Here it came. She could tell by the husky tone of his voice. "I had a chat last night with my friend Thomaii at Security. You know him."

She nodded without looking up. Her father went on.

"And you know what we were talking about, don't you?"

Again she nodded, and this time peeked up to see him standing there, chin in hand. She took a deep breath.

"I was going to tell you, honest. But Mrs. Eraz was rushing around, and—"

He held up a finger of warning, and she almost bit her tongue.

"I don't need to hear any of it. All you need to know is that's the last time you'll be taking joy rides with that boy ... what's his name, Leek?"

"Margus. He's okay."

"Okay and irresponsible. He could have gotten you into more trouble than you can imagine, and it's not going to happen again."

"Just by flying through that field of—"

"Stop." He cut her off with a shake of his head. "I do not want to hear about where you two went, and you don't want to tell me. Believe me. Not another word."

"What? Dad, I'm just trying to tell you that it wasn't my fault." She paused to catch her breath at the lie. "Not totally."

"It doesn't matter whose fault it was, Oriannon. What you did was dangerous. But more than that, the Leeks are simply not the kind of people with whom you should associate. Period. You know what's written. You of all people know what it says."

Yes, she did—every page, every verse of the sacred Codex. Name a chapter and she would start at the top. How could she forget? But ask her what it meant, and that was a little different. She sighed.

"Dad, I'm sorry. I just don't see how it makes any sense that some families are 'in' and some families are 'out' just because of that old story in the Codex."

Her father squeezed his eyes shut and cradled his head in his hands, as if the words hurt him, especially coming from his own daughter.

"Oriannon, Oriannon. You're an eidich, and you still don't understand?"

"I understand that the Leeks are nice people, and being an eidich has nothing to do with that. You just write them off because of what you think the Codex says."

"That's enough. I will not have my own daughter questioning the Codex."

"I'm not, Dad. I just don't think it says—"

"No more!" When he raised his voice the veins in his temples stood out, until he caught his breath again and he reached out toward Oriannon. "Listen. I have to leave. I trust this is the last time we'll talk about it."

She pressed her lips together and bit her tongue.

"And you'll say nothing about this to anyone else. Especially not about where you two went. There are things up there none of us should know about, and I'm only thinking of your own safety. Understood?"

"Why won't you tell me what you're protecting me from?" But she knew it was no use asking as her father turned toward the front door.

"Don't be late for class," he told her.

And then it sunk in, she'd been handed no punishment, no being grounded for the next two hundred years. Just don't talk about where you've been and stay away from that Leek kid.

Margus couldn't help it, though, if his family was considered beneath the Hightowers. He couldn't help what was written in the ancient book of the Codex, book twelve, verses fifteen and sixteen, where it was written that one of his far-removed ancestors had once been a servant in the House of Hightower.

Of course, her father knew all that. He should, being a member of Corista's Assembly. The question was, what could she do about it now? She asked herself that question as she stepped up to the glass-paneled front entry of her school ten minutes later.

"I'm even early to class, Dad," she mumbled to herself and paused for a moment as the little hovering security probe swept her eyes with a shaky red laser beam.

"State your name," it demanded, as it always did. Same voice, same way. She refused to look straight at the probe, which was enhanced with an animal's eyeball, plugged right into a titanium socket in the side of the biomechanical hybrid. Ninety percent machine, ten percent spare parts, one hundred percent obnoxious. If it had a neck, she could just strangle it.

"State your name," it repeated, a little louder, a little closer.

"Oriannon Hightower of Nyssa, as if you didn't know."

Satisfied, it flashed a green entry light, her signal to go ahead.

"Please pause for a summary of today's classes," it told her, but she ignored the annoyance and hurried down the cool, tiled hallway. *Stupid probes.* Gracious limestone columns flanked her on either side, set off by arches that made the place resemble an ancient Coristan temple more than a prep school. But today she paid no attention to architecture. Her footsteps echoed down the nearly empty hall as she pushed to catch up with the boy who had just turned the corner ahead of her.

"Margus, wait!" she called. "I have to tell you something!"

She would have to obey her father, fair or unfair, and the probes would make sure of it. But at least she could tell Margus what happened that morning, couldn't she? When she turned the corner, though, Margus had already slipped into the main office. The door buzzed and locked shut in her face when she tried to follow him.

"I'm sorry," said a soothing digital female voice next to the door. "You're not scheduled for access at this time. If you feel an error has been made, please check your security code and try again. I'm sorry, you're not scheduled—"

"Heard you the first time," snapped Oriannon, and she punched a six-digit code into the keypad next to the door—one she knew would open the door no matter what. It did.

Only thing was, this time of the morning the school secretary still hadn't reported to her station. Oriannon stood in the front office alone, wondering which of a half dozen doors had swallowed her friend, maybe her *ex*-friend. And wondering why he hadn't been stopped.

In a moment another security probe would come snooping around the corner, alerted to her presence by a motion detector. Until then, she chose the first shaded window panel and leaned closer. This one? She should have been able to see through, but the first meeting room looked pitch dark.

She lifted her shades to see better, and tried the next set of windows, where a light flickered.

"There he is," she whispered, leaning close enough to touch her nose. On the other side, Margus Leek was sitting in a stiff-backed chair, watching the view screen where someone had queued up a video. Her mouth went dry as she recognized the oddly familiar scenes, and she cupped her ear to the glass with her hand to hear better.

"What were you thinking, Mr. Leek?" came the muffled voice of their headmaster, Mr. Knarl. "This is very serious, stealing an interlunar pod."

"We didn't steal it," replied Margus, his voice shaking, and not nearly as loud as the headmaster's. She pressed even closer. "We brought it back, all in one piece."

"We?" asked Headmaster Knarl. The video clearly showed Margus crawling out the top of the pod, just the way she remembered. But then the plexi bubble just closed back up, with no sign of Oriannon!

"Uh . . ." Margus sounded as dumb as Oriannon felt, watching the security film that had to have been changed, doctored, erased—as if Oriannon had never even been there. Who would have done this? And why?

Friend or no friend, this was too strange. And Oriannon knew she had to set things straight, no matter what, right now. She stepped around to the door just as a security probe caught sight of what she was trying to do and set off an alarm.

"Please back away from the door," warned the probe, hovering just over her shoulder. "Security breach! Please back away—"

The door slid open and she looked up at Headmaster Knarl, blocking the doorway with his arms crossed and his dark moustache twitching. *Knarl* had always seemed like such an appropriate name.

25

"What are you doing here, Oriannon?" he demanded. Margus looked around from behind the towering man, probably wondering the same thing.

"Security breach!" continued the drone. "Please back away from—"

"That's enough." Headmaster Knarl's deep-voice command stilled the probe.

"Clearance code alpha-two-five. Headmaster." The obedient probe turned away and headed down the hall to continue its rounds. But the principal was still far from satisfied.

"I was just ..." Oriannon had to spill it, and now. She took a breath. "I mean, I need to tell you that I was there on that pod yesterday too. It wasn't Margus's fault. Or it wasn't *just* his fault."

Why am I saying all this? Oriannon asked herself. From behind the headmaster, Margus was doing his best to shake his head and wave her off. She wasn't going to let him be a martyr, though. Not this time.

"Oh, really?" Headmaster Knarl never unfolded his arms, and the frown never left his face. When had it ever? He looked over his shoulder at the view screen in his office while the scene replayed Margus crawling out of the pod and hopping down on the landing mat. Margus, just Margus.

"That's right, sir." She went on, knowing she had to be digging her own grave. First with her father and now with the headmaster. "I don't know why it doesn't show on the replay, but I was there just as much as Margus was. If you're going to punish him, you should punish me too."

There. She said it, and it felt pretty good. He looked back at her, as if considering what she told him, though his raised eyebrows made him look as if he didn't believe a word of it, not for a moment.

"As much as I'd like to," he finally began, "I have no grounds to punish you today. Next time, though, okay? Remind me."

"But, Headmaster Knarl." She pointed at the screen. "Somebody must have messed with the security video. What you see is not what happened."

When he laughed it didn't really sound as if anything was funny. Rather, it made her shiver, and she still wasn't sure how a man could laugh without smiling.

"Nice try, Oriannon, but I think you've been reading too many spy stories. Believe me, I am disappointed I can't accommodate you, but I promise we'll work something out for you to be in some other kind of trouble—as soon as possible."

He probably meant it. Before she could find out, however, he had backed into his office and turned back to Margus as the door began to slowly self-close with a soft puff of air. She watched him as long as she could.

"And now, Mr. Leek," He rubbed his large hands together, and his eyes glittered with obvious pleasure. "Let's discuss your disciplination, shall we?"

Hey, Ori! Wait up!" Brinnin Flyer trotted up behind Oriannon, who had just passed her hand across the front panel of her locker to unlock it. "I hear your boyfriend got busted."

"Would you stop it already with the *boyfriend* thing?" Oriannon could just strangle her sometimes — Brinnin the schemer, Brinnin the sneak, Brinnin the ... But Oriannon wheeled around to face the other girl, lowering her voice to make sure no one else in the hallway could hear. "You *know* he's not my boyfriend."

Brinnin smiled in that crooked way of hers but didn't back down.

"How do I know that? You've been spending more time with him than you do with me lately. Your dad know?"

"Does now."

Brinnin raised her eyebrows and held up her hands like a mind reader.

"Ooo, I see a huge argument. I see Oriannon Hightower of Nyssa grounded for life. I see — "

"Stop. You're worse than Margus."

"So you *do* like him."

Oriannon displayed her best frown to show how displeased she was with Brinnin's act.

"Brinnin, when you grow up — *if* you ever grow up — you're going to be a professional pain. But it's not going to work this time."

"You're sure?" Again that crooked, conniving smile. "Because I just heard some really good dirt."

Oriannon sighed, parked her hands on her hips, and shook her head. Brinnin was impossible sometimes. A lot of times. Most times. But she also had the best ears in Regent Jib Ossek Preparatory Academy, so it was usually good to stay on her happy side. If there was a rumor worth hearing, Brinnin heard it first.

"Okay." Oriannon leaned back on her locker. "What did you hear?"

Though less than an hour had passed since Margus had been called into Headmaster Knarl's office, already Brinnin was spreading the news.

"He's getting detention after school, work detail, everything."

"But he didn't get expelled? I thought for sure — "

"So did I, but no. I don't know why not. I hear he stole a rovercraft, almost crashed it."

"Not a rovercraft." Oriannon shook her head to set things straight. "It was only a little — "

She bit her tongue. It would be better not to say so much, especially not to Brinnin.

"At least," Oriannon added quickly, "that's what I heard."

And with that she turned back to her locker to fetch her music pad and be on her way. No use being late to orchestra too. If Margus hadn't been kicked out of school, maybe she would see him there. But she stopped short. What was that in her locker? Before Brinnin could see, Ori slammed the door shut.

Brinnin ran off just then to spread more rumors so Oriannon didn't have to explain anything else — like, what was that earbud stuck to the inside of her locker door?

She waited for a moment while another couple of girls passed by, then scooted a little closer to her locker and opened it again, slowly. A TunePlayr? Not exactly, though it was obviously wireless, tiny enough to fit in her ear, and clear enough so no one would ever see it there.

Question was, who had put it there? She rolled it around in her hand, wondering. A TunePlayr would need an add-on controller; this one had none.

She was just about to toss it back into her locker when she felt it vibrate slightly, and when she held it up to her ear, a whisper of a voice called her name.

Hey, Ori!

What was that? A little closer still, and she could hear it clearly.

Just plug this thing into your ear, would you?

Margus! She looked around again to be sure no one else had noticed; by that time the hallways had nearly cleared. Only, where was the nearest security probe? She bent forward, her head nearly inside the locker, and plugged in the tiny earbud before brushing her long black hair around to cover her ear. There. Not even the probes would notice.

Finally! Now she could hear Margus clearly enough to almost make her believe he was standing next to her in the hall.

I've been waiting for you.

"What are you doing?" she whispered, covering her mouth with her hand. "I'm still by my locker, but where are you? What is this thing? Why weren't you expelled from school? Can you hear me?"

Whoa, whoa. I can hear you, all right? I wasn't expelled, and you don't have to talk. I'll explain everything later. But right now you're three minutes late to orchestra class. Did you forget? He laughed at his own joke. Oriannon? Forget? *The new mentor is about to call attendance, and if I were you I would get here in a hurry.*

Did he say the new mentor? Of course she had not forgotten, as her friends might have. That would not be possible. Eidichs didn't forget. She knew all about Mentor Noor having a baby and the substitute mentor starting this new term with them.

But something awful and foreign and foggy now hung at the back of her mind as she sprinted down the hall, like nothing she'd ever felt before. It made her shake her head, as if she could leave it behind or outrun it. Yet the fog hung on, chasing her from a distance. She even turned and looked back, just to be sure she couldn't see it.

Nothing. And what was she expecting? Seconds later she stepped up to the music room door, paused as it silently slid open, and did her best to not make a big entrance. It shouldn't have been too hard. Only a few students noticed her from their seats; almost all were busy preparing their instruments. She tiptoed past the boys in the percussion section tuning kettle drums, past woodwinds trilling a scale, and past viols and erhus plucking a C. Kids from each instrument section gathered on their own level, higher in the back and working down in a series of small terraces to the lowest level at the front of the room. Of course it wasn't that large, more like a small performance hall. She paused before stepping all the way down, acting as if she had been there all along, or early even. Good thing their new mentor still had his back to them.

"Oriannon. Glad you're here. Please join us."

Every warm-up stopped dead at his words. What? This man seemed to have eyes in the back of his head. He pivoted behind his plexi conductor's podium, smiled at her, and motioned toward the empty seat in front.

"Yes, Mentor . . ." As she headed for her chair she glanced up at the large slab of glowing blue slate mounted on the front wall of the classroom. He had written his name across the top in large flowing white letters, kind of old-fashioned looking, with curled edges. The words slowly floated off to the side of the illuminated slate, arranging themselves next to moving images of musical techniques such as proper fingering and note reading. She had memorized the techniques years ago, but what kind of name was . . .

Jesmet ban Saius?

Maybe from the North. She couldn't be sure. But he wore the flowing forest green robe and beard of a mentor. Average height, average looks. In fact only his eyes seemed different as they smiled hello with a kind of electric blue twinkle that nearly matched the slate board in vibrancy and intensity. And they seemed quite large compared to what she was used to here on Corista. Perhaps Northers had larger eyes.

"Something you need, Oriannon?" he asked. And she realized she hadn't sat down, but her feet had rooted to the floor right in front of everyone. She felt her cheeks flush and heard a couple of snickers.

"No. Sorry, Mentor ... Jesmet. I won't be late again." She finally found her place — three-stringed erhu, first row, first chair. The chair reserved for the best string musician in the orchestra. Eleven others fanned out behind her, each one holding the carved wooden base of their erhu in their laps. The shapely long necks of the instruments reached up like swans' necks, each stroked by the attached bow that wove itself through three strings.

Spooky eyes, huh? Once more her earbud crackled to life, and she glanced back at the percussion section to see Margus sitting on his stool with the four other boys who hit things. *I just about did the same thing as you when I first stepped into the room.*

The strange thing was, even though she heard his voice Margus wasn't moving his lips. And almost as strange — Mentor Jesmet glanced over his attendance book and straight at Margus — as if he heard every word too. Oriannon would have pulled the earbud out if she thought no one would notice. But now ... too late.

No worries. Margus sounded as if he was back in the cockpit of the shuttle pod. *Nobody else can hear us with these earbuds. Closed channel.*

"But ..." Oriannon caught herself mouthing the words, then added a fake cough and a hand over her mouth to shield it.

Just listen, he told her. Or she thought he told her. *And whatever you do, don't talk. It's a thought transceiver, okay? So I'm thinking these things at you, and you hear them. And vice versa.*

What? She couldn't help looking back at him again, just so he could see the stern expression on her face.

You'll get the hang of it, he told her. *Just think. Don't speak. See?*

Okay, but ... She had to concentrate hard about forming the words in her mind, slowly and clearly.

But where did it come from?

The transceiver? It's new-tech. He smiled as he answered. *My dad has been working on it.*

That didn't quite answer her question, but never mind.

And what ... makes you think ... I have any use ... for this toy?

Toy? Well, for one thing you can honestly say that you never spoke a word to me. Isn't that what your father would want?

She thought about that for a minute. He knew.

But, she wondered, *you can hear anything I'm thinking? I don't think that's a good idea.*

Not anything. Just what you choose to send me. I can't just read your mind.

How do I know that?

Can you read my mind? Right now? Tell me what I'm thinking.

She waited and listened, concentrated, even. Nothing.

That doesn't prove anything, she told him. *Just because—*

All right. He rolled his eyes. *Tell you what. Think of something but don't think the words. Okay?*

She thought of hitting him over the head with one of his drumsticks.

All right, I'm thinking. Are your receiving?

All I get are your words. I have no idea what you're really thinking.

You're sure?

Trust me.

Where have I heard that before?

So she was stuck with the earbud for the time being as Mentor Jesmet finished attendance and introduced himself. He looked sideways at Margus in the back row.

"And Mister Leek, trust me, I'm going to require your full attention as we get to know each other."

As if he'd heard every word. Or rather, every thought. But no, that couldn't be possible. Could it? And who was this new mentor, really?

Not from around here. They learned he was actually from the North, from one of the small mining settlements that dotted the drier, more arid places, beyond the irrigation channels that watered their fertile south. She hadn't known too many people from the North, and often it was hard to understand their singsong twang of an accent.

He also admitted this was his first position as a mentor, replacing Mentor Noor. But as he continued, his words flowed like music with lyrics begging to be heard, and Oriannon found herself leaning forward, listening to every word. Strange. She couldn't help feeling as if she had already known this man for a long time, almost like a favorite uncle she'd never met. He stroked his dark beard and paced as he recalled a story of how he had learned to play the erhu when he was a boy. The part about how his little brother switched the strings around as a prank made everybody laugh.

I'll have to try that sometime, said Margus. Or rather, thought Margus. Once more their new mentor seemed to know.

"I wouldn't try it at home," he told them, but his eyes danced when he said it. He nodded at Margus, who seemed to swallow hard as he slouched behind his njembe-skin drum. But then it was time for the rest of them to introduce themselves, and Mentor Jesmet turned first to Oriannon, his eyebrows arched.

"You've been first chair, Oriannon, for quite a while, have you? I assume you've worked hard to achieve this position."

What was she supposed to say? But once again the smile in his eyes made her relax in that strange way. He pointed up to the slate to bring up a string of written notes, black dots on a checkerboard grid, the kind they read to learn their music. Of course Ori recognized the pattern right away.

"She doesn't need notes," said Brinnin, from back in the third row, third-seat flute. "Not like the rest of us common plebes."

A couple of the kids snickered.

"Oh?" Mentor Jesmet looked at her with his head turned curiously to the side. "And why doesn't she need notes?"

"Because she has everything memorized. Probably memorized it when she was three years old."

Not true, thought Oriannon. *I was four.*

Which was more than eleven years ago. Brinnin kept up her whining.

"She just looks at it once, and—"

"I think I understand, Brinnin." Their mentor finally held up his hand for Brinnin to stop before shifting his gaze again to Oriannon. "You're an eidich then."

Oriannon gave him a little shrug along with her nod as she straightened in her chair to the proper playing position. Well, if he really wanted to know, maybe she would tell him. He would have found out eventually.

"Then you wouldn't mind playing for us?" he asked. The *Aria Corista,* third movement?"

Of course. The one where the erhu carried the delicate melody. She knew the part the same way she knew her own name. Of course she remembered every note of it, and had since the first time she'd picked up the music. She nodded and fingered her instrument, settled the blonde pluqwood base in her lap, leaned the neck against her shoulder until she felt its cool touch, gripped her bow, and launched into the piece.

One measure, two ... and the fingers of her left hand flew over the strings the way they'd always known to do. She couldn't help it. Perfect, right down to the difficult counts and rests, the tricky progression of eighth notes. Their mentor nodded and smiled as if he knew the melody well.

Four measures, five. Here the music heightened, and Oriannon filled with the assurance that no one in the school played better.

Bring it on, Oriannon! Margus whooped in the earbud.

Not now! she managed, but something deep in her mind had already taken over the music, the way it always did and would, through to the end. She closed her eyes and swayed, let the aria come alive through her fingers, her bow.

Seven measures, eight. And then ... what crept into her thoughts? She hardly recognized a whisper, a faint touch of fog, as before when she'd been running down the hall. For a moment she thought an unwelcome stranger had entered the room.

Twelve measures. She felt a faint hesitation catch hold of a note, just a faint one, but then another as if her fingers were asking for directions for the first time in her life, or stiffening up. The strange feeling startled her, actually brought butterflies to her stomach. And without warning the fog dropped down on her in the middle of the fifteenth measure, halfway between notes, and she snapped her eyes open, startled.

The music had disappeared—as if it had never existed.

"Go on." The mentor urged her. "Finish that section. It was beautiful."

Now she could feel a cold sweat of panic trickling down her back. And if she could have, she would have backed up a couple of notes to get a running start on the part she'd suddenly and totally ... *forgotten!*

Is this what it felt like?

She looked down at her fingers, rebels that suddenly would not obey as they always had. She bit her lip and couldn't keep the tears from filling her eyes. No!

Go ahead, Oriannon! Margus urged her in the earbud. But the only thing she could do now was cover up—pretend this is what she intended to do the entire time. She didn't finish because, well, simply because she hadn't felt like it. They'd heard enough. And she said as much.

What are you talking about? Margus, again.

"Shut up!" She didn't think the words this time, just blurted them out as she turned around in her seat. The expensive instrument fell from her lap and clattered to the floor, but that only freed her to stand up and run towards the door through the shocked silence.

"It's all right, Oriannon," she heard the mentor tell her, but she couldn't look at him, couldn't look at anyone. "I didn't mean to put you on the spot."

"I'm sorry," she said, stepping through the doorway and finally pulling the earbud out. Now she didn't care if anyone noticed. "I'm not feeling well."

Which was as true as it got. And a couple of minutes later the school nurse had settled her in the Health Center, the warm, padded room with changing portraits of trees and wildlife on the walls. Treb bears and tree frogs, little yellow terramole lizards, viria songbirds, and the elusive black yagwar. Recorded bird songs and the gurgle of water. Whatever it took to make sick students feel better.

"Take a deep breath, Oriannon." Nurse Anno rested her warm hands on Ori's shoulders as she waited for the sobs to settle.

"But I c-couldn't remember." Oriannon had no one else to tell. "That's never happened before."

"Welcome to the real world, dear." She brushed a glowing multimeter across Oriannon's forehead.

"Am I ..." Oriannon wasn't even sure what to ask.

"You're fine. All your readings are normal. But let me explain. It's not uncommon for eidichs to lose some of their memories as they become teens. It's called pu—"

"I know what it's called," she snapped, not meaning for it to sound rude. She paused. "But I'm sorry. Are you saying I'm going to forget everything? I never heard that before."

"Hold on, dear. It's just part of growing up—even for an eidich like you. But tell me about your new mentor. Please. Perhaps it could help you. Do you remember?"

"Of course I remember."

And she did, now. Every word. Every story.

"He told stories?" asked Nurse Anno. "What kinds of stories?"

Oriannon nodded and repeated the story of his erhu playing, word for word. The nurse listened carefully, nodding as if she was taking careful mental notes. She looked over her shoulder every once in a while, though no one else was in the small Health Center.

Or was there? At first Oriannon couldn't see what Nurse Anno was looking at, not even when her eyes were fully adjusted to the dim light. That took a while for most Coristans, used to the bright sunlight that bathed their planet, waking and sleeping, always bright—except inside.

But then for just a moment she saw it—the slight movement of a probe in the far corner, hiding in the dark. She might not have noticed, as the probe's normal lights had been switched off, its usual hum silenced. But for just a moment the light from Nurse Anno's multimeter blinked brightly enough to reflect off the probe's brushed stainless steel. And then Oriannon knew exactly what she had seen.

"And that's all ..." she said, her voice trailing off.

"It's good to just talk, isn't it." Nurse Anno once again rested her hand on Oriannon's shoulder, and her honey-smooth voice helped Oriannon breathe once again.

"Sure." Oriannon caught her breath. "It is."

"So if you have any other ... uh, incidents, you just let me know and I'll take another look. Right now, though, you just go back to class. Nothing to worry about. I'm sure you'll be fine."

Oriannon tried not to notice where the probe hovered, silent and unblinking, once again hidden in the darkness. She felt for the earbud in her pocket, got up and backed away, while Nurse Anno took her hand.

"And ... Oriannon?"

Oriannon paused, waiting.

"If you ever hear anything, ah ... unusual in your orchestra class, anything the new mentor might say that makes you ... uncomfortable, I want you to know you can always come to me. Remember, I'm your friend. And I'm here to help, understand?"

Oriannon wasn't quite sure what Nurse Anno meant, but she nodded her head and took her hand back.

"Thanks," Ori whispered. But even in the cozy, warm room, she couldn't help shivering.

4.

ey, he hasn't put you on the spot again. You okay now?

By the third day of the new term Oriannon hoped everyone had forgotten the scene she'd put on after forgetting the *Aria Corista*. Fortunately her instrument hadn't suffered any more than a tweaked string after she'd dumped it on the floor that first day. Easy to fix.

She was also getting used to running earbud commentary from Margus Leek, comic relief, as if he was sitting in the chair right next to her and chatting the whole time. Which was kind of amusing, considering the rest of the class still couldn't hear the two of them trading thoughts. Especially not Brinnin, since it would only fuel the silly romance rumors that girl was only too eager to spread.

Shh, she told him, and she had the hang of it now. No moving lips, no funny stares. Not even Mentor Jesmet seemed to notice. *I want to hear this story.*

"So the drummer from Shadowside quit his group," the mentor told them, pacing the front of the room, his green robe flowing behind him. To make his points he tended to wave his own erhu like a baton, though it was nearly the size of a guitar. He should have known better than to treat it so, but he seemed more intent on the story than on the instrument. "He thought he would go solo."

Which brought a laugh from the percussion section. Solo?

Jesmet shrugged and grinned. "Well, he was an excellent player. Gifted by the Maker. His dream was to make it big in the city, become rich and famous over the border in Corista."

"But wait," objected Carrick Trice, who played viol, third chair. She wrinkled her nose in confusion, the way she often did. "That doesn't make sense. Everyone knows no one lives over there — in the dark, even! So how could they come here to Corista? That's not realistic."

Mentor Jesmet was about to explain himself, but Margus stood up in the back to wave her down.

"It's just a story, Carrick. Let him finish."

Now *he* was the one who wanted to listen. That was almost as funny as some of Margus's jokes.

"My father says stories are a waste of time," she snapped back as she adjusted her hair in the traditional tied-back style. "Unless it's written in the Codex."

Count on Carrick to make it sound spiritual, thought Oriannon. Maybe she didn't mean anything by it, or maybe it just came out that way.

"If that's true," answered their mentor, his voice gentle and a smile playing at the corner of his mouth, "then perhaps you should think about not playing the viol."

"Pardon?" Carrick's face went pale and she sputtered a bit.

42

"I just meant that your viol isn't mentioned in the Codex, either. It's what you do with the instrument that matters, whom you play for. Not what goes into it, but the music that comes out."

She opened her mouth to say something back, but must have changed her mind. Margus still obviously wanted to hear the rest, like everyone else in the room.

"So was this guy good enough to play the Grand Hall?" he asked, breaking the awkward silence. Jesmet smiled at them and went on.

"At first he thought he was, but ..." Their mentor shook his head slightly, back into the rhythm of the story. "But the only jobs he could find were playing backup for groups in fight halls, where lonely people would gather to bet on fights between treb bears and yagwar. Do you understand the kind of thing I'm describing? These were dingy back alley establishments where the smoke and the Coristan beer were so thick no one could see him, in any case — not the type of place he would normally have visited had he still been living at home."

Oriannon looked around the practice room to see everyone else in the band hanging on every word. She wasn't sure where this story was going, or if it even was true. She wasn't sure why they were all so fascinated, either. Perhaps it was more the way he said it, like a brook that you wanted to jump into, to float along and feel the current.

Or maybe it was just his singsong Northern accent. Either way, *something* was pulling them along. And the current of Jesmet's words tugged, and tugged hard.

"His instrument was destroyed after just a few gigs," Jesmet went on. "One of the other men in the fight hall became angry at some imagined slight, put his fist through it, and simply walked away."

"Bummer," commented Margus, and the rest of the orchestra nodded agreement. "Did he get it replaced?"

"Unfortunately he ran out of money, and the rest of his funds were stolen as well. He ended up cleaning the floors around the fight pits, then the bathrooms. You can imagine how distasteful that must have been."

43

Carrick wrinkled her nose at the thought.

"Some solo career," replied Margus. "He probably should have stayed put."

Maybe Margus had forgotten where the drummer in the story came from. At this point it didn't seem to matter.

"Exactly what he thought as he was scrubbing toilets," replied Jesmet. "So can you guess what he did?"

Their mentor paused for a moment, maybe waiting for the question to sink in, maybe waiting for someone to answer. No one did.

"He quit his toilet-scrubbing job," he finally told them, "and walked home—halfway across the continent and back to Shadowside—to see if they'd hire him back just to carry their instruments. Even after what he'd been through, he imagined he could still do that."

"Probably beat cleaning toilets," quipped Margus, and some of the others giggled. Jesmet smiled.

"True. And the bandleader was so happy that he paid for a new drum out of his own pocket. Custom-made. He received his friend right back into the band, just as if he'd never left. They had missed him."

"Happy ending, huh?" Margus obviously liked that part. "But, did all the other band members get new instruments too? Doesn't sound like it would be fair if they didn't, since they stuck with the band that whole time, right?"

"Actually, they didn't." Jesmet shook his head no, which didn't make much sense to Oriannon, either. But it was his story, and she supposed he could end it any way he wanted. And this was all true? She asked, just to be sure.

"You decide." Jesmet told them, and they all groaned. But now he was already heading out the door with his erhu snapped up in its worn leather case. "And while you're deciding, bring your instruments along. It's time for a little outdoor rehearsal in the Glades."

That might be easy enough for those with their smaller instruments. The percussion boys, Margus included, grabbed what they could of the smaller drums and followed. And with a stern warning for them to stay close, Jesmet marched them right out the back door of the school, and out into the dappled shade of the terraced gardens and pools surrounding their whitewashed stone building. Carrick even followed, clutching her flawless viol. Maybe she wanted to hear another unrealistic story after all.

"Here?" asked Oriannon, but Jesmet wasn't stopping at the reflecting pools or the flower gardens. For the next half-hour they kept pushing through fern grottoes and thick stands of elephant leaf and wild orchids. This was the Glades—a circle-shaped buffer of thick, watered forestland surrounding the school. Wilder than the gardens, but not as wild as the Outlying. Never mind the shade; as usual Margus was sweating in the heat—but of course he was always doing that in the seasonless, all-year summer of Corista. Were they outside? It would be warm.

"Concert in the Glades?" Oriannon asked, stopping to catch her breath and let some of the kids go by. She glanced around to see if Carrick had lagged behind.

"Why not?" Jesmet smiled at her, wiped his brow, and pointed to several moss-covered logs where they could sit down, where it might be a little cooler in the shade. Water trickled from a nearby irrigation pipe. "I always think music sounds better out here, where it's designed to be played."

"As long as Headmaster Knarl doesn't find out." Margus looked around at the dense green forest, and Oriannon thought the same thing. She also wondered why a security probe hadn't followed them out here—or maybe it had, and it was just hiding in the flamboyan branches.

Did it matter now? Here she breathed in the heavy, perfumed scent of lonicera vines, sweet as honey, entwined around broad-leafed flame trees that helped form a canopy against the ever-present suns. The gentlest of breezes fanned the leaves around them, which set up a soft kind of rustling background. And all around they could hear the soft chirp of viria birds flittering about the branches ... and then a piercing scream.

Oriannon froze for just a moment before running toward the sound. At the far end of the clearing she saw Carrick Trice inching backwards, away from the dark stare of a black yagwar. But way too slowly.

45

Oriannon caught her breath, then clapped her hands and shouted. The large wild cat bared its fangs and ignored them as it advanced on its prey. Still Carrick stumbled backwards, slower and slower, unable to escape the hypnotic stare of the animal. For this was how such a cat hunted, freezing anyone unlucky enough to be caught in its path.

And now the yagwar crouched . . .

But Jesmet knew how to whistle, two fingers in his mouth, and the piercing sound cut through the air like landing thrusters on a shuttle. Every bird that had been twittering in the forest canopy went silent as the echo faded and the students' ears rang.

More than that, the yagwar stood up straight, as if on a leash, then raised his head only enough to meet Jesmet's piercing blue eyes. And Jesmet now stepped across the clearing toward them, helping Carrick to her feet a few seconds later.

"You'll find your lunch elsewhere today," he said, almost too quietly to hear. Talking to the cat? He left no doubt when he stooped to stroke the cat's ears, then motioned with his head. And a moment later the hunter had disappeared back into the dense underbrush of the gardens, while the kids gathered around a white-faced Carrick.

"That was wild!" said Margus, keeping an eye on the bushes like everyone else. "You don't think—"

"He's not coming back." The way Jesmet said it sounded just as final as his command to the yagwar, so much that Oriannon had no doubt. "Just stay by me from now on, the way I told you. Do you understand?"

Carrick nodded slowly and picked up her viol where she'd dropped it in a soft bed of leaves, but didn't say a word.

"And we still have some music to practice," said their mentor, "don't we?"

After all that, Oriannon didn't see how they were going to sit in the Glades and practice the *Simfonia Seramina*. But somehow she still found a place to sit under the flame trees, the flamboyan, along with the rest of the class. She took her erhu out of its carrying case, tuned up the strings, and got ready to play. What else could she do? And then once again she heard Margus's voice in her earbud.

Hey, Oriannon, you know what a faithbreaker is?

She looked around at the group of them, about fifty-five kids, just to be sure no one else heard. No matter what, this thought transceiver still took some getting used to.

Of course I know. She looked straight ahead. Mentor Jesmet was helping a clarinetist find her music.

So tell me, Your Majesty.

He waited. Oh, brother. Was this some kind of exam? Oriannon sighed.

A faithbreaker is anyone who speaks with the spirits of animals and the dead, magicians and diviners, shamans. Someone who tears apart the faith and undermines what we believe. Which is, of course, all forbidden in the Codex — chapter twelve, verse two.

And the penalty? He wasn't giving up on this.

You know it's banishment, Margus. Being sent away for the rest of your life. But come on, that's just in the Codex. Stories. It's not like there are any real people today who are as evil as a faithbreaker. Like we have to worry about it or anything.

Margus had an answer for everything.

That's what I used to think, Ori, but I think we just saw one in action.

She had to ponder for a moment before she realized what he was trying to say. Could he really mean ...

You're kidding. Not Mentor Jesmet?

He didn't answer, which meant yes. She felt a shiver run up her spine.

Now you're just being weird, Margus. The heat's getting to you, again. This always happens when you go outside.

But I'm not being weird, Ori, and the heat is not getting to me. Didn't you see what happened when he whistled?

Anybody can whistle. She wasn't giving him this argument quite so easily.

Maybe. But what about when he talked to the yagwar? Didn't you see that?

Sure, but just because he chased away a wild animal doesn't mean he's talking to spirits.

I'm telling you, Ori, he's a faithbreaker, and if he is ...

He didn't get to finish as Mentor Jesmet raised his arms for them to begin. For a moment Oriannon thought the horrible fog that had once made her forget might be returning, but she choked it away, the same way she choked away Margus's crazy words. Why did she even bother to keep wearing the earbud? She should have taken it out a long time ago.

"Ready?" Jesmet asked them. "Everyone please put their handhelds down. No handhelds. Just real life. Real music."

As a couple of students groaned, Oriannon looked up at their mentor's concentration. There was no mistaking that the life had left his eyes. No laugh remained, no sparkle. He wiped at the perspiration on his forehead with the back of his hand. When he glanced at her, she had to look away.

And she didn't know how, but once more she had the feeling that somehow he'd heard. Somehow.

"So we begin," he told them, and the students all raised their instruments in unison. Oriannon caught a glimpse over her shoulder at Margus, still staring at Mentor Jesmet with a frown on his face.

A faithbreaker?

5

Oriannon *felt* more than *heard* the gentle knock, which could only mean her father. Who else?

"It's open." She looked up from her Seer Codex study book to see him peering in through the doorway to her room.

"Oriannon?" He hadn't yet changed out of his green Assembly robe, meaning he must have come home early from his meetings. "Got a moment?"

She caught her breath, wondering what was coming. After what had happened in school that day — or actually, what had happened in the Glades with Mentor Jesmet and the yagwar, she'd actually been waiting for her father to say something about it. But of course he couldn't already know what had happened unless someone had told him. She decided quickly she would not be the first.

"Sure." She put down her stylus and scooted back the chair. She was bored with memorizing precepts anyway.

"Actually . . ." He didn't uncross his arms and the wrinkles never left his forehead, and he waved his hand at her holo media screen to mute the sound. "Why don't you take a little break from your studies, get some fresh air with me out on the terrace."

49

She hesitated a moment, but grabbed her shades and followed him out the back door and onto the gravel path. Their landscaped terraces cascaded to a show pond fringed with royal palms and cerise bushes, always studded with unscented pink blossoms. They looked nice, but unfortunately smelled like nothing.

Beyond the valley below and off to the north stretched the gently rolling Plains of Izula, dotted by low white stucco homes and criss-crossed with the tidy patterns of irrigated gardens and orchards in all shades of green, carefully tended and watered, covered with a fluffy violet blanket of haze to match the always clear sky. Shuttles broke orbit here and there, returning to land after voyages to other nearby moons.

And if she could have seen it, in the farthest distance lay the Security Zone and the forbidden border with Shadowside. Only a cooling breeze from that direction gave any hint of the place. But of course no one even *talked* about the Security Zone, much less Shadowside, which was just wild darkness and dead ice, period.

Right now she just wondered why her father would drag her out here in full sun with only the brief shadow of their palm trees for protection. Still he removed his own shades and looked at her directly, blinking away the brightness. His face looked pale and tight, with black circles under his eyes, as if he had not been getting enough sleep.

"You're ready for Seer Codex?" He shaded his eyes with his hand, and his voice sounded friendly in a forced sort of way.

"Almost. I've got it memorized to page three hundred."

She dipped her fingers in their pool of cold, clear water, watching ripples glitter in the sun. Here the supply came directly from Shadowside, from melted ice, with a light blue tint that spoke to her of glaciers and darkness, a weird contrast to their world of bright suns that never set.

"Your mother would have been proud of you." He smiled, and Ori nodded. The mother she'd never known, except in videos.

"Well, good thing they won't ask me to recite it all."

She meant it. Memorizing was one thing. Standing up in front of people—quite another. So as long as she didn't have to say too much, she might yet survive her upcoming Seer Codex, the coming-of-age ceremony every young Coristan faced before turning sixteen.

Margus, on the other hand, would still need help just memorizing the first precepts. She hadn't yet figured out how they were going to accomplish that.

Her father went on. "And school?"

He was probably working his way up to what he really wanted to know. She would wait. Meanwhile she told him what old Mentor Narrick had been upset about today, though everyone knew he was always upset about something. She mentioned her other classes and even added how they had a different music mentor this term, a substitute. Her father picked up on the music mentor part.

"Ah, yes. I heard he took your class on a little ... field trip earlier today."

There! Carrick Trice must have told her parents what had happened; her father was a friend of another elder. That was it.

"Mentor Jesmet thought it would be good to practice outside."

"Yes, but did anything strange happen? Anything out of place?"

She pressed her lips together, wondering how to answer honestly without making it sound too alarming. After all, she still wasn't sure Margus was right about the faithbreaker thing. And as a matter of fact, maybe she actually *liked* this mentor.

"He scared a yagwar away that got too close. Carrick was a little shook up, but nobody was hurt. It wasn't such a big deal, though."

Her father frowned and tapped his fingers on the stone terrace railing bordering their low stucco home. She heard it coming—what he *really* had wanted to say.

"Maybe it didn't seem like a big deal to you." He twisted the silver tassel of his tunic around his fingers and faced her head on.

"But listen, Oriannon. What I'm going to tell you is just between you and me, do you understand?"

She gulped and nodded. What choice did she have? He paused and went on.

"Mentor Jesmet's name came up in the Assembly meeting today. We've been hearing things ... complaints from parents."

"The field trip?"

"Not just the field trip, but things that make me worry about the way he's teaching, and what he's teaching. Perhaps kids might not know if he's speaking against the Codex."

"So why don't you just check the records from the security probes?" she asked. "They've been in our room every day this past week. They're all over the place lately."

"That's exactly the problem." He sighed and began pacing. "The probes have been malfunctioning. They're not recording what we would like to see, and they come back from your music classes with completely blank memory files."

"It's not the mentor's fault though?"

"I don't know. It's possible he's been erasing them because he has something to hide. Something he doesn't want us to see. Do you know what I'm saying?"

"I know we haven't been playing all that well," Oriannon offered, brushing away a buzzing tremilo gnat. "Maybe that's what he's hiding."

"It's no joke, Ori," he replied, holding up a finger of caution. "See, I'm telling you all this because I need you to be my eyes and ears for a day or two. At least until we get this technical problem ironed out. Will you do that?"

"Oh." She tried not to frown, now that she heard what he really wanted. "Your spy, you mean."

"Just think of it this way. It's for your protection, for you and your friends. There may be something going on, something we've never encountered before."

"So why don't you talk with *him* about it instead of me? Why doesn't Headmaster Knarl just sit in on the class, see for himself?"

"I wish it were that simple." Her father shook his head. "We don't want this Jesmet to think we're concerned."

This Jesmet. He talked about him as if he was a criminal, instead of a music mentor at Ossek Prep. And the Assembly didn't want him to know? How could he not, the way probes had been following him around on campus?

"He is different," she finally admitted. It wouldn't hurt to say as much. "He says the music has a heart, and he wants us to find it."

But her father acted as if he hadn't heard her.

"I promise you, Oriannon, if you're ever in danger, your safety comes first. You just need to help us help you, and you have to trust me, all right?"

She nodded, but didn't like the feeling. From now on, she would be a spy. They would want to use her eyes and her ears, the images that attached themselves to her memory like stubborn burrs on her socks.

Of course, she could stay silent if she wanted to. Hold it back. But she also knew there were other ways to harvest an cidich's memories, ways she didn't want to think about. She'd heard about them. But surely her dad wouldn't let anyone do that.

Would he?

6

No, try again." Oriannon didn't need to look at the page to know which verses Brinnin had fumbled. "You missed the last half of verse twelve."

Brinnin rolled her eyes and blew dark hair out of her eyes.

"What good does it do to memorize all these verses, anyway? We're only going to forget them again. I mean, *I* am."

True. Oriannon bit her tongue to keep from saying what was really on her mind. Instead she moved a little deeper into the shade of a flamboyan tree and stretched out on her back, finding a more comfortable spot. They'd found their place again, behind a low, vine-covered brick wall in a grassy courtyard next to the sparkling white Coristan Temple. Daddy always said this was the center of everything important and anything holy; maybe he was right.

She adjusted her shades and squinted up through branches at a pair of moordoves as they fluttered across the gleaming red roof tiles, probably seeking shade too. Did the birds think it holy?

Holy. Now there was an interesting idea. The Temple's three copper-topped, pointed bell towers cast their own shadows below — long fingers with sharp fingernails, each one pointed at the three suns of the Trion. Did the towers stand guard over something holy?

Inside, she had never been allowed to see the inner Temple, but she knew it to be a dark, high-ceilinged place, filled with clouds of sweet sandalwood incense, the aroma that clung to her father's robes when he came home. It's where the priests spent all their time praying and where the Assembly elders spent all their time deciding.

But ... holy? Outside, well-tended gardens and gurgling fountains surrounded them on three sides, hemmed in by more Temple buildings and a maze of waist-high stone walls. All this ... holy too?

At least it was quiet. Aside from the moordoves, only an olive green-robed apprentice ventured out into the simmering heat, shuffling along vine-covered walkways that hugged each building, probably running errands for his Temple superiors. She wasn't sure if there was a better place to study, to soak in their Seer Codex lessons.

If only it didn't take Brinnin so long to get the words. How hard could it be? You memorize a few passages of the Codex, a few canned answers to a few simple questions. You get ready to stand up in front of everyone in the Temple's outer court, where you were supposed to say your piece. The priest would tell them they'd graduated from being a child to a *Seer,* a grown-up Coristan. Someone who sees and knows. And that, from what she understood, would be the end of the story.

There would be nothing to it, as far as Oriannon could tell. Now, if Brinnin could just get a clue. Oriannon counted the moordoves: five, six, seven ...

"Uh ..." Brinnin paused once more in the middle of a verse. "I know it, I know it ... Just give me a hint, Ori?"

"For thus saith ..." Oriannon quoted the next words to her, which helped a little, and Brinnin finally finished that verse, and the next. Now they were getting somewhere. But then Brinnin paused for a moment, turning her head to the side.

"You hear that?" she asked.

A moment later Oriannon did too. Low voices and the soft clicking of shoes on a shaded tile walkway surrounding the Temple proper. Only, something sounded more familiar here. When Ori and Brinnin peeked over the nearby wall they sighted Mentor Jesmet and a handful of other kids from the orchestra, including Carrick Trice, and even Margus.

That's interesting, thought Oriannon. Especially after what he'd been trying to tell her the other day about Jesmet being a faith-breaker. Had he changed his mind about their mentor, already? Jesmet gestured with his hands as he walked, as if he was telling another of his stories.

And he was. Brinnin raised her head, but Ori pulled her back down.

"What are you doing?" asked Brinnin. "I'm just trying to hear."

"Shh." Oriannon put a finger to her mouth and kept low enough behind a full-bloom cerise bush to stay hidden. No one had seen them yet, probably not even the probe floating at a respectful distance behind the group. When Oriannon pointed it out, Brinnin's eyes widened as she finally saw—and understood.

"And what if someone from Shadowside was up there in a shuttle pod," Jesmet asked his little group, "engines offline, nearly out of oxygen. What would you do?"

"Why do you keep mentioning Shadow—er, that place?" Margus raised his hand as he asked. "When no one has ever lived over there, and never could?"

Oriannon thought she could hear the smile in Jesmet's voice, even from where they watched.

"All right. We'll save that for later. Let's just say for now that the shuttle pilot is from the North, where I came from. He's not your typical next-door neighbor; he just needs assistance. And along comes a young boy who stole a shuttle pod for fun, just to see the sights. Do you think he's going to stop, thereby risking everything?"

"What if he doesn't?" asked another voice.

"The Norther has only a few minutes of O_2 left. He's out of air. So he's breathing hard—and burned from an on-board explosion. He's in poor condition, and is undoubtedly going to die unless someone helps him."

By this time Oriannon and Brinnin had both keyed into the story as well, waiting to hear what would happen. So much that Oriannon almost didn't see the ironwood gate slowly swinging open at the far end of the walkway. Never mind; Jesmet only continued with the suspense.

"A scheduled shuttle already went by; they don't stop for Northers. Neither did the blue-and-gold government shuttle, carrying three Assembly members to a meeting on Zed–3. They were going to be late, and they estimated a call back to Corista would be sufficient."

By this time, two Temple securities had slipped through the gate and quietly made their way towards where Jesmet and the others were sitting. Dressed in their traditional black coveralls, they blended in well with the shadows along the covered outside Temple walkway. And for a minute they paused, as if listening to the story themselves.

"See that?" Brinnin whispered into Oriannon's ear. Of course she did. And the sinking feeling in Oriannon's stomach reminded her that these securities weren't just coming out to listen to a story. They had both unsheathed their stun batons, and the brutish weapons glowed a deadly green behind their backs.

But still the securities waited in the shadows as Jesmet finished his story. That would give Oriannon a chance, maybe. To do what? Run out into the courtyard? Scream a warning? As she kneeled in their hiding place, frozen in place behind the brick wall, she felt Brinnin shaking beside her, and the tiny earbud still in her pocket.

That's it!

She only fumbled with it a moment before plugging it into her ear and sending her silent warnings. Brinnin didn't even notice. Of course, what were the chances that Margus was also wearing his earbud?

Margus! She wasn't sure how to scream without opening her mouth, but she would try. *Margus! I don't know if you're listening, but there are a couple of Temple securities coming your way, and I don't think they're happy. Margus?*

She waited for a moment, not really expecting to hear anything back. She certainly did not expect the voice she now heard, as clearly as if he was standing right beside them.

I appreciate the thought, Oriannon. Really.

Jesmet?

She peeked over the wall once again, just to be sure. Jesmet was laughing with the guys in his little group even as the securities approached more closely.

So you have one of those earbuds too. She managed to send the thought.

Not exactly, Oriannon.

She couldn't believe she was having this kind of conversation with her music mentor, if that's what was really happening. Not here with the little earbud toy, and certainly not now. Did he know?

Did you hear me about the securities? she tried again. And this time she couldn't help getting to her feet. Brinnin tried to pull her back down, but she stood firm. *They have stun batons, and they look like they want to use them!*

I know. He sounded as if he was taking attendance. *Thanks, Oriannon.*

He most certainly did not know. He couldn't. Oriannon had seen everything, and the man had his back to the securities the entire time. He hadn't turned. He had to be lying.

In fact, he continued in that utterly calm voice of his, *you and Brinnin are welcome to come on over, join the discussion.*

Oriannon blinked and looked over at Brinnin. How would he have seen them? And then her feet betrayed her.

"I'm going to get a little closer," she told Brinnin. "See what's going on."

Brinnin nearly tore the sleeve of Oriannon's blouse, trying to hang on.

"What are you, crazy? You know they don't charge up those batons unless they're going to use them!"

True, but by that time Oriannon had pulled herself free and started across the grassy courtyard. The securities quickened their step from the other direction, their batons glowing brighter and brighter and more menacing. She had of course never felt the sting of one of those weapons, only heard they could knock out a full-grown treb with a single tap. So why was she walking straight into this face-off?

Margus noticed her first, and gave her a curious look. She still didn't understand that part—why he was even there, after all the things he'd said. But the securities had a three-step lead, and parked themselves in front of the group with all the puffed-chest authority they could probably muster. Oriannon pulled up short as the two big men drew their batons out from behind their backs.

"Excuse me," she said, but the nearest security held his ground. He looked much taller up close.

"We're going to have to ask you all to disperse," announced the security in a loud voice. "Unless this is an Assembly-sanctioned training session or school-sponsored meeting. I'm asking you to leave the premises. Now."

Oriannon still wasn't quite sure why the securities were acting as if this was an uprising instead of just a mentor telling his students stories. Who was hurting anything? She also wasn't quite sure what she was doing there.

To back up their threat, though, their batons now sputtered and spit with glowing green energy. Nothing you'd want to get close to, and the boys in the group who were sitting scrambled to their feet. Jesmet, on the other hand, only looked at the securities the same sad way he'd looked at Oriannon that first day of class, the time she'd walked in late.

"You wouldn't want to hurt someone with those things, would you?" And as he spoke the words both batons sputtered and fizzled out.

"What?" The first security muttered and tried the handle-mounted switch of his weapon, on and off and on. Nothing.

"I said, you wouldn't want to—"

"No, I heard what you said." Now the security huffed as he slipped his baton back into a belt holster. "Question is, did you hear what *I* said? Temple staff sent us out here to keep the premises secure."

"We don't want to cause any trouble, gentlemen." Jesmet hadn't even broken a sweat. "I am curious, though. Did someone complain?"

"None of your concern. You just need to—"

"I'm sorry to interrupt," Oriannon cut in. "But I'm looking for my father, Tavlin Hightower. Have you seen him?"

So she would play that card, but was that supposed to help? At least it got their attention. Both securities looked over at her, as if for the first time.

"You father is Tavlin Hightower?"

"You've seen him?" she asked innocently.

The taller security studied her through slit eyes.

"Not lately, miss. But when I do, I'll tell him you're looking."

That didn't sound very promising, but that would be the end of the face-off. Weapons sheathed, the two men turned to go. One had kind of stared at Margus, a question mark on his face, as if he was waiting for something. But this meeting was definitely over.

"You didn't need to say that," Jesmet whispered at Oriannon as his audience split up too. "Unless you really were looking for your father—which you weren't."

How did he know? But he had a parting word for the securities too.

"By the way, boys," he called after them. "You might want to check your batons, in case you left the switch on. Wouldn't want to have an accident with one of those things."

The taller one just sneered back at him as they stalked off. As if a lowly mentor would know anything about handling stun weapons, right?

"He probably has a collection of them at home," murmured the other, and they both laughed—until the first man's baton suddenly powered back on in its holster.

"Yee-OWW!" The man yelped in pain and danced on the spot until he was finally able to yank the weapon out of its holster and toss it aside. It flew through the air and clattered to the pavement, but he still moaned and clutched the side of his leg where it had stung him. Meanwhile his partner bent over double in laughter, while everyone else could only watch.

"Didn't he say to check the switch?" The other security hooted.

Even some of the boys smiled at the accident—but not Jesmet. He just shook his head sadly and told everyone it was time for them all to go home. They headed for one of the several iron entry gates that were set into tall, thick white stucco walls encircling the Temple complex.

Beyond that lay the Walking Street, a quaint cobblestone path that circled the city in a neat loop. Its bushy blue-green cerulean trees offered welcome shade for healers and artisans, silversmiths and dressmakers, lev-scooter mechanics, tea shops and bookstores, each in their own tidy little space. Any other day she would have loved to peek in some of the windows with Brinnin, who had already run on ahead. Maybe they could have sampled a spicy cirit-bun, steaming and straight from the oven, or looked at new blouses.

Now all she could think of was what the securities might say to her father about her—and what kind of trouble she'd be in when he found out. Why had she told them who she was, anyway?

"I still don't know what you were doing here, Oriannon." Margus interrupted her thoughts.

"I was about to say the same thing about *you*," she told him, but he just shrugged and gave her his "no worries" line, which she'd heard too often before. No worries? After what they'd just seen?

"I'm liking his stories," he finally offered, which sounded rather lame.

"That's it?" she lowered her voice. "What about all that stuff you said the other day about—"

The faithbreaker. But he shook his head at her, as if he wanted her to cut it out, or Jesmet might overhear them. And of course that's when she heard Jesmet's voice again in her ear, as clear and strong as if he was standing next to her.

Thanks for your help, Oriannon, came the voice again, and Margus didn't seem to have a clue what she was hearing. *See you in class tomorrow?*

She looked around, just to be sure Jesmet wasn't walking nearby, after all. He must have already disappeared into the crowd. A woman pushing a baby in a lev-carriage gave her an odd look.

Uh ... sure. She nodded and returned the thought, though obviously Jesmet was nowhere close by and couldn't see her. *Tomorrow.*

And then it occurred to her. She checked her ear and felt nothing.

She had already slipped the earbud into her pocket.

7

Some days she would wear the earbud, other days not. But Oriannon had to admit it was often fun listening to Margus imitating Mentor Narrick's nasal voice, or Margus announcing the mid-day meal in the school's dining room. Like now.

And now, students, you're going to enjoy one of the supreme benefits of living the good life on the sunny side of Corista. Even his thoughts sounded like a media announcer, working the crowd. *Today we have ... glaep dumplings to brighten your day even more!*

Too bad the rest of the kids filing into lunch lines couldn't hear him. Instead they gathered under vaulted ceilings, waiting. Sunlight filtered through shaded skylights arching from marble column to column, set in a careful pattern between long tables in several rows. Dark banners speckled with embroidered planets and stars draped the upper walls. Oriannon thought it all rather pretentious, for a cafeteria. Pretty, perhaps, but pretentious. With tables moved out it had, on occasion, doubled as a grand ballroom.

I'm here, you know. She thought it best to warn him, in case he didn't want to embarrass himself. He wheeled around from where he stood at the front of the line.

Hey, haven't talked to you in a while. His face brightened and she almost forgot what had happened back at the Temple. *Where you been?*

Oh, you know. Around. My dad's making me come right home from class for the next week, after what happened the other day.

Oh. Sorry. But you couldn't miss lunch, right?

Not for the world.

Of course, if Oriannon could have politely plugged her nose she would have. And she imagined so would everyone else in the lunch line. She had long ago given up trying to figure out how an advanced civilization that could send people to nearby planets and produce thought transceivers couldn't come up with better cafeteria food.

She did think of maybe slipping out—except the lunchroom probe had already scanned her entry and she knew what would happen if she tried to leave. Besides, Mentor Jesmet had followed them inside and was coming up the line with his own tray.

Brave guy, thought Margus. He must have seen the mentor come in as well. *You ever seen him in here before?*

She had not. But that didn't stop Jesmet from smiling at the two older women behind the serving line, Deelie Wither and Frax Orrun, and thanking them for the generous helping of glaep.

"Supposed to be good for you," Margus told her the regular way as he passed with a steaming tray and plopped down at one of the ironwood tables draped with a royal blue tablecloth. He glanced up at the hovering probe and switched back to the thought transceiver.

Whoops, sorry, Oriannon. I know your dad doesn't want me talking to you. Wouldn't want to get you in trouble.

Not likely. She never looked to the side as she stood in line, just straight ahead. *I think the probe is keeping busy making sure everyone eats this stuff.*

Yeah, what a job, huh?

Out of the corner of her eye she did keep track of their music mentor, though, who was now holding his own tray and chatting with several kids in the middle of the crowded lunch room. The probe also looked as if it was keeping track, as it flew closer to the mentor for a better look. Meanwhile Oriannon inched ahead in the line.

Stay right there, Margus told her as she neared his table. *Right between me and the probe.*

She looked up to make sure, alarmed by what he'd said. And she nearly ducked away when she saw what Margus was getting ready to do.

"Margus," she hissed out loud, but too late. Step one, he'd quickly loaded one of his glaep dumplings on his spoon. Step two, he'd lined himself up to use Oriannon as a shield from the all-seeing eye of the probe. Step three, he pulled his spoon way back and let it fly.

Oriannon shut her eyes and waited for the splat. Now they were in bigger trouble than ever.

No worries, Margus told her through the transceiver. Yet one peek up at the probe told her Margus had aimed pretty well; spinach-green glaep dumpling had spattered all over the side of the grapefruit-sized unit, probably gumming up the view lens and sending it into a wobbly gyro-spin that threatened to take it down. A couple of other kids who noticed clapped under their tables.

"Yes!" A guy from orchestra cheered.

But then nearly everyone else in the crowded lunchroom suddenly went very quiet, and it sent a chill up Oriannon's spine.

Uh-oh, she thought, *this is it.*

She was afraid to even look at the main doors; perhaps Headmaster Knarl had just walked in. And if he had, surely life as they knew it was over.

An odd thing happened, though, when she finally got up the courage to look around. Because instead of everybody laughing at the glaep-splatted probe, the way she might have expected, they all stared down at their trays. And the busy hubbub had been traded for an eerie silence, quiet enough to hear a plexi fork drop to the floor.

"Holy Regev and Saius," Margus whispered. He poked his spoon where the pile of glaep used to be. But now?

Disappeared, without even a trace on the plate to show where it had once been. Oriannon refocused her eyes to make sure she wasn't seeing things. Everyone in the room could not have suddenly scarfed down their lunch or dumped it on the floor. A quick look under a couple of nearby tables told Oriannon that much. She even picked up a nearby tray to give it a good shake, just to be sure.

Nothing. She sniffed the air, and even the food smell had disappeared, which made no sense, either.

Back in the kitchen, Deelie and Frax scurried around, lifting empty serving trays, bumping into each other and knocking over piles of clattering steel pots in their panicked search.

"Does this mean we don't have to eat glaep today, after all?" asked a girl at the head of the line. Deelie wiped her hands on her apron, parked her hands on her hips, and scowled at the student's question.

"Take a look around, sweetheart. What do you think? It's all gone!"

Except for one. The only glaep left in the entire room finally slid off the side of the security probe and landed with a plop—right on Oriannon's arm. Considering where it had been ... She carefully wiped it off with a napkin and left it on Margus's tray. Meanwhile, the probe had straightened itself out and raced around the room, obviously trying to catch up with what had happened. Someone back in the office was going to be very interested in all this.

By now the noise had reached a new level again, as everyone looked to see what had happened to *their* lunch. And in the middle of it all, a smiling Jesmet looked to the ceiling for a moment, nodded his head, and then threaded his way out through the crowd—as if he was the only one in the room who wasn't completely taken back by what had just happened.

He nodded when he passed where Margus still sat at the table. Their mentor leaned over to make himself heard.

"Actually," he told them, "I don't care much for glaep, either."

And with that he left the room.

"Wait!" Oriannon called out. Maybe nobody else understood what was happening here. But Oriannon wasn't going to let him get away with this so easily. She ran out after her mentor, catching up with him in the hall.

"What happened back there?" she asked.

She couldn't say why she thought he would know. But he looked over at her with that same twinkle in his eye, the one he'd brought to the first music class.

"What makes you think it's for me to explain?"

"But it was you, wasn't it? Everybody saw ..."

He waited for her to finish.

"Everybody saw the food vanish," she said. Did she really have to explain it again? One moment plates were piled high with their lunch, the next minute each one was cleaned off, as if the tray had just come out of the sonic cleaner. That much she knew.

But everything was getting more and more confusing with Mentor Jesmet.

"Would you be less confused," he asked, "if I had made food appear, rather than take it away?"

"So you *did* take it away."

"If I had, where would I have put it?"

"You always answer my question with another question." She sighed and regrouped as they headed down the hall toward the music rooms. "But something weird is going on here."

"You should explain what you mean by *weird*."

"Actually, I was hoping *you* would explain, sir. What happened in the Glades with the yagwar? And what about the other day at the

Temple, when you knew the securities were coming, and then their stun batons wouldn't work. Did you?"

"Did I …?"

He was going to make her finish the question, every word of it.

"Did you fix it so they wouldn't work?"

"I do feel badly about how that happened. The poor man wouldn't listen when I suggested he check the switch. I did not want him to hurt himself."

Good thing the halls weren't crowded yet. But she had another question — the one that, unasked, made her twitch.

"Actually, that was kind of funny. But …" She fingered the earbud in her pocket, wondering how much she could say that he didn't already know. "I have this … well, I thought I heard …"

Oh, forget it.

She yanked the earbud out of her pocket and held it out at him, like a solicitor in a court of law, cross-examining a witness before the Assembly. He had to know what it was.

"Do you have one of these?" she asked. There — a good yes or no question. She would wait for the answer, this time.

They rounded the corner to come face to face with a probe, hovering just above their heads, pointing a red eye straight down at them. Oriannon swallowed hard and quickly slipped the earbud back into her pocket. Mentor Jesmet didn't even seem to care.

"You can speak freely, Oriannon." He looked from her to the probe. "I'm afraid this probe isn't in working order at the moment."

See? One more thing to ask him — assuming he was telling the truth. What about these probes that wouldn't work whenever Mentor Jesmet was around? He had no idea of the kind of awkward position that put her in with her father. Or perhaps he did.

"Actually I do know, Oriannon." This time he answered the question she had not even asked, only thought, and once more without the earbud in place. "And I'm sorry if you're feeling pressure about having to observe my actions for your father."

He knew! By this time they had arrived at the music rooms, and he paused before stepping inside.

"What about the earbud?" she asked once more, her voice low.

He smiled over his shoulder as the sliding door began to slide shut behind him.

"No, I don't have one. Although you and Mr. Leek do seem to get a lot of use out of them."

And then he was gone. Oriannon could only stand there and wonder, alone in the darkened hallway. The overhead light tubes had been dimmed. But she hardly had a chance to think about what the strange mentor had just said when an alarm sounded from the hallway they had just walked through.

This time a security hurried up to the disabled probe in the hallway behind her. He pointed a remote at it and picked it out of the air as he would pick a grapefruit from a tree. Cradling the disabled probe, he looked around for a moment before settling his gaze on Oriannon.

"You!" His free hand pointed straight at her, and she wondered how he could see anything in the shadows. "What did you do to this probe?"

"Me?" She looked around the empty hallway, her heart racing, wishing she could blend into the wall just a little better. Was everybody still back in the lunchroom, searching for their dumplings?

"Don't act dumb." The security beckoned with his finger for her to approach. She couldn't see if he carried a stun baton, but hoped not. "You're the only one in this hall, and suddenly the probe goes offline. Just like it does every time that Jesmet guy sneezes. You haven't seen him, have you?"

Uhh … She paused for a moment, wondering how to answer, when the security's lapel comm chirped for him to answer. He touched his collar and turned aside.

"Yeah I found it." He spit out the words as if they left a bad taste on his tongue. "Just like the others. Offline."

While the man talked, Oriannon shuffled slowly to the side, down the hall.

"What?" said the man. "No, he's not here. I'm close to his classroom, but he's not around."

Keep talking. She scooted away, slowly. Maybe the security hadn't seen her face yet; maybe he didn't recognize her. But if she had to answer any more questions, someone was going to get in trouble.

"Just a student," said the security, "but I think she might have—"

Oriannon couldn't wait any longer. She thought of escaping into the music classrooms; decided against it. No telling what kind of trouble would come from that. Instead she put her head down, sprinted for the exit, and pushed her legs as fast as they would go. If she could just reach the door—

"Hey you! Stop!"

At least he didn't call her by name. That was the good news, if he didn't know who she was. Unfortunately he pounded along right behind her, threatening to catch up before she reached the exit. And if he did, whatever trouble she had been in before would seem like nothing.

And if he used his stun baton on her? She lunged for the doors, ten steps ahead of the security, hoping they wouldn't lock up on her.

Margus, she thought, wishing he wasn't out of range of the thought transceiver. *Where were you when I needed you?*

8

Oriannon didn't stop to catch her breath, just darted around the corner and into the gardens behind the school, past a row of bushes and behind a grove of her favorite orange-flowered flamboyan trees. She blinked at the bright sunshine and nearly fell on her face in the gravel path. Out here the security would catch her for certain.

Yet she did have to breathe, and she crouched between two hedges, gasping for air, listening.

From out on the parkway she heard the buzz of passing levcraft, and overhead the occasional pods, coming and going with their peculiar fizzling buzz. Anything else? She peeked behind her to see nothing. Maybe the security hadn't followed her after all. Problem was, they'd find out she was missing as soon as Mentor Jesmet took attendance at the start of the next period. And then she heard the crunch of footsteps, running down the path in her direction.

Oriannon hesitated only a moment before turning away from the school once more, toward the narrow garden lanes and pretty whitewashed stucco buildings of Seramine.

"Wait!"

She thought the voice sounded familiar, but between heavy breaths she couldn't quite be sure. Steps grew louder behind her, and she couldn't help crying out as someone stepped on her heels.

"I said wait up, Oriannon!"

She might have, but instead lost her balance as her legs folded. She hit the mossy ground with a grunt, rolled once, then stared up at her pursuer.

"You're not the security," she said, still gasping for air.

Margus offered her a hand up, which she ignored.

"You figured that out by yourself?" he answered.

"But why did you tackle me?" She rubbed her elbow, moving it gingerly to see if it still worked.

"I didn't. You just wouldn't stop. And after what happened in the dining hall, I needed to see you. What made you think I was a security, anyway?"

So she had to tell him the story, or most of it. Margus just started laughing.

"What? I don't see what's so funny."

"Sorry. I thought *I* was the one who was crazy. But you're totally insane."

"Or getting that way." She sighed and looked around the garden, just to be sure no one else was listening in. "Are you sure it's okay to be talking?"

"You see any probes?" He pointed his thumb back at the school. "After what happened in the dining hall, there's an army of programmers running around in the hallways, resetting them. Never seen such a panic."

She shook her head.

"You could have gotten us both in big trouble," she told him. "And we still might, if someone tells. I mean, *you* still might."

"I don't think so."

"But you didn't come out here and tackle me just to brag about what a good shot you are with a blob of glaep."

"Not exactly." Now he started fidgeting. "I was just wondering ... what you saw. I mean, if an eidich —"

"If an eidich sees what really happened, that would be proof in a court of law. Right?"

He shrugged. "You said it. Everybody knows it."

She didn't answer, so he tried again.

"So, what did you see?"

"I have a feeling you're not going to be the last person to ask me that." Finally she raised herself from the path, dusting off her pants. "But I hate to disappoint you. I didn't see anything, except what you saw."

"Oh, come on. Really?"

"Really. With everything going on, I saw people with trays full of food, then I saw people staring at their empty trays, and then I saw Mentor Jesmet leaving. Not much proof, huh? Although ..."

Something made her not want to repeat what their mentor had said to her in the hallway. Not that it meant anything. Margus scratched his head and stared at her, then kicked at the moss.

"I was hoping you'd be able to tell me something else." He turned to go.

"Wait a minute." She grabbed his arm. "My turn. Now you tell me."

She wasn't going to let him go until he gave her a straight answer. He hesitated but didn't turn around.

"The other day you were saying how you thought Jesmet had to be a faithbreaker, right?"

He shrugged and she went on.

"So now you don't think he is? And that's why you were listening to his stories at the Temple?"

"Uh ..." Now he sounded as if he was looking for an excuse, but she just crossed her arms and waited for him to explain. Finally he sighed and turned around.

"Okay, you really want to know? There was just a group of us hanging around, and we weren't really looking for him or anything."

"So?"

"So when he walked by," Margus went on, "a couple of the guys just started talking to him, and then he got into this story, and then … well, I guess you know the rest."

They continued on toward the school building.

"But it still doesn't add up," she said, "And you're lying to me about something."

"What?" He puffed out his chest and put a hurt look on his face. "I come looking for you, trying to help you out, and you call me a liar?"

"But look at the way you're acting — all huffy. The shrugs. The looking at the ground. It all says the same thing: Something's going on that you're not telling me."

"Oh, wow." He kind of spun in a circle, looking up. "So now the great eidich is a great lie detector."

"You can stop bringing up the eidich thing. You know that has nothing to do with anything."

He stopped to let a probe scan him as they re-entered the building.

"I shouldn't have followed you," he said.

"Look, I appreciate it — except for the tripping part. But I still don't know what you really think."

"Okay, then. You know what I really think? I think there's something very messed up here, starting with the field of mirror satellites we flew into, to the thing with the yagwar, all the way down to this whole Jesmet deal. I didn't think so before, but now I do. And now I think it's all tied together, somehow, and I think we need to find out what it is, before it's too late. Before somebody gets hurt — like you."

"You're sounding like a big brother or something." She supposed it was nice in a way if he really cared whether she got hurt or not. Slightly creepy, but nice.

But by that time they'd reached the hallway in front of the music rooms, and at least three or four more probes now circled overhead, recording who was coming and going, scanning hall passes. They'd obviously been brought back on line in a hurry.

"There's one other thing, Margus," she whispered. "About the earbud."

He shook his head and pointed to his ear.

Tell me later.

She nodded, and the earbud still worked. She just hoped Mentor Jesmet wasn't listening in too, as she let herself be swept into the music room with the stream of other kids. She saw no sign of the security who had confronted her earlier, and she still wasn't quite sure if he'd seen enough of her to know who she was.

Mentor Jesmet, on the other hand, stood waiting behind a music stand, waiting for everyone to settle down so they could begin. He looked as if nothing had happened back in the cafeteria.

But honestly? Right now, Oriannon thought losing herself in the music sounded pretty good. Maybe that way she wouldn't see anything that would get her into even more trouble.

For now.

"What do you mean, you didn't actually see him do anything?"

After school that day Oriannon's father paced back and forth across the living room, and he sounded exactly like Margus. Mrs. Eraz the housekeeper hadn't returned from working her other jobs yet, or she might have warned him to calm down and that getting excited like this wasn't good for his blood pressure.

"I'm sorry, Daddy." She sat quietly in her favorite comfy chair, twirling slowly to keep him from getting too close. "I was there, just like everybody else. But I wasn't really watching when the food disappeared."

"You heard him say he did it, though, right? That's what several other witnesses said."

She shook her head. And she couldn't help wonder what kind of "witnesses" he was talking about. Mentors? Or other students?

"All he said was 'Actually, I don't care much for glaep, either.' And then he left."

And her father knew that would be a word-for-word recollection.

"Nothing else?" Still he looked as if he was having a hard time believing it. She shook her head no.

"Nothing else. That doesn't prove he made all the dumplings disappear, does it? Sounds like a great magic trick to me, though. People were pretty excited about it."

Finally her father's face relaxed, just a little bit.

"I can understand glaep doesn't sound like a great meal." He turned back to serious just as quickly. "But it's very good for you. And the Assembly is interested in getting to the bottom of this."

You and Margus both, she thought, and it seemed odd to her that the Assembly itself was so interested in something at her school.

"In fact," he went on, "just a few minutes later, another probe was taken down — out in the hallways. We received a report that a young girl was at the scene, but that she ran away. You don't know anything about that, do you?"

Her mouth went dry. So here's where the new trouble began. And she couldn't lie to her father, though she opened her mouth to try a couple of times. The words just wouldn't come, as if frozen in her lungs.

"That's what I was afraid of." Now he stopped pacing as he stared straight at her, leaning in and holding the arms of the chair so she couldn't squirm away. "So was it you, Oriannon, or someone else you know?"

His eyes told her she couldn't escape his question. She chewed on her lip and finally managed to force out a squeak.

"Me. But—"

That was all he needed. He stood up with a heavy sigh, hitting his forehead.

"That is the last thing I want to hear about my own daughter. What were you thinking?"

"Dad, I—"

"Do you know how much trouble you can get into for vandalizing one of those probes? You could be refused for Seer Codex, you know. And that's just for starters."

Part of her bristled that he would even think she could do such a thing. Vandalize a probe? Margus might, maybe, but not her. But a second part of her breathed a sigh of relief that he didn't know the whole story. And a third part wished he did.

"I know all about that, Dad. But I didn't do anything. I didn't touch any probes, and I didn't have anything to do with it breaking down. The security just saw me in the hall, and he asked me a couple of questions, but then he started talking to someone else on his comm, and I sort of left."

Sort of. He looked back into her eyes. Did he have his own ways of seeing if she told the truth?

"It's the boy, isn't it?" He snapped his finger. "The Leek kid? Ever since you started hanging around with him, you've been acting differently."

"I've been trying to stay away from him, Dad. Honest. He just followed me today."

Once again, all true.

"Well, you tell him to—no, you don't tell him anything. You just stay away from him, the way I told you before. How else can I explain that you shouldn't spend time with a boy from a lowborn family? And if he still bothers you, I'll see to it that—"

"Daddy, please. It's not his fault. He's not evil, and he's not making me act any different than I always act."

She realized how that sounded, tried to back up. How did she always act?

"I mean, it's not him, and it's not ... it's not me. It's ..."

Oriannon might have finished the sentence, except that it would have meant heaping hot coals on Mentor Jesmet's head. And still she could not do that, not yet. Fortunately her father let it go.

"All right, then," he told her, pacing back to the windows again. "But listen: We still don't have a handle on what's going on at your school. Just remember it's more important than ever that you keep your eyes and ears open. Especially during your music times."

She frowned, the not-so-willing volunteer.

"I don't know how much I can help."

He reached down and rested his hand on her shoulder, the way he always did when she was a little girl. "You've all been practicing for your big concert, no?"

She shrugged and nodded. Practicing, and then some. Their performance loomed in three short weeks.

"All right, then." He went on. "That gives you a chance to watch what he's doing."

The *he* in this case, of course, would be Mentor Jesmet.

"So even if it seems like a little thing," he said, "you be sure to tell me if you see—"

"I know." She interrupted him. "If I see anything strange."

If the last few days were any clue, that would be very soon.

Good thing no one asked her what this jumble of sound seemed to taste like. Like burnt rubber boots, or moldering peaches. Like mud. She would not try to explain how the sound of school orchestra instruments tuning up could take on these humble, horrible tastes. They just did.

And Oriannon would have popped another peppermint lozenge in her mouth if she didn't have to tune up her own instrument just then. She straightened her long black dress and tried to block out everything else: sights, sounds, smells, and tastes.

But really, how often did they get a chance to play in a grand performance hall like this? With a lofty, ornamented ceiling with carved twin suns above, gold leaf on the wall, balconies, and chandeliers. This was a place to hear a symphony.

Too bad it was just the Ossek Prep Academy orchestra.

Even so. Mentor Jesmet had promised the Corista Assembly a performance, and a performance they would receive. Everyone in the orchestra had been practicing weeks and weeks for this. She closed her eyes for a moment, just to be sure she could still see the notes, hear the music they'd learned.

"How's this?" Brinnin called to them from the top of a tall ladder where she was hanging a woven cerulean leaf wreath. Not that the grand hall needed any more decorating, but Brinnin thought so.

"Perfect!" Oriannon called back without opening her eyes. "Now just get down from there. You're making me nervous."

And so was Margus Leek, for that matter. Those boys with the drums always had a bit too much time on their hands, a fact which Margus demonstrated for them as he sauntered up to the empty conductor's platform.

"All right, young people!" He raised his hands in his best Mentor Jesmet imitation. "I want to hear those last three measures again, only this time put your hearts into it. Give me the *soul* of the music. Understand?"

Some of the other kids giggled, which only encouraged him more.

"Play it with all your heart, see?" He wrinkled his face in concentration, the same way Jesmet did when they played — or when they practiced. "And when this is all over, I'll bring you a special treat at our next practice: spinach dumplings!"

Even Oriannon had to smile, but for a different reason. She just sat still and waited as the real Mentor Jesmet made his way quietly into the auditorium, from the back. Maybe he was enjoying this as much as everyone else. The giggle level went up, and Margus brightened at his success as a comedian.

"Oh, but I forgot, sorry. I got rid of all those dumplings. Just like I got rid of all the probes in the school building. But does anybody miss them? I thought not. Are we ready?" He picked up Jesmet's baton and waved it at them. "A one and a two and a . . ."

By this time all the kids were pretty much doubled over, watching Jesmet standing behind his student with his arms crossed and a smile on his face. The smile told them Margus had nothing to worry about, except being embarrassed.

"Here, I'll take that." Jesmet gently lifted the baton from Margus's hand, which of course made Margus jump out of his skin and the kids laugh even more. But the smile drained from Oriannon's face when she noticed Brinnin out of the corner of her eye, still decorating from the top of her ladder.

Brinnin had leaned precariously to fix just one more golden ribbon to the wall, and her weight shifted just enough to tilt the ladder dangerously to her left. If she called for help, no one heard her over the laughter.

But now Oriannon could only stand and point, a silent scream on her lips as Brinnin clawed for a way to stop her fall, grabbing handfuls of ribbons as she tumbled down and down, two long stories down to the rows of chairs below.

Now everyone heard the clatter of the ladder, heard the awful thud of Brinnin's head hitting the chairs—a horrible snap. And all the laughter stopped while Oriannon vaulted from the stage and rushed up the aisle to see what had happened.

"No!" Oriannon held back tears of shock when she reached Brinnin, or Brinnin's body. The poor girl had been thrown free of the ladder and now lay sprawled between two rows of seats, broken and not moving. Her arms had twisted horribly and her head lay in a way that said she was no longer with them. That had been the snapping noise—her broken neck. And Oriannon heard the yells from behind her, panicked but well-meaning.

"Don't move her! Don't touch her!"

Instead she leaned her face down close to Brinnin's, holding her breath, listening and feeling for any spark of life.

She heard nothing, felt nothing.

"Brinnin?" she whispered, and by that time several other horrified students had gathered around too. "Brinnin ..."

"Somebody call for help!" yelled another, and Oriannon wished it would help but knew it could not. Her tears dropped to wet the dead girl's own cheeks. Because even though Oriannon had never seen a dead body up close before, she knew without a doubt she was touching one now. Of course Oriannon couldn't claim to be a healer, a doctor. But she knew.

Brinnin didn't breathe, didn't move, had no pulse in that spot below the jaw where a person could always feel a pulse. The life had left her. The girls next to Oriannon began to wail too.

No. No. No! Why did Brinnin have to insist on climbing up the ladder, just for those silly decorations?

"Brinnin, why did you do this?" Oriannon sobbed. "How could you be so ... stupid?"

But she felt strong hands on her shoulders then, lifting her to her feet. Mentor Jesmet, pain written all over his face, gently moved Oriannon to the side.

"Why did you let her do this?" Oriannon spit out the words before she could think. She just needed someone to blame. Someone to hit. "You shouldn't have let her work on a ladder like this. It was too dangerous. It's your fault she's ... she's dead!"

He didn't answer back, only closed his eyes and nodded his head slowly. And when he finally opened them again he gave Oriannon the chills with his long face, as if this had been his best friend.

"I'm glad you care," he finally told her, but in a voice softer than she'd ever heard him speak. "That means a lot."

He paused for a moment, sighed, and glanced up at the ceiling. And then he simply reached over for Brinnin's hand to pull her up from between the chairs, pulled her up straight as if her arm wasn't all broken, as if none of this had happened. Just reached down and pulled her to her feet, just like that. When he let her go, she balanced on her own, like a corpse whose legs had suddenly stiffened.

"See?" he told them. "No harm done."

And then Brinnin blinked, gulped for air. She stared at them now with wide eyes. Oriannon nearly swallowed her tongue at the sight.

"So, you think the ribbons look good up there too?" Brinnin asked them, sounding a little hoarse and a good deal confused.

Oh, but if *she* was confused, what would Oriannon be? The crowd backed away with a gasp, while Brinnin walked over to the fallen ladder as if nothing out of the ordinary had just happened.

"That's weird." She stopped and looked around as if she was trying to figure out a puzzle. "How did the ladder get down here? Did I do something wrong? Did I —"

The back doors flew open just then as a security rushed into the room.

"Where's the accident?" The guard noticed their ladder and hurried over. "Who's hurt?"

Brinnin couldn't explain any more than could the rest of the orchestra, and no one seemed in the mood to volunteer details. But she picked up her ladder and pushed it off to the side against the wall.

"My fault, sorry," she told him with a funny shrug and one of her lopsided smiles. "I guess I need to be more careful. But I'm fine. You didn't need to come running just because we dropped a ladder. We didn't break it or anything."

Give it to Brinnin, thought Oriannon. *She sure knows how to talk to those securities.*

This security glanced around with a frown, obviously not happy about being summoned to an emergency call that was no emergency at all. Of course if he'd arrived a minute earlier, he might have seen things far differently.

But now Oriannon knew without doubt what she had just witnessed, and it made her head spin. Where to put this kind of thing in her mind? Mentor Jesmet saw the security to the doors while the rest of the orchestra drifted back to their seats on the stage, shocked silent. A couple of girls hugged Brinnin and started bawling, while one of the boys tried to tell her that she had died, but of course that sounded outlandish.

Oriannon could only stand in the middle of the grand hall, her body tingling. Replaying her memory over and over. The tipping, the thud, the snap, the broken body. And then Jesmet's touch, the way Brinnin stood up.

Would this be one of those *strange little things* her father might be interested in hearing about?

He'd be there in an hour, along with their housekeeper and everyone else in the family, along with everyone else's family, friends, cousins, great-uncles and aunts ... Probably all twelve members of the Assembly too. Here in Seramine, they took this kind of performance seriously, even if it was only the Ossek Prep orchestra playing in the city's best venue.

Which was fine, but when Oriannon finally took her chair she could only sit there in a daze, just like all the other the kids around her. They heard no jokes from Margus, no whining from Carrick Trice. Just an otherworldly quiet. And though Oriannon waited for Margus to say something in the earbud, he never did. In fact, he had disappeared for a few minutes, probably to the bathroom or something.

Brinnin, on the other hand — the only one who didn't know exactly what had just happened — leaned over from the next row and whispered loudly enough for everyone to hear. "I know we just ate before coming, Ori, but did you bring anything to munch on? I'm totally starving!"

Perhaps the fall really *had* done something to her head.

"I'd be starving too," answered Oriannon, reaching into her bag for a piece of starfruit to share, "if I'd been where you were."

Which brought the first smile from anyone after the accident, and still more questions from Brinnin.

"Come on you guys. What's going on? That's a pretty good joke, but — "

"Brinnin, think for a minute." Oriannon turned to face her. "What do you remember?"

Brinnin's face went a little pale.

"You're serious, aren't you?"

"What do you remember?" Oriannon repeated, louder. "You were up on the ladder, and then what?"

Brinnin bit her lip and looked around at the group. Everyone leaned closer to hear her answer.

"Yeah, I was leaning over. It slipped, I think. And then next thing I know Mentor Jesmet was helping me up."

"You fell two stories, snapped your neck, and now you don't have any bumps or bruises?"

"Uh ..." Brinnin felt the back of her head, rotated her shoulders. "No, actually. I feel great. Kind of like warm all over. Really good. Are you going to tell me what I did? I must have blanked for a second."

"Brinnin, you didn't just blank. You died." This time Oriannon's voice caught on her tears. "You weren't breathing. Your heart wasn't beating. And you were all twisted and broken ..."

Oriannon couldn't say anything else, just dissolved into the tears she didn't want. Brinnin held her hands and looked at Oriannon as if she had just told her a tall tale.

"I do remember falling ..." Brinnin's voice trailed off as Mentor Jesmet returned down the main aisle of the auditorium and Margus slipped back to his place behind the drum row. Where had he been? Soon their audience would begin filling the seats below.

"Brinnin." Now Mentor Jesmet eyed them all with that twinkle of his, pacing around as if he was going to tell another of his stories. Instead, he stroked his beard and seemed to think for a minute. "I'm glad to see you're up and well."

She looked at him with the same question in her face.

"Was I really?" she stammered. "Did you really?"

"Sometimes you'll see and experience things you don't have words for," he told the whole orchestra, leaning forward so they could all hear him. "And right now you still might not own those words. Not yet."

He strolled to the edge of his conductor's platform and smiled.

"But I promise you, you will. In fact, that's what this music we've practiced is all about—giving you a way to express what you can't express in mathematics, or astronomy, or planetary history. Song gives us wings. A way to touch people's hearts with your own. Do you understand what I'm saying?"

For the first time, Oriannon caught a glimmer of something that finally made sense, a door slowly opening. She could memorize the notes, but until she shared them like this, no one else knew. And now behind Jesmet's baton the music finally *meant* something.

She nodded but didn't notice if anyone else did too. It didn't matter either way, as he went on.

"All right. Good. And by the way, Brinnin, in answer to your question, since you were the only one in the orchestra who really didn't see what happened, yes, you really were. And yes, I really did.

"But in the meantime, we have a performance to give, don't forget. You've been practicing for this for a long time. So where's the soul of that music? Let's show them that soul. Let's show them what we can do!"

10

By this time the electricity in the air had picked up in Seramine's Grand Opera Hall, onstage and in the audience. With everything she had, Oriannon focused on Mentor Jesmet's hand, the wave of his arm, his baton raised. He whispered a final comment as the curtain went up to show a sea of curious faces. Her father sat at the end of the aisle by the rest of the Assembly, minus the Regent, whose seat remained empty. She hardly noticed.

"Now," Mentor Jesmet whispered so only the kids in the front row would hear, "as one of your favorite orchestra leaders, Mr. Leek, would say—a one and a two and a ..."

The applause thundered in their ears, though the crowd quickly backed off when they realized Mentor Jesmet would offer no traditional words of welcome to their annual concert. He would give them no introductory speech, the way they were used to. That would be a little unusual.

But everyone politely hushed to the sweet sound of flutes, soft at first, then building louder and louder. With a nod from Jesmet the low roll of drums began, building to a crash of cymbals. This was where the strings and the brass joined in. Oriannon waited for Jesmet's signal as she sat up straight, positioned her fingers on the strings and let them follow in the rise and fall, the swell and the retreat.

And the audience blurred even more into the background as they followed their conductor, each little shrug and each little blink, each sweep of his baton, each smile and wink of his eye. Just then it was as if nothing else existed in all of Corista, only the music and only this conductor. Here she lived in the blend of viol and erhu, kettledrum and horn, but now with a sound enormously different from any they had ever produced in rehearsals.

For the first time Oriannon could taste the sweet sound they made together — like a pomegranate from the tree, picked ripe, full of juice, and surely she had never tasted better. Was this really the same music they had tried to play out in the Glades, weeks ago, stumbling and missing and butchering?

Certainly not this time. Jesmet's broadening smile told them they had begun to touch something far beyond what they'd ever played before. They had finally touched a nerve, uncovered the soul. And for a moment it seemed every bit as magical as when their mentor had reached down and pulled Brinnin to her feet.

Only now — after sixty spellbinding minutes — they'd pulled the audience to their feet, as well. Because when the final notes echoed from the ceiling and Jesmet finally lowered his baton with an exhausted sigh, Oriannon couldn't see anyone in the audience still seated. Even members of the Assembly had risen to clap their hands, though Oriannon had to note they were the last to rise. And no, they weren't whistling and grinning like many of the others in the audience, just politely putting their hands together.

No one else in the orchestra probably noticed, though, behind giddy smiles and little squeezes of the hand or pats on the shoulder. They simply must have understood they had pulled off something very special, and the tears in Jesmet's eyes only sealed the experience for them.

Still the applause kept on for a full minute, then two. Even from where she sat Oriannon could make out the glow on the face of Mrs. Eraz. Who could not be enchanted by the magic they'd just heard?

But before the applause had finally stilled, a messenger in a starched yellow suit hurried down the center aisle from the back door, stopping only at the front row to hand the nearest elder a message. Tavlin Hightower scanned the note quickly in the midst of the applause that would not stop, and the stormy expression that washed over his face sent a chill down Oriannon's spine. Anything wrong enough to crack her father's usual calm expression had to be very bad news indeed. And as the orchestra stood to take a final bow her mind worked to guess the message. What now? Had Jesmet noticed? Would he even know to look?

If he did, he didn't let on and didn't stop smiling as they took another bow. However, Oriannon's father leaned to his side, passing the note and his grim scowl from person to person, all the way down the front row line of Assembly men and women. One started to leave, then changed his mind. Several whispered to each other, and as the audience finally sat down from their standing O, Oriannon's father stayed on his feet and turned to face the crowd.

"I'd like your attention, please." Of course no one could ignore Tavlin Hightower's booming voice. He didn't need a microphone any more than a person needed a magnifying lens to see how bright the Trion was. Especially not when he held up his hand and everybody went silent.

"We've just received word of an extremely urgent issue, one that requires immediate attention." Oriannon's father looked around the auditorium before gesturing to an usher standing by the back exits, so the bright house lights came up. "Unfortunately I'm not yet able to share with you all the details, other than the fact that an extremely serious incident has come to our attention that cannot be ignored or left unaddressed. I can tell you that it is grave enough to cancel the rest of this performance as of this moment, and that it requires everyone to leave in an orderly fashion, without panic—but immediately."

Naturally that sparked a considerable buzz as everybody in the auditorium tried to make sense of his speech. The rest of their performance, cancelled? Once again he raised his hand.

"If you have a child in the orchestra, they will leave their instruments on the stage and come down to join you as you exit. Please be assured that there is no danger to anyone, so there is no reason to panic."

Still no one moved; perhaps everyone else was as shocked as Oriannon. Her father raised his voice even more, putting on the same tone he did at home when it was time for his daughter to clean up her room.

"Listen to me. I am as disappointed as you are at this turn of events, and I realize this seems unusual or perhaps a bit extreme. But I am certain everyone here on the Assembly will concur that we have no choice but to dismiss you at this time."

He glanced at the other Assembly members, who nodded quickly and in unison. Finally Oriannon's father wrapped up his message.

"I assure you we'll do everything we can to clear up this matter *expeditiously,* and we'll be certain to give you further information as it becomes available. Mentor, you will remain for a moment."

That was it. By this time families started shuffling toward the doors, all of them behaving as if they suddenly understood what the word "expeditiously" meant. Or they were working their way through the crowd and looking over people's heads to find their kids. Oriannon's father caught her eye and signaled for her to stay, so she filed down the steps to a safe place in the shadows. Meanwhile, confusion ruled for several minutes before all the orchestra kids and their families finally cleared the Grand Hall. That left only the Assembly members to face a tight-lipped Mentor Jesmet. Finally Oriannon's father broke the awkward silence.

"I assume you know what this is all about." Elder Tavlin Hightower looked around the auditorium, probably checking to make sure no one else heard them.

"Why don't you explain," replied Jesmet, "so we might all be enlightened?"

"Oh, please." Her father slumped his shoulders and sighed. "We've given you as much latitude as possible, mentor, but there comes a time when we cannot ignore the complaints any longer."

"What kinds of complaints are we speaking of?"

"You know as well as I do." The elder shook his head. "What you did in the Glades, for instance."

They hadn't called off the concert to ask him *that* again, had they? He answered quietly that he'd done what any mentor would do, scaring away the yagwar.

"Isn't that what you would have wanted me to do?" he asked, but they obviously weren't in the mood to answer any questions, just ask them.

"And what about the probes?" asked another elder, an older man with a gray-speckled beard.

"I've had quite a few sent to my classroom," Jesmet answered. "Is that how all new mentors are treated?"

Typical Jesmet—answering a question with a question.

"Listen." Oriannon's father pointed a finger at the mentor. "Only a faithbreaker would do or say the kind of things we've heard that you've done and said. And you know the Codex condemns—"

"If I were a faithbreaker," Jesmet interrupted, "I would not be able to bring this kind of music to you. Even the kids know what the music is all about. Or rather, *who* it's about. Do you know who it's about?"

"Don't confuse the issue. We're not talking about the music now." Now Oriannon's father left his seat to approach the platform. "Although I hear you've been teaching the children some rather strange songs. But we might have been willing to work through these differences—misunderstandings, perhaps—if we had not just been informed of this latest incident."

Oh no. Oriannon slumped to the floor where she stood, off to the side of the auditorium. And now that she realized what her father was getting at, she wished she had slipped out with the rest of the orchestra.

Still Mentor Jesmet faced his accusers with a peaceful expression as they lined up to accuse him. He was, in their words, an embarrassment. A heretic, teaching things forbidden in the ancient Codex — though they never explained exactly what. Still they didn't seem to have any trouble calling him a bad influence, a faith-breaker, or worse.

And what about the incident in the cafeteria?

"That's surely not why you stopped the concert today, is it?" This time he actually smiled. "As you saw yourselves, the kids played their hearts out. But something else must have come to your attention that made you afraid to let it go on. Quite a drastic step, I'd say. Personally, I think you owe me a better explanation and you owe the students and their families an apology."

Oriannon could only see the back of her dad's head, but she could imagine his face turning red at such a challenge. And sure enough, he now waved the note he'd been given in the middle of the concert, holding it high with a trembling hand.

"You force us to act, *Mentor*. The reason we're here is that I was informed of a highly disturbing incident taking place only minutes before we arrived at the concert." Tavlin Hightower's voice quavered, and then he gestured at Oriannon to approach. "Assuming it's true, you know this could be cause for dismissal."

That was it, then. Her father and the Assembly were here to fire Jesmet, sweep him away. And now Oriannon felt her own cheeks heat up when she realized that someone in the orchestra must have told what happened when the ladder fell and . . .

Odd. What happened after that? Oriannon tried to call up the memory but suddenly found herself grasping at nothing. She tried again, then dismissed it as due to the stress of the moment. She shook her head, searching desperately for anything she could bring back to mind.

"Oriannon!" Her father wasn't sounding patient and he looked back at her with a glare that made her jump to her feet and hurry down the aisle. "I assume you witnessed the incident. I'd like you to simply tell us what you saw, right from the start."

But with each step Oriannon only felt the horrible fog thicken, just like the time she'd been called on to play her instrument in front of the class. Where was it? The harder she tried to push through, the thicker the fog got, leaving her empty-handed. She rubbed her temples, feeling lightheaded. But then she could only stand at the front of the auditorium, feeling mute, wrestling with tiny memory fragments of nothing that made sense.

"We came to practice early," she finally blurted out, and some of the Assembly members gave her a curious look. She paused once more.

"And then?" her father crossed his arms.

"We played well." That part hadn't left her. She could still taste the sound of the music, the pleasure of their audience. "We played from our hearts."

This time her father rolled his eyes and sighed.

"Everyone enjoyed the performance, dear. But we're talking about before. What happened to your friend ..." He glanced at his note. "Brinnin Flyer?"

Oriannon wrestled once again for the memory, but once again came up clutching zeros. And with each attempt it became that much harder to understand what her dad was so upset about. Mentor Jesmet had done something her father and the Assembly didn't like. And by this time she only knew that she had once known — and now did not. But then she started to doubt even that. What a strange dizzy feeling, as if she was trying to pull back a forgotten dream. Then, as it faded more and more, she wondered if she had really dreamed it.

"I'm sorry, Dad. I ... I can't remember."

"What?" His eyes widened and his mouth fell open. She supposed he had never heard her say those words before. "You ... you know how utterly unacceptable that is. Especially from you."

By this time she couldn't hold back the tears as she shook her head.

"I know there's something there, Dad. But I can't find it. It's weird, but I'm telling you the truth!"

He studied her for a long moment, looking as disturbed and as torn apart now as when he was first handed the note. Meanwhile Mentor Jesmet had climbed down from the stage to join them.

"You know that the ability of some eidichs fade when they reach her age," he told them. "Or actually, it's all there, but they lose the ability to recall."

"And now you're a counselor too," snapped her father, grabbing the front of Jesmet's robe and facing the mentor nose-to-nose. His voice raised to a fever. "Or is this something else a faithbreaker does? Break the memories of his students? Scramble their brains? And what did you do to Brinnin Flyer?"

"Daddy, stop!" Oriannon tried to tug her father away. "He didn't do anything!"

But her father only shoved her aside, waiting for an answer. Oriannon would have pounded her head on the floor if it would have helped her bring back what had happened, what her father wanted so badly.

"Are you going to tell us?" As Oriannon's father waited, his chest heaving, one of the other elders finally spoke up.

"That's enough, Hightower."

"Tavlin." Mentor Jesmet held his hands out as he used her father's first name. "I know you only want to protect the children. But I think—"

"No, let me tell you, Mentor." Oriannon's father finally let go of Jesmet's robe but still wagged a finger in his face. "We're not done here, and we have plenty of ways to bring the facts out into the daylight. I intend to utilize them, in case you're wondering."

"Dad—" Oriannon tried to put in a word. She still couldn't remember what had happened before the concert, but she was pretty sure her music teacher hadn't done anything wrong. Or had he? Either way, her father wasn't quite done.

"You're going to take your black magic out of our school." Tavlin straightened his robe. "Because the Codex warns us about people like you."

"You wouldn't say that," replied Jesmet, "if you really knew who wrote that book."

If Tavlin Hightower's face looked stormy before, Jesmet's new challenge brought on a dark rage. He grabbed Oriannon's arm, jerked her away from the group, and marched them back up the aisle.

"You're through messing with their minds, Mentor," he called back over his shoulder. "You're through teaching your strange songs. And I promise you this. You've got a very short career at this school. A very short career."

hether Mentor Jesmet's career at Ossek Prep would be brief or not, Oriannon couldn't be sure. But then, she wasn't sure of very much of anything anymore. Oh, once in a while it almost cleared. But all she could think to do the next day before the sleep cycle was to get away from the house, away from all the grim people with grim faces coming and going, whispering to her father, disappearing into his book-lined study. They didn't see her watching from the second-floor balcony, didn't know she heard bits and pieces of their angry words.

"Dangerous example," said one. "Nothing but a false hope." And of course she wasn't surprised to hear the evil word "faithbreaker" whispered over and over again. Each person seemed to spit the word like a sour lemon into a sink.

"And his music!" grumbled another. "Infects their minds."

If they didn't appreciate Jesmet's music, that would have been one thing. But with each minute she stood listening Oriannon knew this wound went much deeper. She rested her forehead on the railing, wishing she couldn't hear all the poisoned words and sharp accusations, but hearing them all the same. Finally her father emerged from his study, his jaw set and fists clenched. His eyes met

Oriannon's for just a moment, and the chill she felt made her turn away.

"Oriannon?" He called up to her, and she had to pause in the middle of the hallway.

"I'm sorry," she answered. "I have to go out for a little while."

He said that was all right with him. But where could she escape to? Out. Anywhere would be fine; her favorite place in the world might be even better. On Seventh Day like today, though, it might be crowded with people out walking and relaxing.

Never mind. She slipped out the back and hurried down to the tiled walkways of the central city, through busy avenues filled with Seventh Day shoppers and security probes, lev-craft and the usual shuttle traffic landing on roof pads. As always the suns cast long shadows in the cooler part of the city, where arched doorways led to private gardens, and fountains granted her relief in small pockets of cooler air. She stopped at one, closing her eyes, took a deep breath, and smiled at the way the scent from the cerulean tree tickled her nose. Maybe no one else would be at her favorite little garden.

"You going too?" Brinnin cut in on her thoughts.

"Why do you always do that?" Oriannon twirled and tried to look as if she hadn't nearly jumped out of her sandals.

"Whoa, girl." Brinnin held up her hands in surrender. "I'm your friend, remember? Or did you forget that too?"

Was that supposed to be a jab? Oriannon studied the other girl's face for a clue, didn't find one, just a hint of a smile. Who else could she trust? Margus, maybe, though lately she wondered.

"Sorry." Oriannon lowered her gaze as they walked together up a flight of stairs to the next level, past whitewashed stucco walls covered with creeping lonicera vines and cerise blossoms that made her head spin with their heady perfume. "The worst part is, I'm not even sure what I forgot, only what people told me. But my dad ... I don't think he believes me."

Stairs finally brought them up to more covered walkways that connected on their way to Oriannon's favorite rooftop garden.

Funny—neither of them said where they were headed; they both seemed to know.

"So you really don't know what happened to me at the concert?" asked Brinnin. "I mean, before?"

"Only bits and pieces. And that my dad and the rest of the Assembly are still pretty worked up about it. I think they've been meeting all day."

So they traded stories as they walked. Oriannon told Brinnin about the fog; Brinnin told Oriannon about falling off the ladder, and how she woke again—standing up. No bruises, no sore neck.

"Tell me again. You really don't recall?" Brinnin tilted her head to squint at her, and Oriannon could only shake her head no.

"Like I said, it's all a—"

"A fog, yeah. That's so weird. You of all people."

"You're starting to sound like my dad."

"Is that bad?"

"No. I just don't know how I'm supposed to be around him anymore. I mean, he's still my dad, and I love him and everything, but ..."

Her words hit a dead end; she didn't know how else to explain. But as they rounded another corner she caught a flash of sunlight behind them, perhaps off a piece of metal. Just a tiny flash, but enough so she caught her breath.

"What?" Maybe Brinnin hadn't seen.

Without making it too obvious, Oriannon covered her double-take with a laugh, as if they'd just heard the best joke all year. She leaned toward the other girl, cupped her hand around Brinnin's ear, and whispered a warning:

"Don't look now, but there's a probe following us just a few steps back."

Brinnin only paused a moment. She had to understand everything they said could be heard now. Monitored by some faceless security running the controls to this probe, or the probe could be self-directed, feeding the surveillance data into a larger Security center somewhere.

In either case, somebody was having them followed.

Only, why? Two fifteen-year-old girls, a threat to Corista?

"You're sure?" asked Brinnin, which could mean just about anything. *You're sure* Truly has a boyfriend? *You're sure* she really said that? *You're sure* you would wear that to class tomorrow?

"Absolutely." Oriannon had to give her credit. Brinnin could put on as good an act as anyone. And now her face looked as if Oriannon had just told her the latest gossip.

They also both knew the alleyways and walkways of their many-layered city better than anyone — probes included. They knew from playing here since they were little where the maze of walkways opened up into gardens that hugged hillsides, where sunken alleys led off under market squares, where doorways opened into cool hiding places.

"Well, then, there's only one thing to do about it." Brinnin laughed too, maybe a little too hard. And Oriannon could feel the sharp disconnect between the pretend laughs and the very real hair on the back of her neck standing on end. Probes didn't follow people around the city for no reason.

So as they rounded yet another corner they nodded at each other and quickly broke in opposite directions — Brinnin toward a covered patio that overlooked the Rift Valley, and Oriannon toward a service entry that led down to a food court. This would force the probe to choose one of them; but by running they also let the probe and its handlers know they knew they were being followed.

Oh well. Oriannon tried not to look behind her as she darted through the doorway and around another corner, stepping into a busy kitchen and bumping into a table piled high with dirty dishes.

"Sorry," she mumbled. One of the dishes clattered to the floor as she dashed on through the steaming room filled with white-aproned men.

"Hey!" yelled one who was bent over a sink, up to his elbows in simquat peels. "Out of here, kid!"

"Nothing I'd rather do." Oriannon weaved her way through the crowd of cooks and ducked behind a wood counter piled with vegetable scraps just as the probe followed her inside. If she had only been a couple of steps faster, she could have. . .

Thwaang!

Everyone in the kitchen stopped at the sound of metal on metal, and Oriannon froze in fear to see the probe bounce off the wall and spin to the wet floor. Meanwhile the head cook, a burly man about her father's age with a prominent belly, examined the bottom of his frying pan for damage.

"Hmm," he told them, dabbing at the pan with his greasy finger, "I think I may have dented it." He shrugged and grinned at the admiring kitchen crowd, showing a line of crooked teeth. "Accidents happen, right?"

Oriannon slowly got to her feet, while the kitchen's biomice released from a little floor-level door in the corner, scurried out to the stunned probe, and dragged it out of the way. The little collars on the enhanced robotics blinked green until they'd completed their task and cleared the mess from the floor. The sight of biomice always made the skin on the back of her neck crawl, through she supposed biomice were better than real ones. Maybe. And now the rest of the men backed away as the head cook stepped over to Oriannon.

"Not good to have someone following you." He squinted at her.

"Uh . . ." How was she supposed to answer?

"Well, doesn't matter. Let's just say we don't allow probes in this establishment, understand? Now get out of here. And stay clear of those probes!"

"Right." She nodded, her throat suddenly dry. "Thanks."

But would these cooks get in trouble for helping her? One look at the floor told her the biomice had taken away every scrap and had disappeared back into their compartment with a click. All that remained was the dent in the cook's pan, which he now waved at her in warning.

"Now!" he growled. "Before you bring more friends with you."

No sense getting on his bad side. She did as she was told, leaving the way she came, scurrying back out to the patio where Brinnin was pacing. And when Oriannon stepped closer the other girl gave her a puzzled look.

"What happened to you?" she asked, looking around and behind her. "You look like you took a swim somewhere. And what about the probe? I saw it follow you."

Oriannon looked down at her clothes, still wet from the adventure in the kitchen. She brushed off a blue aplon rind from her knee.

"I took a little detour." She straightened her shirt too. "The good news is I don't think we need to worry about that one anymore."

For now. But for how long? There were plenty more probes where that one came from, each one sent out from a Security monitoring station scattered around the city. And whoever had sent it was bound to come looking for it, wondering what happened when the lights went out.

So Brinnin nodded and led the way through the upper courtyards again, this time toward the gentle sound of a lonely erhu, its haunting melody floating through the third level gardens along the hillside city. Who could possibly play that well?

"This is where you were going in the first place," asked Brinnin, speeding up the pace. "Wasn't it?"

Oriannon nodded. And it didn't seem to matter now that dozens of others were making their own way toward her favorite courtyard, the one with a quiet goldfish pond surrounded by ferns and pink flowers but now filled with people, elbow-to-elbow, trampling the ferns and listening to the strange, sad tune played by . . .

Mentor Jesmet! Oriannon should have known he wouldn't just crawl away and never show himself again. She stopped to listen in on an older couple as they watched him cautiously from a distance.

"You don't think this is the one they were talking about on the media?" asked the woman, squinting a little. The man shrugged and scratched his ear.

"Don't know. But he doesn't sound like a faithbreaker to me."

Of course, Oriannon wasn't sure how a faithbreaker was supposed to sound, either, but like everyone else she couldn't help but get closer. She'd never heard a voice quite so clear, like a crystal pool of water. The words, though, didn't all make sense to her.

"In the morning, when all is new ..."

Morning? The word was new to her, but perhaps it made sense in the North, where he came from. She would find out.

"Pardon!" A woman with a baby in her arms bumped into them from behind, so now they could not have backed out if they'd wanted to — though leaving was the last thing on Oriannon's mind. And when she looked up again Mentor Jesmet's smile and nod seemed to prove he'd noticed how she had joined the crowd. How did he do that?

Even more, how did he pull such a song out of a simple instrument like the erhu? It very much resembled hers and a dozen others in the orchestra. Now he leaned into the music, swayed from side to side, as if he was attached to it. Like the way he'd made them play the other night before her father had sent the audience home. Now she could taste the sound just like the other night, all over again. The fruit of the pomegranate tree, sweet and full of flavor — even better than when they'd played.

And she hardly knew he had stopped playing until moments later, when the crowd wouldn't stop clapping until after he finally held up his hand and nodded to them with a smile. Still the music played in her head, and she didn't want the echoes to stop.

Was this the kind of music the Assembly didn't want her to hear? she wondered.

"I appreciate the applause," he told them after everyone had hushed. "But really it's not that hard to learn. I've taught Level Eight students the same tunes. Oriannon will tell you. And Brinnin. Even my friend Margus Leek, who plays percussion in Ossek Prep's orchestra."

Oriannon turned pink as he pointed her out of the crowd. So he *had* noticed. Brinnin smiled and nodded as people turned to look at them. And for the first time Oriannon noticed Margus standing over on the other side of the people, arms folded across his chest. He'd knit his eyebrows, as if fighting back a headache. And when he saw her he pointed to his ear.

Oh. Oriannon hesitated for a moment before finally slipping in her earbud. A woman in the crowd said something about never having heard the songs before.

"Oh, the songs have been around." Jesmet smiled. "You just have to listen for them."

Which made no sense, and all the sense in the world. An older man asked for another song, and then Oriannon heard Margus, louder than she cared to hear him.

I'd get out of here right away if I were you.

His thought sounded almost breathless.

Are you kidding? We just got here. What's wrong with you?

But across the courtyard, his expression didn't change.

Take Brinnin with you and get out, now.

What? she fired back, *and miss another song?*

Trust me. There's not going to be another song today. And you wouldn't want your dad seeing you here.

Maybe. But how did he know? And what did he know? Once more she heard his words:

I can't keep looking out for you, Oriannon.

Now his eyes pleaded with her as Jesmet joked with a couple of people near the front of the crowd and tuned up his instrument again. When had he said something like that to her before?

Back in the school garden, the day Jesmet had made their school lunch disappear.

Leave, Margus insisted. *Now.*

Which only made Ori dig in her heels and cross her arms, especially as Jesmet by this time had turned back to the crowd with another song. What right did Margus have to tell her that kind of thing, especially now? And why did he look so serious about it? But that's when Brinnin leaned in and whispered in her ear.

"They're back, Ori. I think we'd better get out of here."

They?

Unfortunately yes, if one could properly call ten or twelve probes *they*. One by one they lifted above the edge of the surrounding stucco wall, peering through tree branches and pushing aside vines. Each one scanned the crowd with their unblinking red eyes, sending pencil-thin beams of light from person to person, undoubtedly cataloging each one. And Oriannon would have wished for the cook to be here with his handy fry pan, if only there weren't so many targets this time.

Of course, the probes were only the first wave. As the crowd backed away from where Jesmet had been playing, Oriannon heard scuffling and muffled protests, and then the sound she dreaded the most: the horrible high-pitched whine of a security's stun baton, charging up and surely aimed at the people who were making trouble. Even from across the courtyard and even aimed at someone else, just the thought of what it could do nearly turned Oriannon's knees into tofu. And the sound she nearly tasted — this time she didn't want to give it words as her stomach turned.

"This is an illegal gathering!" the probes announced in unison as three black-suited securities pulled people away from the front, where Jesmet still stood with his instrument. "For your own safety, return to your homes immediately."

In other words, concert over. The securities had made sure of that. And if anyone wondered why they were being asked to disperse, most people didn't take the time to ask. Now three or four more securities joined in, circling the musician as if they would surely arrest him.

"Oriannon," Brinnin urged her, "Come on. *Please!*"

"No, wait." She stood on tip-toes to see her music mentor calmly replacing his scarred old instrument in its velvet-lined hard case. Brinnin nearly tugged her arm off before giving up.

"You're crazy," said Brinnin, finally pulling away and disappearing into the crowd.

Crazy? Maybe Brinnin was right. But Oriannon couldn't help watching as the silent crowd separated down the middle and Jesmet himself walked past gape-mouthed securities. One of them raised his hand as if to activate his baton once more, but something changed his mind and he lowered it again. A moment later Jesmet stopped short directly in front of where Oriannon stood, and Oriannon could hardly look up.

"Sorry your friend had to leave, Oriannon." He smiled and rested his hand on her shoulder, as if they were discussing a piece of music in the lunch line. As if nothing had happened. "But as they said, the concert's over. Better to go home now."

Not yet! Actually, she would rather have sat and listened to his music just a little while longer. But she wasn't about to admit that to Brinnin or Margus. Not to the mentor, and maybe not even to herself.

But she had no choice. Because without another word Jesmet simply walked away, leaving behind all the probes, the securities, and the wondering crowd.

12

Oriannon Hightower!"

The next day Ori snapped to attention at Mentor Narrick's words, but a moment too late. He looked over his astronomy text-book and frowned at her.

"Mentor?" She brought up her most innocent smile; it was worth a try.

"Since you seem so interested in staring out at the sky today, perhaps you could answer a couple of astronomy questions that, by the way, you might expect to appear on the upcoming Level Eight examination."

She could do that.

"So tell us," droned their third-hour mentor, "how many klicks to the nearest of our three suns?"

Caught off guard! She felt her face redden a shade and promised herself this would not happen again. Slowly she brought her hand to her ear.

Want to know the answer? came the small voice.

No! she answered, then paused. *I must not have read that book.*

If she had, she would have known. He laughed. Margus—not the mentor.

Either that, or you're forgetting, again.

I am not!

"Did you hear me, Miss Hightower?" Mentor Narrick tapped the toe of his sandal on the floor. Good thing he didn't hear any of the back-and-forth.

Fifty-two million ... Margus sounded smug. *Three hundred, sixty-two thousand...*

Margus, don't!

But she couldn't help hearing. How would Margus know? The numbers sounded right, so she repeated them aloud as if from memory, watching Mentor Narrick's expression melt from nasty to somewhat less harsh.

"Hmm." He frowned once more. "Close enough. But in the future, Miss Hightower, I'd appreciate your entire attention during the lesson. Even eidichs need to study."

"Yes, of course, Mentor." She added the proper amount of meek, submissive tone to her voice so he would continue with his speech about the volcanoes of their twelve moons circling the big planet.

I thought you knew that answer, Oriannon. Margus was all business now. *Didn't we study that, once?*

I don't care. She sat up straight to stay awake and gave him a hard stare to let him know she meant it. *I want to know what happened to you at the concert. What were you doing there?*

Same thing as you.

"And when these volcanic eruptions ..."

Yeah. But why did you tell me to leave?

Margus shook his head and pressed his lips together, as if he wasn't going to answer.

You saw what happened. I just didn't want you to get hurt.

But you knew it was coming.

Sure I did. Jesmet playing, the Assembly looking for ways to fire him. Didn't you expect it too?

Fire him, sure. But that was something else.

Margus didn't answer. And perhaps she should have known the answers, the way he said. But by now old Mentor Narrick was on a roll with his planetary lecture. He would talk for at least the next thirty minutes on everything from orbits to the pull of gravity, in detail. He would explain anything, of course, except the shadow-side of Corista, one of the twelve moons of . . .

Ori's mind drifted once more as she gazed out the tall bank of ornamented glass windows facing the school's central plaza and its hanging gardens full of bright yellow orsianthius flowers. Nothing made sense anymore except Jesmet's music. But now even that was gone.

A rap at the classroom door interrupted Mentor Narrick's lecture and Ori's daydream, and all the Level Eight students turned in their seats to see a pair of black-uniformed securities quietly step inside. Mentor's face went pale—for just a moment—but he recovered just as quickly and stepped forward to intercept the two men.

"A problem?" he asked. Obviously. Why else would a tight-faced security interrupt a class? Usually they hardly even came on campus; only for problems.

They said nothing at first, only opened a hand-held comm at him to show an image. The apprentices didn't have to wonder long when Mentor Narrick cast a worried glance straight at Oriannon.

"Oriannon," he told her, his voice low. "Please go with these securities to the Health Center. Immediately."

Still the two securities didn't even look at her, just stood with their arms crossed, now in position at the door. Mentor must have seen her eyes widen too, and his voice softened even more.

"Just go, Oriannon. You don't have to take your books; they'll be here when you get back in a few minutes. It will be fine if you do what they say."

For a moment Ori wondered what would happen if she launched herself out the window to the garden below, wondered if Jesmet might be up to healing every broken bone in her body.

But now the two securities shifted at the door, waiting.

Be careful. Margus whispered in her earbud, and she glanced over to where he was slouched in his back-row seat, in the corner of the room.

Easy for him to say. She had no choice about going this time, but she didn't have to open her mouth. She could hold back the memories, hide them in some secret part of her mind, cling to what she knew was inside. So she drew herself up like a Hightower, glaring at the securities the way her father might have done.

The securities ignored her until she reached the door, then gripped her arms on both sides as they hurried down the hallway.

"Health Center, huh?" She tried to keep her voice from breaking. "But I'm feeling great. Haven't been sick in years. Not even the sniffles. Dad says it's the air around our house. The altitude really clears out our lungs. What do you think?"

Neither of the men answered, just continued around the corner and into what would have been the sparkling, bright white domain of Nurse Anno, the school Health Center Supervisor. Only instead of cheery sunlight the nurse had shaded all the clinic's windows with black, casting them into dark shadows. What was this about?

Ori shuddered when she saw how most of the nurse's regular equipment had been shoved into a corner and covered by a gray tarp. The fact that the room had been chilled at least twenty degrees didn't help either. Another cart had been wheeled into place, topped by a small, humming laptop computer projecting a blank blue hologram screen into the air just above.

Where had she seen this before? She locked her legs at the sight, which only meant the securities grunted and nearly knocked her onto her face as they all entered the room.

"No!" Ori tried to backpedal and wiggle free, screaming and flailing at the securities with all her strength. She even tried to grab the nearest face shield, but her fingernails didn't even scratch the polished black plexi surface. "Do you know who I am? You can't do this!"

But they could and they did. Even over her screaming and thrashing they lifted her onto a cold magnesium examining table. A moment later she heard a buzz and felt her skin crawl as the hair on her head stood straight up and they strapped force field grips to her forehead, wrists, and ankles. Not before she managed a swift kick to one of the securities, though — straight to the chin.

"Ow!" Ori murmured. Her toe throbbed; the security had hardly flinched. Time for Plan B.

"I'll call my father," she threatened, and her heart beat so wildly she could hardly make herself speak straight. "He's in the Assembly, you know. He'll have your badges so quick — "

"No need to get excited." Nurse Anno made her appearance through a side door, sweeping the securities off with a wave. Finally!

"What are they doing to me?" Ori tried to move against the force field straps across her legs, arms, and forehead. But the more she struggled, the tighter they clamped down on her, pressing her back and shoulder blades down even more painfully. "Somebody's making a big mistake here."

"Unfortunately no, sweetheart." Nurse Anno crooned and leaned closer, then cast an annoyed glance over her shoulder.

"She resisted," explained one of the securities with a nameless shrug. If he'd stood any closer, Oriannon might have managed to spit in his face shield.

"But you didn't have to be so rough." She turned to Oriannon and rested a more gentle hand on her shoulder.

"Now, Ori, they're just doing their jobs, honey. I'm sure they didn't mean anything."

"Yes, they did. They — "

"All right, never mind. I just need you to hold still for me a moment. Relax. Can you do that for me?"

"Do I have a choice? This is crazy! When my dad hears about this, he's going to ..."

Oriannon tried every threat she could think of, but the nurse just smiled sweetly as she pulled down a small scanning head attached to a spring arm and positioned it just over Oriannon's forehead. The scanner's blue light bathed Ori's face, instantly numbing her lips and making it hard to speak or even blink her eyes.

"Why ..." Ori managed to mumble, "are ... you doing this?"

Now the nurse went on in a sweet, chirpy voice, as if she was simply cleaning a patient's teeth or fixing a bloody nose—instead of getting ready for something obviously much more sinister.

"I'm so sorry, dear. I know this is unpleasant for you, because it's unpleasant for me too. But all you have to do is relax and we'll have this over in just a few minutes. You won't feel a thing."

"Won't feel a thing? No! Please! I'll tell my father, and he'll ..."

She wasn't quite sure what her father might do. One of the securities chuckled, the one who'd spoken just before.

"Does she know her dad was the one who signed the brain scan order?" he asked under his breath, but Oriannon heard him all too well.

Nurse Anno snapped her head around to glare at him.

"You're not needed here any longer. Leave us."

The security took a step backward but crossed his arms in defiance and stayed inside the door. No, he wasn't leaving. So the nurse sighed as she leaned closer and held Oriannon's squirming shoulders down with her two hands, but gently.

"Please, Oriannon. I'm afraid he's right. Our instructions come from the Assembly itself, and there's nothing you or I can do about it."

"The Assembly?" Ori couldn't believe what she was hearing. It had to be a lie. Not her father! "But—"

"It's for your own good, so just sit still or it will take even longer. I promise to make this as painless as I can."

Still Ori wiggled and squirmed, trying to scream, trying to ignore the bitter taste that had come to her. Maybe she shouldn't have been so surprised, the way her father had talked about Jesmet.

So now it had gone from "you won't feel a thing" to "I'll make this as painless as I can." She fought it for as long as she could, but the blue light did its numbing work on her face, as tingling spilled down to her neck, as far as her shoulders and beyond. Finally she could not even feel herself resist any longer. The nurse stepped back.

What had happened to Ori's great idea of hiding her memories? Because as the humming from the laptop grew louder, she could see the first of her thoughts projected right up into the middle of the room for all to see.

Oh, great.

The images came slowly at first, blurred and scattered, random. Views from their home on the Rift Valley Rim, where the air was thin and violet in Corista's rare upper atmosphere. There was her Blue Terrier, Tunni, and her mother laughing over a meal, just the three of them, before her mother had died, when they used to laugh. If Ori's tear ducts hadn't been numb by this time, she would have sobbed. Nurse Anno adjusted the program, and the pictures cleared, flashed more frantically.

And the faster those pictures flashed, the more Ori could feel the horrible, dull ache, now from deep within her memory. The kind of memory her father called a special gift, given to only one in a million girls on Corista. The kind of memory that lingered for years and years, clear to the very detail, easy picking now for Nurse Anno's projector.

One in a million? Thanks but no thanks. What good was a memory that she herself could not enjoy, that could only be stolen from her while she was strapped to an operating table? She winced at the sight of her school friends, orchestra performances out in the plaza, the rehearsal in the Grand Opera Hall ...

"Does that hurt?" Nurse Anno made another adjustment. By now Ori couldn't even move her mouth to complain. But yes. Perhaps not the way the nurse thought, but yes it did.

And finally the securities took notice, leaned in a little closer to see.

"Don't worry," the nurse told them blankly as she slowed down the memory transfer. "You'll get what you came for."

And that would be the crisp, clear images of Mentor Jesmet. There he was standing in front of the class, the first day he'd arrived at the school. Laughing with the kids. Jesmet leading them in their music, thrashing at the air with an ironwood baton. Jesmet with tears in his eyes, telling them another story about Shadowside.

"There it is!" One of the securities grunted and pointed. That would probably be her memory of the healing. He chuckled. Oh, they'd gotten what they'd come for, all right. Except—

Ori! Good thing she couldn't flinch at the voice in her earbud. She was sure Nurse Anno would be able to hear it, though.

But the nurse only paused and looked around the room for a moment, then wrinkled her forehead as if she wasn't quite sure of something. Perhaps it hadn't been loud enough.

You hear me, Ori? Margus Leek sounded as if he was screaming at the other end of the line. Obviously he couldn't be sitting back in Mentor Narrick's astronomy class anymore. *I'm in the utility room. Hello?*

What was she supposed to do, yell back at him?

Okay, he went on, *so I don't know if you can hear me, but I'm going to cut the power real quick. I saw this on an old movie once. Everything goes dark for a couple of seconds, right? When it does, run like crazy.*

Like crazy? She wasn't sure she'd ever heard a plan that sounded crazier, more insane.

Margus cuts the power like some kind of movie terrorist while I run around with a numb head and half a brain, and two securities chase me down in the hallway. This is perfect.

But she had no time to complain, even less to worry. Because a moment later everything in the room went black—including her memory scan in progress. The straps on her head and body let loose without a sound, and she felt as if she could have floated to the ceiling. She heard shuffling and grunting, someone bumping into a cabinet and things crashing to the floor.

"Hold on to her!" yelled one of the securities, just before a backup light glowed orange for a second, then flickered back out. Now was her chance, maybe her only one. Because Margus had obviously thought of everything—even the backup power supplies. Perfect.

"Oriannon!" cried Nurse Anno. "Please stay where you are. Your memory isn't stable yet! You may cause permanent damage if you move."

But the damage was already done. What else could happen? Besides, by then Oriannon had already rolled to the side and hit the floor. Her head tipped as if the tide of all her memories had just washed over her, around and back again. And she was just driftwood now in this vast sea, unleashed, set loose, tossed about.

I have to run! Stung with a fright she'd never known before, she gasped for breath and forced herself to the surface of remembering. It might all wash over her again, any moment. Her head flopped to the side like a rag doll's.

Move! She inched away from where the securities and Nurse Anno stumbled into each other. Too dizzy to stand, she crawled on all fours and headed for the exit. She knew she had only seconds to get out of there, so she'd better move faster.

Right now.

117

13

Out in the hallway Oriannon finally pulled herself to her feet, and she stumbled in circles for a few minutes as backup power switched on and lights returned.

"Oriannon!"

She heard a girl's voice, not sure who it was. Brinnin, maybe. Or Nurse Anno. Didn't matter. Get away.

She ran, stumbled, picked herself up. Voices buzzed around her head, voices she could not understand. And dizzy. So dizzy. She ran straight into a cluster of girls in the hall; they scattered with a little scream of surprise. Still she knew she had to —

Get away!

But her head would not let her, her eyes would not focus, her legs would not obey. Nothing worked the way it was supposed to. And she was really only sure of one fact:

She'd lost everything.

Not just a memory or two this time, and not just a little bit of annoying absentmindedness. This time it was much more. And the worst part was, she wasn't even sure how much — only that it was a lot. She could hardly make her way through the fog this time as she leaned against the wall, panting.

Which way was the door? She couldn't go back to her class like this. She did remember that much. Mentor ... started with an N.

Only this time, she couldn't go back to the nurse's office. Why not? She worked it through for a moment, trying to recall everything that had just happened to her.

The securities. Of course she remembered it now, like a dream in the morning. And the blue light—the memory scan ... A seventh-year girl hurried by her clutching an armload of books, passing by on the opposite side of the hall with a worried glance. Oriannon thought of saying "Boo!" but held back. Instead she put a hand to her hair, which now felt wild and windblown. No wonder.

Do I really look that scary? she wondered.

She hurried down the hall once more, but came up short. Something told her she'd been running the wrong direction, away from the exit. Would she trust the feeling? Right now she had nothing else to go on. If she turned around and slipped back through the halls, maybe she could still get out of here. Maybe, before Nurse Anno, or a probe, or a security caught up with her.

And then she heard footsteps running down the hallway, coming her way. Before she could make up her mind to run again, she turned to see ... her father!

"There you are!" But his look wasn't so different from the seventh-year girl's. Of course Oriannon couldn't run away, not now. She couldn't say anything.

"I meant to be there, Oriannon." He went on. "I'm sorry."

She studied her father's face, trying to decide if she still recognized him. Once again her memory washed in and out like a tide, coming and going. First it was here, then it faded.

"Can you walk?" he asked, and he sounded a little bit like the father she used to know. The one she remembered ... vaguely. Something deep down told her to trust him and she let him lead her by the hand down the hall.

"I can't believe that nurse let you go after the treatment." Now his voice darkened to a growl. "Incompetent idiots. They're going to hear from the Assembly after this is all over."

She tried not to look back at the kids who now watched them from the windows of doors, from both sides of the halls. No one said a word to them, good thing. Not the mentors either, who just looked at her father with wide eyes.

And then the dizziness returned, the confusion. She wondered who she was, and where she was being taken. Her feet buckled, and she felt her father's arms around her.

But that was all she remembered, and she could not hold back the heavy fog as it covered her.

"Oriannon?" Once again she heard her father's voice beside her, felt his hand on her arm. And maybe it was a good thing she recognized her father's voice. Maybe it was a good thing she actually knew who she was. But she groaned and held on to her head to try to keep it from throbbing.

"We're almost home, Oriannon. That was a little too much for you."

No kidding. She heard the hum of her father's pod as it skimmed around a corner on a cushion of air, then jerked to a stop.

"Headache," she explained, not letting go of her forehead. Even saying the words made it worse. But finally she opened her eyes to see where they were, and her father had already come around to open her door. Still the little pod hummed and shivered below her.

"I've got to get right back to the hearing," he told her, "but I want you to rest here."

"Hearing?" She squinted at him, let him pull her out of the pod, and made her way up the brick steps in front of their hillside home. Still she said nothing. She had no idea what he was talking about, anyway.

"Don't worry about it. Everything was set up; all we needed was the testimony of an eidich."

He smiled down at her.

"That's you, and I'm proud of you. But listen, Mrs. Eraz and I will both be back in a few hours. We'll talk."

"Mmm."

The front door slid to the side and she stumbled inside, waved at her father, fell into the sofa. Whatever. It didn't matter now. Maybe nothing mattered. And still she held on to her throbbing headache as she pointed at the far wall, and the media screen came to life.

She didn't know how long she dozed there on the sofa, in and out of sleep. Maybe a few hours; maybe five or six. Voices woke her up and she sat up straight.

Where am I? She wondered. Back in music class, with Mentor ... what was his name? She heard his quiet voice, didn't quite follow what he said, but still she recognized it for now, and knew what she was supposed to do. Never mind the pain that tried to collapse her head from both sides.

"Ready." She looked for an instrument, the one she thought she played. Her fingers felt for the strings, the comforting feeling of polished pluqwood. She sat up straight in her music chair.

And then she realized where she was. By then his voice had faded, replaced by another.

"You're watching continuing live coverage ..."

Her eyes finally focused on the wall screen, the local community news feed, and the figures flickered, life-sized.

" ... where startling new testimony just downloaded earlier today from an unidentified eidich witness is expected to help close the case against a local mentor accused of ..."

Jesmet! She remembered his name again. And on the display now she saw him standing off to the side in the Court of Justice, flanked by two grim securities. Stern-faced men in sky-purple robes surrounded him, each at their place in a horseshoe-shaped table. Though she didn't see his face yet, her father would be among this Assembly; she knew that too.

Oh yes, there—at the end of the table, one of the junior members, but looking as stern and grim as anyone.

Now she heard every word, every charge they brought against him: Speaking to animals. Abuse of power. Encouraging unlawful thoughts. Divination. All strictly forbidden in the Codex.

She heard a flutter of people and paper as the final and most serious charge came up. Worse yet, she saw her own thoughts played back like home movies for the whole world to see: the trip to the Glades and the ruckus in the dining hall, when all the food disappeared. And then the clearest pictures of all, and the ones she didn't even remember firsthand: Brinnin laying dead and twisted, and Jesmet pulling her to her feet.

Almost against her will, Oriannon found herself rising to her feet as well, as everyone in the hearing room hushed and her father cleared his throat. She held her head in her hands. He ran a hand through his thinning hair and looked from side to side before finally facing the accused.

"I only have one . . ." He cleared his throat, started over. "Only one question for you, Jesmet. We know you're a musician. But are you a faithbreaker?"

Jesmet almost smiled before answering. Didn't he know how serious this was?

"You don't recognize me, do you Tavlin?"

Oriannon's father frowned back as the accused went on.

"You've heard my song, and you know the Codex better than anyone else in Corista—except for perhaps your daughter. So let me just ask you: Who do you say I am?"

Oriannon didn't hear the answer, but jumped when someone pounded on the front door, long and hard. She couldn't tear herself away from the drama happening on the screen.

Another thunk-thunk-thunk, and she heard a muffled yell from outside. Finally she sighed and turned to the door.

"Open!" she said, and a green light flickered on the wall before the door slipped open. A boy about her age nearly fell on their tiled entry floor, ready to knock a third time.

"Oriannon!" He sounded out of breath, desperate, his face red and blotchy. Almost as if he'd been ... crying. "You see what's happening?"

She didn't answer, just turned back to the wall, filled corner to corner with the images from the trial. She still couldn't make her mind work the way it should, couldn't fight off the drifting fog that came across her, then lifted.

"Come on, then," he said, stumbling inside and grabbing her arm. "You can't just watch it here. We've got to be there, where it's happening."

"Why?" She dug in her heels. Who did he think he was? And what was he doing?

But he wouldn't take no for an answer, or any other kind of answer, just pulled her toward the door. "You saw the evidence they're using. It's all your memories, right?"

"Stop it!" She yanked herself free from his grip. That much she knew. "I know what they're using. But you think you can just march in here and take me along, whenever you want?"

"I'm the one who got you out of the nurse's office today, don't forget."

She paused for a moment, rubbing her arms where he had squeezed them, and tiny pieces of the memory drifted just out of reach, while others fell back into place — for now.

"You did, didn't you? Thanks. I think."

"We really don't have time for all this." He started for the door. "And if you don't come with me, I'll just go myself."

"What?" She crossed her arms. "You think we can march right in there and tell them to stop? What are you thinking?"

"I don't know. I just know we have to be there."

She studied his face for a moment before another flicker of memory played at the back of her mind. Something important.

"I'll go with you," she finally agreed. Maybe he could help her fill the holes in her memories that now threatened to erode away completely. "As long as you tell me one thing."

He waited by the door with a frown as she went on, squeezing her memory for everything she could get.

"That time when Mentor Jesmet was playing his music in the Temple courtyard, right? You remember that? Before he was arrested."

"Sure I remember. What about it?"

"You told me to get out before all the probes and the securities got there. So how did you know something bad was going to happen? You *did* know."

He stiffened as he looked back at her, and now she noticed how red his eyes looked. It looked as if he was debating whether to tell her something. Finally he shrugged and sighed.

"I was just trying to do the right thing, Ori. *Somebody's* got to look out for you."

"That's not much of an answer."

But he wouldn't tell her any more, only motioned for her to follow.

"Are you coming?"

Once more she glanced at the wall screen, where the report showed one of the more long-winded elders giving his speech about cleansing the nation and following the precepts of the Codex. About the mentor's evil music.

All right. If she followed him she might find out what was going on somehow. So finally she nodded and followed Margus out the door to his waiting lev-scooter.

"I should have walked!"

Minutes later Oriannon was white-knuckling the lev-scooter's double saddle as Margus skidded around the last turn in front of the Court of Justice, the tall domed building that, aside from the nearby Temple, reached higher than any other in the city. Designed to impress, a row of tall marble columns topped a long flight of wide ivory steps, framing the imperial-looking white edifice with the kind of solemn dignity Seramine's leaders held dear.

As Margus shut down the force field, they scraped the scooter's foot, bounced twice, and came to a stop nose first in a hedge of cerise bushes. Here, some of the city's oldest landmarks faced the plaza—stately, classic white stone buildings serving as homes to generations of judges and priests, solicitors and leading business-men. Low black iron fences protected the front entries of most. None would appreciate scooters parked in their landscaping, but Margus didn't seem to care.

"Are we in that much of a hurry?" she wondered aloud.

Margus slapped the side of his scooter with the palm of his hand to silence the whining. He pointed to the side of his head.

"Maybe you should keep your earbud plugged in, just in case."

In case what? For a moment she honestly wasn't sure. Because with the wild ride her head had started throbbing once more, and worse yet, the fog crept back in with it. In and out, here and gone. She rubbed her forehead and temples. Not again!

"Hey." He glanced back as he pushed through the edge of the crowd, gathered ahead of them on the plaza. "You okay?"

She debated whether she should tell him about her headaches, about what had happened to her in the clinic. But of course now was not the time. Maybe later.

"Your driving, that's all."

"Oh. Well, I got you here, didn't I?"

Sort of. Still Oriannon wrestled with the pain and the dizzi-ness, doing everything she could to hold it back and stay on her feet, to stay and look normal. Margus elbowed his way past a sea of media crews and cameras, working toward the front, across the plaza and toward the Court of Justice steps.

I will not get dizzy, she told herself, trying not to step on people's feet. *I will not get dizzy.*

Halfway across she reached out to grab the shoulder of a woman standing nearby; better that than falling to the ground. Margus didn't seem to notice; he didn't look back anymore, and she could hardly see him now for the people. The crowd surged forward as several securities appeared at the top of the front steps, leading Mentor Jesmet out of the tall, golden-domed Court of Justice.

Handcuffed.

"Is the trial . . ." Oriannon stumbled over the words, still taken aback by the horror of what she saw. "I mean, do you know what's going on?"

The woman looked at her curiously, then down to where Oriannon gripped her for support.

"Are you well, dear?"

Oriannon tried to catch her breath as she felt another wave of confusion, coming and going. What was she doing here? What was happening? She fought it as best she could, but feared this forgetting sea would soon wash over her again, perhaps like the sea of people.

Even so, she had to know.

"I'm good." She looked at the building again. The crowd looked on as more securities shoved the man in handcuffs into a transport. She knew him, yes, of course, but . . .

"Well, then you must have heard." The woman patted her hand the way a grandmother would. "The Assembly found him guilty of divination. That was the least they could do, if you ask me."

"Oh." Oriannon gulped and nodded. "Yes, right."

Divination. Claiming a holy link to the Maker. Assuming powers no normal Coristan should claim. Expressly forbidden in the . . . somewhere.

"But can you believe they're not going to execute him?" The woman shook her head and clucked her tongue. "Imagine, divination in a school . . . the children!"

"Then what are they going to do?" Meaning the Assembly, of course, not the children.

"Banished to Shadowside, if he can survive over there, which I doubt. Serves him right, of course. No one survives over there."

"Banished ..." Oriannon repeated the word as people moved aside enough so they could see the gray Security transport. Even over the murmur of the crowd she heard a crackle as glowing green force fields engaged and lifted so the vehicle could skim over the fitted stones of the plaza.

"Instant death, of course, if he ever sets foot again in Corista." The woman looked at her curiously. "Don't they teach young people these things in Codex classes any more? The Principles? The Law?"

"I know the Principles ..." All Oriannon could do was repeat the words, as if hearing them for the first time. She forced herself to focus, but her light was seriously slipping away this time, and she knew it. "The Law."

Or perhaps she used to know them. And there was no fighting it this time. She jammed her hands in her pockets as they watched, felt something small. What was that? She pulled out a tiny ear-bud, wondered for a moment why she'd been carrying it around, plugged it into her right ear with a shrug. This, like so many things, seemed very important to her, though she could not immediately bring to mind the *why*.

If only she could remember. The tide of her memory ebbed once more, pulling back more than ever. Would it return? Up ahead someone was pushing through the crowd, yelling, moving toward the transport. It was someone about her age and very familiar, as if she'd known him in a dream.

"It's not right!" The boy yelled, and people backed away from him as if he carried a virus. Oriannon struggled to focus on his face, but now the headache was taking over as it closed in more and more tightly. "You can't do this!"

Strangely enough, Oriannon knew she was supposed to know who this was, but now she just couldn't make the connection. By this time that's all she clung to: knowing she was supposed to know.

Still, even across the crowd she saw his tears, recognized the desperate look.

Oriannon! She heard the boy's voice clearly in her earbud, and she jumped. *A little help, huh?*

And then everything happened so fast: the boy pressing his palms against the transport's glassteel windows, crying. The securities jumping on him, tearing him away, searching him, pinning him to the ground. His pitiful sobs.

You've got to follow him, Oriannon! came the boy's voice once more. *Find out where they're taking him!*

What? Who was he talking about? And then the voice stopped as the transport glided away with its prisoner, metallic orange lights flashing. The crowd parted to let it advance, and it advanced straight at Oriannon, as if they would take her next.

But instead of jumping away, she couldn't make her legs move. Finally the woman she'd been talking to pulled her aside, just before the transport sideswiped her, jolted her to the side with its force field. And through tinted windows she saw the calm face of the condemned man who looked straight at her with piercing eyes, as if he knew her.

And he did. If she lost touch with everything else, she knew her name — the name this man clearly spoke as he passed by.

Oriannon.

Through the glassteel? She pulled the earbud out, creeped out by the voices. First the boy's voice, now the man in the transport. But they echoed in her mind.

You've got to follow him, Oriannon.

By that time she thought the crowd might have attacked the transport if its force field had not been active. A couple of kids actually tried but bounced away. Others yelled, "Faithbreaker!" and waved their fists. And where was the boy who had caused the scene up front? Oriannon shook her head to make sure it wasn't all a dream.

Shook her head again, and the crowd had vanished.

129

14

How long had she been standing there, by the side of the road? Oriannon couldn't be sure. The way her memory had been coming and going, she couldn't be sure of anything. Her hands shook.

I'm coming unglued!

And what did she really know? Just that she'd been standing there in a fog, maybe ten minutes, maybe an hour. By this time the crowd had disappeared, and so had the boy.

Yet even though she somehow knew she was supposed to, she still couldn't remember his name, no matter how hard she tried. And now the tears blurred her vision — tears for what she had seen, tears for the headache that throbbed in her temples. Now all she could really remember clearly was the man looking out through the transport window at her, calling her by name.

"That's it!" she yelped, glad that no one was watching her talk to herself. A few meters away she spotted a familiar-looking levscooter, half hidden in a cerise bush. Something about that bush. She stepped closer for a better look.

"Hey you!" A man stuck his head out a second-floor balcony window, just above the street. "Is that your scooter?"

Oriannon looked closer at the blue-and-white two-seater, sleek but good and beat up. She had to admit it looked awfully familiar, as if she had ridden on it, even.

"Uh ..."

"Well, you need to get it out of my garden, you hear? What is it with you people? You think you can trample all over the place, and just leave your trash anywhere you please? The show was over a half-hour ago."

Oh. That told her how long she'd been out of it, anyway. Just standing there, or wandering around in a daze, she couldn't be sure. She didn't answer.

"You hear me?" he went on, "Because if you don't get out of here now, I'm calling a security!"

"No, no. I'm sorry about your flowers." Oriannon threw her leg over the worn saddle and slapped the side of the scooter just below the steering wheel. The little machine came to life, lighting up a little control panel and winding up its force field.

How had she known how to do that? Didn't matter now. The scooter finally worked up enough power and bobbed up on a bubble of air. She rocked back and forth for a moment, smashed a few more blooms, and finally managed to back away.

"NOW what are you doing?" yelled the unhappy homeowner. He brought a comm to his ear and started shouting all over again. "Hello, Security? I have a girl here in front of my home, smashing all my flowers, and ..."

Oriannon didn't hang around to hear the rest of his story. She wheeled around and put the Court of Justice behind her, retracing the route the transport had taken. Strange. Even if she had forgotten most everything else, she knew exactly which street to follow, which direction led out of the city.

And she remembered the man, the prisoner taken away. The way he'd called her name through the window. The strong pull she felt now, the tug to follow.

You've got to follow him!

This way? Here in this part of the ancient capital, streets hardly seemed wide enough for a person walking and a little lev-scooter like hers. But she wound her way through the mid-day crowd, some taking shade under brightly colored blue and green awnings strung over the narrowest parts of the street. She picked through the market crowd, ignoring tantalizing smells of pluq fritters and spiced teas, weaving right and left and eventually turning onto a wide, tree-lined avenue past five-story clusters of ivory stone apartment buildings and neighborhood shops, moms walking little pet treb bears, and bustling open-top transporters full of people on their way to and from work. Bright red and yellow banners hung from balconies, fluttering lightly in the breeze, and she gazed at them to try to remind herself. She knew this place, but still the fog held her in its grip, making her feel like a stranger in a strange land.

I can't even say where I live, she told herself, *or who my family is.*

So she pushed on. Twenty minutes later the avenue took her into rolling hills, where the traffic thinned and trees began to outnumber the white stucco buildings and rooftop gardens of the city. Beside her she noticed a mass of giant water pipelines — at least ten or fifteen of them — all painted a mottled tan to blend into the landscape, but sticking out even so. Who could miss Corista's lifeline, where all their water came from? She'd just never seen them so close before.

She glanced over her shoulder one last time to see the suns reflected in glittering domes and red tile roofs, then twisted the handle grip all the way towards her and held on as the scooter surged ahead and the scenery flashed by. What was her hurry?

Find him!

Crazy, but she knew she'd taken the right way, past checkerboard fields of ebony-flowered waspseed plant, and she ducked down behind the little plexi windshield so the bugs would not *splat* in her eye. And, as the world flashed by, every hour brought her closer. Four hours, then five ... She lost track.

At length the paved road turned to gravel, which turned to dry, hard-packed red dirt. Didn't matter. She hadn't seen another scooter, another vehicle, for the past half-hour — until now.

Whoosh. Backwash from the big gray truck-sized transporter knocked her sideways, nearly throwing her into a spin. She squeezed the brake and applied rear thrust, which only spun her more. Finally she pulled to a stop in a dusty ditch, but only after bouncing off a couple of small boulders.

One more dent in this thing won't matter. She coughed and watched the back end of the familiar-looking transporter disappear over a hill, back the direction she'd come.

Was that what I was following? she asked herself, biting her lip in concentration. No, she decided. Maybe it had been, but not any more. So she waved away the dust, pushed away from the boulder, and continued on her way. The scooter complained and whined beneath her. Maybe it had taken one too many bumps.

Still something told her this was the right way to go, and she urged her little lev-scooter on as fast as she dared, flying up and over hills, almost losing her way except for the washed out trail of dust left by the transporter's force fields. That, and the ever-present pipelines snaking their way over the hills. Yes, this would be the way.

But something else was happening, something odd, and every once in a while she checked over her shoulder to make sure. Trees had long since disappeared, replaced by ragged outcroppings of rocks. And now as she crested yet another hill she was sure of it.

Look at the shadows! They lengthened and darkened in ways she'd never seen before. And behind her, instead of being overhead? The three suns of the Trion had lowered in the sky. She pulled off her shades and still felt as if she was traveling deeper and deeper into a darkened closet.

At the same time she shivered at a wall of cooler air, though she had to admit there was something here that cleared her head. New smells, pungent and prickly, tickled her nose, almost like spices Mrs. Eraz cooked with in their kitchen. They seemed to soothe away the last of her mind-splitting headache. She breathed deeply, then noticed something new on the side of the road. This time she had to stop.

"Weird." She thought no one had ever told her that white ice lay on the ground like this. And cold! She giggled when she touched it for the first time, then picked up a handful and squeezed. It even smelled like this strange land—dark and full of secrets. Had she crossed over into Shadowside yet?

Not yet; she probably still had a ways to go until the border, and she guessed it would be marked. So she shivered and squeezed her shoulders, trying to set aside all the reasons she should turn back. It wasn't too late yet.

Oriannon only felt the pull to follow, as if she was standing in a stream and the current would take her if she let it. And still she knew this was the right current, the right direction. Never mind the shivers and the fear. So once more she mounted the scooter, and it moaned beneath her this time, hesitated for a couple of seconds—and finally sputtered back to life.

"Come on ..." Oriannon willed it up the next hill, but the higher she climbed the slower it crawled. She tried not to think of what she would do if it decided to break down way out here. On the next crest, though, it seemed to jerk less and speed up more. Good.

Only now with each kilometer the shadows grew longer, the sky turning from light violet to maroon to nearly jet black. Just like up in the shuttle, with ...

"With who?" A particle of memory had just hit her, she knew. Something about riding into danger, very much like today, only they were high above Corista and ... and that was all she could remember. She just didn't know where the thought had come from, or if it was real. Maybe it had been a dream of some kind. In any case it was out of reach, like the lights that had started to blink above her head—stars that they could never see in the always-daytime of Corista.

Only problem was, pretty soon she wouldn't be able to see where she was going. The shadows had grown so long that they'd melted into each other. It did help a little that the white ice seemed to glow with pale blue and green sparkles that showed her where the hills rose and fell. Still she pushed the scooter, kept the throttle turned full, and it responded by screaming and whining louder than ever. Maybe this place that was pulling her on, kilometer after kilometer, maybe it would help her put everything back together.

Or not. Now she crouched behind the cracked windscreen, shivering, wondering if maybe she should give up this quest and turn around. But to where? The city and her foggy past had disappeared far behind her. The only thing that made sense — in a strange sort of way — lay ahead. Never mind the weathered orange warning sign that leaned precariously over the road: Restricted Zone Ahead.

At least she knew the border was just ahead now. A single light blinked in the distance. And only a few minutes later she slowed at the sight of a lone guard tower set on rusting metal legs but tall enough to overlook several hectares of barren scrubland.

The light, it turned out, was a slowly spinning yellow warning blinker, bright enough to shine for many kilometers in the twilight. She eased back on the throttle even more, letting the scooter coast the last few hundred meters, and held her breath.

I haven't come all this way to stop now, she told herself.

"Hello?" At first Oriannon expected a security to jump out of the little shack at the base of the tower, but she couldn't make out even a dim light through the window. The scooter finally wheezed to a halt, though she pumped the throttle to try to keep it alive.

"Don't die on me now!"

But the scooter's force field had already slipped away, leaving her no choice but to park it in the gravel. She took another breath, stepped clear, and checked out the guard house once more.

"Anybody here?" She raised her voice, though it occurred to her she really didn't want to know the answer to her own question. Still she ventured closer, heart beating loudly, ready to run.

Still nothing.

What about the door? She knocked quietly, leg muscles tensed, and tried to slide it open.

No luck.

The window? It was covered with a fine layer of dust, but she wiped it aside with her fist and peered inside.

Completely dark.

"This is really creepy," she told herself, and she wasn't sure if she was shaking now from the cold or from something else, or both. She looked up again at the top of the tower, where the yellow revolving light cast a blink of daylight on her once every other second. In between, she thought she heard the faintest glimmer of music—but so faint that she couldn't tell if it was her imagination or real. She paused. No, the only sound was the wind whistling through the tower legs, reminding her that—

"This is a restricted area!" A distant probe's voice broke the silence, nearly giving Oriannon a heart attack. "Turn back immediately!"

She sprinted to the idling lev-scooter, worked the starter switch on and off, on and off.

"This is a restricted area!"

She heard it again, just wasn't quite sure which direction it came from. Perhaps a ways off, but getting closer—fast. Still, she should have known this part of the border between Corista and Shadowside would have been patrolled by probes. She should not have been surprised.

She glanced quickly back in the direction of Seramine, far away now, and all she could see was a thin sliver of light on the horizon where the suns used to be. Ahead, over the border, darkness completely closed in.

"Restricted area!" came the probe again, sounding closer than ever.

But she had already decided which direction she was headed—if the scooter would only cooperate. Too bad it didn't have its own

137

lights on it, though that would have given her away this time. She tried the ignition one more time, and it finally powered up.

"There we go." She lifted and coaxed it up to a hover position a few centimeters off the gravel, but this time it sagged under her weight, scraping the rocky ground. Her little control panel indicator between the handlebars flickered. And as she applied full power the scooter fussed and fishtailed.

"Oh, please." She squeezed the handlebar grips and crouched. "Don't give up on me now."

She might have stepped off and pushed if it would have done any good. She did try to lean out with one foot and give it a boost. But that only sent her spinning in circles once more, and the more she tried to make the scooter move ahead the more it complained, until—

Thwump! One of the thrusters came to life, and she rocketed away from the yellow sentinel light, though tilted to the side and almost falling off. Just ahead she could see a stringed red curtain of laser light, about two meters tall, stretching from right to left as far as she could see and hugging each curve of hills.

So this was the border, the edge of Shadowside.

Would she just pass through? Oriannon had no idea, but whatever memories had been driving her on through all these kilometers, all these hours, only pushed her faster now, as fast as the poor little scooter would take her. It bobbed and weaved and wobbled, but even half-thruster power sent her careening dangerously toward the light fence.

And even if she had been able to see the probe in time, she probably could not have done anything about it, or steered clear. One second she saw it, outlined for a brief second in the blinking light from the tower behind her. She winced and ducked, but that was all. The next second ...

Bam! The scooter shuddered, igniting a fireball and sending a world of sparks and flaming shards of metal in all directions. She must have hit the probe head on.

And not only that; her little windshield peeled off to the side, opening the door for an icy blast of wind to hit Oriannon in the face. She grimaced and held on with everything she had as the scooter writhed and twisted, like a terramole lizard caught by the tail, trying to escape the accident.

That flash of red light gave her a tingling sizzle of raw energy. Probably the border fence. She thought she heard the harsh buzz of an alarm somewhere behind her too. Though at this point, that was the last thing Oriannon was worried about.

Right now getting off this scooter was the only thing that mattered. Brakes? She squeezed the handle again and again. No effect, except that it seemed to speed up even more insanely and rocket over a low series of hills. Steering? None of that, either. Maybe that was because she'd left the front end of the scooter behind, in pieces, on the other side of the border.

Now she had no idea what was left of the crippled lev-scooter to help jet her up yet another barren hillside, then around another set of hills and far across a rugged plateau before plunging down, down into a sudden ravine. She could only hold on, her knuckles raw and cold, waiting to be dashed against the hard face of this forbidding landscape.

Instead the reactor whistled in its final agony before the scooter glanced off a boulder to the right, spun off another hard outcropping to the left, and then finally dug in to launch Oriannon off the saddle — still holding to a now-useless pair of handlebars.

She remembered hitting hard enough to knock her breath out, but sliding for quite a ways upside down on a carpet of white ice. The blue and green glittering crystals looked pretty as they sprayed all around her. And then when she slipped to the side — the handlebars finally jerked from her hands — she tumbled into a low spot, on her head and not sure which way was up. Her arm twisted severely, and she felt an ugly snap in her shoulder just before finally coming to rest in a horrible twisted heap.

FINDING SHADOWSIDE

How long have I been lying here?

The pain woke Oriannon more than anything else. And it was not just in her head this time, but over every inch of her body. Her legs felt bruised or broken, her back and neck twisted beyond hope, and her arm ...

Oh, her arm! She tried to pull it back into place, but just the thought sent flames of pain shooting up from her elbow to her shoulder. At the same time, it throbbed almost enough to make her sick to her stomach.

Not to mention the cold that made her feel like a piece of meat in a freezer. What kind of combination was this—freezing flames? She couldn't stop the freezing, but every shake only made it worse. Even the tears—which she also couldn't stop—didn't help either.

Still, she knew she could not stay this way, twisted and broken in the dark and the white ice. If she died here, who would know the difference? If she could just move the arm around to the front again, maybe even sit up ...

No worries, she told herself, and the words reminded her of something. Someone. Who? The fog still hadn't left her. But she imagined sitting someplace warm, back in the city where she'd come from, with people who cared for her. And because she was trying to remember it, did that make it true?

She squeezed her eyes shut and bit her lip, reached up her free left hand, and screamed.

"Oh!" Did it get any worse? Still she fought to sit up, to free her right arm pinned beneath her. She clawed at the dark as if she could pull herself up, while her shoulder gave a large *pop*.

And she screamed in pain once more, now clutching her injured arm in front of her, sitting up in the white ice and crying with even more tears that she didn't know she had. But she had to get up, so she rolled to the side and hoisted herself to her knees.

Don't stop! she told herself. And finally she stood panting and exhausted, still clutching her arm. She stood that way for a while, catching her breath, waiting for the pain to subside just a little. And she listened—there!

This time she thought she heard it, resembling a faint whisper more than a real chorus. And whether it was above or simply off in the distance, she still could not be sure. But she smiled at the song, even if it was yet hardly more than pretend.

Oriannon tried not to think too much about what had happened. But she knew her shoulder had popped out of its socket, and now was hopefully back in. The pain now throbbed, aching, pushing her to the edge of lightheadedness. And then she heard something else—a faint rustling, pebbles falling from a height.

"Who's there?" she shouted up into the darkness.

And now she found perhaps it wasn't as dark as she'd first thought. Dark, yes, compared to where she had come from. But a bright canopy of stars offered a bit of light. The blue-green glow of the white ice added a bit more. And with these nightlights she could see how the three-story walls of her little canyon were pock-marked with ledges and caves. But again she heard the rustle. And when she ducked away behind a rock, the pain from her shoulder nearly made her faint.

Don't black out, she told herself. Her stomach growled, and she couldn't remember the last time she'd had anything to eat. Or drink. With her good arm she scooped up a handful of white ice; she let it melt on her parched tongue. Better, but it sure didn't warm her up. Tasted like ... space, and was just as cold. The only way to warm up, she thought, would be to move. And that, given her arm, wasn't going to be the easiest thing to do.

"Okay, then!" she yelled up at the ridge above. "If you don't come down, I'm coming up."

It might have been better if she'd been able to explain why she'd come here in the first place, or where she was going from here.

"Well ..." she mumbled, and talking to herself only seemed natural in a lonely place such as this. "I know I can't stay down in this canyon, right?"

She felt in her pocket, finding a small wireless earbud. She held it up in the dim star-glow, wondering what she had used it for. Once again her memories floated just beyond her reach, taunting her, but she knew at least they were there to forget. Now, if she didn't even know that she was *supposed* to know, *that* would be frightening. She slipped the earbud back into her pocket and started up the canyon wall. Slowly, slowly.

Oriannon could have retraced her steps the way she'd tumbled down the side of the hill into the gorge, but this other side seemed a little less steep. Besides, she wanted to keep going the same way she'd been traveling on the scooter.

"This way," she told herself, breathing heavier from the climb. Didn't matter what was up here. Even with just her one arm she found her way up a series of broad natural rock steps, each one steeper than the last. And now she could climb, but slowly, using her good left arm to reach up and grab a handhold in the sandstone ledges above her head. Where the rock had been worn by wind and rain, small puddles of sand made her grip that much more slippery. And, of course, it would have gone faster with two hands. But she just reached and pulled, reached and —

The hiss startled her more than the slimy rope feel of the thing she grabbed. But only for a moment. With a yelp she let go as a snake tumbled off the ledge in front of her, covered in a sort of glittery ooze that made it look like a huge worm. As thick around as her own leg, it stretched longer than she was tall.

And the stench! She covered her nose as an odor like dog vomit assaulted her, only worse. When the worm spit hit her in the shoulder she tumbled backwards, trying to blink away the burning pain and wipe off the caustic venom at the same time.

"Get away!" she screamed. She thought of stomping it, but figured that would have made it madder than it already was, hissing and squirming its way down the rock wall and burrowing into the loose sand at her feet.

Stupid worm. And she crouched there on a rock ledge, halfway up the rise, wondering how many more surprises this horrible, cold, dark place held. Her eyes watered and her shoulder and arm still throbbed. At least she wasn't shivering as much now, though she could feel the raw wind picking up as she climbed higher.

Only now she slowed even more, tossing handfuls of gravel up to the places she couldn't yet see.

"Away!" she called at each step. Right now she just wanted to make her way to the top and out of the canyon without getting sprayed again by giant worms, these ... sand worms. She kicked at another one without thinking, and it hissed but slipped away without doing any more damage. Strange how quickly they could bury themselves in the sand. She stepped lightly, hoping not to disturb any more than she already had.

Finally the wind told her she'd made it to the top—a chilling breeze loaded with the scent of heather and ice, chiseled with a raw power that slapped her cheeks and took her breath away. Her hair stood out like a flag as she stood at the edge of the ravine, hands on her hips, turning to see what this place really looked like.

Dark, yes—but it could have been worse. Now it almost made her think she was looking at the world through shades—but of course she'd lost hers long ago, back on the scooter. Yet even in the shadows of this darkened world she could make out the rugged, rolling hills, stretching as far as the horizon, decorated with the blue-green glow of white ice and warmed by the thick canopy of stars overhead.

"I can't believe it." For a moment she forgot even the pain of her arm, just blinked back the tears—and those not from the sting of the sand worm, but from seeing the fierce beauty of so many tiny lights, so close. She reached out to touch them, staring at the patterns that began to blink out of the stars. There—a face! Or a hand holding an ancient sword. She even recognized a jet-black yagwar, crouched as if ready to pounce on its prey.

For the first time in her life, Oriannon saw so far past herself that she wondered who had put so many stars in this sky. This couldn't be the same cold, lifeless Maker she'd always read about.

Could it?

No. These stars sang and danced to music she'd never before heard, like a window to the universe she'd never witnessed. Like they'd been created yesterday.

She didn't know how long she stood there staring at the stars, wondering about things she'd never wondered before, when the rumbling beneath her feet shook her out of her wondering.

What was that? The rocky earth rumbled below her, deep and quivering. She leaned over to hold onto a large stone, larger than herself, but it rumbled with the rest of it. And then the dry waves came, one after the other, nearly knocking her off her feet, and she heard this earthquake as much as felt it.

"What kind of place is this?"

The earthquake jolted her back to now, back to the real world of shivering cold and a shoulder that still throbbed. What was she doing here? Alone and lost, cold and hungry, in a place where people were sent to ... to die?

How did she know that? The thought tickled a memory somewhere deep, and though she couldn't quite bring it up, it pushed her to start walking once again.

147

Keep walking, but which way? She knew without thinking, even walked faster, though her shoulder and arm throbbed worse than ever with each step. She put the canyon behind her, the borderlands and the crossing, grateful the probes had not tried to chase her. And she tried not to step on anymore sand worms. Tried not to sink too deep when she came upon a glistening field of dark, dusty ash.

Was she just imagining it, or did it suddenly feel much warmer? She coughed and waved her hands as the dust covered her. And then she heard what she'd been hoping not to hear, ever since she'd climbed out of the ravine.

Another hiss. Only this one came from several directions at once, even as she hobbled a couple of steps and sank knee-deep in the warm, dusty ash. And the harder she tried to lift her legs to walk, the harder the ash seemed to tug at her.

Stop! she told herself, holding her breath and hoping for the hissing sounds to go away.

They grew louder, closer, like a sucking vacuum cleaner. The ground quivered beneath her feet — not like an earthquake this time, but more like a bowl of glaep dumplings, and she thought it odd to be recalling food at such a time.

No going forward. She tried to lift just one of her legs, slowly, and imagined a family of sand worms nibbling at her toes. Maybe the creature couldn't see her, but she knew better. And when she smelled the telltale vomit odor she knew it was even closer.

Could she back up? She knew of no other solid ground, no place else to go. Even if she met this sand worm, better to be able to run than to be mired in this pit. Her foot finally worked free, leaving behind her shoe. She reached all the way down and hooked it with one finger, fishing it from the dust. But she looked back up to face three sand worms, each one following her movements like a tracking laser.

Oriannon screamed.

And for a moment they recoiled, before weaving their heads back around and hissing at her shoe, following it from side to side. Almost without knowing it she held her breath, and by this time her eyes were watering from the smell. But after a long minute's standoff, Oriannon couldn't stand it. She sneezed, which drew the instant attention of the sand worms. Which made her wonder: *Could they only see things that moved?*

This time she was ready for what came next. She dove to the side as all three creatures reared back and spit wicked streams of bile straight at her. One stream caught her on the knee, spinning her around, but that wasn't going to stop her this time. Shoe in hand, she scrambled to the side looking for firm ground. She hoped they couldn't squirm that fast.

Up ahead and to the right, she leaped over an odd bubbling pool set into a cluster of rocks where the steam smelled like rotten eggs. Right now she needed to put as much room as she could between her, the ash pit, and the angry sand worms. She didn't stop until she had climbed another rise a half kilometer away, where she fell to her knees and gasped for breath.

They wouldn't follow me, she told herself. *They can't.* But still she wasn't at all sure, and so she listened once more to the wind. She only heard her own heart beating, and again a rustling sound in the bushes that seemed more like footsteps than worm creatures. But she couldn't be sure. She picked up a rock and threw it at the sound, wincing at the pain in her shoulder.

Nothing moved.

"Yah!" She stomped in the direction of the sound, but that only hurt her shoulder even more, so she crouched low, listening and catching her breath. By this time the day was catching up with her, the deep fatigue settling upon her, pushing past her adrenaline rush.

She licked her dry, cracked lips, wishing for just a little more of that white ice. Something to cool her throat. But up here on the rise most of the ice had melted. She tried to swallow; it didn't

149

help. Never mind noises in the shadows—where could she find something to drink?

What's more, how could she find what she came here for? How would she know what she was looking for in the first place?

She would figure that out, in time. The answers would come. For now she just wondered how it might feel to stretch out on a comfortable bed again after a long, steamy shower. That would be so nice. Maybe she could just close her eyes for a minute or two. She nodded.

"Just for a minute or two," she mumbled. Still shaking, she dropped to the ground behind a cluster of boulders and curled up into a ball. Never mind the worms. Never mind the sounds in the shadows.

Just sleep.

16

It took a moment for Oriannon to sort out the dream from reality. Even then, she huddled behind the shelter of boulders so the probes wouldn't find her. And she tried to shake away her nightmare, shocked that she could remember every detail: the fear and the running, the tripping, the attacking probes, and the sand worms wrapped around her ankles.

She could not recall ever having had such a dream, couldn't even remember recalling a dream in such detail. The dark must have brought it on. Where was she? Oriannon pulled a thick, handwoven cloak to her chin, sweating, shaking, wondering. Only the dull, throbbing pain in her shoulder convinced her this Shadowside was real, rather than the bizarre chase she had just tumbled through in her sleep. She held the cloak a little closer; it smelled of cook fires and garlic, earthy spices and fried fish. It was obviously not hers.

So where did it come from? She knew she had not fallen asleep with it wrapped around her shoulders. Would the owner return to reclaim it? She sat up with another mystery added to the list, right behind "What am I doing here?" and "Where am I going?"

Without answers she studied the cloak's weave for a minute, tracing her finger along an embroidered golden thread, a pattern of three suns against a dark background. She thought it quite beautifully made, really, with its intricate stitching and a sort of rustic charm. The suns reminded her of the place she had left, the place where it was always as bright as this place was dim. Perhaps if she just studied the cloak long enough she would remember.

Or not. She sighed as she pulled herself to her feet and looked around, trying to decide which direction to follow. Every stiffened muscle in her body protested, and her right shoulder throbbed worse than ever. Her eyes followed the outline of distant barren hills, a deep purple set against thousands upon thousands of stars dashed across the western sky. To the south a small, distant moon meandered into view, lending its own pale, yellow light and a certain sense that she was not completely alone. A reddish-blue glow danced above the eastern horizon, illuminating a familiar sight.

The pipeline.

"I've seen that before," she told herself, and with her eyes she traced the paths of three good-sized pipes snaking their way across barren hills, much as they had on the other side of the border. She approached them carefully, pausing here and there, unsure just how close she should get.

Each probably measured three meters across—big enough to drive a large transport inside. She guessed they might be for water, and even leaned close, listening to its rushing pulse. This had to be a good trail to follow, one that would lead her somewhere.

So as she continued her hike she listened for any sign of life. A crow, maybe. Even the rustling footsteps of the person—or animal—that she thought had followed her. Just in case it had, she stopped and shot a look over her shoulder, strained her eyes to peer into the shadows.

Nothing moved.

See? she told herself. *Nothing lives here. No animals, no people, no birds. Nothing except the sand worms.*

Other than that, the wind and the sky seemed to carry all the life in this Shadowside. But still she wondered: *How far can this pipeline go?* Several hours later she leaned up against it once more, felt the thrum of liquid inside, and thought she heard the faintest of new sounds—like a river far off. It made her hurry on, hopping over rocks, downhill once again.

Pretty soon she was certain she heard rushing waterfalls, which meant they weren't cold enough to freeze entirely. Several nice-sized streams trickled down a nearby hillside, adding to the music. Oriannon tried not to stumble as she kicked pebbles and sand down the hill in front of her, while the scent of water quickened her step.

Water! Now she came upon a small, stream-fed pond, not much bigger than a ragball field. Ripples reflected from dozens of tiny waterfalls emptying here from surrounding hills. Finally a place to drink! She tried to ignore her aching shoulder as she ran the last few meters to the icy edge. Just then she didn't care how the ice ledge cracked a bit under her weight. She got down on all fours and reached over the edge, down to dark waters.

It did call to mind a pot of clemsonroot tea that had been steeping a few minutes too long. Or maybe it was just the shadows. Steam from the water caught her in the face, and she actually giggled.

For the first time Oriannon had something to feel good about, as she scooped handful after handful of dark water, lapped up like a dog, and she didn't mind that it felt lukewarm. It tasted as dark as it looked, though—earthy and rich, in any case not the kind of refreshment to bottle and take home. She imagined some kind of warm springs here.

But what was that?

When she paused to catch her breath, she heard the start-up of a distant hum, then a faint sucking sound like a bathtub emptying. She guessed it had something to do with one of the huge pipes terminating here. In fact, she could see such a pipe lurking only a few meters away, only half underwater. A pump must have activated, because now it was sucking the pond dry like a giant straw.

She kept drinking and didn't hear the ice cracking again until it was too late to back away from the edge. This time it cracked all the way through, catching first her leg and then sending her slipping down, down toward the water, face first.

"It can't—!" she cried, but what could she do but claw at the ice for a handhold? She even waved with her crippled right arm, ignoring the deep ache. But she found nothing to grip, just ice. And she could do nothing but slide helplessly over the edge, landing on her head in the water.

After the first shock, she spit a mouthful of water, gasped for air, and wrapped her fingers around a fat icicle hanging off the edge. The good news was that the water felt warmer than the air around her. The bad news was that she couldn't hold on to the icicle forever, and no matter how hard she tried, she wasn't able to lift herself out of the water and up over the slippery edge of the shore. And she couldn't touch the bottom of the little lake either.

So what now?

There had to be a way out. But even if there was, Oriannon wasn't sure she had the strength anymore. And as she floated in the warm water, she felt the strong pull of the pipeline sucking at her feet, sucking everything in the pond toward the opening. She shook the water out of her ears and heard the horrible sound all too clearly.

"Please help me," she whispered, and the words to a prayer came to mind.

154

Maker who formed the waters, keep watch over Corista and me.

She had no time to wonder where the words had come from. Pleading took strength she couldn't spare as her fingers began to slip from the icicle.

"Please!"

The cloak floated up around her shoulders now and wrapped around her arms. In a moment her only real clue to this strange land would drag her down into the dark tea waters. Now the open mouth of the pipeline gargled as loudly as ever, seeking to swallow her as well. And if it didn't shut down immediately she really only had two choices:

One, she could hang on until she dropped off and was sucked away.

Or two, she could push away from this spot, taking a chance that maybe she could swim clear of its underwater grip and find a way up on the far side of the pond. Who knew?

"So here goes." She might not make it more than a couple of strokes. But at least she'd have a better chance swimming, compared to just slipping off to her death. So she pulled off the cloak and set it adrift, watching where it would go and how fast.

No surprise—it drifted directly toward the pipeline's open maw, joined a swirling eddy of dark water, but then caught right on the corner of the pipe, pinned against the sheer weight of the water, half in and half out, flapping like a flag.

That's how I'm going to be sucked in, Oriannon told herself, *unless I can kick away from here a lot better than that piece of wool did.*

Granted, that piece of wool could only drift helplessly. But Oriannon was pretty sure she knew what would happen as soon as she let go of her handhold. Even so she looked up through the swirling fog, up at the stars, and wondered once more.

"Maker," she whispered, "can you hear me?"

As she looked up, the stars sang just as they had before, the first time she saw them. Was that the Maker's voice, or something else?

"If you can, please help me swim!"

She held her breath, closed her eyes, and pushed away from the slippery bank with all her strength.

155

17

I s she being alive or dead?"

The voice didn't wake Oriannon; the bump and the pain in her shoulder certainly did. She snapped open her eyes with a low groan, wondering where she was and why she couldn't move. Was a tightly wrapped blanket holding her flat on her back as she rode in some kind of stretcher?

"Still alive, I'm thinking," observed an older man in a thick sing-song accent unfamiliar to her ears. He didn't seem to open his mouth all the way. But yes, she did understand the words, except now she wanted to turn away when his lean, bearded face leaned in close. "She just opened her eyes."

He stared at her with a curious look and his own enormous bright eyes that reminded her of Mentor Jesmet. In fact, she'd seen animals in the zoo with eyes like this.

"Well, how about that, Suuli," replied the stretcher-bearer, who dragged her down a path with the feet end of the stretcher bumping along the rocky ground. "And all this time I was thinking I was pulling up a body."

"You're knowing better, Becket. He would not be leading us all this way for a body."

"Hmm. Well, my wife isn't going to be as pleased as you. I can just hear her now: 'Becket Sol, I'm sending you out to get us a string of fish for dinner, and all you come back with is a half-drowned stranger!'"

"Fish, yeh!" When Suuli chuckled he revealed a crooked line of teeth, small and pale white, to match his features. "Figured you had a good bite didn't you, the way she was splashing around."

Ori remembered that part—the pipe pulling her closer, the grip of the water, the helpless feeling as it sucked her under. All her paddling made no difference. And then ... what? Strong hands had lifted her by one arm like a doll, hauling her clear of the water. And now she still coughed, and it took all her strength to breathe.

"Easy." Suuli's voice sounded soft like that of a nurse. They stopped, and Ori felt herself lowered to the ground—or rather, dropped like a sack of flour.

"Easy, I'm saying!" Suuli scolded the other man as he squatted next to her, tucking in the blanket and prodding at her face, maybe to see if she had any color.

But Becket Sol the stretcher-bearer just stood off to the side, arms crossed. He looked her father's age but only half his height, not much taller than Suuli but more broad shouldered. Both men wore simple lace-up boots and rough wool frocks resembling the one she'd woken up with, with the same three-star design embroidered into the sleeves.

"Still don't know if we should be keeping her," said the younger man. Maybe he was still disappointed because she hadn't been a fish. He ran his fingers through his beard and scratched his short button nose. "She's going to be nothing but trouble for us."

"I'll be pretending I didn't hear that, Becket. You're knowing what he says about helping strangers."

Becket spit off to the side and shook his head.

"Nothing but trouble."

"I ..." Oriannon sputtered, hoping they would understand. "I'm from Corista. You know, the bright side."

"We know." Suuli poked at her eye with a gnarled little finger, the same way he would examine a curious little bug. "Don't know how you people can be seeing anything with those tiny little eyes, though."

"Tiny?" She flinched and tried to hold up her hand, but couldn't work it free. "They're certainly not tiny."

"Around here they're tiny."

She coughed again, and the older man brought out a small flask from a fold in his frock. He uncorked it and acted as if he would pour some down her throat until she jerked her head to the side.

"No!" she cried. "I mean, I'm fine."

She peeked back to see him frown and replace the bottle, but not after taking a swig for himself.

"Half-dead is what you're being. And rude, besides."

Conversation over. This time each of the little men took a handle of her homemade stretcher and dragged her at a jog over the rough up-and-down of the rocky hillsides. She felt like the catch of the day, tossed and well seasoned.

"So how did you ..." Oriannon looked to the side; saw more of the same kind of landscape she'd been through, the rugged hills and canyons, the treeless twilight. Strange how much better she could see things now, even without the sun. "How did you find me?"

Suuli laughed as they hurried down another slope. His age didn't seem to slow him down, if he was really as old as he looked.

"Pretty hard to be missing a big fish like you, splashing around at the pipe. You must have fallen in just before the pumps started working again. And ..."

He paused, as if trying to decide if he'd tell her the rest. His voice went serious.

" ... and he told us where to look."

"He?" asked Oriannon. Who was this *he* they kept talking about?

But he didn't explain, just kept pulling her across the rugged Shadowside landscape. Oriannon grit her teeth as they teetered on the trail, kicking rocks out to the slope below.

"Go gentle, Becket," said the older man. "What if it was your daughter?"

"It's not my daughter, and she's asking too many questions." Maybe Becket didn't enjoy dragging girls like Oriannon for endless kilometers across rough trails and hillsides on a blanket stretched between two sticks. Especially when she was as big as either man, maybe taller.

"Then I'm sorry for all the questions." She winced as they hit another rock. Smooth it was not. Didn't they have lev-scooters around here? "But why won't you tell me where you're taking me?"

They jogged on in silence for several minutes, until Oriannon almost dared repeat her question.

"Just a little way yet," Suuli finally told her. "We'll be getting you to someplace warm."

That would be good, she thought. Even with the rough blanket wrapped tightly around her, her damp clothes still made her shiver.

"We'll be there soon?" she pushed her luck for another question.

"Soon enough," answered Suuli, and he wasn't even breathing hard. She tried to look over her shoulder to see their direction — mostly uphill. And now when they finally paused again, the younger one pulled a scarf from his pocket, folded it several times, and fixed it as a blindfold around Oriannon's eyes.

"Hey!" she protested, wiggling to the side. "What are you doing?"

"Hold still," he told her, his voice hardening. "You'll be needing to wear this for a while."

"But why? I haven't done anything!" As the panic rose, she shook her head, trying to move the blindfold, but Becket was too strong. "Did he tell you to do this to me?"

That did it. Of course she still didn't have a clue who *he* was. But the men dropped her right there and argued while she lay shivering. Maybe they would just walk off and leave her on the rocky hillside.

"But I'm telling you we can't be letting a Coristan just come in here," argued Becket. "Once she knows where the city is, well ... you know what will happen."

"Becket, Becket. You think they don't already know? And if you were that worried about it you might not have fished her out of the lake in the first place."

"Aw, what was I supposed to be doing? Leaving her there? You know what he would have said."

"All right, then we both know she's here for his reason. He wouldn't have told us about her if it weren't so."

And that seemed to settle the argument. Because a moment later they'd picked her up again and continued on their bone-jolting hike. On the ragged edge of panic, Oriannon didn't stop wiggling her nose, doing all she could to rub off the blindfold. After a couple of interminable hours, they paused once more.

"Open your mouth, then," commanded Becket.

"No." She remembered Suuli's bottle and stuck out her chin, as if that helped any.

"Open up your mouth so I'll be able to take off your blindfold."

"What?"

Becket wasn't fooling around. She felt it in her mouth, either a tree root or a stick of candy. She could have spit it out, but the taste reminded her of licorice, and after a moment she hungrily sucked at the honey-sweet root.

"Is this to eat?" she wondered aloud.

"In a way. Chew it. It will be making you feel better. In fact, you ..."

But she didn't even hear the rest, just blinked her eyes and felt her head grow heavy. She couldn't have kept her eyes open if she'd wanted to. So she sighed and gave herself to sleep once again.

●●●

When Oriannon woke again, the first thing she noticed was that her headache had disappeared, that her mouth still tasted of licorice, and that the heavy comforter she rested under smelled of sage and the desert.

"Where am I?" She tried to roll over and sit up—too quickly. Her head spun.

"Don't." A girl about her age moved quickly to keep Oriannon from tumbling off the side of the tiny bed.

Back on the pillow, Oriannon looked around to see a small room with stucco walls and a ceiling so low she would certainly bump her head if she stood. A flat stone etched with a design of those same three stars hung on the opposite wall, next to a meager window framed by yellow curtains. A wall lamp was perched next to her bed, giving off a steady blue-green glow from a glass tube filled with a kind of luminescent soup.

"I always heard that Coristans never slept," said the girl, who was dressed in simple gray overalls and kept her large brown eyes on Oriannon. Her face reminded Oriannon of Suuli, the old man. Just like Suuli, her curious but kindly stare made it seem as if she had never met anyone from the other side of the planet. "You sure did."

Oriannon rubbed her shoulder. "I sleep two-point-two hours each day cycle."

Once more Oriannon realized that a random memory had just bubbled to the surface. She would have to get used to this, not knowing where—or when—she might suddenly recall pieces of trivia from her past life.

"Only two—" If the girl's eyes got any bigger they might pop out of her face entirely.

"Why?" Oriannon interrupted, "How long have I been sleeping?"

"Two days, not counting the time it took for them to bring you back. You must have been needing it."

Oriannon looked at the girl closer to see if she was lying. Nothing could be more bizarre.

"I've never slept longer than two hours in my entire life," Oriannon finally told her.

"But if you don't sleep," asked the girl, her eyes still saucer-wide, "how can you dream?"

Oriannon thought for a moment before answering.

"I dream," she replied. "I just never remembered ... until I came here."

She yawned and found her eyelids drooping, even after all that sleep.

"I'm sorry." The girl talked as if she thought Oriannon still needed help. "I should be letting you sleep more. My grandfather said you almost drowned and that you were hurting, and that we should be praying for you."

Oriannon rubbed her shoulder once again, searching for the pain but finding none.

"Well, either you're a pretty good prayer, or that root they gave me must have done something. My shoulder—" She rubbed it good and hard. "Feels pretty good. Stiff, but not bad."

"Good." The girl brightened. "Then you'll be up soon."

"And the root?"

Again the smile.

"Lakris root. Some people say it cures ailments. Makes you sleepy too. Not two days sleepy, but—"

A worried shadow crossed her face when she looked toward the door on the far side of the room.

"But what?" asked Oriannon.

"Some of the Owlings are arguing. When they find out you're awake, they'll be asking you a lot of questions."

"Owlings?" Oriannon looked up at her, and the other girl hid a giggle.

"Owlings. The people of Shadowside."

Again, Oriannon let the words soak.

"I never knew there were any people over here," she finally admitted. "Just thought it was dark and ... you know, nothing."

"Nothing?" She laughed softly. "Sounds as if we're knowing a bit more about you than you do about us."

"Oh, really?" Oriannon took it as a challenge, throwing off her covers and doing her best to stand. But her head would not cooperate; she saw stars and teetered backwards into the mattress.

"I told you not so fast!" warned the girl, just as they heard a knock at the door. A bearded man holding a tray with a steaming bowl poked his head inside.

"Are we all right in here, Wist?" asked the old man, and it was Oriannon's rescuer. The nice one, Suuli. He hovered at the entrance for a moment before the girl waved him inside.

"She's awake, grandfather."

Oh. So he was her grandfather, and her name was Wist. No introductions needed, then.

"Hmm. Good." He set the tray down on a small table. "Did she tell you her name, and what she's doing here?"

Wist looked over at Oriannon, who had settled back onto the bed.

"Oriannon." Oriannon straightened and opened her mouth, still afraid nothing would come out. The way her mind had betrayed her lately, who could say? "Oriannon High — Hightower. Of Nyssa. And I'm here because ... because ..."

She tried to grab bits and pieces of the fog here and there, mixed in strange ways, like a child's puzzle thrown together and stirred. For the moment knowing her own name seemed like a good start.

"I'm sorry," she went on, feeling their stares. "I know I came here to find someone, and I know it's very important."

"I can't imagine anyone here on Shadowside that a person such as you would be needing to find." Suuli frowned and his eyes seemed to darken. "Unless you're sent here to spy on us, the way my friend Becket believes."

"Please." Oriannon looked from one to the other. "I don't mean you any harm."

"You said you didn't know of the Owlings," said Wist, "but then you said you were looking for someone. That doesn't make sense."

"I know. None of this makes sense."

"What about your parents?" asked Suuli. "They'll be worrying about you."

"I've tried to remember my parents." She sighed. "But I just can't."

"You remember your name but you don't remember your own family?" Suuli didn't look as if he believed her story. "And you don't even know who you're looking for, but you know it's important enough to sneak across the border?"

Oriannon swallowed hard and smelled the soft fragrant steam of the stew Suuli had brought as it filled the little room. She couldn't help staring at it and her stomach rumbled loudly enough for everyone to hear. Suuli shook his head at her.

"You're going to have to come up with better answers than that," he told her. "Becket and the others will be having more questions for you shortly. But in the meantime ..."

He nudged the bowl her way a couple of centimeters.

"In the meantime you'd better be eating something."

Oriannon didn't need to be told again. She picked up the bowl and slurped it down with the simple wooden spoon, hardly taking the time to chew bits of a potato-like vegetable and stringy pieces of mystery meat. Though it tasted different from anything she'd ever had before, she couldn't help licking the bowl down to the last bit of gravy. And Wist watched her take each bite.

"Do you thank the Maker after you eat instead of before?"

"Thank?" Oriannon choked a little, clearing her throat. "You mean, like *pray?*"

The question made her think of the stars, how she had asked for help. Suuli rested his hand on his granddaughter's shoulder.

165

"Coristans aren't like us, Wist. She doesn't understand."

"I understand praying." Oriannon thought she did. "I ... ah ... just never thought of it that way."

Wist wrinkled her nose at their guest.

"What's to think about?"

"It's just that where I come from, the priests do most of the praying. Or they tell us what to say and we say it. You know, everybody has their own job."

"So you do remember where you came from, at least?" asked Suuli.

Oriannon thought for a moment.

"I remember the city. The Temple. The trial."

"Hmm," he answered, obviously not understanding. A couple of memories trickled back to her. The boy she had ridden with ... what was his name? She gave her spoon one last lick, and Wist looked at her with a little smile.

"You like it?" she asked. Good of her to change the subject. It hurt to try to remember things that would not untangle themselves.

"Sure." Oriannon nodded. "What was it?"

"Sand worm. It's really tasty grilled."

She said it with such a straight face that Oriannon was entirely uncertain whether she was joking or not. But the look on Oriannon's face must have been too much for Wist, who broke out in giggles.

"Just kidding, all right? Come here, I'll show you."

So the other girl took her hand and helped her stand — slowly, this time. And this time Oriannon held on as her head spun just a little. Wist pointed out the window, and it made Oriannon dizzy all over again.

"Look at that view." Oriannon took in a breath. "We're pretty high up."

Wist didn't seem to notice.

"There's another moon out now. One of the twelve. My grandfather says Coristans can't see the same way as us. Can you see?"

Oriannon took another look. Far below, the silvery landscape twinkled with the now-familiar blue and green lights from patches of snow. She could see a deep canyon with a twisting riverbed at the bottom, dotted with gnarled, low trees. Each side of the rust-red canyon was decorated with cliffside huts, stuck to the canyon walls like little wasp nests. Oriannon had no idea how people living there would be able to reach them, but most showed faint golden yellow lights in windows and smoke rising from chimneys. Even beyond that she made out another twinkle of soft lights, perhaps a distant cliff village such as the one in which she found herself. And directly below, at the foot of their own cliff, a winding river glittered bright silver in the moonlight, met head-on by the ugly dark mouth of another pipeline.

"I see it."

"Then you're seeing that flock of birds in the ironwood bushes, on that far hillside?"

"Maybe your eyes are a little better than mine." Oriannon squinted. No way could she make out anything as small as a flock of birds, not from this distance.

"That's what you had in your stew. Plock. They're small, but they taste pretty good."

"Oh." Oriannon's stomach turned, though she had to admit this was better news than thinking she had eaten sand worms. "I've never eaten meat before."

Wist laughed again. "You Coristans really *are* strange."

And then she looked over at Suuli.

"Can I take her around?" she asked. "Show her Lior?"

So that was the name of this odd place. Li ... They pronounced it with a kind of gargle, li-*ORhh*. Not a sound she'd heard before. But Suuli shook his head no.

"Becket and the others will be wanting to speak with her, now that she's awake." He headed for the door. "She's not to be leaving this room until it's time for her to go, before she's had a chance to clean up a little, get some fresh clothes. And Miss Hightower of Nyssa ..."

He paused, looking back.

"For your own sake, I hope you'll be finding your memories soon."

With that he left them, and Oriannon would have asked him more, but Wist held her back with a warning hand and a look before following him out of the room. Alone again, Oriannon could only look out the window, wondering what kind of strange place she had come to — and if she would ever find what she had come for.

18

Not an hour later the door creaked open again — this time without a knock or a word. Two straight-faced boys — each a head shorter than Oriannon — peered at her with their Owling eyes.

"Do you speak?" asked the taller of the two, turning his head to the side.

Oriannon frowned. "Of course I speak. But I wish you would have knocked. It's only polite, you know."

Now the two messengers — if that's what they were — looked at each other and straightened their rumpled brown tunics before the taller cleared his throat and answered back.

"Sorry. But we're to escort you to the Great Hall, where you will be questioned by the Council of Safety."

"Council of Safety? Whose safety?"

The young Owling looked at her as if he really didn't understand her after all.

"Owling safety, of course."

"What about Wist?" Oriannon had to know. "Is she going to be there?"

The two boys stiffened at the name and held their spots on either side of the door. The younger pointed. She was to fall into place between them.

"Too many questions," said the older. "Follow us ... please."

So she did, out of her room and into a narrow tiled hallway, then threaded her way down tiny one-way corridors and small balconies overhanging a great height under the overarching red rock cliff. She gawked once more at the rugged hills and canyons stretching out below them, but from a height each detail seemed more clear and sharp. This whitewashed city seemed as if it actually belonged on its impossibly high perch, halfway up the side of an impossibly tall mountain.

She kept step between the boy in front and the boy in back, but they didn't let her dawdle. Here and there odd-smelling springs bubbled from little bird-shaped fountains in the side of the cliff, and Oriannon stopped for just a moment to dip her finger in one.

Hot. Even warmer than the pond she'd fallen into. The younger boy stepped on her heel.

"Sorry," he mumbled, but neither of her guides said anything else as they made their way through this maze of a city, with narrow walkways barely wide enough for two people to pass, lined with little two-story apartments or shops—all of chiseled white stone, right into the side of the cliff, floor upon roof upon floor. At first glance she couldn't tell how tall the city was, but guessed it could have five or six levels, maybe more.

"Makes me dizzy up here," she told them, tripping over a crooked stairway leading down from the level they'd been walking. "So just this place here is called Lior?"

"Just this place," replied the younger. "This is Lior."

But they weren't stopping. They trooped down and to the left along a damp passageway lit by more glowing blue vials. And every few paces Owling people stopped what they were doing to stare curiously at her. A woman rested on her tattered broom and tilted her head. An old man looked up from the shoes he was sewing and gave her a cautious nod. The nutty smell of tanned leather drifted to the street from the open door to his shop, blending with the warm aromas of spices and coffee from others. Laughter floated out of several windows where people sat around rough wooden tables, eating flatbread together, and Oriannon thought she caught a whiff of the same stew she had been fed. Some played a board game that reminded her of chess, but that used carved white and blue stones and a round board.

Just ahead on the narrow pathway, two little girls chased each other in a game of tag, but stopped when they caught sight of Oriannon. Like all the others, they stared at her curiously. Maybe they, like Oriannon's two escorts, had never seen a person from Corista before, from Seramine.

"Hey there." Oriannon waved, but the girls only squealed and ran away. A window opened above their heads, and Oriannon looked up to see a startled mother looking down at her with those wide eyes.

Let them stare, she thought, doing her best to keep up with the boys. These strange little people very much resembled the snowy white owls that sat above their heads on wooden perches, their feet tied with little leather leashes. Most, she imagined, had a view of the valley below. And at the end of this alley one of the Owling men stood at the edge of his raised patio with a bird on his leather-gloved forearm.

"What are all the owls for?" Oriannon thought she'd ask, in case her escorts decided to become talkative.

Of course they didn't answer, just kept walking. But she could see well enough as the bird took off from its master's arm and disappeared over the railing with a *screee!* Oriannon slowed down to see what would happen, bending down to adjust the sandal on her foot, taking as long as she dared. Out of the corner of her eye she watched as the man whistled and the bird finally returned with a limp white rabbit in its claws.

A hunter!

"Come on," the older told her, waving with his hand. Impatient kid.

"I've never seen that before." Oriannon would have stood there for the next hour, watching the man and his bird catch rabbits, if the boys hadn't hurried her along again. But one overlook led to another, until they pulled up short at a rock ledge directly above the silvery snake of the river, far below. From this wide outlook they would have an even better view. Oriannon dared to lean over the rock railing for a better look.

"What's that?" She pointed at the place where two pipelines joined the river hundreds of meters below. In this kind of setting they looked sorely out of place, like a giant wound on the landscape. But she focused on something else too: a huge mound of rocks had been piled at the opening, a plug of some kind, with tree trunks and mud … a jumbled mess. From a flood, or built there on purpose?

"You're from the other side." The older raised his eyebrows. "And you're not knowing what that is?"

"Am I supposed to?" Oriannon leaned a little closer, trying to figure it out. Again the boys looked at each other, as if they were wondering if they should tell her or not. Finally the older one shrugged.

"It's to stop the water," he explained. "If we hadn't built the mound there, the river would be sucked dry."

"Oh!" Now she was getting it. "A big plug. And you need the water."

The older sighed, as if explaining basic arithmetic to a young child who didn't yet understand.

"You think we could be living without water?"

"Why don't you just tell the people who put in the pipeline that they should stop?"

At that both boys burst out laughing.

"I'm not trying to be funny," she explained, but they weren't listening anymore, just chuckling and pointing for her to get moving again. So they continued down another crooked alley, moving in and out of the narrow outer terraces hugging the vertical side of the cliff. What a place to build a city!

"Left," the older finally told her, and they turned into the shelter of an arched entry carved directly into the rock, much taller than it needed to be for the little Owling people. Someone had carefully chiseled a design of three stars and twelve moons into the overhead, while ornately carved double ironwood doors blocked their way. While her escorts knocked, she studied the design.

"Why does everything have a picture of those three suns?" she asked. The younger couldn't dodge her question this time.

"You don't know anything, do you?" He crossed his arms as they waited for someone to open the doors from inside. "Regev, Saius, and Heliaan ... The Trion. They're the symbol of Jesmet."

It took a moment for the name to register. But when it did Oriannon grabbed the boy by the arm.

"Did you say Jesmet? I know that name! He's—"

She didn't have a chance to finish, as a huge blue flash—like lightning—lit the sky behind them. The Owlings fell to the pavement, covering their faces. Oriannon blinked back the bright pain too, but still she stepped back over to the railing to see what was going on. The shockwave from a tremendous boom, like a mighty clap of thunder, nearly knocked her off her feet.

"Get down!" yelled the boys, and one of them reached across the cobblestone walkway to grab her ankle. But she had to see, and she pulled free long enough to sight a large shuttle craft hovering just over the river below, directly in front of the mound at the mouth of the pipeline. Red and blue lights flashed at the top of the shuttle, then dimmed again while a high-pitched whine grew louder and louder. And she saw the wicked blue fireball spit from extended disruptor tubes at the front of the shuttle, tearing into the makeshift dam like a tornado unleashed, a second before the *boom!* knocked her over backwards.

Rocks and shreds of red tile tumbled everywhere in the city as people scrambled for cover. A little girl ran screaming to her mother, blood streaming down her face. A small chunk of the outside terrace railing cracked and tumbled over the side, and Oriannon heard a roof splinter.

This can't be happening! The stone shook beneath her feet, while a small but worrisome crack opened up in the pavement from end to end, as if the little city was preparing to peel away from the hillside.

No!

But Oriannon recognized the blue and gold striped markings on the shuttle, and in an instant she knew exactly where they came from. Coristan Security. If she hadn't been able to recall *that* memory before, now she wished she could not. With it she also remembered a panicked jumble of images: probes in a classroom, securities, men in black coveralls chasing her down school hallways … like a bad dream it paralyzed her on the spot. In a moment she might slip down the hill right on top of the shuttle, along with the rest of this precarious city.

"Are they attacking us?" she asked the boys. They wouldn't answer.

Once more the blue light flashed, just as a black cloud emanated from the shuttle. Anyone else might have thought it a swarm of hornets, perhaps, except these stainless orbs were bigger and they knew exactly where they were going. And as they flew up the side of the cliff Oriannon noticed a flicker of red light sweeping from their eyes, scanning rocks and crevices, scanning the steep trail leading upward to the city. Halfway up they caught sight of an Owling man, crouching in the shadows but not out of their reach. Four — no, five — swept him with their light — up, down, and side-to-side. He cried out as he tried to duck but couldn't hide.

The probes hovered just out of reach, scanning him for a few more seconds before flying off to rejoin the swarm. While these pests moved up the cliff Oriannon could only stare, her feet glued to the ground, her hands shaking. No one told her, but she remembered the feeling of running from these things, of hiding. Or was it her nightmare from the other day?

Are they coming for me?

She had no time to wonder when the boys grabbed her from behind and dragged her through the opened portal in the stone wall. And once more the ground shuddered, dislodging cobblestones and bringing small pieces of the city down around their heads. But a moment later the boys slammed the huge ironwood doors behind them and rammed home a heavy crossbeam. The sound echoed around Oriannon's head, blocking out muffled screams of panic and warning bells outside.

It took just a moment for Oriannon's eyes to readjust to the dim light of their cavern, even darker than the rest of Shadowside. Candle sconces set along the wall cast pale circles of light, still shaking from the impact of the attack. They coughed in the cloud of dust that had followed them into the high-ceilinged cave-room.

"Come in, Oriannon Hightower of Nyssa."

Still breathing hard after the shock of the attack, Oriannon turned slowly to face the deep voice.

19

This is the "Council of Safety" they told me about? Oriannon wondered.

Seven older Owlings sat in straight-backed black leather chairs arranged in a large half circle around a crackling fire, looking as if they might be enjoying an after-dinner cup of tea and a good book. Only this was no social visit, to be sure. Oriannon recognized the gray-haired Suuli and the slightly younger, dark-eyed Becket Sol — but none of the others — two women and three men, none quite as old as Suuli but perhaps close. Each wore a variation of the woolen pullover most Owlings seemed to favor, comfortable and simple, shapeless and gray.

"I said, come in, Oriannon." Suuli repeated his greeting. "No one's going to be hurting you."

The fire created a halo of flickering golden light around them and the dark animal skin that served as a rug in front of the fireplace. Beyond and above, only the shadows hinted to her that the cave — this "Great Hall" — was bigger than she knew. So Oriannon stepped into the circle of light, feeling like a moth. What other choice did she have?

"What's it like outside, boys?" asked another man. "What's going on?"

The older shrugged as if he hadn't noticed anything unusual.

"Another attack from the water thieves, like on the Lake of the Trout." He sounded cool, not like the way he'd been screaming a minute ago. "They're using disruptors this time to open their pipeline back up. Sending out a swarm of probes too."

"You mean this isn't the first time this has happened?" Oriannon couldn't believe it. "And you all just act as if it's no big deal?"

"Silence." The younger warned her with a poke in the ribs before he went back to warming his hands by the fire.

"Not the first time, young lady." Suuli leaned back in his chair. "And certainly not the last."

"I'm sorry. It's just that this place is so different from what I'm used to. And nobody wants to explain things to me."

Becket Sol finally set down his mug on the stone floor next to his chair and turned to face her. "We were thinking perhaps *you* could explain it to *us*."

"Becket, not so fast." Suuli frowned as he looked over at the other Owlings. "I thought we agreed."

But Becket only frowned and stood up to pace in front of the large stone fireplace.

"Agreed what? To not upset our visitor? Well, even though I was the one to pull her out of the lake, I have to confess I'm still wondering if I did the right thing." He paused, allowing his words to sink in. "Am I the only one here who sees a connection between coming to Lior ... and now this latest attack, this threat to our survival? What do you think the probes are looking for?"

"Becket, please—" Suuli tried get the other Owlings to sit down, but Becket only shrugged him off.

"You have to admit it doesn't look good," said one of the others, a dark-haired woman who reminded Oriannon of someone she knew.

"That's right." Becket wasn't done yet. "The Coristan girl comes, and ..." He clapped his hands. "Just like that, we're getting another visit from the shuttle. Do you think anyone was hurt this time?"

"I'm sure they've left by now," said Suuli. "They always do, and life goes on as it always has. We trust the Maker; we take precautions."

"And they take our water — every last drop, if we allow it. That's not 'life goes on,' my colleagues. Those people out there, those Coristans, they think we're just some kind of animals to be exterminated. Most of them don't even know we're alive! You know I'm right."

Becket's speech made Oriannon's ears burn. How much of it might be true? Even Suuli closed his eyes as if the argument had worn him out, as if he'd heard it all before. The light of the fire flickered on his serene expression.

"I also know he says we should be helping the helpless," Suuli said as he opened his eyes again. As he did he pointed at a large book with a leather binding, sitting open on a nearby wooden stand. "That's what you did at the lake, and you did the right thing."

"I don't know. What if I've endangered the city by bringing her here?"

"I don't believe that's the case."

"Then what about this?" Becket raised his voice as he marched over to another low table in the shadows behind their chairs. Oriannon recognized her old clothes there ... and something else. He picked up a small item and held it in the air.

"Oh, that." Oriannon recognized the earbud. "It's just — "

"A transmitter of some kind." Becket didn't let her finish. "Our people have already had it apart and back together again. *Neurocircuits*, I believe they're called. Do you really think we're so simple that we couldn't figure this out?"

"I don't think you're so simple." By this time Oriannon realized she was on trial here. "I didn't know anything about you before I got here."

"What else didn't you know?" Becket continued pacing like a lawyer, his hands knit behind his back. His dark eyebrows furrowed as he spoke.

"I ... I'm not sure what you mean." Oriannon wondered now what to do with her hands.

"Perhaps you're conveniently forgetting that too? Who sent you here? Did they track you with this thing? Is that how they found us so quickly this time? Will they use it to map our city, plan an invasion of Shadowside? Why do they want to destroy us? We know you know!"

"Becket!" This time Suuli pointed at his friend. "I am still the Council Presider for this term, and you will not treat our guest this way. He has called us to welcome, not to—"

"Yes, that's fine for you to say, but where is he now? Gone for over a year. I think he went over to Corista and he's never coming back. I say he abandoned us!"

Suuli's jaw dropped for a moment before he snapped it shut.

"You're not meaning that, brother. He calls us to hope. He could be back any day."

"You say so. But in the meantime we only have a few days of water without the living river, perhaps less. And then what? We can't be drinking from the hot sulfur springs. And here we are with the reason for all this trouble standing right in front of us. What did I tell you when we picked her out of the water?"

"But I didn't do anything wrong!" Oriannon protested. She tried to keep her voice from going shaky and the tears from escaping her eyes. "I think the earbud—*transmitter*—is just to talk with friends ..."

"You think?" asked Becket, his arms still crossed. "Sounds like another convenient memory lapse."

"It's not convenient at all," she replied. "You have no idea how inconvenient this all is."

"All right then. Let's just be saying for the sake of conversation that we believe what you tell us about your memory. But friends?

What are their names? And where are they? On the Coristan ship?"

"I . . . I don't remember."

"I see. And we're supposed to be accepting this because you took a swim, and then you just lost your memory?"

"No. That's not it. I . . . there was . . . that is, something happened at my school." She closed her eyes, searching for bits of the past. "They called me an . . . eidich. That's it. And they took part of my memory because . . . I'm not sure. That's when everything got all mixed up. Sometimes I remember things here and there, but most of the time it's just not there. You've got to believe me."

"An eidich?" Now Becket raised an eyebrow. "I've heard of that kind of thing. Never seen it. This is ironic. So you once remembered everything you saw and heard?"

Oriannon looked at her feet.

"Used to. Someone told me I was changing, that I might be growing out of it." For a moment she remembered, as if a small passage had cleared through the fog, just for a moment. But just as quickly as the memory appeared, it curled back on itself and collapsed once more. "You've got to believe me: I know I had nothing to do with the shuttle that came here."

"If you can't remember," asked Becket, "how can you be sure? That's assuming you're telling the truth."

"I *am* telling you the truth. And I don't know how they found this place, but it couldn't have been that hard. They have satellites that can take pictures, you know."

Perhaps she could have left off that last part. Now all of the Council looked at her with wrinkled eyebrows, leaning forward in their chairs. Becket still had not rested his case.

"I'm not accepting this story," he told the others, chopping with his hand for emphasis. "I'm saying we send her back where she came from as soon as we can and keep her under close watch while she's here. And furthermore—"

He paused to look around as the floor shook again, this time a gentle rattling that wouldn't let up for nearly half a minute. Everyone held onto his or her chairs, fear on their faces. Oriannon held onto the fireplace for balance until the shaking had settled back down.

"The Coristans again?" asked one of the women. Her kindly face had wrinkled with concern.

"I'm not thinking so." Suuli looked at the others with a serious expression to match. "They would be gone by now. And the Codex says that when the ground shakes and the three stars return, so will Jesmet. Let's not be losing sight of hope. Because—"

"Not the three-star prophecy again, Suuli," Becket interrupted. "Listen, we've been waiting for three stars to be appearing for generations, and what has ever happened? Forgive me, brother; I'm following the Codex as well as the next Owling, but let's not be fanatics about this."

The same Codex? Oriannon wasn't sure she even heard him right. And three stars? This time she couldn't forget what the younger Owling had told her: *Regev, Saius, and Heliaan are the symbols of Jesmet.*

"Becket, I just wish ..." But Suuli sighed and shook his head sadly. Finally he waved his hand at the two boys who now flanked Oriannon. "All right, then, boys. Once we're sure the immediate danger is past and the Coristan ship is gone—and I'm assuming it must be by this time—why don't you take Miss Hightower back to her guest room at my house. Perhaps if she gets some more rest her head will be clearing a bit, and we can be figuring out a way to get her home."

"Pardon me?" Oriannon wasn't sure what to tell them, but she had to say it. "I know the man you're talking about. Jesmet. Or I used to. He was ..." She squinted, searching hard for the memory. "He was in my school, I think. And then—"

"See?" interrupted Becket. "She's lying, again. How can she know Jesmet? Coristans can't be knowing Jesmet."

"Why not?" asked Suuli, rubbing his chin. "Didn't he say—"

An aftershock jolted the Great Hall just then, throwing Suuli off balance and Oriannon to her knees. This time the sharp earthquake shook loose the ceiling, dropping a rain of small, colored mosaic tiles on their heads. And where they had once scrambled to find shelter inside the Great Hall, this time they pushed away the bar across the main door and pulled at the handle. Even Oriannon planted her feet and joined the others to pull as hard as she could. So much for their Jesmet discussion. Because even if the probes waited outside, right now anything was better than staying in that cave to be buried alive.

But the mighty doors wouldn't budge, the floor shook even more, and a chunk of rock the size of Oriannon's head smashed with a thud into the floor—not a meter from where they stood. Oriannon grunted once more as she pulled with all her strength, and announced what they already knew.

"It won't open!" she cried.

20

Strange how ten seconds in the middle of an earthquake could seem like ten minutes. And as they pulled together at the big set of double doors from the inside, Oriannon heard pounding from the outside.

Good, she thought. *Someone out there knows we're trapped.*

But when the door still wouldn't budge, the older of the two boys leaned his ear against the door once more, listening.

"He's saying the probes are gone, but the men are going to help someone else."

That seemed to satisfy everyone except Oriannon.

"Don't go away!" She nearly skinned her knuckles raw from knocking so hard. "We're going to die in here!"

"You might as well relax and wait," the younger told her. "Nobody's going to be opening that thing for a while. It's at least ten centimeters thick."

Too thick to cut through or break through without a battering ram. And that, the boys explained, was the point.

"They built the Great Hall as a hiding place," said the younger. "In case anyone attacked."

"Like the Coristans?" Oriannon asked. The boys just shrugged their shoulders and sat down on the cold stones. After one more useless tug on the door, she joined them.

"I still think you should complain about the water problem," she said. "Tell them how you feel."

"We sent ambassadors once," explained Becket, looking off into the darkness. "Long ago. They never came back. That was before your time too, wasn't it, Suuli?"

He looked over to where Suuli had been sitting, but the older man had disappeared without anyone noticing.

"Suuli?" Becket stood to see what had happened to him, walked over to the edge of the light. Oriannon thought she heard a soft groan, and she followed the two boys to the deeper shadows, where they nearly tripped over a body on the floor, sprawled next to a good-sized piece of the rock ceiling that must have fallen on him and rolled away.

"He's over here!" she called back, kneeling at his side. She touched a finger to his neck, feeling for the faint flutter of pulse that would tell her the man still lived. And for a moment she thought she felt something.

"Out of the way!" Becket bumped her to the side, leaned down close as if to feel Suuli's shallow breathing. The others circled around and closed their eyes. Oriannon could see their lips moving but couldn't hear their words.

"You people need to do something!" she told them. But what? Back in Corista, none of this would ever have happened. They'd have a rescue squad here in moments, complete with paramedics and a mercy lift.

"Do you even have doctors?" she asked the boys. They didn't answer, but of course it made no difference if they couldn't even open the doors. And right now that was either going to take a battering ram ... or another earthquake. She wandered over to the table, came back with the rolled-up clothes she'd worn back on the other side. It wasn't much, but maybe it would help.

"Here," she said, kneeling back down. "He needs a pillow for his head."

The pale grimace on his face and his shallow breathing told her he needed much more than that. But Becket accepted the bundle and slipped it carefully under Suuli's neck. The older man's eyes fluttered before he looked straight at Oriannon and smiled.

"Thank you." And he looked up at Becket, gasping for each breath and each word. "Sorry for wandering off like that. I was just wanting to see if anything was damaged, and—"

"Don't talk." Becket bit his lip. "We'll be getting you to a healer in just a few minutes."

But Suuli only shook his head slowly.

"It's all right," he whispered, lifting his trembling hand to take hold of Oriannon's sleeve. His eyes looked far away one moment, focused the next. "But you must be telling me, my young friend."

Becket had to give way as she leaned closer, and Suuli closed his eyes once more, as if looking for a last bit of strength to speak.

"Suuli," Becket interrupted, taking his hand. "Save it. I told you we'll—"

"No!" Suuli snapped open his eyes again, ignoring everyone else, focused only on Oriannon. "You must tell me!"

Now his breath rattled, and she knew that perhaps he had few words left to give them.

"What?" she whispered. "What do you want me to tell you?"

He licked his lips and swallowed hard before forcing out the words.

"Did you really know Jesmet?" The question hung in the still air. "I know you'll be telling me the truth. What was—what is he like?"

Becket's jaw tensed, but he said nothing this time. And Oriannon closed her own eyes, desperately looking for the answer to his question. Did she know him? What was he like? A carousel swirled by in her mind, spinning, spinning, and if she reached out at just the right time she might grab the right memory. She reached, and it nearly knocked the breath out of her.

"I knew him," she finally whispered, and she clung to the memory shreds she had gathered, tattered and scrambled as they were. "He was kind. A good teacher. And ... he taught us a different kind of song."

"The song." Suuli smiled and looked to Becket. "See, Becket? How would an outsider be knowing his song, if she had not actually been with him?"

"That's enough," Becket warned her, now, holding up his hands for her to stop. Really, she wasn't sure what else she could add to what she had already said. But it looked as if that was enough for Suuli, who smiled and nodded when he closed his eyes for the last time. When he coughed, Becket lowered his own forehead to the older man's chest, weeping silently.

"Don't go, old man." Becket forced out the words, gripping Suuli's shoulders. "Please."

But the old Suuli just sighed as his lips moved and he held the hand of his friend. Oriannon leaned closer to hear.

"Let me go now in your peace," he whispered, at once hoarse and soft. "For I have heard your song with my own ears, as they will too. A song for all your children, both Owling and Corista ..."

● ● ●

She had not known Suuli, of course, though he had been kind to her, defended her even. So three hours later Oriannon wondered at the tears still streaming down her face. She stood aside as the Owling men finally forced open the double doors with large steel pry bars and a log that pounded the corners with a thud that made her wince. The door splintered and screeched as they forced it open, past where the entry had settled in the last earthquake.

Of course, the sound couldn't bother old Suuli anymore. After a whispered conference with their rescuers, a red-eyed Becket directed them to carry out the partly draped body as the others stood silently by. As Oriannon headed for the opening she nearly stepped on her little earbud—the one that had gotten her in so much trouble with Becket. Pretending to dust off her foot, she scooped it up and once again slipped it into her pocket.

But she had to know something else before she left this place. So she paused at the opening, wondering if the Coristans had left behind any of their probes. She peeked out into the twilight, slowly, ready to duck back in and run, if she needed to.

She saw nothing that would remind her of the danger, even as she looked left and right. Apparently the Owlings who told them the Coristan ship had left were correct. But she didn't expect what she found back out on the streets of Lior.

Singing?

Sad songs, perhaps, slow and mourning. But still a song. A woman on a terrace above hung out her blankets and sang about a light in the darkness, but what kind of light did these Owlings know, away from their candles and dim lanterns? And what kind of light did they have now, with their city battered and bruised?

Oriannon stepped out into Shadowside twilight, confident now that at least the probes had disappeared. She couldn't tell which damage was from the Coristan attack at the water pipe though, and which was from the deadly earthquakes that followed. No one seemed to care as they scurried about with shovels on their shoulders, or trundling little wheelbarrows full of rock and gravel, or straightening up walls that had leaned or caved in. A couple of Owling men on crude ladders were already replacing a roof of red tiles.

And yet the time was full of tears, as well—especially as people on the street saw the men carrying Suuli's body.

Only Becket, following behind, didn't let tears come to his eyes. Out in public he kept his arms crossed and fisted them away before anyone could see. But Oriannon saw. "Oh, Suuli!" cried an older woman as they passed slowly by. "You were Jesmet's friend."

"And if Jesmet had been here," mumbled Becket, softly so that no one else could hear, "this would never have happened."

189

Oriannon guessed he didn't know she'd heard, and he didn't seem to care that Oriannon slowed down to let the death march go on ahead. He didn't even look her way, just shuffled slowly on. She would follow, go back to Suuli and Wist's house, the way they wanted her to. But on the wings of the cool breeze, lofting up from the canyon floor, she heard again the notes to a song she knew, a song she could not ignore.

She'd heard it before, only where? Slipping away from the rest of the funeral procession, Oriannon stepped carefully over a jagged crack in the cobblestone, hurried down an alleyway, over a pile of stones from a broken wall, and down a crooked stairway made even more crooked by the events of the day. She followed the music from a simple erhu, music so familiar to her that she had to know.

And as she came closer, she ran past a couple rebuilding their garden wall, past a shopkeeper sweeping broken pottery off the tile floor. She paused as the picture flashed into her mind of an orchestra, and she heard the same notes, the same music, as it blended into one.

We played that song! Then she knew. *I played that song!*

And then she was almost afraid to turn the last corner in front of the two-story stucco building where she had slept, Suuli's home. A few bricks on one side had peeled away, but it still stood straight and proud. Must have been well made. Up on the roof Wist sat with her erhu, playing the sad song Oriannon had heard drifting across the city.

So Oriannon just watched and listened, all the time wondering where Wist had learned the tune. And she knew the others would be there any minute with the body of Wist's grandfather, after they'd paraded it around the city. She'd just taken a short cut.

Someone needs to tell her what's coming, she thought. And she gripped the ladder leaning against the side of the house, stepped up to the first rung, and wondered if she could do it.

21

riannon!" Wist's face lit up when she saw who was climbing up the ladder; she held out her hand to help Oriannon up over the side. "I'm glad you're all right! Did you see my grandfather?"

"I saw him."

How was she going to tell her?

"That's good. I was hoping he wasn't hurt. Several people were."

"Right." Oriannon swallowed. The girl could find out on her own, without Oriannon's help. It wasn't Oriannon's place to tell Wist her grandfather had been killed. Or if it was, she just couldn't. Instead she tried changing the subject.

"Heard you playing." Oriannon nodded toward the three-stringed instrument Wist held. It seemed exceptionally small and fragile, smaller than the ones in Corista and hardly able to produce the kind of sound she'd heard. "What was the song?"

"Oh." Wist hesitated, fingering the simple instrument. "You wouldn't understand."

"Why not? What is there to understand? It's just a song, isn't it?"

"That's what I mean." Wist shook her head. "It's about—"

191

"Here." Oriannon reached for the instrument. "Let me try it. Please?"

Oriannon wasn't even sure why she did that. And at first Wist didn't look too sure either, but she slowly handed over the erhu. It felt good in Oriannon's hands, a little different, but still right and familiar. And before she could think, she positioned her fingers on the strings, took a deep breath, and drew the bow.

At first the notes came slowly, but then faster and faster, like ice melting or a stream tumbling through woods. And she felt as if others played next to her, their music filling her ears, though she couldn't make out their faces. She even imagined a man standing in front of them, his face blurred, but just as much a part of the music as anything—more! She followed his hands, leaned into the music, and played.

"Where did you learn that?" Wist burst the bubble when she snatched back the violin, her face a storm cloud of questions. "How did you know that song?"

"I'm sorry." Oriannon backed away, looking at her hands, and now she wasn't even sure what she had done. She could only turn away while Wist stepped around to grab her by the shoulder.

"You didn't answer me," said Wist, her eyes blazing. "Where did you—"

"He taught us."

"What did you say?" The other girl blinked as if she'd been slapped in the face.

"I said, he taught me, Wist. Jesmet taught me."

Wist just stared.

"Jesmet," Oriannon repeated. "The same Jesmet you're always singing songs about, right? Or is there another?"

"Only one." Wist's eyes widened even more. "But is my grandfather knowing who you are? Did you tell him you know Jesmet?"

She had to explain now. But now the tears threatened to choke her.

"I told him, Wist. He knows — he ... knew." She took a deep, ragged breath and wiped away the tears, but they would not stop. "We were in the Great Hall when the earthquake hit. Everything was shaking, stuff was falling from the ceiling. And then when we turned around, a rock must have fallen on him, and he ..."

Oriannon couldn't finish her sentence, just draped her arms around the other girl in her pain. And now they both could see the procession coming down the street, coming their way. Wist looked into Oriannon's eyes, then back at the street, then pulled away and shook her head. She understood.

"No. Please. Don't say anything else."

Oriannon couldn't find a dry eye in the small crowd that gathered at the base of the cliff the next day to lay Suuli's body to rest. Hand in hand they circled a small knoll overlooking a bend in the dry river, where small stone markers gave testimony to lives lived while the red earth of a freshly dug grave revealed where Suuli's body had been covered.

Oriannon stood a few steps back from the mourners, crying and wondering. It's just that she had never seen people act this way when someone died. Or she didn't think so. Because when it really came down to it, did she remember how people acted back in Corista? She couldn't say yes; she couldn't say no. Yet it could not have been like this.

For one thing, what kind of a funeral could they have without a proper priest? She knew that much. Here, three older men took turns leading the group in sung prayers, as if they were making them up on the spot. That couldn't be right.

Later, another Owling read from a book whose words Oriannon only vaguely recognized.

"Out of the darkness he's showing us the key to the mystery," read the man, wearing bandages on his head that told everyone he'd been injured in the recent earthquake. "And he will turn the deepest darkness into light."

Everyone nodded while Oriannon fidgeted. Because once again these words tickled the edge of her mind, just out of reach, like a stubborn dream that refused to step out of the shadows of her night.

And then they started talking about how much Suuli cared about people, and how much he loved Jesmet, and how he walked in the light. As if these Owlings knew what *real* light was!

"This is so strange," she whispered to Wist, a few minutes later. "People act as if they're almost happy to see your grandfather go."

Wist shook her head and frowned back a warning at Oriannon.

"You know that's not true. We're just glad for him, that's all."

By that time they had finished praying and talking about how much they'd loved Suuli; now someone led them in another song. Wist joined in, wiping the tears from her eyes and smiling at the same time as others reached out to put their arms around her.

"And why does everybody sing so much?" asked Oriannon. "And then smile when they sing it?"

At first Wist didn't answer, just kept singing with the rest of them. And in a way they sounded just like the woman sweeping the street or the men whistling as they repaired their broken city. The same kind of music, joy and sorrow blended, but mostly joy. Oriannon would never admit it, but she would have given anything to be able to make music that way. Never mind that it didn't make sense.

But while the singing went on around them, Wist finally stopped long enough to look straight at Oriannon.

"Maybe it's because we have something you don't have over on Corista."

"You mean darkness?"

Wist humored her with a smile.

"No. Hope."

Oriannon had to think about that one for a moment.

"But ... hope in what? I'm sorry, Wist, but your grandfather's dead. That doesn't seem very hopeful."

Once again Wist looked at her as if for the first time. Everyone else kept singing.

"You're really not getting it, are you?"

"I didn't know there was anything to get."

But even as she spoke she knew she was lying. These people, these strange Owlings, it almost made her mad how happy they seemed, and she knew they had something she did not. How could she miss it?

"I didn't think you were that dense, Oriannon."

"I'm not dense. I just don't see what you have to sing about. Look around you! It's always half-dark and you never see the suns."

"They reflect off the other moons. And we will, someday. Meanwhile, we—"

"Meanwhile you sing about how the Maker painted the colors of the Southern Lights on the sky, for goodness sake, and the moons, and the blue glowing snow ..."

A faint smile crossed Wist's sad face. "You were paying attention, after all."

How could she not hear it? Even now, at this funeral, they were singing about the Maker in ways she wasn't sure they were supposed to sing. As if he wasn't even in the Temple, but was strolling somewhere in the next courtyard. As if they expected him to show up here at the funeral with them. Was that allowed?

Oriannon shook her head and crossed her arms as the funeral finally started to break up and they drifted toward the long, winding stairway that would take them back up to the city. Without elevators, they would take ten steps up, turn, take ten more steps, and so on. Going down was easier, of course. She wasn't sure why she had come down all this way, anyway. Just to be nice to Wist? What if the shuttle returned?

She tripped and Wist grabbed her elbow.

"Thanks," she murmured. As they trudged up the stairway, someone started singing another of their low, sad songs, this one about how the people who walk in the dark will see the great lights ...

Hey, wake up, people, she thought. *The light is on the other side of the planet!*

And what was hopeful about that?

"Who are they kidding?" she wondered out loud, gasping for air. The people ahead and behind her didn't seem to mind the long climb back up to the city, and their words echoed off the face of the cliff, along with ...

The bells of the city?

Oriannon paused to listen as she hung on to the rope railing.

"You hear that?" Oriannon turned to Wist, then cocked her head to the side and craned her neck to look up and around. Now the singing dropped off as the others must have heard too.

"I hear." Wist grabbed her hand as if something new had happened. Warning bells?

Oriannon glanced back down at the river where Owling workers had already started rebuilding a dam to block the water once again, piling rocks and timbers at the opening. No shuttle—yet. Good. Wist, on the other hand, must have heard something else. She pointed up at the city, shining white in the dim light and pretty, really, with twinkling lights in every window. Someone waved a lantern at them from the large overhang at the top of the stairway, from the city plaza.

And still the bells rang out, only this time they sounded different—not crying, like a funeral, but quicker, louder. Or maybe it was the young boy, almost falling down the stairs.

"He's here!" shouted the boy, taking the steps three or four at a time and waving at them as if he brought the most important news they'd ever heard. "Here! Jesmet is back!"

22

So these Owlings must have short memories.

Not that she herself was one to complain about memories — or lack of. But Oriannon couldn't help wondering as she surged up the stairs with the rest of the crowd. Actually, Wist nearly flew the last few meters, Oriannon tripped along behind her, and the people behind boosted her up each step.

And the strangest thing was, now everyone acted as if they'd forgotten that their city's lifeblood had been attacked just a few hours ago. The all-important water supply had been cut off, hadn't it? People had been killed, including Wist's grandfather, hadn't they?

Forget the whitewashed adobe brick walls that had collapsed and the cracks in the street and the market in disarray. Forget that the hanging city could be in danger of sliding right off the side of the cliff into the deep ravine below. This funeral had just turned into a party, if the buzz of people above them was any sign. Oriannon paused at the edge of the plaza, taking it all in.

And here he came, the grand marshal of a walking parade, right down the crooked little alleys of Lior, surrounded by nearly every Owling in the city. And all who didn't join the street mob waved and cheered out their windows. So by this time Oriannon had to yell at Wist to make herself heard.

"We should get up on a roof if you want to see," shouted Oriannon, pointing at the nearest high spot. It seemed like a good idea. Wist only shook her head and crowded in closer, stepping into the middle of the cobblestone plaza. Oriannon could only follow.

She almost didn't recognize him, though. Because this time he wore plain Owling clothes, gray-brown and roughly woven. He seemed shorter too, not the way she imagined he would look, and his eyes seemed deeper and even more full of sadness than before.

Before? A dim picture of the same man came to mind, but in her memory he used to wear a dignified Coristan forest green robe reserved for ... mentors.

"Mentor Jesmet!" she called through the crowd. "Over here!"

If he'd heard her, she couldn't tell, and at this point no one knew the difference. By this time Jesmet had made his way through the crowd to stand in front of Wist, and when he stopped the crowd settled down too—from a roar to a whimper as the man raised his hand to speak.

"I'm so sorry about your grandfather, Wist." He rested a hand on her shoulder as if he'd known her all her life, and the tears glistened in his eyes too. "I know how much he loved everyone in the city. And of course you."

"Thank you." Wist bowed her head. But Oriannon wondered how he could be acting like some kind of long-lost uncle, as if he knew her. And another thing—

"You could have healed him," Oriannon blurted out, "if you'd wanted to."

Some in the crowd gasped at her impudence, and Oriannon clapped a hand to her mouth, too late to recall the thought.

"What did you say, Oriannon?" Now his voice carried over the crowd, as if he wanted them all to hear. Of course, by this time they could have heard a baby whisper. Someone coughed from a second-story window.

"I ..." Now Oriannon couldn't get her voice to work, and Wist backed up a step.

"He knows your name, Oriannon," she whispered. "Say something. Anything."

"Of course he knows my name," Oriannon hissed back. "He used to be my ..."

My mentor. And there came the memory, again, dancing at the edge of her mind, mocking her. But right now Mentor Jesmet wanted an answer, and she had the weird feeling she'd been in this exact same situation before.

"I said ..." She swallowed hard, wishing now that she'd been able to keep her big mouth shut. "You could have made him better, if you'd been there."

She felt the eyes of everyone in Lior resting on her. Of course, it was too late now.

"I mean," she went on, trying to dig herself out of this hole, "I saw you heal people. I think I did. Pretty sure. I saw you pull a girl back from being dead. She *was* dead, wasn't she?"

He nodded, answer enough. And when he looked at her, she knew how real it was. Maybe she got the pieces mixed up, but not those eyes.

"Why are you here, Oriannon?" he asked her, and she supposed it was up to him if he wanted to change the subject.

By this time Wist had grabbed Oriannon's arm and was digging her fingernails in a death grip. Oriannon hardly noticed, and now she couldn't tear herself away from Jesmet's gaze.

199

"I lost everything I knew ..." she couldn't help explaining what little she remembered, as strange as it sounded. "Everything I was."

"Back in Corista, you mean."

She nodded. "Kind of like it was all smashed, and I was left holding the pieces."

He waited, and it was still her turn to explain. Why was she telling him all this? She opened her mouth and it came out.

"And the only way I could think of to find it was over here. I know that sounds stupid, but—"

"Not stupid." He shook his head. "Not stupid at all. But tell me what you thought you would find."

She turned away, feeling her cheeks flush. Everybody could hear this. But she knew she had to answer.

"Not me," she whispered, confused. "I wasn't looking for myself. I was looking for a mentor. A song, maybe."

"And did you find it?"

She looked back at him, forgetting the crowd that still pressed in all around them, forgetting the people hanging from their balconies and leaning over the edge of their roofs. Forgetting Wist.

And now she recognized the music she'd been looking for, the same way she had once known it by heart. Strange, but now the song actually stood in front of her—only ... how could she ever explain that to anyone without sounding very odd, indeed? A man, a mentor, a song.

"People who walk in the dark will see a great light," he said, and the words sounded oh so familiar. "And those who live in a dark land—the light will shine on them."

"I'm supposed to know those words, right?"

"You memorized them, once. From the Codex." He pointed to the side of his head. "And they're still living up there for you, Oriannon. We just have to get them back."

"But—"

"No. Don't worry. I'm glad you came here, though you didn't really know where you were going at first. Did you? And I'm glad you found real light here in Lior. But now it's time for you to remember again."

This time she didn't argue, just nodded and waited. And then she remembered the feeling of taking off her sleep blindfold every day after her nap, and the feeling of blinking back the sunlight.

She remembered her room and her house on the hill. Her dad, as if he had just stepped out of a cloud. She remembered!

Her friends at Ossek Prep, Brinnin Flyer and Margus Leek. Their names! She smiled at the returning flood of memories as each one found its proper place once more.

She remembered Mentor Jesmet, the things he'd done and said, and the music he taught them. She remembered it all again—heard it!—each note and each tune, each verse from the book; it all rushed back at her in a wonderful pure torrent, cleansing her mind and making her want to shout. She held back, though, grinned instead. Because now the fog was history—gone, gone, gone. Everything she'd lost or that had been scrambled had been put right back where it had been.

But different, somehow. Better. Sharper and in focus. Neat and in order. Clear, just like the notes to Mentor Jesmet's music. *His music*, the music she'd heard echoed here in Lior. She held her head and stared at this man with wide eyes, wondering how he'd done it, how he'd restored all this to her. And he just nodded and winked, like no one else would know. How could they not?

"It was always there, Oriannon Hightower of Nyssa," he told her. And by that time the crowd was pressing in on him again. "But now you're going to need what you lost. You're going to need it very soon."

What was that supposed to mean? He turned to go, paused for a moment.

"Oh, and by the way," he added, "I'll see you and Wist two days from now ... in the Great Hall."

23

Two days later Oriannon tried not to return people's stares as she walked down the city's main cobblestone avenue with Wist, on their way to the Great Hall and their mystery appointment with Jesmet.

"They're just curious," Wist explained in a low voice, looking up at two stories of balconies fronting the narrow passageway. "They've never seen a Coristan before who knows him."

"Do I?" Oriannon wondered how to explain what had happened to her mind as she fingered the little earbud in her pocket. Funny that Becket hadn't asked her about it again, not since that first time in the Great Hall. "Sometimes it's been hard to tell who I really knew."

"Well, he sure knew *your* name."

"Mine and everyone else's. He has the kind of memory I used to have."

Wist looked at her sharply, expertly sidestepping the outstretched wing of a snowy owl perched on a street-level window ledge.

"Don't be comparing yourself," she told Oriannon.

"I know, I know."

Oh, she knew, all right—more than Wist could guess. Now Oriannon knew who she'd been and exactly where she'd come from. The only thing she didn't know yet was why she had come to this cliffside refuge, this faraway world, where everyone sang but never performed.

A woman washing her clothes in a spring-fed stone basin paused from her humming—and her scrubbing—to watch Wist and Oriannon passing by. Oriannon tried not to giggle at the thought of Mrs. Eraz trying to clean like that. Washing with water! How quaint.

Of course, even the smells were different from what she now remembered. As they walked past a tea-seller's shop, exotic aromas wafted out to tickle her nose with the rich perfume of snowy mountainsides and deep purple canyons—and for a moment she almost forgot where she was.

"There she is!" A couple of small kids on the next level pointed and waved down at her. They hung out of their balcony ledge until their mother pulled them back.

But when Oriannon pulled her hand out of her pocket to wave back she felt the earbud tumble to the pavement, so she stooped to pick it up before someone behind her trampled it.

"What's that?" asked Wist, who got a good look.

"Nothing."

But the Owling was too quick. She grabbed Oriannon's wrist. Not hard, but not to be ignored, either.

"That's what Becket was asking you about, wasn't it?" She wasn't as sleepy as she seemed. "I heard him mention it."

"Oh?" Now Oriannon tried to shrug it off, too late. "I don't know what they were worried about. It's just an earbud, see?"

She wriggled loose from the other girl's grip, slipped it into her ear out of habit and combed her hair back across, then sighed. What would it hurt to explain?

"My friend back in Corista has one just like it. We used to talk to each other. It's really no big deal; just a toy. Nothing anybody needs to worry about."

"Wait a minute." Wist frowned. "You're remembering again? I thought you couldn't recall those kinds of things."

Oriannon looked around to see if anyone was listening. She wasn't sure why it would be such a secret, but she drew Wist back into the quiet alcove formed by an arched doorway, out of the main flow of people.

"Promise not to tell?" she asked, holding on to Wist's sleeve. The other girl put on an extra-serious look and nodded, and kept nodding all through the story.

"All of it?" she gasped, minutes later. "You're remembering everything now?"

"Just like that." Oriannon snapped her finger. "And then he told me I was going to need it."

"I should tell my grand—" Wist stopped in mid-sentence when she realized what she'd said.

"I'm sorry," whispered Oriannon. "These past few days have been hard, haven't they?"

Wist nodded. And her slip of the tongue made Oriannon think of her own home, her father. Dad had probably rousted every security in Corista looking for her. But how long had it been? In a place where day was night and everything else was the mirror opposite of what she'd been brought up to believe, she'd lost track of time. Only Wist's words shook her from her worry.

"I'm sorry too, Oriannon." She gripped Oriannon by the shoulders and looked up at her. "But if you found what you were looking for, maybe now you want to ... go home?"

Oriannon opened her mouth, not sure what would come out.

"He gave me my memory back," she admitted. "But some of it, I don't know ..."

She looked at the cobblestones at her feet.

" ... Some of it doesn't look so good."

Wist waited for her to go on.

"Compared to here, I mean, it's much lighter over there in Corista, sure." Oriannon felt a streak of honesty. "The suns are shining all the time. But in a lot of ways it's really dark."

So, did she really want to go back? She wondered as they continued down the narrow street. A few minutes later she stopped, turning her head.

"What?" Wist looked at her as a man with an armload of baskets swerved around them.

"Did you hear that?" Oriannon turned her head again.

"Lots of sounds around here, sister." Wist waved her hand at the compact little city. "Which one are you meaning?"

Which sound, indeed? A furniture maker hammered on a chair in his workshop. An older Owling woman tapped her cane on the street. A baby squalled from an open window above their heads. And everywhere excited little knots of people seemed to be comparing notes about the latest Jesmet sighting.

"There!" Oriannon heard it again, only this time she realized which direction it came from.

Her earbud.

She put her hand to her ear, plugged the other one, and there it was — faint, but now clearer than before. A boy's voice. Margus Leek's voice, to be exact. She jumped at the sound as he went on.

... all this way, and what good did it do? Zero, zip, nada. Hang it, Oriannon Hightower of Nyssa, I'm sick and tired of trying to get through to you, especially since you're obviously not listening.

Margus. She tried to interrupt his thought transmission, but he obviously wasn't listening, either.

And if you're really here, what are you doing here? You know what else? You're nuts, number one, and as soon as this is over I am going right back to Corista and I'm going to forget I ever came to this miserable dark place. And number two ...

Margus! She tried to up the volume.

And number two, he went on, *you don't need to interrupt me when I'm ...*

His thought trailed off.

Well, I didn't mean to interrupt you, she told him, *except I thought maybe ...*

Oriannon! His thought blasted so loudly she almost had to yank out the earbud. *That's not really you, is it? I mean, you're really there?*

Of course I'm really here. It's you I can't believe I'm hearing. I never thought I'd be so happy to hear . . . I mean, you know what I mean.

Exactly, he replied. *I'm just sitting here on this shuttle, looking out the viewport at a lot of nothing, and all of a sudden, bam! You sound pretty good. A little fuzzy, but good.*

So are you the cavalry to the rescue? she asked. *I used to read stories like this, when I was a little girl.*

Sorry, no, Ori. His voice went serious for the first time, and it sent a chill up her spine. *You can call this the cavalry, but there's no rescue, except for your dad sending out a team of securities to try to find you. Only they couldn't, and some of the media said you were dead. You're not, are you? Really? Tell me you're not.*

She laughed.

A couple of times I thought I was. But no. I'm here in the city above where the water pipeline ends. Lior. It's built right up in a huge cliff, roads and homes and people and everything. And you'll never guess who else is here.

She switched to real talking as she grabbed Wist's hand.

"It's Margus!" she pointed to her earbud, saying the words aloud. "Margus Leek!"

Wist nodded and smiled, as if she understood, which wasn't likely.

Listen, Ori. Margus broke in, again. His far-off voice crackled. *Are you still there?*

I'm still here, Margus. And—

Okay, listen. I don't know who you're with or what you're doing. But if you're in that place by the pipeline you've got to get away, do you understand me? You've got to get out of there, now!

What are you talking—

207

I told you this isn't the cavalry. They found out the pipeline was all blocked up again, so the guys on this ship are supposed to tear apart what's blocking it, once and for all. Did you know the creatures there plug it up all the time?

I know, I know, Margus. I've seen it. In fact—

Yeah, but this is different. They're ticked off this time, and they're talking about doing something to the place where the things live.

Owlings, Margus. Owlings. And they're not things. They're people. They're good people.

His voice faded.

Margus? She adjusted her earbud. *I didn't hear—*

I said, I hope you're really not there with them.

That's what I've been trying to tell you!

Oh, wow. He paused again. *Well then, you just have to do what I say, 'cause it's going to get ugly, is what I hear.*

Where had she heard him tell her that before?

What do you mean, ugly?

Don't you get it, Oriannon? They said they're going to teach those owlers a lesson.

How soon, Margus? She couldn't believe what she was hearing. *How soon before you're here?*

How do I know? All I know is we're getting really close, and . . .

His voice faded once again.

Margus?

● ● ●

208

"Hey, wait a minute!" A half-hour later Oriannon bounced on her toes as yet another young man ran past her and through Becket Sol's front door, a narrow townhouse over a bakery. "Can't you tell me what's going on?"

The rough-cut door slammed behind him, but she already knew the answer, actually. With city bells ringing and people running about, she didn't have to look down the cliff to know the Coristan shuttle craft had arrived. She thought about hurrying down the street to a place where she could get a better view, but in all the confusion decided it was better not to lose track of Wist.

What was taking her so long to warn Becket Sol? And why wouldn't she let Oriannon come in with her?

"Excuse me?" Oriannon tried to flag down another young man as he burst through the door and back out onto the street. "Do you know if my friend Wist is still in there?"

She had to be. But the young man didn't know or didn't care.

"Sorry." He raised his hands as if parting the waters and hopped over a set of clay jugs on the walkway. "No time to talk."

"But can't you just tell me—"

Apparently not, and that was enough for Oriannon. She marched up to Becket Sol's front door the way she had been told not to, took a deep breath, and rapped three times.

"Come on, come on." Oriannon crossed her arms. Didn't they know how serious this was?

She watched the street while raising her hand to knock again—just as the door reopened and Wist finally appeared.

"There you are!" said Oriannon. "What did he say?"

"Becket said not to be worrying about it." She dragged Oriannon along, away from the house. "Said it happens all the time, and the Maker will be taking care of us."

"He took all this time to tell you that?"

"Lots of visitors. I had to wait my turn."

"But didn't you tell him they're coming back to finish the job? And this time it might not just be the pipeline they're clearing! Look, I'll go back and explain to him if you won't."

Wist held up her hand and shook her head.

"I told him, Oriannon. That's all we can do. Let it go."

"But—"

"Listen! Are you hearing the warning bells anymore?"

Oriannon stopped and had to admit she did not, which only gave Wist the opportunity for an "I told you so" moment.

"Besides," the Owling girl said over her shoulder as she started down the street again. "Jesmet is here now. You know he wouldn't be letting anything bad happen."

Oh, was that it? Well, Jesmet was there yesterday and look what happened.

"Wait a minute." Oriannon ran to catch up. "Is that all he said?"

"He said he'd meet us at the Great Hall, and to stay clear of the plaza until we're sure the Coristan ships aren't coming back, and ..."

Her voice trailed off when they heard the shouting.

"I'm telling you, I'm a friend of hers!" The voice echoed off the sides of buildings as it came closer. "I know she's up here, somewhere. Oriannon! Do you hear me? Oriannon Hightower of—"

The voice stopped in mid-sentence as two Owling men dragged him around the corner to face them. One on each arm.

"—of Nyssa." His voice dropped to a whisper.

"Your friend?" asked Wist.

"Boy, am I glad to see you." Margus tried to shake the two men's grips but they held on.

"Margus!" Oriannon ran up to him.

"We were bringing him to Becket Sol," explained one of the men, never smiling. He raised an eyebrow at Oriannon. "You're knowing this boy?"

"He's my friend. But what happened down there?"

Margus waved his hands as he tried to explain.

"I don't know, Ori. It was a circus. Guys running everywhere, yelling, things blowing up. Total mess. I stepped out of the ship for a minute and these guys here jumped me and dragged me all the way up that crazy staircase."

"What about the ship?"

Margus shrugged, as if it was none of his business.

"Don't know, but I think they may have sent up some more probes."

"Oriannon?" Wist nudged her in the side. "I think Jesmet is going to be waiting for us at the Great Hall. Maybe your friend should be coming along. He could tell us the rest of his story on the way."

So now Wist was worried about being late? Oriannon looked to the men, then nodded at Margus.

"He knows Jesmet too."

That did it. Without another word both men let go and stepped back. Margus straightened his light white Coristan shirt and shivered. He certainly wasn't dressed for this side of the world.

"That's right," he agreed, but Oriannon could see the sweat on his forehead, despite a chilly breeze whistling through the narrow alleys and snaking walkways of Lior. "I know him."

Without waiting for the men to change their minds, Oriannon grabbed Margus by the hand and dragged him along. But she still had to know.

"Do the men on the ship . . . ?" she asked Margus. "Do they know I'm here?"

"Doesn't matter either way." He shook his head and lowered his voice to a whisper. "I'm telling you, Ori. If they don't attack the city this time, it's going to be next time. All they needed was a green light from the Assembly, and — "

"So this is your famous friend Margus?" Wist interrupted as they walked.

"Oh, I'm sorry." Oriannon waved her hand. "Yeah. This is Margus; we go to school together back in Seramine. Went. Margus, this is Wist. She's one of the *Owlings* I told you about."

Wist's shy smile never left her face as she led them toward the Great Hall entry. But Oriannon froze when she noticed a blinking light out of the corner of her eye, just above street level. Not again! She reacted almost out of instinct.

"Duck!" She pointed at the probe and looked for a place to hide. But as she did, a white blur of feathers flashed overhead and they heard a little *skree* of satisfaction as hunter connected with its prey. Wist glanced up as well, and nodded grimly at the owl flying away with a probe in its talons.

"I'll tell you about the owls later," Oriannon told Margus as they hurried toward the huge ironwood entry door, this time staying low in case more probes lurked nearby. Because where there was one . . .

as this the same place, the same Great Hall?

Oriannon gasped as she gawked at the soaring high ceilings criss-crossed by sturdy timbers, the surviving stained glass windows set into the stone, the rainbow of colors glittering down on them and bringing marble floors to life. So much had already been repaired and cleaned up. She studied an elaborate tapestry hanging from just below the windows, a scene with flowers and trees and the Trion that naturally reminded her of Corista.

And for the first time in a long time she felt a twinge of homesickness, mixed with something else far deeper than she knew.

"Why do we have to come here?" asked Margus. "Can't we get something to eat instead? I'm hungry."

"Shh!" Wist signaled to him as they heard Becket's booming voice echo through the chambers.

"We only light it up for special occasions."

They turned to see Becket entering through a door by the fireplace, this time dressed in a tan linen robe, and flanked by the other six members of the Council. Minus Suuli, of course. Becket said nothing else but motioned for them to remain standing.

"So this must be a special occasion," Margus whispered.

Oriannon didn't answer, just glanced at the massive front door barred shut, and a good thing too. She could just imagine what would happen if a probe found them in here. This time there would be no shadows to hide in; every torch and wall sconce flickered with bright golden light. And from the sides of the Great Hall they noticed even more torches approaching like flickering lightning bugs, carried by the people of Lior. Before, when the hall had been dark, she hadn't realized how far it stretched in either direction under stone archways and beyond.

And then Jesmet himself stepped into the light, joining the crowd and standing in front of the fireplace where Suuli had stood before. He dressed like all the other Council members. But unlike the other members, his face almost seemed to glow in the torchlight as if he was a part of the illumination himself.

"Oh-oh." Margus quietly groaned at the sight, but Oriannon wouldn't let him hide behind her. Why would he want to anyway?

"Well." Jesmet smiled at them the same way he had when they walked into his orchestra class. "We seem to be safe in here for a while. Very nice of you to be here, Oriannon."

She opened her mouth to say something but decided against it for now.

"Mr. Leek," Jesmet went on, and what could Margus do but stand there? "The last time we saw each other I seem to recall you putting in several good words on my behalf. I appreciate your enthusiasm."

Owlings on each side of them murmured their approval. So Margus had already made a few points here in Lior without saying a word. But still he stammered and shook his head as if the words rebelled in his throat. Finally he sighed and looked straight at Jesmet.

"Listen, I'm not who you think I am." He carved a circle in the stone with the toe of his bright blue running shoe. "I can't stand up here and pretend that—"

"I hate to argue the point, Mr. Leek ... Margus." A smile escaped Jesmet's lips for a brief moment as if a joke had been told between them. "But I know exactly who you are, and I know exactly what happened back in Corista. That's all behind us now."

"I'm sorry, I—" Margus's face went pale as Jesmet went on.

"I know you are." He stepped over and rested a hand on Margus's shoulder. "But it's all right, Margus, really."

Margus teared up as he nodded his head. And now Oriannon couldn't help wondering who this man was, dressed in a simple robe, telling Margus not to worry.

"I thought you used to be a music mentor." She wasn't sure she should ask, as all eyes turned her direction. She took a deep breath. "But who are you really?"

It seemed like a reasonable question at the time, even if Margus poked her in the side to keep her quiet. Jesmet just rubbed his forehead as if he'd just been hit by a killer headache.

"You of all people should know, Oriannon," he answered. "You've seen it all, and you remember it too. No one else can say that."

"Maybe there's a difference between remembering and knowing?"

"Yes." A little smile crept over his face, the look he got when he was looking for the right answer from one of his students. She'd seen it more than once before. "Yes, there is. But does that mean you have no idea?"

"I didn't say that, exactly ..."

Once more Jesmet had backed her into a corner. How did he do that? He waited for her to explain herself.

"I just wanted to hear you say it," she said. "That's all."

"After what happened with the yagwar, you don't know?"

Of course Oriannon remembered everything about how Carrick Trice had been frozen in fear and nearly attacked, how Jesmet had turned away the wild animal with a whistle and a sharp word.

"After what happened in the dining hall, you don't know?"

The smell of those horrid gelatin-spinach dumplings flooded her mind, and how he'd swept them all off their plates, just like that.

"And after what happened to your friend Brinnin Flyer, you don't know?"

Now Oriannon remembered every detail of Brinnin falling off her ladder, of Jesmet pulling her to her feet, from death to life. No doubt about it: Brinnin *had* been dead.

"And are you telling me you were with me all those days in orchestra, and you still don't know?"

She opened her mouth to defend herself, but that wasn't going to amount to anything. What was her excuse? She was just asking a dumb question.

"All that music?" He went on. "All those songs, and you still can't tell me?"

No one else said a word. Did everyone else in the Great Hall know the answer to his question, everyone but her? But she knew. Every detail, every word, everything he'd done. All the music he'd taught them, the same music the Owlings sang. She remembered, and then ... then she knew. Not just remembered, but really *knew.*

"The song." She finally managed to un-stick her dry tongue from the roof of her mouth. "You are ... you're the song. I don't know how, yet, but you're the Maker's Song."

And then he smiled wide and bright, as if he would burst out laughing for her having said so.

"Well. You're finally getting it, Oriannon. And you know what? You don't have to be an eidich to understand our music. Only the Maker can clear your head that way."

Only the Maker? Then who had cleared her head just the day before, given her back her mind?

Jesmet waved his hand at the Owlings around him, and they nodded as if they knew exactly what he was talking about. Well, they probably did. And yet Jesmet was only just getting started.

"But that's not why we're here today." He looked at the other Council members, to the right and to the left. "We're here because Miss Hightower missed an important date by coming to Shadowside, and now we're going to see what we can do to make it up to her."

"You are?" Oriannon wasn't sure what was going on with Margus and Jesmet, but now it was her turn to get shaky-kneed. What was he talking about? "I mean, we are?"

"We are. And so the rest of the members of the Council have graciously allowed us to hold this special Seer Codex ceremony for Oriannon Hightower of Nyssa. A reminder of the Maker's promise to everyone on the planet, Coristan and Owling ..."

Oh! So this is why they were summoned! And now Jesmet had slipped into the language of the Seer Codex, the words she'd heard dozens of times before when it was for older cousins or friends—but never for her. The Owlings stood quietly to the sides, their torches still flickering, as Jesmet turned once again to her.

"Do you remember the words, Oriannon?"

The words she'd known since before she could walk? Her turn:

"You are the light of Corista." Words from the Codex tumbled from her lips. "There is no hiding a city high on a cliff ..."

How many times had she read those words and never known what they'd meant! Of course even though no one had ever tried to explain them, she had never asked. She wiped a tear from her eye and looked around at the torches these kind people held up for her.

"Torches were never meant to be hidden," she went on, and the words tumbled out of her mouth like a stream whose ice-dam had just melted and broken loose. " ... but held high for others to see. Lift up yours so the shadows will flee, and so all of Corista can know whose light you bear."

Her words echoed now in the Great Hall, and after a few more verses Jesmet motioned for her to come forward. He pulled out a plain silver necklace from a fold in his frock and held it out to her. A small black stone dangled from the end of the necklace, set with even smaller white stones in the pattern of the Trion.

"Now that you see, Oriannon Hightower, wear this to remind you of the song we sing, the light we seek, the promise of your Maker."

She looked at the three tiny, blazing stars and nodded before taking the necklace and fixing the clasp. The symbol of Jesmet.

A few Owlings began to clap, quietly at first, then more and more, until they all joined in their cheers. For Jesmet. For Oriannon. For all of Lior. Jesmet smiled at her as the cheers turned to singing, the way only Owlings could sing. Even Becket smiled as a young messenger hurried in from outside and whispered something in his ear.

"Wonderful." He looked different when he smiled. And now he cleared his throat and straightened up, the way a new head of the Council probably should when announcing something important. He raised his hands and waited until everyone finally hushed.

"Er, sorry to interrupt the singing. But I'm told the Coristan probes that were released this time have all been destroyed, and their ship has once again left us, the way we'd prayed."

Wist gave Oriannon a quick look, as if saying, "See? I told you not to worry about it." This time Oriannon couldn't help cheering with everyone else, only catching herself when she thought of her father, and what it would have been like for him to be here too.

But by that time the songs started all over again, chorus after chorus. How these Owlings could sing! When Wist pulled Oriannon into their circle dance, though, Margus headed for the corner of the room.

"Come on, Margus!" Oriannon laughed and held on to the hands of the Owlings on either side of her. "If I can do it ..."

But Margus only shook his head no and went to warm his hands by the fire.

"Is your friend shy?" yelled Wist, passing by in another line.

"Or cold!" Oriannon tried not to worry about it as she twirled about with the rest of them, clapping her hands and joining in their wonderful but complicated storytelling music about the lights in the sky, of brave Owling warriors from long ago, of the Maker and his Song.

If only more people in Corista could hear this! she thought. *If only Daddy could hear this!*

Even the Song himself joined in, and at one point the dance came to a full stop as Jesmet added a short chorus to the epic tale of a hunter and his brave little owl. Oriannon stood with the others, swaying in time, listening to his clear, true voice.

But Jesmet would not sing for long. Because with a little nod he finished his line and stepped back into the line as their dance began anew.

"Here we go again!" Wist skipped past, never slowing. But a few minutes later Oriannon finally dropped out of line, gasping for breath yet still giddy with the celebration. She stepped over to join Margus at the fireplace and rested her hands on her knees.

"What a workout!" she told him, between breaths. "You really should try it."

"Not unless you want me to step all over your feet." Margus kept his place, leaning against the warm stones. And now several Council members even came over to clap her on the back, as if she was the one who might have chased the Coristan invaders away. She accepted their congratulations with a puzzled smile until Jesmet finally made his way over to see them as well.

"You enjoy the songs?" he wondered.

"Of course!" Oriannon glanced over at Margus but couldn't quite read his face.

"Then," replied Jesmet, "perhaps you'll share some of them with your friends back in Corista."

"If I ever go back." Oriannon surprised herself with her own words. "I mean, of course. Eventually."

"Or sooner." Jesmet rested his hands on their shoulders, looked straight into their eyes. "Because actually, Oriannon, you do need to return to Corista right away."

She coughed, wishing she had heard him wrong.

"You're not serious? You want me to leave Lior, just when I'm starting to get used to it?"

"And go back home. Yes. You and Margus both have family who are terribly worried about you. And things are going to change very soon."

"What kind of things?" she wondered.

"Yeah, actually, Oriannon." Margus finally joined the conversation, though he steered it off-track. "I do need to get back. My parents are going to kill me for being gone like this. I just don't know when the next Coristan ship is coming."

"Margus!" Oriannon looked around, hoping no one else had heard him. "Don't say that."

"What? Oh, right." His voice fell. "I guess Coristan ships aren't exactly too popular around here. But how else do we get back?"

"Wist is going to show you another way," Jesmet told them, pointing toward the back of the Great Hall.

"But if the Coristan ship does return?" asked Oriannon. "I could, I could ..."

She could ... what, exactly?

"It's not all about what you can do, Oriannon." Jesmet broke into her worries. "You start with what you know is right, but then you let go—and let me take care of the rest."

"Let you?" She thought she understood, or maybe not.

"That's right." When he reached over and mussed her hair, she remembered how her father used to do the same thing. "But now I believe it's time for you and Margus to go."

Of course not before saying good-bye to Becket Sol, who had taken a breather by the fireplace as well.

"Thanks for saving my life, Mr. Becket ... Becket Sol." She held out her hand and he hesitated for a second before taking it. "But Jesmet says it's time for us to leave."

Becket nodded as if he understood, finally unlocked his grip and pointed toward one of the Great Hall's wings.

"Wist will show you another way out. But ..." He looked Margus over and frowned. "You're not going out there dressed that way, are you?"

"Well ..." Margus didn't have a swift answer, so Becket held up his hand for them to wait, stepped away through the crowd, and returned a moment later with two wooly coats. Each had a blond fur hood, the kind Owling hunters wore out in the cold.

"Here then." He held out the coats. "Wouldn't want you to freeze, would we?"

Oriannon tried to thank him but wasn't quite sure what came out of her mouth. And before she could turn away Becket wrapped his arms around her shoulders and gave her a big hug.

"Jesmet will go with you," he whispered. "But you'd better hurry. The danger is coming."

THE
WAY HOME

fter saying their goodbyes to Jesmet and the rest of the Owlings, Oriannon and Margus followed Wist away from the crowd, away from the high-ceilinged Great Hall and through the arches, away from the wonderful multicolored windows and bright torches, down a long, marble-tiled hall that disappeared into darkness.

"That was kind of different," Margus told them, but back-tracked when he saw the expressions on both the girls' faces. "Uhh ... I mean, *nice* different, the way I would have wished my Seer Codex had been. You know. Simple. Meaningful. Without a lot of—"

"We get the point." Oriannon fingered her Trion necklace and couldn't help breaking into a smile. She had to give him credit, just stepping into this place the way he did, not knowing what was going on — even less than she did. "You'll have to tell me how yours went sometime."

He didn't say anything for a moment, as if he was thinking about it. When he finally answered, his voice sounded hoarse.

"Oh, you know. They wanted to have it right after Jesmet was sent away. So the priest stood up, read a bunch of stuff nobody understood, and then he waved his hands over us and that was

225

pretty much it. Now we're supposed to be grown-up all of a sudden. You missed out."

"Isn't that how you thought it would be?" she asked.

"I don't know. Maybe it was just strange because you and Mentor Jesmet weren't there. So it wasn't anything like what they just did here. Everybody back in Corista was so serious."

"Serious is okay," said Oriannon.

"Serious can be good sometimes," agreed Wist.

Who were they kidding? Oriannon knew what Margus was trying to say. And before they got too far away from the Great Hall she had to pause just once more. The faint sound of singing and clapping echoed faintly down the hall.

"That song . . ." She remembered it this time, every note, every harmony, just as before. And since Wist didn't need to remind her, they just smiled in the shared memory and continued down an echo-filled hallway that sloped downhill, steeper all the time and dimmer with each step. Here and there a glow vial cast a weak blue circle of light, but after a couple of minutes they left those lights behind them as well.

"Slow down, Wist." Oriannon tried to hold on to the other girl's sleeve. "We can't see as well as you can in . . ."

Oriannon's voice melted when she saw a blinking red light in a dark corner, a tiny glint of metal. Or thought she did. She caught her breath and skidded to a stop, trying not to stare.

"What are you doing now?" Margus asked her.

"Shh!" She grabbed his shoulders and whispered into his ear: "Look over there to the right. Only don't look. I think there's a probe."

Which was probably the exact wrong thing to do, now that she thought of it. So instead of acting as if she had noticed anything, she kneeled on the damp floor and pretended to adjust her shoe.

"Where?" Margus didn't lower his voice enough. Did he want the probe to know he'd seen it too? "I don't see anything."

"The red light!" she whispered. She couldn't point. But the next time she looked, it had disappeared. No blinking red light, no probe.

"Here." Wist reached into her pocket and handed her a small glass vial, shaking it as she did. It came to life with a bright ice blue that bathed them all in its strange night light. "I didn't think we'd be needing this for a while, but you two are blinder than I thought. You're probably going to be wanting it from here on."

"Let me see." Margus took the vial and held it high, casting blue shadows all around them. He tiptoed over to where Oriannon had been pointing, lighting up a corner of the hallway ceiling and a good collection of cobwebs but not much else.

"I'm pretty sure I saw it," said Oriannon, but maybe she wasn't so sure now, after all. It could have been one of those things a person imagines when they're feeling jumpy, the face in the closet. How could it have slipped inside the Great Hall, anyway? Unless—

"Wist, is there any other way in?"

Wist shrugged. "Lots of tunnels and corridors I'm not knowing about. I've only heard of one other way out, but that doesn't mean there aren't others."

That didn't help her much.

"Maybe we should just keep going," Margus suggested. So after one last look into the corner, Oriannon was happy to hurry on behind Wist, while Margus held the vial up so they could both see where they were going—deeper and deeper into the mountain, into a solid rock cave.

They didn't talk for the next little while, said nothing to each other as the tile floor gave way to rough rock. And after a few minutes Oriannon had to wipe a trickle of sweat from her forehead.

"Is it just me?" Margus loosened the collar of his shirt, a light white Coristan fabric that would have been cool to wear under the three suns. "Or is it getting really warm all of a sudden?"

"This is where all the hot springs are coming from," answered Wist, and at this point she wasn't slowing down for anyone. They also didn't need Becket Sol's coats down here yet, though Oriannon held on to them for later, when they would.

"Wait!" This time Margus stopped short and looked around. "Did you feel that?"

Feel what? So they all had to stop again, and when Oriannon rested her hand on a rocky outcropping, she could feel the stone vibrating too—faintly at first, then more serious and impossible to ignore. A moment later she wasn't just leaning on the rock for balance, but holding on with both hands to keep from being shaken off her feet.

"Whoa!" Margus braced himself by stretching out his legs and holding his arms out to the side for balance, until finally the shaking let up. "Do you people have a lot of these?"

"Sometimes down here in the lava tubes." Wist looked around and cleared her throat.

"Third one since I've been here," Oriannon added as they continued down the tunnel. She coughed on a mouthful of dust and tried to clear the air in front of her. After a few more minutes they had to slow down, then stoop, then crawl on all fours.

"If this gets any steeper—" said Margus.

Then what?

"We're almost there." At that Wist tugged off her small backpack and pulled out a length of roughly braided rope. She looped one end around an upturned knuckle of rock on the tunnel floor and tossed the other end into the darkness below, just ahead of them. How had she known? Oriannon thought she heard a splash.

"Are we going down there?" Margus's voice sort of wavered, the way Oriannon felt too.

"I'm not; you are." Wist looked at them seriously, and in the blue light her eyes seemed even bigger if that was possible. "This is as far as I'm supposed to go. But look, it's only about four meters down, and then you hit the bottom. It's an underground stream down there, but it should only be up to your ankles, and the water's warm."

"Warm?" Margus didn't look too sure. But Wist nodded and smiled.

"Nothing to it. When you're down there you just follow the stream until it comes out of the side of the mountain, and you just have to keep an eye out because there's a little bit of a waterfall. Once you're past that, you just head east until … well, I've never been out that far. But you have, Oriannon."

Oriannon rolled her eyes.

"Yeah, when my shoulder was sprained and I was half out of my mind. And is it really the same way I came?"

"Not quite. I think you wandered a bit, came by the lakes. This route could be a little quicker."

"Are you sure you don't have a lev-scooter?" asked Margus. "I'm not so big on walking all the way home."

Wist handed Oriannon the pack. "Becket said it should only be a couple of days, depending on how quickly you walk. He goes out fishing in the borderlands all the time."

"I know about his fishing." Oriannon hefted the pack, and her shoulders sagged under the weight. A little heavier than she'd thought. "What's in this thing, anyway?"

"Food, fire starter, a couple flasks of drinking water." Wist tested her rope with a quick yank. "You might have to find more to drink on the way. Don't be drinking the sulfur water though, or you'll be getting sick."

"No sat-nav system?" asked Margus.

"I'm not knowing what a sat-nav is," she answered, handing him the rope. "But I gave you a lodestone, which will point you toward the Trion. That's east. You'll be finding your way."

"I'm glad you're so sure." Margus tried the rope, planted his feet at the edge, and hesitated.

"Go ahead," she told him. "Really. It's not far."

He nodded as he gripped the rope and stood at the top of the little shaft. Oriannon draped their two coats over his shoulders.

"Okay then." He took another deep breath. "We'll text you a message when we get home."

Of course, Wist probably didn't know what he was talking about. But she smiled and waved as he eased himself down slowly, gripping the rope with white knuckles. And then he disappeared into the darkness.

"Well, I guess I'm next." Oriannon swung the backpack over her own shoulder and looked at Wist. "Wist, I—"

"It's okay." Wist's eyes were brimming with tears too. But she returned the warm hug and wouldn't let go first. "I'll be praying for you, Oriannon Hightower. And Jesmet will be going with you. Both of you. Just hurry. Please hurry."

Jesmet? Oriannon wasn't quite sure what her friend meant. But yes, she would hurry. She knew what could happen soon. The Owlings could hide down here in the tunnels, but what good would that do them if Lior was destroyed? Wist straightened her arms and held Oriannon out by the shoulders.

"I know you'll convince them not to come back."

"Yeah." Oriannon nodded and wiped the tears away with her sleeve. So it was all up to her. Or not. What had Jesmet said? She reached for the words, and this time they popped right back at her:

You start with what you know is right, but then you let go—and let me take care of the rest.

All right then. She still didn't know how he proposed to take care of *anything* when they were down here and he was up there. That part still didn't make sense. But she supposed she had seen stranger things since Mentor Jesmet had shown up at Ossek Prep. She called down the hole to Margus to make sure he'd landed safely.

"Just don't let the rope slide through your hands too fast, Ori." His voice floated up at them and she could barely make out his shape in the blue light. "Or you'll get blisters."

Easy for him to say. But now what choice did she have? Slowly she eased her way down the hole, step by step, hand over hand, until she looked down and saw water beneath her scuffed white Coristan flex-shoes. Sure enough, it was barely up to her ankles, smelled a little like rotten eggs, and felt toasty warm.

"Good place for a warm bath." Margus joked but his voice cracked. Oriannon coiled up the wet rope after it dropped down with a splash. They might need it later.

"Remember," Wist called down to them, "use the lodestone. East."

"No worries," Margus called back.

Oriannon looked up to see if she could still make out Wist's face. All she saw was a flicker of a red light. Perhaps Wist waved; she couldn't be sure in the dim light.

And then they were alone once more.

26

So how far did your friend say this stream goes?" Margus splashed up ahead with the backpack and the blue light while Oriannon kept back several paces.

"She didn't."

"Oh." His voice fell. "I got the impression it wasn't supposed to be far."

"Depends on your definition of 'far.'"

He didn't answer, so they kept walking. She thought it sloped down, not too steeply, but steady. Of course, it had to or the water wouldn't be gurgling around her feet.

"Of course," she mumbled to herself, and an hour slipped by, then two, as they walked on.

Every once in a while her foot slipped out from under her on smooth stones, so she kept her head down and her right hand out just in case she had to catch herself. Margus kept up the pace, never looking back. And as she studied the back of his head, she wondered once more.

"Hey!" she called at him. "Tell me again how you got here? I never really got the whole story."

He shrugged as if it was no big deal, as if he stowed away on Coristan shuttlecraft every day.

"Well, like I said before, after that big mess at the Court of Justice I wanted to get my scooter back again." His answer echoed off the tunnel walls. Had he really said this before? "They found what was left of it, and then they found a few footprints in the frozen ice, a ways over the border. But then it got covered over, and they never found you."

"Yeah, I kind of kept going."

"They were even doing satellite searches and everything. You really disappeared."

"I'm sorry about the scooter."

"Not as sorry as I am. You owe me."

"I know. But there's another thing I was wondering, Margus. You came all this way, and you know I appreciate that."

"It was nothing."

"But when Jesmet showed up, you pulled back. What was that all about?"

She could actually see his neck tighten, but he didn't turn around.

"I was hoping to find you; didn't expect to see him. That's all. I was surprised. You understand."

"Sure." Oriannon wondered why he sounded so defensive. "But you know he brought back all my memories, don't you?"

"I guess I just assumed you got better on your own."

She told him about the fog, and what it was like.

"Now you know how the rest of us feel, all the time."

"No, you don't feel like this. Not like this. But Jesmet brought it all back. Of course, some of it I decided maybe I didn't *want* back."

"I know what you mean."

And she wondered how he did. Still they continued on, and Oriannon almost didn't see the low piece of rock that would have caught her in the forehead. The good news was that she reached up just in time to block it.

The not-so-good news was that she fell over backwards in the process, sitting down in the stream.

"Duck!" Margus warned her, turning back just in time to see her scramble back to her feet. "The ceiling is getting pretty low again."

She scowled at him. "Thanks for the warning."

But now Margus couldn't stop laughing.

"You should have seen your face," he told her with a smirk. "And the way you popped up. Priceless. I think I used to have a toy like that."

"It's not funny." She scowled at him as best she could. "What happens when we get out in the cold?"

"Well, then you're going to have a frozen—"

"Margus!"

"I didn't say anything. Look, if it makes you feel any better, I'll let you borrow—"

"No, thanks." She grabbed the light from him. No way was she going to wear any of his clothes. Was he kidding? "I'll just go first this time."

And she did, wondering now how much longer they would have to hike until they reached the end and the waterfall Wist had told about. Hopefully not long. Wist hadn't mentioned anything about a low ceiling, either.

"Hey, hold up again," Margus called out from four or five steps behind her. "Feel it?"

What now?

"Another earthquake?" She turned with the light. "I don't feel anything."

But Margus shook his head no and raised a hand in the air.

"That's not what I mean. Don't talk. Feel it?"

At first she wasn't quite sure what he was talking about. But a moment later she felt her hair flutter in the breeze pushing out of the mountain with the stream. She turned her head to the sound of rushing water.

"I think the falls are up ahead," he told her. "Better let me—"

Oriannon blocked him with her hand.

"I can see the waterfall as well as you can." And she charged off without another word, bending as low as she could to keep from bumping her head, holding the light out in front, and with her ears perked so she wouldn't step off into nothing.

"I think we've joined up with a few other streams!" yelled Margus. That would explain all the water now. The stream tugged at their feet as they surged ahead toward the dimmest of gray showing out of the gloom. Of course, anything seemed lighter than the pitch black of the tunnels. With each step Oriannon could hear the waterfall that much more clearly, until its roar overpowered everything but a shout. Was that Margus?

"What did you say?" she yelled back over her shoulder. And perhaps she should have been more careful, knowing what still lay ahead of them. But the mossy rocks under her feet were just too slick, the current now too strong. Why hadn't Wist told them about this? Before Oriannon knew what had happened, once again she found herself sitting in the swift stream.

"I said ..." Margus stepped up from behind and hoisted her to her feet. "I said it's getting too slippery to walk any more. I almost fell, the way you just did."

"So maybe there's another way," she yelled back. This time she didn't care so much about her wet pants. If they could just get out of there, she'd worry about it later. For now she held onto Margus's backpack with one hand and the lantern with the other as they picked their way along the rushing creek bed, one step at a time, sideways. Finally Margus pointed to a little ledge, off to the side, and she held the light up higher for them to see.

"I think we can get out of the water over there," he told her, and that would suit her just fine.

The ledge actually did widen a bit too, so they could keep going in the right direction. Only here the air had turned to a heavy mist where warm air met cold, and Oriannon had to feel her way along the wall of the tunnel, hunched over the way a blind person would. Eventually the light did them no good. Now cold blasts hit her face, now warm fog, always swirling around her.

"The falls have to be here somewhere," she yelled back over her shoulder. "Don't let me step ... oh!"

Oriannon felt nothing under her next step, heard nothing but water tumbling over the edge. All she could do was try to lean back and windmill her arms to keep from tumbling over the edge ... into nothing.

argus did grab her — by the hair.

"Ow!" She breathed hard and hugged the uphill side of the ledge, away from the drop-off that had nearly swallowed her.

"Sorry." Margus backed away too, and at this point there was no telling how far down the falls fell. He pointed down at the narrow ledge of a path where it seemed to lead away and to the right of the steam where mist obscured the top of the falls. "Let's keep going that way, and then — "

Oriannon cupped a hand to her ear to signal that she had missed his last words.

"I said," he raised his voice another notch to be heard over the falling water, "I think we need to get off this cliff and then find out where we are."

Of course that would have been wise. And with a narrow trail to follow, they did manage to lower themselves slowly past boulders and outcroppings to the rugged terrain below. Oriannon did her best to ignore her wet pants, though now the rising wind made her shiver and brought goose bumps to the back of her neck. Finally they stopped at a level spot in the trail to reconsider.

"Now what?" wondered Margus, turning around slowly. "These hills and rocks all look the same to me."

As they did to Oriannon, though it proved less difficult to make out their surroundings from their new position a stone's throw from the roar of the waterfall and the blinding mist cloud. She tried to imagine which way the city could be from here, and which way they would have to travel.

"I almost forgot." She rummaged in Margus's pack until her hand closed on a smooth, palm-sized rock. "Wist said she gave us a lodestone, remember?"

"Whatever that is." He didn't sound as pleased as she. "I'll bet the power cells are dead."

She turned the rock in her hand, felt its polished ebony, and ran her thumb across its flattened, rounded edges.

"I don't think this kind of thing has power cells, Margus."

It didn't have any markings either. No view screen, no button to turn it on. Margus leaned closer for a better look, tapped at the rock—and frowned.

"This isn't going to tell us where to go," he announced. "It's just a rock, for crying out loud."

"She said it would show us the way east, toward the Trion."

"She must have meant something else." Margus dumped out everything in his pack onto the top of a big flat boulder where he'd been resting, and started picking through their supplies: two rabbit-skin flasks of drinking water, stopped with a cork. By now they'd already drained one to half empty. A cloth-wrapped bundle of jerky, the origins of which she would have to reveal to him later. Several pieces of dark, pungent Owling flatbread, none of which would require further explanation. A small bundle of sticks dipped in a waxy coating, probably intended to start a fire. And a dozen dried pear halves, sliced thin and strung like a necklace, sprinkled with that peculiar nose-tickling spice Oriannon had never smelled back in Corista.

Margus sneezed at the spices but did not uncover anything else that even remotely resembled a lodestone, or anything that suggested the black rock was not what it was supposed to be.

"Well that's great." Margus sighed. "We've come all this way through the mountain and now we don't have the instrument to get us home. I thought you took care of that."

"Now you blame me?" she snapped back, still holding the stone. Why hadn't Wist told her how to use it? And why was Margus acting this way? "She probably just assumed we knew all about these things."

"Surprise." Margus parked his hands on his hips and kicked at a chunk of ice, spreading odd sparks of blue-green that helped light their way. "We don't."

But Oriannon wasn't giving up that easily. Never mind the cold that now numbed her face and frosted her breath. What were they supposed to do, climb back into the tunnel and slog all the way back to Lior for instructions? Not now. She squeezed the stone between her palms.

"There has to be something to it," she said. "I believe Wist. And she didn't just put a strange old rock in the backpack for nothing."

"Well, pardon me for saying so." Margus crossed his arms and shivered. "But I still don't see how a black rock is supposed to help us. That's a lodestone? Give me a satellite positioner any day."

Now would have been an excellent time to plant a good kick to his knee. Instead, she squinted out at the hills in the distance, dim as always but lit by the moons and the lights. The same landscape she'd even started to enjoy during her time here in Shadowside. And sure enough, the grit of wind-whipped dust and sand made her blink and her eyes water. If it got any worse this could turn out nasty.

So it seemed an odd time to hear Jesmet's voice once more. Not as if he was actually there this time — but still just as real. She almost looked behind her to be sure.

"Then you let go — and let me take care of the rest."

Literally? She loosened her grip on the lodestone, looked down at it, and sighed. Maybe Margus was right, though she would not admit it so soon. She turned away from him trying to decide which direction looked east. Nothing seemed the same as before — the shape of the hills, the slope of the land, nothing. How could she be certain? Margus peered over her shoulder and poked at the stone.

"Are you sure it—"

"I'm sure, all right?" But when she yanked it away from him it sailed from her hand, landing in fine volcanic ash a couple of meters away. "Now see what you've done!"

They both jumped for the rock, bumping heads and stirring up dust in the process.

"Back away!" Ori snapped.

"No. It's right here!" Margus dug for the rock but came up empty. Oriannon thought she knew where it had landed but didn't feel it right away either.

"If it's lost . . ." she muttered under her breath, continuing to dig. But the more she dug, the more confusing it became.

"I just wanted to see it," said Margus. "And you act as if I was trying to steal it or something."

"You didn't need to steal anything when it works just as well to bury it."

By this time Oriannon felt her cheeks flush with anger, and it was all she could do not to throw handfuls of volcanic dust at her traveling companion.

242

"Maybe we should back off for a minute," Margus finally suggested, clapping his hands of dust and leaning back on his heels. "That way—"

"No, there!" Oriannon bent closer to be sure, then pointed to a faint blue glow just to the right of where they'd been searching. "I think that's it."

This time Margus let her pick it up, so she carefully blew the dust from the rock as it glowed even more brightly. She turned left and right, testing her direction. And while the glow dimmed to nothing when she faced the waterfall, it lit back up as she faced directly away.

"Hmm." He leaned in a little closer. "Maybe we have something here after all."

"What did I tell you? Wist said it would work. She said it would point toward the Trion. It's going to take us home, Margus. Or at least it's going to take *me* home, and if you want to follow along ..."

Margus looked in the direction she pointed, sheltering his eyes from the blowing sand and probably wondering, as she did, how they would actually get there. But she could walk with her head down now, her eye on the lodestone. If they ran into canyons or hills too steep to climb over, they would walk around them and continue following the lodestone's leading.

"Hey, wait up!" Margus could follow along, and for the next several hours he did. Neither said much of anything above the howling wind that seemed to grow louder with each step. After a while though, Oriannon could feel her stomach beginning to growl.

"How long ... do you think ... we can keep this up?" Margus's voice sounded muffled from beneath the wool scarf he'd wrapped around his face. That would be partly for the cold, partly for the sand. She looked over at him, and his hair already looked peppered with the stuff, like an old man. Sand in his ears, sand in his nose, sand everywhere. She guessed she probably didn't look any better.

"As long as it takes," she answered, and that was the best she could manage. She didn't know the answer either. But every time she wanted to just curl up in a ball and cry, she imagined the Coristan ship on which Margus had traveled to Lior, hovering just below the city, just waiting for permission from Corista's ruling Assembly so they could destroy it.

The thought haunted her for a few more hours, through open fields of loose red volcanic rock that shifted under her feet, and over low hills of boulders full of crevasses—deep holes that would catch and turn her ankle if she didn't place her feet with care.

What will happen next time they return? she asked herself, and the question made her hurry her steps even more. Maybe she could talk to her father. Maybe she could prevent a disaster.

Or not.

Here and there they ran into fields of icy snow, but covered thick with a layer of gray sand, and she couldn't tell what was beneath until her feet slipped out from under her. From then on she had to test her steps.

"Faster," she told herself, checking the lodestone for the hundredth time. She changed course a little as they crested another barren hill, and was about to slog down the other side when she felt a weak hand tug her arm.

"We've got to stop for a minute, Oriannon," Margus begged her. "Please. We've got to rest."

"Are you kidding? You're just slowing us down." But Oriannon paused, breathing hard, hands on her knees. The longer they rested, the longer this was going to take. And already it was going to take way too long.

Yet she hadn't noticed how her lungs burned and her legs ached. Her eyes still watered from all the sand in the air, and she started coughing.

She gasped when she looked over to check on Margus, who had collapsed to his knees in the little sand hill. His forehead almost touched the ground, and his chest heaved. And for a moment she thought it was just the wind stirring things up, sending little twisters across the surface. Almost too late she recognized the way the sand was moving, and she grabbed Margus by the arm.

"Margus!" she cried. "Get up!"

Of course, she had no time to explain what popped out of the sand with a hiss, only centimeters away from where Margus rested his head. And when he looked up with surprise, the huge sand worm timed its stream of bile perfectly, hitting him square in the eyes.

He screamed and clutched his face as Oriannon did her best to roll him away. The sand worm only spit once more, this time missing Margus but hitting Oriannon on her bare hand.

"You picked the wrong person to spit on!" she pulled away for a second, and it felt as if she'd stuck her hand in a flame. Welts rose on the back of her hand, but all she could really do was kick and scream at the attacker while poor Margus rolled away in agony.

"Jesmet, please help me!" The plea slipped from her lips before she realized what she'd said. By this time the worm had crawled all the way out of the sand, showing it was at least as long as Oriannon and Margus put together. She wasn't sure if it could bite too, but in one wild attempt she managed to connect her kick with the head of the creature, sending it sprawling and quivering.

"Oh, oh, oh ..." Margus staggered away, hands still on his face. She couldn't imagine the pain, perhaps like on her hand but so many times worse.

"Margus, are you okay?" She knew better. But she knelt next to him, wondering what to do, while still keeping one eye on the sand worm. It still quivered, only not as much. And Margus didn't answer, just moaned in pain.

"Okay then," she told him. "Let me see what's going on here."

"Wait, no," he finally managed. "Where's that thing?"

"You don't have to worry." She checked again to make sure nothing had tunneled its way under the sand. It was probably a good thing Margus couldn't see the worried look on her face. "It's gone."

At least she didn't see it anymore. So she finally pried his hands back enough to see that Margus's eyes had taken a direct hit and were starting to swell shut. The sand worm's saliva still covered his face and hands, and any other time she would have gagged at the sight. Now she only had one worry: How to clean it off?

"My eyes," Margus moaned, "my eyes ..."

"I know. Listen." She grabbed one of the remaining water flasks from their pack. "I'm sorry it hurts so much. But you've got to stay still and let me wash this out."

Which she did, using the water from one jug and part of another. Margus just grit his teeth and trembled, but he let her. And he did seem to relax slightly after she'd done as much as she could. Next she took the scarf that had wrapped their jerky and laid it carefully across his eyes, mainly to keep sand and grit from blowing at him and making things worse. Although, come to think of it, she wasn't sure if it *could* get much worse.

"You're going to be fine," she told him, hoping she was right. "But let's just rest those eyes for a little while. How's it feel now?"

"Like somebody took a blowtorch to my eyeballs. Other than that, never better. What happened to that snake thing?"

Oriannon looked back over where she'd last seen the sand worm.

"Uh . . ." She stood up to make sure.

"Tell me." He started to stand up too, but Oriannon pushed him back down. No reason to have him stumbling around yet.

"I told you before that it's gone."

"I don't believe you."

She glanced around once more, looking for telltale waves in the sand. Maybe he was right to doubt.

"Okay then. We'll get a little farther away, just in case."

"Just in case is fine with me." Margus stood up and held out his hands, looking for help.

She slung the pack over her own back and guided his hand to hold onto her arm so they could keep going. At this rate it could be many days before they made it back to Corista, and the thought crossed her mind that, given these new circumstances, maybe they'd be better off turning back to the Owling city after all.

And what about their water? She didn't tell Margus how much she'd used to wash out his eyes, but he had to know. She tried to swallow, but could only cough on a mouthful of dust and sand.

Still, she tried not to think of it, leaning into the wind that still howled at them and clawed at her coat without mercy. She checked the lodestone once more just to be sure, and Margus now gripped her arm as if his life depended on it.

Perhaps it did.

28

What did she expect us to burn?" Margus wanted to know. He held his hands out, shivering, as if a fire would magically appear. A fire that he still wouldn't be able to see, even if Oriannon ever managed to get something going with the starter sticks Wist had packed for them.

"I'm sorry, Margus. I've never done this before. I'm working on it."

To which he didn't answer.

"I thought maybe this tumbleweed stuff would burn," she went on, "but it just kind of fizzles and smokes."

"I noticed." Margus waved his hand and coughed. "Keep trying."

Oriannon looked around their little shelter—just an over-sized dimple in the face of a large rock, really, and it seemed to her almost like sitting under a large umbrella, tipped on its side. In other words—not much. At least they could hide here from the full blast of the windstorm. But without a fire and with no more water to drink, the shelter would not be enough.

"So tell me again why you went to Shadowside?" Perhaps Margus was just trying to make conversation while she worked on the fire.

249

"You know why." She struck the piece of steel against a stone and cupped her hand around the flickering sparks, which the wind threatened to snatch away. "I had to find Jesmet. *We all* had to find Jesmet. Didn't you see how it all came together?"

Margus tilted his head back, as if he was thinking long and hard.

"I saw. I just wish I wasn't the blind man now."

"You'll be fine in a few hours . . ." She paused.

"You're hopeful. They still feel swollen shut."

"When we get home we'll get you to a healer."

As if that would help. Maybe it would, maybe it wouldn't.

"Hmm." He hugged at his own shoulders and stomped his feet. "Can't you get your friend's fire starter working?"

"Like to see you do better." Oriannon cradled a shy, smoky flame in a pile of twigs she had gathered from underneath a small bush. But before she could see it graduate to larger sticks, it retreated into a sad little plume of smoke, just as the ground shook all around them. But by this time, they were both getting used to the constant quivering and shaking of Shadowside's latest earthquakes.

"Again?" he asked, sniffing at the air.

"I'm no good at this." Whoever had to make a fire back in Corista? She sighed and threw the whole mess down to the ground. "I know in my head what I'm supposed to do, but my hands just won't do it. I'm sorry, Margus."

"Yeah. What do we need a fire for, anyway?"

"Not just about the fire." She didn't know how else to say it, or when. "I'm sorry for yelling at you back at the waterfall when we were looking for the lodestone. I didn't need to be that way."

"That was yelling?" A small grin spread underneath his eye bandages. "I'm sorry too. But let's forget about it. At least we still have plenty of food and water."

Oriannon looked over at their open backpack just in time to see a cat-sized rodent scurry away, dragging away their jerky and flatbread.

"Hey!" She dove for the disappearing food too late. "You can't do that!"

It could and it did—even though Oriannon scrambled after it, out into the storm's blinding clouds of sand.

"Come back here," she cried, diving at the rodent's tail as it darted toward a nearby jumble of rocks. "No!"

She only came up with gravel between her fingers. By this time the wind had grown into a hurricane, blasting her in the face with sand so hard she cried out and covered her eyes with her hands. If she stayed out here any longer Margus wouldn't be the only blind one.

But she wasn't going to give up that easily, and she crawled toward the rock pile.

"I know you're under there," she told the rat, tossing rocks aside, clawing frantically to get their food back. A sharp gust of wind nearly pushed her over, but she crouched even lower.

"Oriannon!" She heard Margus cry out from the shelter, a distant voice barely sounding over the cry of wind and sand and dust. "Where did you go?"

She didn't answer at first, just kept grunting and screaming and pulling rocks aside until her fingers were bleeding. And of course, when she reached the bottom of the pile the rat was long gone.

"Stupid!" She pounded on the rocks with her fists, bending low to protect herself from the storm. If she lifted her head again, her ears and nose would have been sandblasted right off her face.

"Oriannon!" Margus shouted once more. He sounded weak and far off, though he couldn't have been more than four or five meters behind her. "Are you out there, Oriannon?"

"I'm here," she answered back, knowing her tired voice would only be carried off by the winds. So it was probably a good thing he was yelling. Certainly she couldn't *see* her way back; she would use his cries as a beacon. And with a final glance to make sure the hungry rat had really escaped with their food, she turned back toward shelter.

"I hope you choke on it," she muttered as she slithered back on her stomach, face down, listening for each time Margus yelled "Oriannon!" That close to the ground, she could almost hear the planet's heartbeat, a shuddering giant.

● ● ●

"So you were surprised at what you found in Lior?" asked Oriannon.

Two hours later she still huddled against the inner cave wall, arms around her knees, shivering and waiting for the wind to let up enough for them to leave again. How long? How soon? Talking didn't help much to keep warm, but she couldn't think of anything else.

"Are you kidding?" answered Margus. "Sure I was surprised. That city stuck to the side of the cliff, the crazy Owlings with their bird eyes, the whole weird deal here in Shadowside. How could I not be surprised? I mean, imagine old Mentor Narrick saying, 'Margus, I want you to find me the city of Lior on the holo-map.' Ha! We sure didn't learn about any of this in school."

Oriannon nodded as she stared out at the storm. So he went on.

"I'll bet your dad knows the place is there, though. Elders in the Assembly know that sort of thing."

Of course an elder would know that kind of thing. So why had her father never told her? And if he knew, why hadn't he been able to find her?

"We'll see if he knew," she finally managed.

"Yeah." Margus's voice wandered off again. "I wonder what my folks are doing now ..."

"Same thing as my dad. Going crazy. I'll bet everybody thinks you're dead too."

She tried not to think about it, just wondered how quickly they could get going again.

And then he laughed.

He laughed in spite of being blinded by the sand worms ... in spite of them being stuck in this tiny cave in the middle of a horrible sandstorm, dust swirling around their faces, without food or water — though Oriannon couldn't bring herself to tell him it was *all* gone. In spite of the bone-chilling cold, he laughed.

"What's funny?" she asked, because nothing was.

"I was just thinking what they would say at my funeral. Maybe 'He was always good for a joke' or something like that. I'm sure going to surprise them when we get home."

"Assuming we make it home."

She bit her lip.

"Don't talk that way, Oriannon." Without warning Margus ripped off his eye bandage and squinted at her. "I didn't come all this way to have you say that."

She caught her breath at the sharp rebuke, and she knew she deserved it. Of course he hadn't come all this way to have a sand worm attack and blind him, either. But she didn't have a chance to answer as Margus brought a hand to his face again, bent down and moaned. It must have hurt — bad.

"Margus!" She picked up the scarf and tried to tie it back around his eyes. "You need to keep this on your face for now."

But he only shrugged her off and kept his hands to his face, as if he didn't need her help, or anyone else's.

"We still have a little food left, don't we?" he asked.

She didn't answer. And so they sat there together, shivering, not saying anything more, waiting for a break in the storm, for someone to rescue them, or for sleep — whichever came first. One good thing Oriannon had learned about Shadowside was that over here it wasn't hard to sleep, wasn't hard to dream. Even in their miserable cave, that's what they'd do.

Wait. Sleep. Dream.

Maybe the storm would let up soon, and they could hurry home to Corista. It couldn't just keep blowing and blowing this way, could it? But she had to ask him.

"Did you see anything, Margus?"

At first she thought he'd already fallen asleep since he didn't move, just rested his forehead on his knees. But finally he shook his head slightly.

"No," he whispered, and she had to lean almost next to his face to hear. All the fire had drained from his voice again. "I still can't see a thing."

29

riannon had no idea how long she'd slept, only that every centi-meter of her body ached, and that sand had covered everything. She would discover sand in her ears, sand up her nose, sand that scratched her eyes when she blinked. She groaned and sat up.

"Is that what people do over here on Shadowside?" Margus sat in the other side of their little cave, chewing. He had picked up the scarf bandage and slipped it back over his head and eyes. "Sleep all the time?"

"Not all the time." She straightened and shook herself off. "What are you eating?"

"It's not bad," he told her between chews, then flinched. "Except for the sand."

By this time she checked the backpack to find four cloth-wrapped packages of Owling flatbread and rabbit jerky—every-thing the rats had run off with and more before she'd fallen asleep. What kind of strange dream had brought it all back?

"Weird," she muttered. She picked up the pack and one of the skin flasks fell to her feet—full.

"What's strange?" asked Margus, between mouthfuls. "This bread? It kind of tastes like ... I don't know, strong, but it fills you up. You should try some."

255

"I know what it tastes like," she whispered as he washed it down with a swig from his flask, and it looked just as full. What was going on here?

"Glad the rats didn't run off with all our jerky," he told her, taking another bite. "You did good chasing them off."

She swallowed hard, still wondering.

"Oriannon?"

"Right." She shivered at the thought of a visitor, however benevolent, sneaking around as they slept. "I guess so."

"Sounds as if the storm let up too."

So it wasn't a dream? Or if it was, Margus was part of it as well. Oriannon looked around outside the shelter, and this time she could see the dark, jagged hills, the bright moonlight from Zed – 3, the stars . . . and a clear set of footprints in the sand, coming and going.

"It did let up," she replied, and now she knew what they had to do. Nothing else mattered, really. They'd slept far too long. So after taking a long drink of sweet water and a few bites for herself, she stuffed everything back into the pack, swung it over her shoulder, and took Margus by the shoulder. Her stomach still ached with hunger.

"We need to hurry," she told him, starting off in the direction of the footprints. Her lodestone told her they headed east as well, toward Corista. Her words turned to little puffs of fog in front of them. "Hold onto the strap of my pack and I'll make sure you don't fall."

● ● ●

"I thought you said — "

"Sorry." Oriannon didn't let Margus finish complaining as she reached down to help him to his feet. After what seemed like several long days of walking and climbing and scrambling up and down through bone dry canyons and around boulders the size of small houses, they were both tired enough to drop.

"You're sure we're still going the right direction?" he wanted to know.

"Margus, just look up ..." She caught herself. "I mean, I can see everything up ahead. We'll hit the borderlands soon."

"How soon?"

"How do I know? I've just been following the lodestone. I know the direction, not the distance."

"And you're sure ..."

"I'm sure, I'm sure, okay? Trust me. We'll be there soon."

And if he kept pestering her with questions, maybe she'd just step out ahead and let him find his own way. She sighed. *No.*

"Sorry." His voiced sounded much softer now. "I just thought you'd know the way since you came here before."

"Look, I already explained it to you. First of all, I was totally out of it when I crossed over. You don't know how horrible it felt. Second of all, Becket and Suuli carried me most of the way to the city, and I wasn't really paying attention. I think those guys must have run, considering the distance they probably covered. And third of all—or maybe this should have been first of all—your crazy lev-scooter was zooming out of control and I have no idea how far or where it took me before it crashed."

"Yeah, we could use it right about now."

But Oriannon wasn't listening. And she was plenty sick of dragging this ungrateful boy halfway across Shadowside, sick of his complaining, sick of his arguing, sick of the way he hung on her backpack. But now grabbing her around the neck was too much.

"Margus, what are you—?"

But he cupped his hand on her mouth, nearly wrestling her to the ground in the process.

"Shh!" He hissed in her ear. "Don't say a word."

Something told her he was serious this time. She stood still and listened to the gentle wind whistling through a nearby grove of tangled thorn bushes. And off in the distance a low growl made the hair on the back of her neck stand up straight.

"Now do you hear it?" Margus whispered, and she nodded. "I thought I did before, but I wasn't sure."

"What do we do now?" she whispered back. And she looked all around them with wide eyes, looking for any sign of the predator that had obviously found them. For there could be no mistake about the sound. "I didn't think they had yagwar over here."

"Well, maybe that means we're closer to Corista than we thought. You don't see it?"

Again she looked, searching the hills and canyons around them. Here and there small shrubs pushed their way out from between boulders, and patches of crusty snow waited in the shadows. The cat, if that's what it was, could be hiding anywhere. And when they heard it again Oriannon jumped.

"From that way." She pointed behind them, once more forgetting Margus couldn't see her. But she didn't waste any time and dragged him away down a hill and through a narrow canyon — hopefully in the right direction, away from the yagwar.

"Don't panic," Margus mumbled, but Oriannon wasn't sure if he was saying it for her or for himself. Either way, they both scrambled through the gully double-speed, until they pulled up behind the shelter of a large boulder.

"We can't stop." Oriannon's chest heaved with each word and every breath. She knew who would win if it came down to a running race between them and the yagwar — particularly if it was hungry enough. She picked up a stick the size of her arm and snapped off the end into a point.

"What's that?" Margus wondered. He could probably see a lot more with his ears than Oriannon realized.

"A sharp stick. Got any better ideas?"

Margus nodded and gently pushed her ahead once more.

"Let's just put more distance between us and the cat. I don't like being stalked."

She didn't argue. In fact, the cane-sized stick actually helped; Margus held on to one end while Oriannon ran on ahead with the other. He didn't trip over her heels and she could jog on ahead. Every few minutes, though, they had to stop to catch their breath. And every time, Oriannon imagined she heard footsteps scuffling along the trail, or a rustling of branches.

"Did you hear that?" she asked after their fifth or sixth rest.

Margus cocked his head to the side like a weathervane casting about for a gentle breeze.

"Not sure. But we're getting pretty close to the borderlands, right?"

Oriannon studied the bushes behind them, her heart beating wildly. She could almost imagine it behind every shadow, getting ready to pounce.

"The cat's not going to stop at the border, Margus. You know that fence can be breached."

"Sure, but maybe we can get some help on the other side."

"Help? You mean from a security? I hope not. Let's go."

Out of habit she glanced down at her lodestone, checking for the blue light that told her they were still headed the right direction. Only this time she could hardly make out the glow in the stone — probably because of the glow in the sky up ahead.

"Still the right way?" asked Margus, pushing his stick out ahead.

"Come on," she told him, grabbing her end of the stick. She only paused for a moment when she sighted a flicker of light up ahead, low on the horizon.

"What?" Margus leaned forward. "The yagwar?"

He frowned and reached up to adjust his bandage as the sound of a breaking twig behind them made Oriannon jump. Now she didn't answer, just pushed on toward Corista at a run, wondering what waited for them beyond Shadowside.

"Is this where you crossed over?" Margus asked her a few hours later. Even if he couldn't see, she assumed he could now smell the sweet scent of cerulean trees in full bloom. And surely he would feel the warming breeze that greeted them as they crested the last hill before the borderlands of Corista.

"Not sure." Oriannon didn't have time to stop and smell the wild cerise flowers by the side of the path. Not with a hungry yagwar still stalking them. "But there's a border tower."

Topped by its familiar spinning yellow warning blinker, it could have been the same one she passed on her way to Shadowside, though Oriannon didn't think the landscape quite matched.

"So are we as close as I think we are?" Margus was smiling, though Oriannon feared it was still too early to celebrate. Even if they could outrun the yagwar, they still had at least one more obstacle to navigate.

"Listen, Margus." She studied the ground ahead, looking for clues. "I'm not sure how we're going to get through that fence."

"You did before, didn't you?"

"Yeah, in the scooter. You should have seen all the sparks and stuff. I think because I was going so fast."

"Well then, that's how we'll get through from this side too. Is it flat up ahead?"

"Well yeah, but—"

Margus didn't wait for her to object. He started to trot across the flat, open field, still blind but not sounding as if he cared anymore.

"Oriannon!" he called back. "Tell me if I'm going to run into anything!"

"Just the fence, Margus. The fence!"

Of course that was enough. But even though Oriannon studied the tower in the distance, she noticed no one and nothing moving to intercept them. No securities. Not even a probe. And when she'd almost caught up to Margus she finally caught sight of the fence's red glimmer just a few steps ahead.

"Four steps to the fence, Margus!" She shouted her warning, expecting him to hold back or slow down. No telling what the fence's force field would do to him. "You'd better stop now!"

Instead he took three giant strides, and now he twisted around backwards, as if running straight into a high jump contest.

"No! Margus!"

But she couldn't reach him in time. Taking her word for it, he launched himself backwards into a flying leap, arms outstretched, whooping. And Oriannon could only watch, amazed, as he hit the nearly invisible fence and the red force field covered him in a cocoon of energy, sputtering and sparkling like a fireworks celebration.

"Margus!" she cried.

But the force field just rocked him once, twice, barely two meters above the ground before rejecting him without ceremony on the other side, seat-first, right onto the far edge of the Coristan borderlands. He crumpled to a heap, limp, and she ran up to the fence to see if he still lived and breathed.

"Margus, are you okay?"

He didn't answer.

"Margus! You shouldn't have done that!"

And now she couldn't do a thing to help him. But a moment later he uncurled himself and grinned up at her from the other side.

"That was pretty cool," he reported. "Almost as good as being weightless."

She rolled her head back and groaned.

"You could have been killed," she said, "and what would I have done then?"

"Oh, come on. You got through in the scooter, remember? It's just a Level Three fence. Just for show, keeping out small animals, that kind of thing. I knew it wasn't that serious."

"How do you know?"

"Remember what my dad does?"

Of course; he fixed things. Even so, Oriannon wasn't sure she could put on the same kind of athletic display to vault over the barrier the way Margus had. Too bad there wasn't an easier way. She parked her hands on her hips and looked around for ideas. And her mouth went dry when she saw the dark figure of the yagwar emerge from a clump of bushes — maybe just a hundred meters away — and sprint straight at her.

30

o, no, no ..." She knew what it would take for her to get across the fence; she just couldn't make her legs move *toward* the yagwar, back to where she could get enough of a running start.

And by now she couldn't help shaking as the yagwar covered the hundred meters between them in huge strides, looming larger every second. At a distance it had seemed small; as it approached it grew nearly as tall as she.

"Oriannon!" Margus had to be hearing the cat's low growl too. "Get out of there. Jump over!"

Oriannon could not—just as she could not make herself scream.

Neither could she know why the beast had chosen this open place to finally attack, after stalking them for so long. But by the way it now bounded across the flatland she knew it would be upon her in a moment.

Didn't anyone from the watchtower notice what was going on? For the first time in her life she might have welcomed a probe or two. She saw and heard none.

And she was only vaguely aware of the shower of sparks and raw energy crawling at her back as she leaned into the force field fence. It shook her violently and held her in place, serving her up to the yagwar like an ancient human sacrifice.

"Jesmet," she whispered. "I'm going to die."

And though Oriannon tried to look away, she could not keep from staring at the big, black creature as it flew up to her—as if in slow motion.

Later she would recall its thick fur, sparkling with purple highlights. Its glassy, red-orange eyes as they focused on her. And its large tongue as it slicked across two rows of wicked-sharp teeth.

But now she knew exactly what would happen next, and she imagined herself as a small meal for the formidable yagwar. She winced at the oncoming black storm, though she could no longer move or even make a sound.

Is this how it hypnotizes its prey? she wondered.

As if to answer, the yagwar opened its sizeable mouth and buried its teeth in her arm.

"No!" Oriannon awoke as quickly as she'd fallen into this dream. Suddenly clearheaded, the pain made her scream as the beast's jaws closed around her bones. And too late, she knew she'd been seduced, tricked just as surely as Carrick Trice had been, back when they'd first run into a yagwar in the Glades. Now she knew how helpless Carrick had felt. Too late, she knew that she could do nothing to fight off such a fierce animal.

Of course no amount of screaming would scare away the yagwar, though Oriannon now kicked and pounded. The cat hardly seemed to notice as it tossed its head, growling. Her body flew back and forth like a rag doll. This was it.

Except ... when a hand reached around from behind and pulled her back by the waist, right back up against the security fence.

"Help me!" At this she cried out even louder, knowing that even if Margus was trying to rescue her through the fence he could never pull her back to safety. Especially not when the yagwar was still tugging on her arm from the other side.

Ohh ... Perhaps shock was taking hold as well. She looked down at the awful tug-of-war between a snarling yagwar on one side, her friend from behind, and her in the middle. She glanced at her torn, mangled arm as if it belonged to someone else. She noticed a broken tooth and an ugly, infected scar on the yagwar's nose, smelled his rancid, infected breath. She could just as easily have been experiencing all this on some kind of awful video game, the kind Margus sometimes used to play.

"Fight, Ori!" Margus screamed at her from behind. "Don't let it—"

"I am!" she yelled back. But realistically, what could she do now? The force field made her back tingle and quiver, her vision blur. Any moment, Oriannon knew she would pass out. So she tried one more kick to the underbelly of the yagwar as hard as she could, while Margus retightened his grip.

Now the fence whined as never before, louder and louder, as if it were overloading.

"If we keep pulling this way—" Margus cried out with the effort, yanking her back into the force field over and over. "And we use the cat's power ..."

What was he saying? The fence showered them all with sparks and glittered with pure energy, lighting up the desperate wrestling match with a bright red glow before finally giving way.

"Watch out!" she cried, though it could hardly make any difference as she and the yagwar tumbled in an awful tangled mess on top of Margus—right through the backdrafted Level Three fence, over the boundary and back into the brightside of Corista.

Strangely enough, the worst thing wasn't the bite of the yagwar, or the pain, or even the horrible thought of being attacked and eaten by a wild animal. Each peril had crossed her mind in rapid succession but none took first place. Rather, the one thing that concerned her the most was bleeding on Margus.

Bleeding on Margus! She did her best to roll away from him, though the yagwar obviously had other intentions. So did the man whose voice stopped everything in its place.

"Enough!" Jesmet's command pierced the chaos. But unlike the smaller animal that had once attacked Carrick Trice, this yagwar seemed far less inclined to give up its prey without a fight. It lowered its head and snarled, displaying bloodstained teeth. And it lifted a considerable paw, dagger claws extended.

Jesmet never flinched. In one fluid movement he reached out and grabbed the big creature by the back of the neck, twisting hard as he did. The yagwar yelped in pain and surprise as it floundered onto its back, while Oriannon gulped to hear a sickening snap and a rush of breath from the beast.

"You weren't created for this," Jesmet whispered. "I'm sorry."

A sad frown crossed his face as the yagwar quivered once before finally going limp. Its once fierce eyes drooped, the fire drained. And for a moment she saw something odd: a nearly hidden collar, fitted with a small device of some sort. On its side a red light flickered and faded.

Jesmet ignored the collar, however, and without another word he dragged the lifeless body away. Oriannon wasn't quite certain how he managed that, since the yagwar easily weighed at least as much as several men.

Of course at this point she wasn't quite certain of anything. Numbness and shock had overtaken her and she lay on the ground watching as Jesmet dragged the carcass off across the line toward Shadowside. A shower of red embers covered him and the cat's body as he pulled it through the fence.

The sparks didn't seem to bother Jesmet, or even slow him down. In fact, Oriannon thought he almost looked as if he'd just stepped out of the Great Hall. He was still dressed in the plain robe he'd worn at her Seer Codex ceremony so long ago, so far away.

"Where did he go?" asked Margus, still sitting on the ground but now holding his hands out in front of him. "What happened?"

"He's coming back," she whispered, and she was barely able to hold her head up, much less update Margus on what was going on. Crossing back again to Coristan soil, their mentor knelt down beside them, concern written in deep wrinkles across his forehead. And before either could object, he had peeled off the scarf from around Margus's eyes.

"You won't be needing this anymore, Margus," he announced. Margus sat up straight and blinked with surprise, rubbed his eyes and looked around. He opened his mouth to reply but didn't (or couldn't) say a word. In fact he didn't have to. Oriannon knew from the way his eyes focused that he was seeing the world clearly once again.

"Anything I say right now would sound very dumb," Margus whispered, still blinking, "so I'm not going to try."

Mentor Jesmet nodded and put on his small, patient smile—the same one he had always worn while demonstrating how they should play a particularly difficult passage in the *Simfonia Seramina*, or when explaining timing or meter or something they didn't understand at first.

Next he hoisted Oriannon to her feet, and she clung to him with her right arm for balance, still worried about fainting or bleeding all over everybody—about bleeding to death, for that matter. After all, how long had the yagwar chewed on her left arm? The damage would be considerable, obviously, perhaps even beyond the ability of a Coristan healer to treat. She was afraid to look, so she cradled the arm against her left side as best she could.

"Am I going to die?" she whispered, and with a smile he shook his head no.

"Some day." He closed his eyes for a moment and leaned his head back. "But not yet."

She waited for a moment until he opened his eyes again. And strangely enough, her arm didn't feel disfigured or mutilated, not the way she would have expected. She felt no pain, though she reasoned it was only on account of the extreme shock to her system. Her head still spun. But now Jesmet took her hand—her left hand—and held it up.

As he did, a very strange warmth flowed through her arm, a clean tide washing over her entire body—a euphoria she had never before felt and could not describe with words.

"It's not how you think it is," he told her, nodding at her arm. "Go ahead. Take a look."

"No, please. I don't want to see it." She turned away, but only for a moment, and her curiosity returned.

"Ori," said Margus, his voice low. "I think you're going to want to check it out."

When she finally did, she gasped in stunned amazement at what she saw. Because when she looked down, she couldn't find a scratch where the yagwar had mutilated and torn apart her wrist and elbow. Not a mark or a scar ... nothing. She wiggled her fingers, all five in their proper place, and they worked as designed.

"Jesmet ..." she whispered, and he nodded his reply. It took a moment for her to understand what she was witnessing. But then she remembered, of course.

She'd seen him do this before—to someone else. Only it was different now that it had happened to her. And it made her shiver. "My arm."

"That's right," he answered. "You're going to need both of them, after all. Your mind, and both your arms."

"But ..." What was she supposed to say now? Thank you for following us all the way from Lior? Thank you for saving our lives? Thank you for rescuing us from the yagwar? Thank you for restoring my arm?

"You're welcome," he whispered, letting her hand go and stepping back. But she still struggled to understand exactly what had just happened to her and Margus.

"Why?" she asked, still feeling like she was in shock, only in a new way. "Why are you doing all this?"

"Not just for you. But if you or Margus had been the only person in Corista, I would have come. And you did ask for help, did you not?"

"Once." Well, she had, actually, back when the sand worm had attacked them and blinded Margus. But how would Jesmet know that? Becket Sol's words came to her then, from when they were leaving Lior.

Jesmet will go with you.

At the time it had sounded odd, but now ... *she knew!* The same way she knew whose footprints had led in and out of the shelter where they'd escaped the sandstorm. The same way she knew who had brought them more food and water. This time she didn't even need to ask.

She wouldn't have had time to, anyway.

"Incoming!" Margus held up his hands to fend off the probes that now buzzed overhead. Finally they'd arrived, after the little incident here on the border. Each little silver sphere blinked fiercely and tried to scan their faces with an ID probe. Margus ducked — too late — while Oriannon watched Jesmet just stand there. She could do the same. Eventually everyone would have to know they were back. Except — she panicked when she realized what side of the border Jesmet was standing on. And she remembered what the woman had told her back at Jesmet's trial.

"Instant death, of course, if he ever sets foot again in Corista."

"You can make the probes go blank, Mentor," whispered Margus. "Remember back in orchestra, whenever there was one in the room, you—"

"Not this time, Margus." Jesmet shook his head no. But Oriannon knew it wasn't because he couldn't do anything about the probes, just because ... why, exactly?

"Looks as if we have a welcoming committee," Jesmet told them. And Oriannon gasped all over again when she realized Jesmet wasn't making any move to escape. What was he thinking?

"You can't be here!" she told him. "You crossed the line! You came back into Corista!"

Margus must have already figured it out; he grabbed Jesmet's arm and tried to drag their mentor back across the fence. But Jesmet only shook his head and dug in his heels.

"No," he told them. "It's too late for that."

And really it was. Because by now a Security lev-sled had whisked to the scene and five fully armed securities jumped off a floating platform to take positions around them. Jesmet couldn't have escaped if he'd wanted to. Three more sleds sped up, filled with reinforcements.

"Remain where you are for identification!" barked one of the securities. With their dark face shields Oriannon couldn't tell which one was giving the orders or which one was moving his mouth. But really it didn't matter, as the probes hovered closer and showered them with prickly red beams of light all over again. Hadn't it worked the first time? At least it gave them a few extra seconds. And before it was done Jesmet turned to them.

"Listen to me carefully." His low whisper cut through all the confusion, all the shouting. "You two need to stick together in the next few days, no matter how you feel about what's happened. Then, when you have a chance, let people know. Tell them what you saw over on Shadowside. And we'll talk again."

"But don't you remember?" Oriannon didn't want to tell him the obvious, but he didn't seem too concerned—almost as if he didn't care about the death sentence he'd just stepped into. "They're going to kill you!"

For a moment Jesmet bit his lip as he looked around at the securities. The unmistakable whine of stun batons filled the air. Certainly he really hadn't forgotten what would happen if they ever caught him on Coristan soil, had he? Oriannon thought she saw a tear in his eye, but then three securities stepped closer, grabbed him, and forced him to the ground, face-first.

"Hey!" But when Margus protested, they simply shoved him, aside as well. "He wasn't supposed to be here. He wasn't part of the deal. Nobody said anything about this!"

The tallest of the securities turned to face him.

"You did a good job after all, kid. I actually didn't think you'd come through. But look at this: the girl and the criminal too. Very good."

"What is he talking about, Margus?" Oriannon couldn't believe what she was hearing; the words hit her with more force than the yagwar's attack. It couldn't be true. "Tell me what's going on."

But by this time Margus was grabbing at the security's arm, causing the tall man to laugh.

"A little late to be upset about it, kid. You'll get your bonus."

"But they promised! All I was doing was bringing back Oriannon! Getting her to safety. Nothing else!"

"You mean they didn't tell you what the real prize was?" He shoved Margus away, his voice dripping with sarcasm. "So sorry. An oversight."

By this time Margus fell to his knees and buried his face in his hands.

"You can't do this!" he sobbed. "They promised me!"

"Mr. Leek!" Jesmet managed to turn his dust-caked face to the side before one of the nameless securities planted a black boot on the back of his head. "It's all right. This is how it had to happen. No one made me—"

The pointed toe of another boot caught him in the teeth, silencing him, and the security waved his glowing green baton in Jesmet's face. And now a strong pair of hands grabbed Oriannon by the arms, but she fell to her knees next to her mentor. How could it have turned so wrong? Tears blurred her vision as she reached toward him.

"He saved my life," she sobbed, as if it would change anyone's mind. "That's all he was doing. He came back to save my life."

But a moment later she was hauled off her feet by her hair and by the arm that had just been mangled and bleeding but which now felt tingling with life and stronger than it ever had. She would scratch their eyes out if she had to.

"Oriannon." She heard Mentor Jesmet's voice once again, weaker this time. "Just do as they say."

She looked back to see them hauling him away by his feet, dragging him through the dirt. His body jerked when they jabbed the end of a stun baton into his side. And then his arms flopped to the side, limp, while the back of his head carved a trail in the dust. His eyes were closed, his mouth bloody.

And he had surely not spoken the words—with his lips.

But what could she do now? She didn't pull against the hands that shoved her back to one of the Security lev-sleds, just stared at Margus as if this really wasn't happening to them.

Margus, the traitor.

"And she really is Oriannon Hightower of Nyssa." Margus was still trying to tell them what to do. "You're not supposed to hurt her. You just bring her back to the Temple. That's the deal. Her father is—"

"We know who her father is," interrupted one of the three securities escorting them to their ride. Oriannon still hadn't seen any of the faces behind those dark face shields. Maybe it was better that way. But the one closest to her looked as if he had already downloaded a scan from the probes; on his handheld she caught a glimpse—a small picture of her own face, along with her ID numbers and address, her school, her height and weight, eye color, everything else about her.

Hightower of Nyssa, Oriannon, read the screen. ID:9907– 2236–0021.

He leaned over and whispered something to the other two securities, pointed to his handheld as they stepped up to the waiting lev-sled. Finally he loosened his grip a little and cleared his throat.

"Hold there for a minute, please, Miss Hightower."

Please. The word stuck in her ears. *How courteous of them.* Before she realized what was happening, he had fastened a pair of titanium security cuffs around her wrists, behind her back, as if she was a common criminal! She winced when the cuffs dug into her wrists. And she looked over at Margus, who stood by helplessly with that same shocked look.

"You can't do this to me!" she shrieked. But of course the more she struggled, the more the cuffs tightened. And when she lost her footing the cuffs burned her wrists with a brief but horrible second of electric shock. Nothing like a stun baton, probably, but serious enough.

"Please!" She bowed her head and tried not to cry. She wasn't sure which was worse—the sand worms, these power cuffs, or knowing what Margus had done. She decided to try another way.

"Please don't shock me again," she whimpered. "Why are you doing this?"

"It's for your own protection, Miss Hightower." The security motioned to the set of four stair steps that lowered from the open, hovering craft, a round platform with no roof, in-facing seats, and a clear, protective windscreen around the edge. "You're being detained as an accomplice to an escaped felon. Understand?"

"No." Margus tried once again. "She's not an accomplice! You need to talk with Regent Ossek. He told me, I mean, I was just supposed to find her and bring her back."

"Which you did. But our orders come straight from the Regent, kid. Talk to him yourself."

Oriannon still couldn't believe what she heard as she mounted the steps to the lev-sled. Detained for being an accomplice? Because she had been caught with Mentor Jesmet, now she would be held accountable too. Maybe subject to the same penalty. Oriannon chose her words carefully as she looked over her shoulder at the other sled, already leaving with Mentor Jesmet—or his body.

"I understand ... you're only doing what you've been told," she replied, and the words felt icy on her lips. But now she also understood it was time to change back into Oriannon Hightower of Nyssa, respected daughter of the elder. If she could.

At the same time, the pain of what Margus had done hit her even worse than her own fate. The liar! She'd stew about that later. Right now she blocked him out of her mind as she desperately tried to think of a way to help the Owlings. Was it too late to stall the next attack on Lior, get help from her father, or beg help anywhere she could find it?

The Owlings still counted on her, if they yet lived.

273

31

By all accounts she had meant well. But as they skimmed back over the rolling Coristan hills toward the city, Oriannon felt her once steely-hard determination slowly melting. This was either where she needed to sit up straight and be strong, or where — as Mentor Jesmet had taught her — she needed to let go, and let him take care of the rest.

Either way, she wasn't sure what was right anymore — though Jesmet certainly would not have wanted her to act like a quivering wreck, crying her eyes out. She'd left her strong will behind, somewhere over on Shadowside — if she'd ever had it. The same way she'd probably lost her earbud back over there somewhere. She felt her pocket again, just to be sure. If she had it now she would have thrown it away.

And how could she let Mentor Jesmet take care of the rest now? If he was still alive, he was lying unconscious, probably still under a security's cruel boot. She stared over the railing of their speeding lev-sled, skimming over greening treetops. Even the view didn't stir her the way it once had. All the greens looked gray, the brightness just ... too bright.

275

And as they neared Corista, she looked up to see the Trion shining at them, rising higher in the sky. The symbol of Jesmet, so familiar to the Owlings. Why didn't anyone on her side of the planet know about it? She squinted and turned away, since she couldn't hold a hand to her face.

Seeing the Trion again did make her think of how Wist was doing, though, and if she was safe. Had the Coristan ship been given permission to return and finish the job it had started? Maybe she should have stayed there with her friends after all, for just a little while longer. If she had, none of this would ever have happened. It would never have turned so horribly wrong.

But no. Jesmet had told them to go.

She took a deep, ragged breath. Even with Margus the Traitor sitting next to her she couldn't help it. She lowered her chin and let the tears fall.

"Almost there," he told her, the way her dad used to do.

"And then what?" she snapped, wiping her face on her sleeve. "You collect your fee for bringing back the prize?"

"Oriannon, you've got to believe me. This isn't the way I wanted it."

"Why should I believe you this time? I'll bet you made a deal with the Assembly to bring back Jesmet just so they could kill him."

"That's not true! After all we went through, you can't really believe I'd do that!"

"I don't know what to believe anymore, or what's an act. All I know is what I saw happen — and that I don't want to speak to you again."

She ignored the rich smells of cerise bushes and lonicera vines as they flew over forest and clearing, farms and homes. What did it matter now?

"Look, Oriannon, I am so sorry. The whole thing got out of hand."

She didn't answer, didn't look at him.

"I was only trying to help you," he said, barely audible above the sound of the wind. "Don't you see that?"

She set her jaw and still said nothing.

"All right, then," he sighed. "But what do you really think you can do now, all by yourself? You think you're going to be able to go back and change things? Save your friends?"

"I don't know." She glared at him. "I have to try."

But already Shadowside seemed so far away, much like the fairy tale it had always been before. As if it had never existed. And if it seemed that way to her now, how would it seem to others when she tried to tell them of the danger it faced?

"No one's going to believe me anyway," she sighed and sniffled. Enough crying.

"Maybe they will." His hair blew into his face, and for a moment he looked as scared as Oriannon felt.

Neither spoke for the next hour, and she let her mind spin in circles between her trek to Shadowside, Jesmet's miracles, the darkness of his arrest—and the part Margus played in all of it. But as they finally closed on the city, she could make out a huge crowd of people milling around the central landing port, near the Temple Square and Court of Justice where Jesmet had been condemned and where they had probably taken him again. The lev-sled shook as they descended.

"Once we land," their pilot told them over the whine of braking thrusters, "you'll walk between me and twenty-two."

That would be the security with the "5022" stenciled on the front of his helmet, as opposed to the "5067" on his own. Their pilot added a word of warning.

"The reporters are going to mob you, but I don't want you talking to any of them. Understand?"

Margus just frowned and looked over the railing down at the crowds on the grassy Temple square. Even from this height Oriannon recognized people from school. Several others carried handcams, pointed at network reporters or even up at them.

"Looks as if the whole city knows we're coming," mumbled Margus.

"Where are you taking us?" Oriannon asked him. Not that she expected an answer. The pilot ignored her as he worked the controls and brought them to a gentle touchdown.

Of course, that really set off the excitement, as the expected mob crushed in on them. Oriannon assumed most were reporters, the kind of talking heads featured on news feeds and screens all over Corista. And sure enough, even over the winding down of the lev-sled's engine, the questions came at them like a hailstorm:

"Miss Hightower, tell us what happened!"

"What about your arrest?"

"Why did you run away?"

"Give us some details about how you survived!"

"Did you know your disappearance has headlined all the news programs?"

"Miss Hightower, how did you escape and get back home?"

"Oriannon — over here! Have you spoken yet with your family? What's your reaction to your father's comments?"

Only the last question stopped her, and she stared straight at the man who had asked her. What did he know?

"My father," Oriannon repeated over the din. "What did my father say? Tell me!"

"Oh. Just about Jesmet ben Saius, you know, and the death penalty. I assumed you knew."

"No," she gulped. "But I need to tell you all—"

"Sorry, everybody." Security 67 faced the mob and raised his hands. "But we'll need to have this conversation later. No more questions."

With his visor down he probably looked just as scary to the reporters as he had to Oriannon and Margus, especially towering above them all in his lev-sled. He pointed at the steps now lowering to the ground, and the reporter backed away as Security 67 motioned him aside.

"Because we're going to walk down this way," continued the security, "and you're all going to pull aside so we can get by. Right *now.*"

None of the reporters moved, until the distinct hum of a stun baton let them know how serious this security really was. Under protest the sea of reporters parted.

"Miss Hightower!" The yelling started all over again.

"Oriannon!" cried another, pushing to the front. "Just one more question!"

"I said you'll have a chance later to ask your questions," Security 67 told them in his booming voice, "but Miss Hightower isn't going to say a word until she's been de-briefed by the Assembly."

In other words, they would make sure Oriannon didn't tell them the truth about what was really happening on the other side of the planet. And even though the reporters would not give up their wild questioning, Security 67 motioned for Oriannon to follow as he stepped off the lev-sled first. She glanced at Margus, who nodded at her to go ahead. Security 22—a clone of Security 67 except for the number on his helmet—would bring up the rear.

"Guess he wasn't kidding," shouted Margus as they waded into the sea of reporters, and Oriannon could feel the eyes on them and on their handcuffs. She stopped short in front of the reporter who had asked her about her dad.

"We're glad you're safely home," he said as Margus bumped into Oriannon from behind. She nodded her thanks. "But can't you tell us more about your role in bringing Jesmet ben Saius back to ultimate judgment?"

"Hey!" Security 22 could shout almost as loudly as Security 67. "Let's not be stopping."

"I'm sorry." Oriannon stumbled and hurried to keep up, as the reporters continued shouting and clicking their compact cameras—everyone focused on her and Margus.

32

Oriannon!" Her father approached her from the Temple complex at a half-run, arms outstretched but with a look of panic on his face. No, this wasn't the way Oriannon had imagined it would be, coming home to Daddy. With her wrists bound she could not return his hug, so all she could do was dissolve once more into tears and rest her chin on his shoulder.

"We'll get this cleared up right away," he told her, patting her back. He didn't seem to care that everyone on Corista would be watching this little family reunion, didn't seem to care that the entire planet would see an elder cry. "I'm just glad you're safe. But I'll have a talk with whoever put those things on your hands."

"Please, Daddy." She tried to swallow back the sobs. "There's something you need to know."

"What did they do to you?" His face clouded over. "Because if anyone hurt you, I swear I'll—"

"No, that's not it. I'm fine. Nobody hurt me. It's what I found out, something that's happening on Shadowside. It's life and death."

"I see." He straightened out and held up his hand to silence her. He no longer listened, if he ever had. "Well first we have to meet with the Assembly for a few minutes. Then I'll take you home, I promise. We can talk all you want, later."

"No, Daddy. Please listen to me!"

But her father had already turned aside to argue with Security 67 about her power cuffs. Margus had disappeared too—not that she cared anymore. If Margus had betrayed her and Jesmet was arrested and her father wouldn't listen, who was left to help? Angry tears now welled up, and she let them.

"Look, can't you see how ridiculous it is to put those things on her?" Her father nosed up a lot closer to the security's unblinking faceguard than she ever would have. "Just take them off for now."

But 67 only folded his arms and held his ground.

"You know the protocol as well as I do, sir. Not until the Assembly—"

"But I *am* the Assembly!" Even when he puffed up his chest and stood on his toes he barely reached the security's shoulders.

"Begging your pardon, sir, but there are eleven other members, are there not?"

So the security wasn't going to budge from the letter of the law, and Oriannon could see her father's jaw working, the vein in the side of his neck pumping. Finally he pulled back a step in surrender and his eyes narrowed as he sighed in frustration.

"You'll leave her to my custody then."

The security shook his head no.

"We'll accompany you both to the chambers, sir. Please follow me."

"I know the way, obviously," huffed her father.

With securities on both sides now, all she could do now was follow her father down the hall to the gilded double doors leading into the high-ceilinged chambers of Corista's Ruling Assembly—one of the many halls and rooms of the outer Temple. She'd only been here once before, as a little girl, for the ceremony when her father was sworn in as an elder.

"Just listen to what the Regent tells you, Oriannon," her father whispered in her ear as they paused in the doorway. "And if he asks you a question, answer with only a few words, nothing more. Don't volunteer. Understand?"

She nodded weakly. The sooner they got this over with, the sooner she could get help.

"Step inside, Hightower!" boomed a white-haired man seated at the head of a large, U-shaped table. The setting commanded much of the conference chambers, where the twelve-member Assembly convened for all those meetings her father spent so many hours attending, but never told her about. She craned her neck to take it all in.

Though the large official room had no outside windows, golden shafts of light flooded in through a crystalline ceiling, brightening through clouds of nose-prickling incense. Oriannon stifled a sneeze. Behind and all around, floor-to-ceiling tapestries told the story of Corista, from the First Parents to the Great Uprising and right up to the Now. Pictures of the Trion shed a filmy light on every panel. Oriannon clutched her own Trion necklace, the symbol of Jesmet. And she wondered:

Do these people even know what the stars really mean?

She didn't notice any probes floating around the room. But now three securities took up stations at each of three doors—two smaller side doors and the main entry. Security 67 pointed for Oriannon to approach and stand at her place on the polished marble floor in front of the Regent and the rest of the Assembly. Her father remained a half step behind her.

"Oriannon Hightower of Nyssa." Regent Jib Ossek used her full family name as he leaned his arms on the polished ebony table and gazed straight at her with a kind of look that froze the blood in her veins. He tugged at his beard but it did little to straighten his permanently crooked expression, one eye open and the other squinted.

Was that a question? After a long silence she understood she would not be officially introduced to him or to any of the other ten, seated five on either side, all decked in their sky-purple robes. Only her father's place at the end of the row closest to her sat empty. He would not take part in this inquisition for obvious reasons. He did prod her in the back.

But what was she supposed to say? She settled for a polite bob and a bow of the head, which seemed to satisfy the Assembly leader.

"I'm so sorry about the cuffs, Miss Hightower."

Probably the same way you're so sorry you recaptured Mentor Jesmet, she thought.

Meanwhile the Regent's deadpan expression didn't change any more than his voice. "But as an elder's daughter, I assume you're quite aware of protocol, are you not?"

She nodded and another Assembly member added his carefully-crafted, conditional apology.

"We do regret that you experienced a certain degree of ... difficulties." This elder looked a little older than the others, his beard a little longer and fully white. His expression, however, matched everyone else's—a tight-lipped, narrow-eyed impatient look that made her squirm. "Though you seem to have brought the majority of them on yourself."

His eyes narrowed even more when he said that last part, and Oriannon's throat tightened until she almost couldn't breathe. A couple of other elders clucked their tongues in agreement as he waited for her to respond. Or perhaps he just paused for effect. She would follow her father's advice and stay silent—for now. He went on.

"In any case, we want you to know—for your father's sake as much as for anything else—that we are mindful of the trauma you experienced beyond our borders, on Shadowside."

How did he know? Perhaps there was more that Margus had not told her.

"Nevertheless," he continued, "it is not our purpose to reward blatant disregard for the Assembly's authority, as we have established travel restrictions for the sole purpose of public safety. Nor, I might add, is it our desire to condone any form of reckless behavior, regardless of—"

"Sir." Oriannon couldn't just let this go. "I wouldn't call it reckless. *Reckless* was when securities came to my school and forced me to take a brain scan. Reckless was when you accused our mentor—"

"I did not ask you a question yet, Miss Hightower." He furrowed his off-kilter eyebrows at her and leaned forward in his chair. "Although I find it highly troubling that you were apprehended at precisely the same location as this ... mentor."

Her father poked her in the back and once more whispered in her ear.

"Ori! Remember what I told you."

She nodded as the Regent unloaded the rest of his speech on her.

"Until we can clear up the connection between you and this outlaw, you will be given a supervised opportunity to recover from your ... adventure. I believe this is more than charitable, given the circumstances. But in the meantime, tell me ..."

He cocked his head to one side, as a terramole lizard would stare down a bug for dinner.

"Tell me," he continued, "what exactly now is your connection to the condemned?"

"He was my mentor. And then—"

"She has no current connection with the man, of course." Oriannon's dad interrupted as he stepped forward to answer for her. "None whatever. I can vouch for that."

"Hightower!" The Regent slammed his palm down on the table and glowered at Oriannon's father. "I don't need you to vouch. You're not the one who's been missing all this time. I only require a simple explanation from the young lady."

"Pardon, Regent." Her father backed down again, just as he'd been forced to do with the security. Oriannon was getting a quick lesson in who bowed to whom around here. Unfortunately her father didn't look as if he was as high up in the order as she'd once believed.

"Keeping in mind," added another trustee in a lower voice, "that this is a preliminary debriefing, not a trial. We simply desire to learn what's actually happened. The truth."

The Regent didn't take his eyes off her, just nodded slowly and pressed the tips of his fingers into a tent. She searched for the best answer to make him go away, and was about to answer when her father interrupted once more.

"Regent," said her father, "forgive me. She's clearly been through some sort of mind control process with this character, against her will. I suggest, with your indulgence, that we postpone this line of questioning. Then I assure you she will be happy to return in a few days after this entire situation with the mentor has settled down."

In other words, after Jesmet had been executed. When it would no longer matter who followed this man's teachings, or not. She cleared her throat.

"I'd like to answer your question, sir."

But as a heavy silence hung over the room, Oriannon knew too well what her father was trying to say. Apparently so did the Regent, and this time he chewed on his words as if he would never swallow them fully. Finally he nodded.

"You'll have your chance." He narrowed his eyes at Oriannon's father. "But for now the Assembly remands Oriannon Hightower of Nyssa to the custody of her father, under the full-time supervision of Security. She is prohibited from leaving the city, and she will return to this room in three days from this hour to explain fully her actions since leaving Corista."

For a moment Oriannon thought she'd been dismissed, but the Regent held up his hand when she took a step backwards.

"In the meantime, however, I have one directive for you."

Everyone in the chambers waited for the Regent to explain his one directive. Oriannon glanced once more at the tapestries, traced the golden threads of the Trion, waiting for her chance. And like the lead actor in the Opera Corista, he milked the silence until Oriannon thought she would scream.

"For the time being you will say nothing of what you saw or heard in Shadowside to anyone outside this room," he finally ordered her. "Especially not to the media, not to your friends, not even to your family. With the exception, of course, of Elder Hightower."

"But ..." Oriannon felt her jaw drop and snapped it back up. "People need to know!"

"Not until we receive a full report from you, young lady, and you *will* show appropriate respect." His cheeks began to turn a deeper shade of red as he waved his finger at her. "Once we've learned everything you've experienced, we will make a determination of how much, if any, is appropriate for sharing in the public forum. You will follow this injunction without question. Do you understand what I'm saying?"

"You want me to keep quiet until you tell me what to say."

"A simple yes or no would be sufficient."

She knew from his stormy expression that she probably should not have continued. But she also knew she might not get another chance—and days from now would be too late. So instead of the simple yes or no, she took a deep breath and launched her plea.

"Mr. Regent, sir, please let me explain. I saw people over on Shadowside. Owlings. They were kind to me. But my mentors never told us about Owlings in school. My mentors never told me that we're stealing all their water to water our flowers. They never—"

"Perhaps you weren't listening, Miss Hightower. Everyone knows about the wild animals found on Shadowside. You yourself were attacked by one, were you not?"

Now he was asking her more questions!

"No! I mean, yes, I was attacked. But not by Owlings. Owlings are people—not wild animals."

The Regent looked to the side and drummed his long fingers on the table before answering.

"And how is it you come to call them ... *people*? You realize, of course, that these wild-eyed creatures threaten our existence, do you not?"

"Oh, no, sir. They wouldn't hurt anyone. They—"

"They steal the water that rightfully belongs to Corista!" he thundered. "And I understand your presence there interfered with an effort to clear out a vital pipeline, did it not?"

"Uh ..." She hesitated. How would he know?

"I'll take that as a yes. I am, however, gratified you will not be there next time, Miss Hightower."

"Next time? See, that's what I'm worried about. What are you going to do to the Owlings? Are you going to allow a big attack on Lior? You can't!"

"Lior? Interesting. The creatures even name their city, if you can call it such." He sighed. "However, all of this is none of your concern. You will be summoned."

"Sir, but Jesmet says—"

"Hightower!" he thundered, and the Regent's eyes blazed with a fury that made her shrink back, as from a fire. Of course now the man was clearly speaking over her head, at her father. And the Regent pointed at Oriannon as he spoke.

"We see now the root of this trouble, do we not? Have you not schooled this girl in the Principles? The Law?"

Oriannon's father held his forehead as he stuttered out a defense.

"She received the training, yes. But it wasn't her fault, as you know. She was kidnapped just before her Seer Codex was scheduled to take place, and—"

"I had my Seer ceremony," Oriannon blurted out, then brought a hand to her lips. Perhaps, she thought, she might have saved that revelation for later. Now the Regent leaned forward once again, and both his crooked eyes narrowed to slits.

"How, pray tell, were you able to accomplish that?"

"Mentor Jesmet called us to the Grand Hall," she croaked, and her mouth had gone dry by this time. "He conducted the ceremony."

Her father groaned as she went on.

"Because the Owlings, they follow the Codex too. Only they *understand* it—not just, you know, repeating what other people tell them. It's more as if they breathe it all the time, sort of . . ."

Her voice trailed off as she realized what she was saying, and where she was saying it. Obviously the Regent had heard enough for one day.

"That's quite enough." This time he waved her off the way he would a stray insect. "You were not brought here to lecture us on theology. But you will return in seventy-two hours with an entirely different frame of mind."

"Please forgive me, sir." Oriannon knew she'd dug her own grave. "But I haven't even told you what's really happening over there. I'm sure you've heard, but   "

"I said that's enough!" When he rose his eyes nearly bulged out of his head, while the three securities left their posts to surround her. "You will bring this child home and see to it that she receives proper treatment and immediate re-education. She will wear a Security locator band around her ankle at all times. And, Hightower—"

"Sir." Her father stepped up and his voice quavered.

"'He who does not handle his family well ...'"

Now he was quoting from Codex, using it as a club to hit her father. Well, she could think of several other choice verses she could quote back to him.

"What about 'Whoever mistreats the poor mistreats the Maker,' sir?" Now she was in over her head. "Or 'Remember the poor and you honor the Maker.' Those are in the Codex, too, sir."

"Hightower!" screeched Regent Ossek.

"I'll see to it, Regent." With a hurried bow Oriannon's red-faced father drew her away from the Regent, who looked about ready to strangle her. One of the securities at long last unlocked her wrist cuffs, only to hold out a silver anklet—that Security locator band the Regent had ordered. She shook her head and drew back, at the same time knowing she could not avoid the indignity of having a security grab her leg and strap it on by force.

"Daddy!" she whispered, hoping. But her father only crossed his arms and backed away a step while the security did his job. She might have kicked and screamed too, if she thought it would have done any good. But once the anklet was clicked into place a small green light came on to indicate the locator was sending out its signal. Security would know where she was from now on.

"And if I *ever* hear that name again in these chambers," warned the Regent, perhaps considering what he might do. He took out a gold-embroidered handkerchief and made a show of wiping his hands clean, over and over, as if he could erase the echo of Jesmet's name from the room, or from his hands. Perhaps it wouldn't be that easy.

"Jesmet saved my life," Oriannon called back over her shoulder as her father guided her out of the chambers. But she thought they should hear it one more time, at least. "He restored my arm. He brought back Brinnin Flyer when she died. And he—"

She couldn't finish with a large hand clapped over her mouth. And her feet hardly touched the ground as her father dragged her through the marble hallways of the outer Temple, around to a back entrance and a loading area where their family's pod sat waiting.

"Get in the pod." Her father shook as he spat the words, and she knew she had never seen him quite this angry. When the plexi doors slid shut behind them he turned to her with a tight-lipped, hurt expression that said everything.

"And don't you ever embarrass me like that again," he hissed.

"I—"

"No more! That was the Regent of the Ruling Assembly, in case you forgot."

He pushed a control handle forward as they lurched over a curb and through a cerise bush, finally backed up and found a clear path. Oriannon secured her safety field.

"He was mean."

"But he's my superior, the most powerful person in Corista. And you disrespected him as if you were arguing with a girlfriend in the hallway at school!"

Oriannon wished she could turn away, but she couldn't. She rubbed a tear from her eyes.

"But Daddy, don't you even care? Don't you even want to know what happened to me over there? I thought—I hoped you would understand."

"You want to know what I understand?" He rubbed his forehead as they nearly sideswiped a row of stopped pods. People crowded around them in the city center, slowing their progress. "I understand my only daughter was brainwashed by a mentor we once trusted, who was banished to Shadowside because of his heresy, and who then came waltzing back over here to defy the Assembly's will. *That's* what I understand."

"He didn't come waltzing back. He came back to help us. And what happened to him, anyway? Where did they take him?"

"That's not for you to worry about." Finally they lurched forward again, careening around a corner into a tree-lined side street. Of course their assigned securities followed directly behind. "But don't you see, Ori? Your mentor-*friend* wanted to tear apart the fabric of everything we believe in. And he wanted to take you and your friends with him!"

"Maybe the fabric needs to be torn a little. Jesmet said—"

"Don't you ever say that kind of thing again!" He slammed his fist on the pod's control panel, causing them to swerve and warning lights to flicker. "I don't want to hear that name, and I don't want you to use that name, ever!"

"But that's another thing. Why is everyone so scared of his name?"

"The name is banished, Oriannon. The man and his memory are banished. You just don't seem to understand the kind of pain he's caused."

"*He's* caused?" She tried to keep from sounding hysterical. "Father, you didn't see what I saw, over there. You didn't see the attacks. You didn't see what they were doing to the Owlings. And why wouldn't Regent Ossek admit to me what's going to happen?"

"Oriannon." He shook his head as if she'd hurt him. Two more turns took them to the outskirts and to the hilly lane that would lead to their home.

"What? Please! I need to know."

"And if you knew, what then?"

She couldn't answer, could hardly breathe. But yes—what then?

"They're going to destroy Lior, aren't they?" She bit her lip until she could taste blood. "They're not just going to clear the pipeline. They're going to clear the whole city. Aren't they? Please tell me! You can't let them!"

He just stared at her as if she'd gone crazy. A curbside warning buzzed and jolted their pod back into the road, but her father didn't seem to notice.

"What's wrong with you, Oriannon? Don't you see? He's warped your mind."

"The only one who warped my mind ..." Her voice trailed off into tears as she recalled what happened back in the Health Center that horrible day, what happened to her memory before Jesmet healed her. Her father tried to rest his hand on her shoulder but she shrugged him away.

"Listen, Ori." His voice softened for a moment. "I'm sorry. Perhaps some of this is my fault."

If he only knew, thought Oriannon. But even in her anger she couldn't help feeling a little sorry for her dad. Still she looked straight out the window at the hillside as he spoke. The view could have been painted over in black rather than the beautiful Rift Valley; she didn't care.

"If your mother were still alive, I—" His voice caught for a moment before he turned back to her again. "No, listen. We're going to get you some help, Oriannon. Whatever it takes. But you need to get your mind back, and it needs to happen before we take you back to the Assembly chambers. I promise you we'll do this. Do you understand?"

"But that's just it! I already do have my mind back. Jes—he's the one who gave it back to me."

She glanced over to see the corners of her father's lips turned up in a forced, painful smile—as if he was trying to find a new way of getting through to her. He turned another bend in the road as it climbed higher and higher.

"I'm sure that's the way it seems to you," he told her, his voice quieter. "Right now I just want you to know I'll be here for you. And if you care about your family, if you respect what we stand for, if you love Corista at all, you'll remember what the Regent told you to do."

She didn't answer. Even the sound of that man's name made her grind her teeth.

"I mean you need to obey, Oriannon. *Obey.*"

Not that *obey* was an evil word. She'd never thought so before, for even the Codex mentioned it often enough. Only now when she thought of *obey,* she thought of the way someone like Suuli or Wist obeyed, as if it was something they really wanted to do for their Maker. Not this.

"I understand," she finally managed to answer. "But obey ... who?"

Her father's tentative smile withered into a frown, but she had to finish her thought.

"I mean, do you want me to obey even if it means forgetting people I care about? I know what forgetting is like now, Father, and I don't want to do that again."

Her father still didn't answer, so she asked him again.

"Or do I obey even if it means doing what I know is wrong?"

By this time they had nearly climbed to the top of the hill, and the securities still followed closely in their own pod. Her father turned into their cobblestone drive.

"I think you know exactly what I mean, Oriannon."

Unfortunately she did.

Finally they slipped into their own garage. Even before their pod sank to the garage floor with a hiss, Oriannon tried to push out the side door—but her father grabbed her arm to stay in her seat.

"Remember what I said, Ori. Don't make yourself confused. Just obey."

She nodded weakly, slipped out of the pod, and shuffled into their house. If only it was that simple. She didn't look at the securities who had already posted themselves inside.

Brinnin! *No one will listen to me!!!* Oriannon typed into her hand-held. *I'm not even supposed to be talking to you, but—*

She paused. They might as well have put her in prison, with the anklet they'd locked to her leg. She tugged at the silvery band, the little transmitter that blinked green and told the Assembly everywhere she walked—from bedroom to bathroom and everything in between.

But I'm sure glad you're alive after all, wrote Brinnin. *So when can you go back to school?*

Don't know. Right now I just need somebody to hear me about the Owlings before it's too late.

I hear you, Brinnin typed. Another message popped into her screen, only this time not from Brinnin Flyer. Oriannon groaned.

Gotta go, wrote Brinnin, a little too quickly. She must have seen the other person's message. *See you soon?*

Oriannon was about to power down her handheld without responding, but couldn't help reading the next line as it poured onto her multi-colored screen.

I know you're upset with me, Ori. But please let me explain!!!!!!!

Ori frowned before hammering in a response: *Nothing to explain. I don't want to see you, talk, or text.*

Again she reached for the power off button.

Margus wrote, *Wait! I only wanted to help you. Don't you believe me?*

Now Ori clenched her jaw as she fired back a question of her own. *Did they pay you to come find me and bring me back?*

Margus paused a little longer than before.

I gave all the money back. They didn't want it, but I made them take it back. I'm sorry.

But why you? Ori questioned.

They came to me. They said that you would run if adults came for you. Easier for me.

The probe in the tunnel? Ori typed. She had to find out. *Did you know?*

Margus apologized. *I should have told you. I'm sorry.*

You mean yes?

Y.

What about the yagwar with the collar? Ori questioned.

They were controlling it. A way to hurry us. But promised no one would get hurt.

Thought so. Ori knew she should have trusted her gut. *And you pretended not to know anything about it!!*

I'm really really sorry, Margus apologized again. *Only way I could think to get you back.*

What about Jesmet? You knew they wanted to kill him?

No! No! I said before. Never part of the deal. They never told me.

So they tricked you. Ori couldn't believe Margus was so gullible.

Again Margus paused a long time before finally answering.

I wish I could make up for it.

"Oh, Margus," she whispered out loud, shaking her head. Her fist wasn't clenched anymore. "I wish you could too."

She turned to stare at the projection screen floating above her bed. By this time another Coristan Security team was probably on its way to take out her Owling friends and destroy Lior, but would they show it on the media?

Meanwhile all the details about Jesmet's arrest flooded into her room, with live interviews, expert analysis from the Temple, and talking heads giving every nauseating detail, over and over again. Didn't they ever stop?

"Residents of Corista are still stunned at the shocking developments," reported a wide-eyed little man on the screen, "as new reports surface about the quiet mentor who traded his music conductor's baton for the spotlight—and who now faces the death penalty for flagrantly disregarding the terms of his banishment."

Are you watching? Margus finally asked. She'd thought he'd already signed off.

Wish I wasn't.

Makes me sick to know it's my fault.

Not your fault, Oriannon typed, then almost wished she could take it back. After all, she was still supposed to be terminally angry with Margus Leek. But she knew whose life Jesmet had come back to save.

I still wish I could do something, Margus wrote.

"Me too," Ori whispered, and was about to write something else when a soft knock at her door made her jump. She tapped her comm so it quickly powered down.

"What is it?" she asked her dad, already knowing the answer.

"Almost time to go, Ori. You ready?"

She set her comm under a pillow and crossed her arms.

"I'm not going."

He only paused a moment before the door swooshed open. And her father stood in the opening, his hands on his hips. He was dressed in his best gold-fringed Assembly robe, the kind he only wore for special occasions. The security posted at the side of the door barely turned his head to look at them over his shoulder.

"You will be going, Oriannon." Her father's voice sounded cold and distant. "It's not a choice."

"I'm sorry, Dad. I just can't." She rolled over on her bed and buried her face in the pillow, still soggy from tears. "It's horrid, it's sick, and it's gruesome—and I just won't go."

But her father wasn't backing down, either.

"Oriannon, listen to me. Nobody's enjoying this. It's just one of those things you have to get through whether you enjoy it or not. It's your duty as a Coristan ... as a Hightower."

She frowned. Did it matter that the security heard every word they said? After another pause her father stepped inside and the door swooshed closed behind him. He waited until she looked up at him, then lowered his voice.

"There's something else too." He pulled out a small e-tablet and held it out to her. "I want you to put your fingerprint on this, right now."

She wrinkled her nose at him but sat up and took the tablet. With a sinking feeling in her stomach she quickly scrolled through the words:

"I, Oriannon Hightower of Nyssa, deny all and any connection to the condemned faithbreaker, Jesmet ..."

She bit her tongue as she whispered the statement and looked back up at her dad, wide-eyed.

"Who ... who wrote this?" she asked, but he shook his head. "Why now?"

"It doesn't matter. The only thing that matters is that we protect you. I was talking with a counselor, and he seems to think this would be the best thing for you right now."

"But Dad ..." She started to hand it back, and he only waved his hand at her. "I can't—"

"You can and you will. Look, it does you no good to have anything to do with a man who's being executed in two hours. Don't you see? This is the best way we can keep you from getting into any more trouble with Regent Ossek and the rest of the Assembly."

"I don't care about them."

"Yes you do." His voice took on that hard edge once more. "You know where it's written. 'Friends of the wicked are dragged into the same mud . . .'"

He didn't have to finish the verse. She knew every word.

"It doesn't apply," she argued, but by this time her vision blurred with tears. "Jesmet isn't wicked."

"Lawbreakers are wicked, period!" he snapped. "And I'm done arguing with you. This man did everything to provoke our response."

He sighed and shook his head before continuing, a little more slowly.

"Oriannon, you have to see this is the best way. You have to trust me. I'm your father."

"Daddy. I know." She bowed her head and cried, wanting so much to trust, grieving for the harsh decision she was being forced to make. "I just think—"

"It doesn't matter anymore what you think. The Regent announced an hour ago that anyone who associated with this man deserves the same punishment as him. That's why I'm bringing you this way out, before it's too late. I can help you now, but I might not be able to later."

He rested his hand on her shoulders and got down on his knees next to her bed.

"Please, honey. Let me help you. You can't do anything more for him. The only one you can help is yourself now. So just put your finger on the tablet and we won't have to talk about it again."

His plea hung in the air between them, and she knew he only meant to protect her, the way he said. Why did it have to be so confusing? She closed her eyes and tried to stop the dizzy swirling feeling, but that only made it worse.

"Please." Her father's pain was almost more than she could bear. And maybe he was right; she couldn't help Jesmet anymore.

So before she could think any more she slipped her thumb over the little track pad and pressed hard, much harder than she needed to.

Of course her father breathed a heavy sigh of relief.

"That's my girl. You're doing the right thing."

Was she? Feeling numb, she just gripped the tablet as he sprang to his feet. Now his voice took on an entirely new tone as he headed for the door.

"So I'll get the pod out of the garage and wait for you. Oh, and by the way, I've arranged with the other elders to have that anklet removed too."

As if he knew in advance what she would do. He went on.

"The security outside your door will disconnect it. I'll give you a minute to wash your face, and then we can leave."

She nodded. But as the door shut behind her father the e-tablet's screen flashed twice yellow and a female voice asked for her name.

"Oriannon Hightower ..." She paused, her voice cracking. "Oriannon Hightower of Nyssa."

The tablet went through its checking routine to ensure the voice it heard was her own.

"Please confirm your assent by indicating 'yes.'"

She looked out her window, her mind racing, wondering if this was how Margus had felt when he realized how the elders had tricked him into bringing Jesmet back over the border—to his death. Was this what it felt to betray someone? And still she gripped the tablet.

"Please confirm your assent—" The tablet repeated itself.

"What have I *done?*" she gasped, and the reality of her betrayal nearly took her breath away.

"No," she whispered, then said it again, louder. "No!"

"Negative response received," chirped the tablet. "Please confirm negative response by repeating—"

"I said NO!"

She held the tablet close to her face, watched as a red light flashed and the treacherous writing faded away.

"Confirmation cancelled," said the voice.

She swallowed hard and slipped the tablet into her handbag. Obviously her father would find out sooner or later. But she would still have to go to the execution, no matter what.

Of course the entire city would be there too—curious and righteous, parents and kids, reporters and high officials. She waved her hand in the direction of the media image in her room, hovering just over her bed, and the sound came back on.

"And for the first time in recent memory," said the reporter, standing with the Temple behind him, "elders have decided this execution will be carried out with a star chamber. For more on that, let's go to Andor Swat in the plaza. Andor?"

The report switched to a science editor, who explained with graphics and simulations all the awful details about how the chamber worked, starting with the orbiting mirrors that would focus deadly rays from the Trion down to a single point on Corista's surface, and then straight at the victim's heart.

Mentor's Jesmet's heart.

"Oh, Maker!" Oriannon had to look away; even the media report was enough to bring tears to her eyes all over again. Especially since she knew who would be placed in the path of that deadly ray in just a couple of hours. "Is this really what you want to happen? Why won't you stop this? Why can't you?"

She heard no answer to her prayer. When had she ever? It just didn't happen that way here in Corista. Not the way it did on Shadowside, where Wist and the other Owlings seemed to hear from the Maker every day.

Today it would have been nice if the Maker could have visited Corista, just this once. Nice if he would say something to her, just a word or two. Even nicer if her father and the rest of the Assembly would also hear from the Maker—who couldn't possibly want someone executed who had never done anything wrong. Crossed the line back into Corista? Jesmet had only done it for *her!* She looked down to see her fingernails dug into the palms of her hands, not sure how she could live with the guilt of knowing someone was going to die—and it was all her fault.

"It's not fair!" She pounded her pillow and wiped the back of her hand across her tears with a sniff. But though a large part of her still just wanted to throw up at the thought of what they were going to do to Mentor Jesmet, perhaps in another way she did want to be there at the end. Maybe just to say good-bye to Mentor Jesmet, from a distance. It would be unbearable, of course, if she had to see him up close. But from a distance, maybe. And so she swallowed hard, sat up once again, and slipped her feet into shoes.

Her father would be waiting.

35

"This will all be over in a few minutes," whispered Oriannon's father as they waded into the crowd and stepped down the main aisle. "Just hold on to my hand."

She shook her head slightly and slipped her clammy hands behind her back. So her father walked several steps ahead, leading them to a pair of reserved seats. With only a quick glance she lowered herself into her place, slumped, and tried to pretend she was somewhere else—instead of at the Coristan pavilion with a front row seat to witness the execution of Mentor Jesmet.

She also tried to pretend a dozen cameras weren't pointed straight at her, ready to capture every muscle twitch, anything that might be worth playing on the day's news. Margus caught her eye from about ten seats over. She rubbed her forehead and went back to studying her shoes.

A few moments later she noticed her father trying to make out the necklace she wore, partially revealed above her collar. She wished she had remembered to take off her Trion necklace, since it now threatened to expose her for the fraud and hypocrite she really was. Her father gave her a questioning look before she managed to stuff it back out of sight. At a moment like this he would probably not care to know where it came from.

"We're filled to capacity here in the pavilion," she heard a reporter tell a camera, "at a place normally filled with music or the voices of fine actors. This time is very different."

The reporter got *that* right. Every seat in the pavilion appeared spoken for, filling its deep, natural bowl in the hillside. Behind them, after twenty-five or thirty rows, the half rings of seating graduated to a grassy hillside where families usually spread out picnics on blankets. Today they simply covered the lawn, sitting nearly elbow-to-elbow.

Above them a blue canvas sunshade cut out the worst of the bright sunshine, except in the very middle—where a rounded stage again opened to the sun. A team of dark-suited securities sweated as they secured the ancient star chamber to the raised stage with anchor lines.

The chamber itself was nothing fancy or high-tech. Actually just the opposite—a simple crystalline ball with a mirrored floor and a small door in the side, barely large enough for a man—in this case, Mentor Jesmet—to squeeze through. It reminded Oriannon of an ancient space capsule, the kind she had only seen in the Seramine Museum of Interplanetary History. Brave Coristan explorers used them on voyages to the other moons generations ago. This, however, would be an entirely different kind of voyage.

Oriannon shivered at the morbid thought. This star chamber looked too festive, really, to do what it had been designed to do hundreds of years ago. Today if they really wanted to kill someone, she thought, they surely could have found a better way with a lot less fuss. And certainly not here in front of everyone, complete with news cameras and commentators. What was wrong with them? What was wrong with her?

I'm the one to blame, she reminded herself, looking down at her arm, touching the places where there should have been scars. *I'm the one who caused all this.*

Each time she repeated the words they dug more deeply than the last.

But this was what the elders had ordered for Mentor Jesmet, the lawbreaker, the faithbreaker. And what could she do but obey?

Obey. Obey the elders and report to the pavilion as a witness. Obey her father and sign the statement, betray Jesmet with her thumbprint. Here there was nothing but obey, even for Mentor Jesmet. But today the word tasted bitter, many times bitter, on her tongue.

Obey.

Oriannon's father sat silently, staring straight ahead. It might have been nice to be able to understand the look on his face. He didn't even move when musicians started to play the familiar Coristan "Song of Freedom" from the orchestra pit just below the stage.

Oriannon felt her fingers move in time to the music, one of the songs they'd learned to play in Level Two music class, when most of the kids hardly knew how to hold their instruments. And she thought it rather amazing that they hadn't tried to force the Ossek Prep Academy Orchestra to play it. Now *that* would have been ironic.

And the song of freedom stirs our hearts . . .

She could not stand to put her voice to the words, only moved her mouth. She knew they would probably burn her tongue if she dared.

But they stood now for the chorus, everyone from the front row and on back to the grassy hillside, ten thousand Coristans here at the pavilion, the rest glued to their media screens in homes and restaurants, schools and workplaces all over Corista. People who would only know Mentor Jesmet as a sensationalized news report over the past several days, nothing more.

"Such singing!" boomed one reporter, and Oriannon could hear his voice even over the singing. "It's enough to send goose bumps up my spine."

For the man being led up on stage, however, Oriannon guessed the music would probably call forth an entirely different reaction. And now as they finished the last verse and sat, she couldn't stop the tears from tracking once more down her cheeks. At the same time she couldn't stop wishing she'd locked her door or hidden under the covers.

"I'm sorry, Ori." Her father leaned over and whispered in her ear. "I wish you didn't have to see this."

She looked over at him for a moment and believed him, wishing there was some way she could take back the pain she had caused him, as well.

"I know, Daddy."

A swarm of ugly drones now hovered over the stage; Oriannon hadn't noticed where they'd come from, or when. Security? Who would try to stop this? Obviously not Jesmet himself. Dressed in his now-ragged mentor's robe, he let three securities lead him up a small flight of stairs to the middle of the blue carpeted platform, toward the star chamber. A stair caught his foot and he almost stumbled, but they held him up. One of them opened the clear glass door and waited for a moment while Jesmet turned to the crowd. The music faded for a moment, then stopped with a little squawk of a horn.

"I'm allowed a word," he told them. It wasn't a question. They knew the protocol, though it hadn't been used in generations. And the protocol said prisoners about to die would be allowed a final word. So it is written, so shall it be.

Oriannon could see her father tense, sitting up a little straighter. The drones lowered a little more and several shot out red scans, bathing the prisoner in an eerie glow. But who could go against protocol? From where he sat off to the side, the Regent raised his hand, palm-up, and gave a little swirling signal for Jesmet to go ahead.

Now everything stopped completely; everything fell silent. Jesmet turned his head slowly, so all could see him. When his gaze reached Oriannon's, he seemed to pause—though she thought she might have imagined it. She did not imagine the little nod of his head though. She glanced over at Margus, six or eight seats away, seated in a place reserved for dignitaries, elders, and betrayers. Margus looked death-white in the face, the way Oriannon felt.

Do you know what I almost did? She swallowed back the bitter confession. Maybe her father had been right. What difference did it make now? No one could stop what was happening. Better to not be dragged down with a condemned man. Better not to be sucked into this deadly whirlpool.

Better? She knew she was lying to herself.

She was pretty sure they wouldn't allow Jesmet to deliver a long speech, just a few words, if that. She didn't realize how few, as they waited in ear-pounding silence for him to speak.

"I forgive you." His voice echoed over their heads, all the way across the pavilion, all across Seramine, all across Corista. Had he really said what she thought he'd said?

"Do you hear me?" He paused again as they all leaned forward in their seats. Who could help it? "I forgive you!"

And that was it. The echo of his words came back to hit them right between the eyes. A baby cried in the back row but no one said anything. Who could? Finally the securities grabbed his arms and forced him through the door of the star chamber. They needn't have been so rough since he put up no resistance. Still, one of them shoved him from behind for good measure, slammed the door, and touched a button to secure it shut. They heard the suction of an air lock before the security was finally satisfied and stepped back. He looked over his shoulder at the lineup of elders, waited for the signal, and nodded back.

Inside, they could see Jesmet plainly through the chamber's clear walls. His lips moved just a little, as if he was speaking with someone, as the securities backed away several steps and ducked behind a small shield. And now his eyes found Oriannon again, and she wished with everything in her that she could look away. Her father rested his hand on hers as if to protect her, since he did not quite know what to expect, either. And she tensed her shoulders as three beams of impossibly bright light came to rest on the top of the star chamber, directed to the surface of the planet precisely, directly from the mirror satellites so many kilometers above their heads.

This part she could not watch. With eyes tightly shut all she could remember was the time she was a little girl, playing outside with a toy magnifying glass, and what she had done to a small beetle. If only she was still playing now!

But now she could not close her ears to the sound of the star chamber, the squeal of super-heated air escaping from safety vents, the horrible gasp as people around her realized what was actually taking place. What had they expected? A school drama? A single person clapped, then stopped short when the ground beneath them began to shake. Even without looking Oriannon knew everyone else had been shocked into silence at the raw barbarity of this spectacle. An earthquake, however, would not be part of the official agenda.

A woman behind them screamed, but as it turned out she needn't have panicked. Their seats shook beneath them, and the sunshade swayed above their heads. Even the star chamber rolled about a little on the stage, held fast by its restraints. But unlike some of the other tremblers Oriannon had felt on Shadowside, this one quickly passed.

And when her father's grip on her hand finally loosened, Oriannon got up the nerve to take a breath, open the slits of her eyes, and look around. The robed man sitting next to her father wore a tight mask of grim pleasure as if he hadn't even noticed the quake.

In contrast, the woman next to him gripped her face with both hands, her eyes wide and her face completely stiff. She had obviously seen more than she'd bargained for. An older woman got up from her seat, blowing her nose in a handkerchief, and hurried off, while the reporter closest to Oriannon pressed his lips together and looked as if he would be ill.

"Just a minute," he muttered to the cameraman. "Please. Just give me a minute."

Moments later the reporter swallowed hard before looking into the camera and nodding twice. Oriannon thought she knew the feeling. The camera's red light flickered on.

"We have just witnessed a historic event for the people of Corista," the reporter told his camera. Oriannon's eyes followed as it slowly panned across the crowd. "The execution of former music mentor Jesmet ban Saius, convicted of violating the terms of his banishment and returning from Shadowside, and ..."

Oriannon knew she had to see, maybe just once, as the camera moved in a slow arc toward the platform and the reporter went on with her story.

" ... And whose body they now remove from the ancient star chamber, unused for a generation. Except for a small earthquake, which we just felt, it appears all went as planned as a high-intensity reflection from the Trion was directed through a concert of low-level reflecting satellites straight to the chamber, heating it for just one point five seconds, hot enough to instantly take the life of the condemned while leaving his body intact."

Oriannon shivered, not wanting to imagine what had just been described.

"However," the reporter continued, "it does appear that dozens of probes have also been affected by the event, and were somehow either disabled by the sudden blast or by the earthquake, which measured a five point two. We're streaming instant reports, and officials are already saying ..."

Never mind what officials were saying. Oriannon could only glance back at the stage for a second, as securities stepped over disabled probes and carried away what was left of Jesmet's body. And never mind who saw or who cared. Oriannon could only bury her face in her hands and weep.

At the same time, she knew there was one more thing left for her, one thing Jesmet would have wanted her to do—if there was still time.

3·6

What did your dad say?" Margus braced his legs for balance as the ground shook once more. Oriannon had lost count of all the earthquakes in the three hours since the execution. Ten? Twelve?

"Another emergency meeting of the Assembly," she replied, looking around at the bustling spaceport. "He ran off when they told him the Temple was damaged in the first quake. But listen, are you sure you want to do this?"

"I have to." He glared at her. "You know how much I owe Jesmet."

"You're not the only one. Here, let me see your pass."

Still he paused, and she pointed at him.

"Better chance of me getting in than you, right?"

Beyond the fence another alarm sounded, and workers in orange coveralls scurried around dozens of stainless metal-sided spaceport hangars, lined up in neat rows. Transport pods taxied from the two nearest hangars, rising and taking off almost immediately.

But first things first. Oriannon took the entry pass and waved it in front of a reader by the chain-link gate.

"Hightower of Nyssa, Oriannon," she spoke to the reader, reciting her ID number. She held her breath, hoping there wouldn't be a problem with Margus's father's pass and her ID. One could hope.

"See?" Margus kicked at the gate when nothing happened. "I should have—"

A buzzer sounded as the gate slid aside. They looked at each other, and she wasn't sure if it was her clearance or his kick. But without delay they stepped through and into the spaceport chaos.

"Okay, then." He took his pass back and nodded toward a building marked C–33. "This way."

So they hurried across the tarmac, avoiding workers and weaving their way around shuttles and cargo ships, coming and going in a confusion of takeoffs and landings.

"Which one?" she asked again, and he pointed at one of the hangar's large open doors.

"In there. Nobody will care if we borrow one of the maintenance pods."

Oriannon paused. "Maintenance?"

"The ones my dad is working on. He takes them out for test runs all the time."

"We just better hope nothing is wrong with it."

"Hold on." He cut her off as he flagged down someone he knew running by.

"Arl!" cried Margus, and the worker slowed down but didn't stop. "What's up?"

Arl shrugged.

"Level Orange Security drill. You didn't hear? Somebody stole that mentor guy's body, and now we're supposed to make sure nobody gets away with it."

"That mentor guy?"

"You know, the mentor they just put to death in the star chamber. Where have you been?"

Oriannon winced at the memory, but Margus didn't seem to let it bother him.

"We're still okay taking one of my dad's projects up, aren't we?"

"I wouldn't. It's pretty crazy right now." The worker paused and looked around at the busy spaceport, then nodded at three long-range shuttles. Workers ran about the craft with tools and charging cables while teams of black-suited securities climbed aboard.

"Where are they going?" asked Oriannon, but Arl shook his head.

"That's what I'm talking about," he told them. "Up to you, but you really ought to stay out of their way. I hear they're headed to Shadowside — don't ask why."

A chill ran up the back of Oriannon's neck as Arl hurried off. And she tried not to run across the huge indoor hangar area filled with two-seater pods, mid-sized shuttles, and full-sized silver transports. A pudgy lunar shuttle touched down with a bump and taxied their way.

"That one." Margus pointed at an even smaller two-seat pod, not unlike the one they'd flown before. This one, however, looked a little more charred around the edges — as if it had seen too many hot re-entries into the Coristan atmosphere, or flown a bit too close to one of the Trion. Oriannon held back a moment before climbing up into the cockpit.

"You're sure it flies?"

"Guess we'll find out." Margus pushed away a pile of tools and spare parts from the cracked leather pilot's seat.

Oriannon guessed she didn't have much choice if she wanted to get back to Shadowside. She strapped herself in as Margus pulled down the view bubble and fired up the engines.

"Hmm," he said, rapping on the dashboard with his knuckles. "Looks as if we may have a short. Nothing serious, though."

"Oh, great," she moaned. "You don't think we should try something else?"

But Margus wasn't listening as they skipped ahead, maneuvering around an incoming freighter and into the clear. The engines whined, then made an odd whirring noise, then whined again.

"Hang on." When had she heard him say that before?

For a moment nothing happened except the whirring and whining, while Oriannon felt her teeth chatter as the whole pod shook with effort. Margus dialed in a course and pushed the joystick forward, then pulled it back and tried again.

"Come on—"

At that the engines dutifully kicked in, Oriannon's head hit the back of the seat, and they left Spaceport Corista in a blur behind them.

"Here we go!" Margus whooped. Oriannon could hardly move her eyeballs to the side and the stars she saw dancing weren't outside. So she closed her eyes, letting the minutes and the kilometers pass by.

"You know the way," she finally asked after they'd cleared most of the spaceport traffic. "Don't you?"

"I thought you were asleep. But yeah, of course I know the way. See, we're here."

When she opened her eyes he pointed at the green 3-D readout, a small revolving globe with grids that would show their position.

"That's us?" she asked him, and he nodded.

"We're in the middle of the screen. The yellow dot there at the top is your cliff city."

She nodded, then watched out the window to find the line on the planet where Shadowside began. Had they really walked all that way?

"I wasn't sure we'd get back so soon," she whispered.

"Mm-hmm." Her friend's face had turned green, but only from the nav-screen, and they continued on in silence. He seemed to be chewing on his lip, trying to say something.

"You okay?" she finally asked. She should have known better than to ask. He shook his head no.

"Not really. I have to tell you one more thing. Promise you won't hate me."

"More than I already do?"

She waited for him to say something else, not sure how to react. Finally he swallowed hard and went on.

"I told you what happened after you went to Shadowside."

"Right."

"But there was something else, before that."

"What do you mean, 'something else'?"

"I mean …" He sighed, his lip quivering slightly. "I mean I didn't just let you down, Ori. I betrayed him too."

Him, of course, would be Jesmet. But that didn't make sense.

"I don't understand. You were always following him around back in Corista. You were so gung-ho."

"But how do you think the Assembly caught up to him so quick at that concert? Remember that?"

She did. The time when Margus told her to leave before anything bad happened. The time when securities seemed to come out of nowhere, as if they'd practiced it all. She felt the pit of her stomach turn as the pieces finally started to fall into place.

"Who do you think made it happen that way?" he asked, looking over at her with tears brimming in his eyes. "Who do you think fed them the information, told them exactly when Jesmet was going to be there?"

"You?" Her eyes widened as it finally all made sense, though in another way it made no sense at all. "Why?"

315

"They had me convinced I was doing the right thing, the moral thing. They even told me they'd wipe my school record clean if I helped. I know that sounds lame."

Now she could have strangled him all over again, and she held her arms at her sides so she wouldn't — until she remembered again that she was just as much to blame as anyone else. Just as much as Margus.

"But why did they need your help?" she wondered. "They could have found him without you, couldn't they?"

He shrugged.

"I guess I made it a little easier. I told them about what happened when Brinnin fell off her ladder too."

Oriannon groaned. So that's how they found out. Now it made even more sense.

"I know they grabbed all your memories, Ori, but I was confused too. I thought it was a fine idea for a while."

"What made you change your mind? Or was that just an act too?"

"No! They told me he was just going to be fired, not sent off to Shadowside. They lied to me. They always lied to me. That's why I went ballistic after the trial. I tried to make it right, but by that time it was too late." He rested his head against the controls. "Maybe that's why I had to come find you."

"Like you'd even the score?" She shook her head.

"Maybe. But even after the trial, I was into it so deep, and then I thought I had no choice that I had to keep going along with them to get you back. And I guess you know the rest of the story."

She did. But now she understood.

"Is there anything else?" she asked, as if anything else could make it worse. He shook his head.

"That's the last of it. I know I said it before, but I'm sorry."

She thought of Jesmet's words as they were about to execute him.

"So am I," she replied with a sigh of exhaustion. But as they flew on, somehow she could not blame Margus any longer for this mess. And a blinking light caught her eye.

"What are those things there?" She pointed to the bottom of the screen, barely visible, at three red blips in formation. She wasn't sure she wanted to know.

"Uh-oh. I was hoping they wouldn't take off so soon."

Neither of them said anything for the next few minutes as the blips grew larger. Finally Margus cleared his throat.

"You know what's happening here, Oriannon."

"I know."

"So are you sure you want to get caught in the middle of this war zone?" he wondered aloud, and his voice seemed to shake a little. "You know where they're going, and what they're going for."

She nodded grimly. "Just so we get there ahead of them."

And then what? Margus tapped another screen, moving his finger across the glass as numbers appeared in front of them.

"I think we will." He frowned and double-checked. "As long as we can keep up this speed, and—"

The screen flickered once, twice . . . and then the entire control panel went dark. Oriannon gasped at the sudden change as they flew ahead blindly.

"Please tell me you meant to do that," she squeaked.

"I wish." He pounded the top of the panel, just below the plexi view shield. It flickered once, barely, then made a very unfriendly popping noise.

"Something's burning, Margus!" Oriannon nearly choked when she sniffed the air inside their pod. A raspy-sounding warning buzzed incessantly. "What do you want me to do?"

"Hang tight, that's all." Margus worked his control stick from side to side, frantically pushing buttons that didn't seem to respond. Oriannon stiffened and gripped the sides of her seat. "And pray."

He'd never asked her to do that before.

"Please don't let us crash," she repeated over and over, hoping the Maker would take it for a prayer. "Please don't let us—"

"I can't see a thing!" Desperation slipped into his voice, while her eardrums popped twice as they descended even more quickly. They would have to level out. And in spite of everything, she thought of the planet below—and their long walk.

"Margus," she asked, "when you were blind before, down there, what did you do?" Now the engines sounded the way they did before take-off, making that peculiar whirring and whining sound.

"Not sure what you mean." He wrestled the control stick.

"I mean, how did you make it home, not being able to see?"

"Oh." He paused for only a second. "I had to trust someone else I guess."

"Exactly." She nodded and held on, praying harder than ever as the engines raced, choked—and finally cut out completely. In an instant all the desperate noises and warning buzzers were replaced by an eerie silence and whistling wind.

"Uh-oh," Margus whispered under his breath.

Powerless now, the pod lurched downward again and Oriannon felt her stomach rise to her throat, saw the dark surface of the planet rise up at them. Up ahead and below she thought she saw a flicker, a glow—but that could have been anything.

"We're on approach," Margus told her, wrestling the control stick. "Getting pretty close. I'm going to head for that light, and hope—trust—that it's your friends."

Oriannon reached out to brace herself as they lurched and twisted through a small patch of clouds. The pod made a poor glider. Breaking through, however, she saw clearly what she'd hoped for: A dim collection of lights, glittering in the twilight.

"There!" She pointed.

"I see it, I see it." Margus stabbed wildly at a control in front of him as the dark ground rushed up at them. "Hang on—"

The bump knocked Oriannon's teeth together, clipping the tip of her tongue. A piece of the pod's outer skin sounded as if it peeled away, and she felt a rush of icy air pull at her feet. But Margus didn't let go of the controls, and she didn't let go of her knees as they bumped again and again, until they finally ground to a stop in a bed of gravel and rocks. They sat still for a moment, waiting, listening to the quiet.

Alive.

"There, what did I tell you?" In light of the circumstances Margus sounded a little too pleased with himself, but she would not be complaining. "Pretty good landing without instruments and without power if I do say so myself."

"Not bad."

"Not bad?" Margus popped the plexi top open to let a full blast of cold Shadowside air hit them in the face. This time it drove a cold, needling rain as well. "I bring us down totally blind from ten thousand meters, dead as a brick, and all you can say is, 'not bad?'"

But she could think of nothing else to tell him as she hopped out onto solid ground, already shivering and wet. It didn't matter that she had not brought a coat. She just shaded her eyes from the blowing rain and looked around to see how close they'd come.

Because if they weren't close, nothing mattered.

3·7

Here we go again." Margus groaned as they clambered over a rain-slicked rock. "I'll bet that snake-worm thing is going to—"

"Shh!" Oriannon helped him to the top of the sand hill and craned her neck. "There! See it?"

"I don't see any ... oh!" He clapped her on the back. "Any closer and we would have crashed right into the city, huh? I told you!"

For once Margus had a point. But right now all she could do was run ahead to the base of the cliff, slogging through puddles and mud.

"How long before those three other ships get here?" she asked over her shoulder.

"At the rate they were going? I'm guessing fifteen minutes. Maybe less."

Which didn't give them much time, hardly enough to climb the stairway to the city. She hurried up to the first landing, only to have a young Owling jump out of the shadows to block their way.

"No farther!" The husky boy hoisted an ironwood spear, pointing it at her chin. "Who are you and what are you wanting here?"

"Oh!" Oriannon stopped short, put up her hand. "Listen, I'm a friend of Suuli and Wist, and I have to see them right away. It's a matter of life and death!"

"Suuli's dead." The young guard growled.

"I know. I only meant that—"

"And how do I know you're not part of another attack?"

"You don't. But I was here before, when Jesmet—"

"You know Jesmet?"

"Of course I know Jesmet. He is—he was my mentor. Now, please." She stepped forward, pointed the end of the spear away and down. "There's an attack coming any minute, and I've got to get up there and warn people right now."

The guard hesitated long enough for Margus to step around and hold him back.

"Let her go," Margus demanded. "She's telling you the truth. Go, Oriannon! I'll take care of him."

By this time Oriannon wasn't waiting for the boy's permission, just leaped past him and up the stairs. And now she would have to take them two or three at a time. She did hear an alarm bell ringing from below, and as soon as she made it halfway she added her shouts to the noise.

"Wist!" she yelled, hoping someone would hear her. "Wist!"

No answer. But the bell below kept ringing, and as Oriannon climbed on she noticed curious faces peering down at her from the railing above.

322

"Get away from there!" she shouted, but they didn't seem to understand. So when she finally mounted the top of the stairway she stumbled toward them.

"You've ..." she gasped. "You've got to get out of here! Hide!"

They only stared at her and backed away, and of course Oriannon couldn't blame them for thinking her crazy. But as she stood at the edge of the main plaza, chest heaving, she heard a gradually increasing hum behind her, then felt a rush of air and mist that stood her hair on end.

They're here, she thought. *It's too late!*

And she turned to see three fully loaded Security shuttles drop out of the gray clouds before coming to a close hover over the pipeline below.

"See what I'm talking about?" Oriannon shouted as she ran up to a man and his wife. Didn't they know danger when they saw it? Hadn't they figured it out from the past attack? Despite the rain the woman held a baby in her arms, and looked back with wide-eyed surprise when Oriannon tugged on their arms and tried to pull them back from the edge.

"Not to worry," said the man, holding on to the railing. "This kind of thing happens all the time."

"Not like this it doesn't. They're—"

"They're just breaking up the logjam." He pointed as if she didn't understand, as if she was a friendly alien who didn't know their language. Didn't any of them recognize her? "We'll be going back down in a little while and plug it all up again."

"No!" Oriannon trembled as she turned to the others. "It's not a game! Not this time. Please listen to me! They're going to wipe out Lior, the whole city. You've got to hide! Now!"

But still they all just stared at her, then moved to the railing as if trying to decide. Oriannon didn't even need to look; she could already hear the hum grow louder and feel static crawling on her skin as the shuttles rose into position.

"Why are they coming up here?" wondered a little Owling boy. Without warning he picked up a fist-sized rock and heaved it over the side. "I'll stop them!"

"No, dear!" His mother grabbed his arm, too late. The rock clattered harmlessly down the side of the cliff. And now Oriannon pulled on the woman's hand.

"Please, I'm just telling you what I know. Go to the buildings next to the cliff instead of those hanging out here. Maybe they're safer. I'm begging you, please go before it's too late."

Perhaps it already was. The parents in the group looked at each other, and a little girl started to cry.

"Please!" Oriannon repeated. "I'm a friend of Wist's. I'm trying to save your lives!"

By that time she knew it certainly had to be too late. Wist and Becket came rushing into the little plaza from one side, while the three Coristan ships rose higher along the cliff to hover only a few hundred meters away. Their blue lights blinked and glittered off titanium skin, painted with the blue and white tri-star markings of Coristan Security.

"Oriannon!" yelled Wist, and her face showed that she understood the danger. How could she not? "You came back!"

Wist reached out a hand while Becket held her back and the three ships maneuvered much closer, deadly silent except for their humming. Without delay, ugly black disruptor tubes disengaged from the front with a whine of hydraulics—and aimed straight at them.

But then Oriannon heard another voice, much lower than Wist's—and much clearer.

"The rock, Oriannon."

She slipped her hand up to her ear, just to be sure the earbud wasn't still somehow in place. Of course it wasn't. And in any case, the voice did not belong to Margus. She glanced around the plaza to see who had called her name. A dozen Owlings all stood like statues, as if hypnotized by a yagwar. And again the voice called her name.

"Pick up the rock, Oriannon! Throw it!"

Puzzled, she shook her head. But she knew the voice, and this time she knew how to obey—no matter how strange it seemed, no matter how much it seemed like a story from the Codex. Pick up the rock? She reached over to pluck a good-sized stone from the little boy's hand, and he didn't resist.

"Now, Ori. Throw it now!"

This time she could not ignore Jesmet's strong voice, even if she was just imagining it. And it *was* his voice. It could be no other. So she backed up a couple of steps and wound up, then let fly so hard the rock might have taken her arm with it.

And as they watched, the rock made a perfect arc and landed with a satisfying *plink* directly on the nearest shuttle's nose, bounced once, and tumbled out of sight.

Instantly a translucent blue force field appeared as a thin cloud around the ship, shimmering with energy. And now Oriannon knew what to do. She stood at the railing, waving her arms, jumping, shouting. Anything to get their attention, including throwing rocks. Now it didn't matter — because whatever they might do to her, they would do even worse to the Owlings.

"OVER HERE!" she screamed at the top of her lungs. If they were going to take down Lior, city of the Owlings, they would have to do it with her standing right here in front of the whole disaster. And they would have to know it was her. "Look over here, you idiots!"

For good measure she scooped up another rock and let fly again. Of course this time it fizzled in a cloud of sparks off the edge of the force field, far short of the three hovering craft. She could still wave and shout, though — even as she heard the peculiar high-pitched whine of disruptor tubes charging. Any second now, the tubes would fire, blowing away anything in their sights.

"It's me!" she screamed, tears now running down her cheeks, mixing with the rain. "Oriannon Hightower of Nyssa!"

Her shouts echoed off the side of the cliff city, yet she had no idea if anyone in the ship would hear her. "My father is an elder on the Assembly. Are you going to kill an elder's daughter? His name is Tavlin Hightower. What else do you need to know? Do you want my ID number?"

Sobbing with emotion, she scrambled to the top of the rock wall, held her arms out to both sides and took a deep breath. Because now she knew:

This was why I came here. To stop this attack, or die trying.

Still the disruptors whined, louder and louder, and she knew she had only seconds to breathe. Wist and the others there in the plaza fell to their knees with their hands covering their ears. Oriannon stood fast and shook her fists.

"And if you destroy this city, I go with it!" Her voice cracked with the strain. "How do you want to explain that to my father? DO YOU HEAR ME?"

Did they hear her? She held her breath, teetered on the top of the wall, hardly noticing small hands gripping her ankles. A long moment later the whining slowed, and the disrupter tubes pulled back slowly, while a probe released from a small hatch on the ship's underside. Still she didn't move, just grit her teeth as the probe flew up to her and scanned her eyes with its obnoxious red beam.

"State your name," it demanded.

"I told you. Oriannon Hightower." She parked her hands on her hips, spit the words out in a challenge. Better to give it the full pedigree than just her first name. "Oriannon Hightower of Nyssa."

The probe paused for a moment until it flashed its green light. It could tell who she was. And now everyone in the shuttles would know as well.

"You will board the Coristan Security vessel immediately," barked the probe.

But Oriannon shook her head.

"Not a chance. I'm not moving from this spot."

She didn't dare look down, but ducked when the probe flew straight at her head without warning. Pebbles worked loose from the wall and tumbled hundreds of meters down, far down to the pipeline. She slipped a half-step backward, and then she was waving for balance, losing it, and tumbling backward.

"Oriannon!"

Falling, she heard her name once more. But this time she tumbled into the arms of . . . Wist!

This time they both nearly fell to the wet paving stones, but managed to stay on their feet. Dear Wist!

"What are you doing?" asked Wist, wrapping her arms around Oriannon in a hug. "What's going on?"

"Immediately!" the probe repeated, buzzing by their heads once more like an angry bird of prey. "You will board ..."

Twanng!

Before she could flinch, a thousand pieces of smoking probe showered across the little plaza, sending Oriannon, Wist, and the other Owlings scurrying in all directions. Had the attack begun? Shards of shattered microchips spiked her in the back of the neck as she dove for cover behind a bench.

"I've always wanted to do that." Margus slipped in next to them with a shadow of a grin on his face. He gripped a gnarly spear in his hand, obviously his weapon of choice, borrowed from the guard at the foot of the cliff.

"Margus!" cried Oriannon. "Where did you come from?"

He nodded toward the top of the stairway a few meters away.

"Same as you. Took me a little longer to climb up, though. That's the longest bunch of stairs."

"Are you out of your mind?" She didn't need to ask what had happened to their guard; the boy came stumbling up to the plaza just then. Oriannon glanced back over the top of the bench to see if the ship had sent out any more probes.

"I was going to ask you the same thing," he answered back. "Did you really think they would call off the attack just because of you?"

"It's not over yet." She took his hand as he helped her up, only to tumble back down again as the earth jolted and shook as never before.

3·8

Oriannon rose slowly to her feet when the earthquake had finally played itself out a minute later—one minute that had seemed like one hour. She held out her hands for balance, just in case, looking around at the damage.

"We're still here," croaked Wist, pulling herself up as well. Just like everyone else, she wore the same wide-eyed expression that told the world she was glad to be alive—but perhaps a little surprised that she still was.

Even more surprising was the fact that their cliffside city still hung on. Bruised and battered, yes, as it had been after previous quakes. Several more cracks had appeared in the plaza, while loose stones littered the narrow lanes. But like its Owling people, Lior seemed just too stubborn to let go.

Yet the thing Oriannon now noticed most was a strange, almost eerie quiet—and it hit her in the eardrums with almost as much force as had all the noise.

No more rumble of earthquake, only the soft crumbling of gravel, tripping down the hillside, and a distant baby squalling his or her little lungs out.

No more drizzle of rain, rare as it had been, only the dripping of water from rooftops.

No more whine of disruptor beams, threatening to take down what the earthquake could not.

No more hum of the three Coristan ships, hovering like dragonflies.

"They're gone, Oriannon." Wist announced the obvious as they rose from their knees. "You did it! They've gone!"

Oriannon glanced over to see Margus's reaction, and she guessed he might be thinking the same thing. Maybe the Coristan ships could have retreated to hide around the side of the mountain.

Why? Oriannon couldn't be sure. However, Wist was right about one thing: The three ships had turned and disappeared, quickly enough and in the middle of the earthquake so that no one had noticed exactly how or when.

Gone, gone, gone! Never mind the terrifying shake-up. Wist began dancing, grabbing Margus by the hands and skipping in circles. She giggled like a little girl as they spun, skipping and singing a tune Oriannon had never heard before. They still lived and breathed, the Maker be praised! To Wist and the others, that was enough to celebrate.

But Oriannon stepped off to the side, away from the spontaneous party—because she knew in her heart that Wist was very wrong about something else.

"I didn't do it," she whispered, stepping closer to the edge than she should have. She fingered her Trion necklace just to be sure she still had it. "It was nothing I did."

She had done nothing to turn back the Security shuttles, only stood up on this ledge, and it made her shake now to realize how close she'd come to falling. She looked down at the plaza, followed a crack with her eye, and noticed the shadow lengthening at her feet.

What was this? She stepped a little closer, just to be sure of what she could not be seeing. She shook her head to clear her mind.

But Wist and the others must have noticed as well, since the dancing had suddenly stopped.

They all saw the same thing she saw, out over the rugged beautiful landscape of Shadowside. And silently they watched what had most surely turned the shuttles around. Not the rock-throwing or the shouting, and not the shaking of her fist. None of that had ultimately made any difference.

Together they looked out at a view that no one had ever seen before, as clouds cleared overhead and the sky changed from its usual dark blue ink to azure and then over to the lightest of gold, orange, and pink. The brightest stars that had always watched over Shadowside began to fade. Even the pretty hues of the Southern Lights slipped away, replaced—if it were possible—by an even more awesome spectacle.

Oriannon's mouth dropped open in heart-stopping wonder as she took it all in, watching what she had never experienced, something she was certain she had no words for. Neither did Margus; he had fallen to his knees. Only Wist knew what to say.

"It's dawn," whispered Wist. "It finally came."

And with this dawn came something else that Oriannon did finally recognize—something perhaps the others would not know. She pointed to the horizon.

"The Trion."

Of course the actual Trion resembled neither the necklace nor the stained glass window picture. Yet even Oriannon's necklace seemed now to come alive. It pulsed with life, warmed but didn't burn. Wist held her hand to her chest the same way, and they exchanged glances with a little smile. Oriannon was not the only one here with the same necklace.

At the same time the other Owlings pointed and gasped as they recognized what was happening. More Owlings filtered into the plaza from the city. Now there was no mistaking the triplet suns, rising for the first time in many millennia on this side of the planet, lighting up the sky as Oriannon had seen them do every day of her life — before she had come to Shadowside.

Some greeted the light of the three suns with their hands in the air, as if they'd been waiting for these three suns to rise all their lives. Others watched the plains come alive in blazing red and gold and everything in between. Had it really been so full of color before, but hidden in the twilight of Shadowside? No longer. From somewhere down the cliff she heard a twittering of small birds, singing softly at first, then with growing confidence. A whisper of warm air hit her face, full of the promise this new day delivered. And then she heard the song.

Now everyone froze with awe as Oriannon heard clearly the voice she had heard with her heart only minutes ago. There could be no mistake this time, no ghosts, no imaginings. Only ... how? The Owlings crowded to the railing, looking to see what they must all be hearing.

"Jesmet!" Oriannon and Margus whispered the name at the same time as they saw him approach the base of the cliff. And there was no mistake: He wore the same robe he'd worn to the execution. She could make out the scorch marks.

But the Song removed all doubt as Jesmet's clear, strong voice drifted up to them.

Who else had ever sung that Song, but him? Only now the words made sense, and the Song finally made sense — glorious sense. Oriannon mouthed the words she'd heard once before, adding her harmony as Jesmet sang them aloud.

"In the morning, when all is new ..."

THEOWLING

ROBERT ELMER

1

Oriannon jerked awake, jolted by the shuttle's sudden dive and the high-pitched whine of ion boosters. The unseen hand of several Gs squeezed her squarely back in the padded seat, and she gasped for breath.

Where were they?

Off course, without a doubt, and certainly not heading home. She managed a glance out a tiny side window, though her eyeballs hurt to focus, and her stomach rebelled at the sudden drop. Outside, space appeared cold, dark, and colorless—not the dense, bright violet atmosphere she would have expected to see above irrigated farms and the well-watered surface of Brightside of Corista.

Just across the aisle, her father unstrapped from his grav seat with a grunt, gathered his gold-trimmed ceremonial robe, and struggled down the narrow aisle toward the pilot's compartment. Several passengers screamed as they banked sharply, and the engines whined even more loudly. Oriannon's father seemed to ignore the panic. He put his head down and tumbled the last few feet to the flight deck.

"What's going on here?" Father was always polite, even when he was pounding on doors. "I'd like a word with you, please."

The pilot would have to listen to an Assembly elder, one of the twelve most important men in Corista, aside from the Regent himself. Oriannon's father continued pounding, and Oriannon gripped the handle in front of her as they made another tight turn. Light from the three Trion suns blinded her for a moment as it passed through the window and caught her in the face. When she shaded her eyes, she saw something else, looming large and close.

"Father?" She tried to get his attention over all the noise. "I know where we are."

But he only pounded harder, raising his voice above braking thrusters as they came online. She felt a forward pull as the shuttle engines whined and then seemed to catch. Still they wagged and wobbled, nearly out of control. Outside, a pockmarked asteroid loomed ever larger, while sunlight glittered off a tinted plexidome built into the surface.

From here the dome didn't seem much larger than Regent Jib Ossek Academy back home, but Oriannon knew it covered what would have been a deep impact crater on the near side of the huge space rock's surface. This was obviously no planet, only a remote way station called Asylum Four—one of twelve ancient Asylum outposts. Why had their shuttle diverted here?

By this time everyone else on the shuttle must have seen the asteroid out their windows as well. Now every viewport on her side was filled with close-ups of the tortured surface, scarred by thousands of hits from space debris and tiny asteroids. But instead of an announcement over the intercom, shuttle passengers were met only with a strange silence from the flight deck.

"I insist that you—" Oriannon's father couldn't finish his demand as he was thrown from his feet by the impact. Oriannon's forehead nearly hit the back of the seat in front of her. A loud squeal of scraping metal outside told everyone they'd made full contact with Asylum Four's docking port.

And then there was only silence, as their engines slowly powered down. Her father rose to his feet, and no one spoke for a long, tense moment. Air rushed through a lock, and they heard the pilot's emergency hatch swing free. Still, the twenty-one passengers could only sit and wait, trapped in their sealed compartment without any word of explanation and without any fresh air. A couple of men rose to their feet and pushed to the front.

"We need to get out of here!" announced one, but Oriannon's father put a stop to it with a raised hand.

"Just be patient," he told them. "I'm certain we'll find out what happened in a moment."

Or two. Several minutes later they heard footsteps and a shuffling before the main hatch finally swept open and they were met with a rush of cool air—and a curious stare.

"Are you people quite all right?" A small man in the rust-colored frock of a scribe looked nearly as confused as Oriannon felt. "Where's your pilot?"

"We were hoping you would tell *us*." Oriannon's father tried to take charge of the chaos that followed, as everyone shouted at once, trying to find answers in a place that only held more questions. Why were they brought here, instead of back to Corista?

"Please!" The scribe held up his hands for silence. He didn't look as if he was used to this much company—or this much shouting—all at once. And just how old was he? Oriannon couldn't be sure, though he appeared as wrinkled as a dried aplon. Wispy white hair circled his ears as if searching for a way inside. Yet his eyes sparkled in an impish, almost pleasant sort of way, and judging by the way his dark eyes darted from side to side, he seemed to miss nothing.

"I'm very sorry for the confusion," he continued, "but all are welcome here at Asylum Way Station Four. As you probably know, it's the tradition of the Asylum outposts to welcome all visitors. Although I must say ..."

He glanced at the hatch beside him, where the trim along the bottom edge had bent and twisted during the rough landing. The ship's skin, though gouged and damaged, appeared not to have been breached. It could have been worse.

" ... Whoever piloted your craft here was either in a very great hurry or perhaps in need of a bit more practice in the art of landing."

No doubt about that. But as her father introduced himself, Oriannon noticed the hatch hydraulics hissing a little too loudly, while an odd thumping sound came from inside the craft's wall, weak but steady.

"I'm Cirrus Main," the scribe went on, bowing slightly to her father. "And we're especially honored to greet a member of the Assembly. I cannot recall the last time we enjoyed a visit from an elder, though I should consult our station archives to be sure. There was a day, several generations ago when—"

"But what about the pilot?" interrupted another passenger, a dark-eyed man a bit younger than Oriannon's father. "Didn't you see him? We didn't fly here ourselves, you know."

The scribe seemed taken aback by the man's rudeness, blinking in surprise.

"Please pardon my lack of an immediate answer for you," he replied, holding his fingertips together and his lips tight. "Most of us were otherwise occupied in the library when this incident occurred. However, in time I will inquire as to whether your pilot was seen disembarking and attempt to discern his or her disposition."

"The pilot will answer to the Assembly," replied Oriannon's father. "We were returning from a diplomatic mission to the Owling capital, on our way back to Seramine. We should never have been brought here."

"Ah, but do not all things work for good to those who are called according to ..." The scribe forced a shy smile, opened his mouth to say something else, and then seemed to change his mind.

"But never mind. Our protocols here on Asylum Four require us to offer sanctuary to all, you see, no matter the circumstances."

"Sanctuary?" barked the dark-eyed man. "We need some answers, and you're—"

"As I said." The scribe raised his hand for peace. "We simply cannot say who brought you here other than the Maker himself. However, we are quite pleased it appears you're all unharmed."

Yes, they were. But then the shouting started all over again, most of it to do with who was to blame for this unscheduled stop, who was going to be late for their appointments, and how soon they'd be able to get home. Finally, their host had to raise his hand once more.

"Please let me assure you that despite the apparent confusion of the moment, we will make every effort to make your stay as comfortable as possible, so that you may return to Seramine in due course. In the meantime, I trust you'll agree to observe our protocol."

"Remain silent before the Codex." Oriannon quoted an ancient commentary. "And at peace before all."

"Who said that?" Cirrus Main searched the crowd with a curious expression. Oriannon shrank behind another passenger so he wouldn't see her.

"My daughter is an eidich," explained Oriannon's father, taking his place at the front of the little crowd. "Oriannon remembers everything she reads in the ancient book. Every word."

That was true most of the time, with certain annoying exceptions over the past several months that no one needed to know about.

"I'm familiar with eidichs," answered the scribe, raising his eyebrows at Oriannon. She couldn't really hide. "Although there were once many more than there are today. In fact, when I first came from Asylum Seven, years ago, we knew of several ..."

His voice trailed off as he seemed to put aside the memory with a sad shake of his head.

"I'm sorry." His face reddened. "You didn't come here to hear an old man's stories. But perhaps you'll find clarity here. That is, after all, the purpose for which this outpost was created. So if you'll follow me, I would be most pleased to show you the facilities."

"We do appreciate your hospitality," said Oriannon's father, looking around at the group. "But we can only stay a short time, until we get another pilot and the shuttle is prepared to return."

Oriannon shivered, but not because of the cool, musty air that smelled of far-off worlds, aging dust, and something else she couldn't quite identify. She followed as Cirrus Main led them through narrow hallways blasted out of rough, iron-stained rock. They walked through a network of prefabricated but obviously ancient modules anchored to the surface of the asteroid at three or four levels. A chalky rust tarnished most of the walls. And through viewports, she could see the sheer face of the crater rising up on all sides around them before meeting the umbrella of the plexidome far above. This place had obviously been constructed generations ago. She craned her neck to see hanging gardens and flowing plants cascading from terraces and clinging precariously to crater walls. The scent of cerise and flamboyan joined rivulets coursing over small waterfalls as moisture condensed on the inside of the dome. She found it odd to discover the faint perfume of Coristan flowers at such a remote outpost.

"I suppose it's a bit like living in a greenhouse," their host admitted, ducking past a stream of spray. "It is an environment, however, to which one becomes accustomed."

They paused for a moment to watch a viria bird flitter across the upper expanse inside the dome. Here, under the plexi and against the cold void of space, the freedom of small fluttering wings appeared strangely out of place.

"Remain close behind me, please," he told them. "Our environment is rather fragile, as I'm sure you can appreciate."

By now Oriannon had made her way to the front of the group, where she could hear everything Cirrus Main told them about the water recycling system, the gardens, and the delicate balance of work and study that made their home livable. Here and there other residents quietly tended the gardens, each one dressed in red work coveralls, harvesting fruit and adjusting irrigation controls. None seemed to notice much that this group had been brought here under such strange circumstances, or even that they had been brought here at all. Oriannon saw a young face staring at them from the far end of the dome, but the little girl quickly ducked out of sight behind a humming generator.

"Some of us have families here." Cirrus Main must have noticed the little girl as well. He didn't stop as he led them up a stairway, through a set of noisy airlocks, and finally back into a large, high-ceilinged room where ten or twelve other red-frocked scribes sat at tables, leaning close to each other in animated discussions. Here the polished stone floor contrasted with the worn look of the rest of the station. The dark pluqwood trim and carefully inlaid ceiling of planets and stars in copper and stone suggested a different type of room. Certainly it looked less utilitarian than the rest. Cirrus gestured at a wall filled with shelves.

"Our library." He crossed his arms with obvious satisfaction and lowered his voice as if they had entered a holy place. Oriannon carefully picked up a leather-bound volume from a stack on a nearby stone table. "Mainly theological, but also a bit of the fine arts and some of Corista's finest ancient philosophers — Rainott, Ornix ... You know them?"

Of course she did — at least every word that had ever been digitally transcribed. Oriannon nodded as she riffed through the pages, sensing something entirely different among them. Here the carefully inscribed words came alive in a way that the ones in her ebooks never could. Each page appeared hand printed in a script that flowed carefully across each line with a sort of measured serendipity. Here a real person with hopes and dreams had actually written the words on a page — laboriously, lovingly, one letter at a time. Some of the pages even showed flourishes and highlights, making the book more a work of art than merely a collection of thoughts.

"I've never ..." She held back a sneeze. "... seen so many old books in one place. Back home they're all under glass."

"Like everyone else," he told her, slipping the book from her hands and holding it up for the others to see. "You're accustomed to words in their digital form. Here we study Codex as it was first recorded — in books and on pages, scribed by hand many generations ago in a day when we still had calligraphers among us.

341

They brought us the words from the Maker's heart, straight to the page."

He sighed deeply as a couple of the other passengers stood off at a distance, arms crossed and muttering something about how old books weren't going to help get them off this rock. He smiled again and lovingly smoothed a page before returning the book to its place on the table.

"We seek the Maker in these pages," he said, closing his eyes and rocking back on his heels. He paused as if actually praying. "Sometimes, if we're very quiet, we can hear his whisper."

In the books? Oriannon thought she might hear such a whisper too. She listened to water tinkling from outside and the gentle murmur of scribes discussing their wondrous, ancient volumes. She could have stayed there much longer, except that the quiet was interrupted by hurried footsteps as a younger scribe burst into the room and whispered something obviously urgent in Cirrus Main's ear. The older man's face clouded only a moment before a peaceful calm returned.

"Your pilot seems to have been found," he told them, "locked inside a storage compartment in your shuttle. We have yet no idea how he came to be there, only that one of our maintenance people located him."

"Alive?" asked Oriannon. She shuddered at the thought.

"Oh, I'm alive, all right."

Oriannon and the others turned to see the Coristan shuttle pilot in his blue coveralls standing at the entry through which they'd just stepped. He rubbed the back of his neck.

"But I'll tell you something," he added, his voice booming through the library. All the scribes froze at their seats. "When I find the Owling who hijacked us, he's going to wish he stayed on his side of the planet."

Carter House Girls Series
from Melody Carlson

Mix six teenage girls and one '60s fashion icon (retired, of course) in an old Victorian-era boarding home. Add boys and dating, a little high school angst, and throw in a Kate Spade bag or two ... and you've got the Carter House Girls, Melody Carlson's new chick lit series for young adults!

Mixed Bags
Book One

Softcover • ISBN: 978-0-310-71488-0

The Carter House residents arrive shortly before high school starts. With a crazy mix of personalities, pocketbooks, and problems, the girls get acquainted, sharing secrets and shoes and a variety of squabbles.

Stealing Bradford
Book Two

Softcover • ISBN: 978-0-310-71489-7

The Carter House girls are divided when two of them go after the same guy. Rhiannon and Taylor are at serious odds, and several girls get hurt before it's over.

Books 3–8 coming soon!

Pick up a copy today at your favorite bookstore!

A Sweet Seasons Novel from Debbie Viguié!

They're fun! They're quirky! They're Sweet Seasons—unlike any other books you've ever read. You could call them alternative, God-honoring chick lit. Join Candy Thompson on a sweet, light-hearted, and honest romp through the friendships, romances, family, school, faith, and values that make a girl's life as full as it can be.

The Summer of Cotton Candy
Book One

Softcover • ISBN: 978-0-310-71558-0

Sixteen-year-old Candace thinks her vacation is ruined when her father forces her to apply for a job at the local amusement park, but when she meets a mysterious "Lone Ranger" there, she finds love and learns the value of true faith and friendship.

Books 2-4 coming soon!

Pick up a copy today at your favorite bookstore!

Forbidden Doors

A Four-Volume Series from Bestselling Author Bill Myers!

Some doors are better left unopened.

Join teenager Rebecca "Becka" Williams, her brother Scott, and her friend Ryan Riordan as they head for mind-bending clashes between the forces of darkness and the kingdom of God.

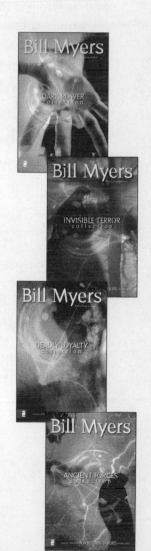

Dark Power Collection

Volume One

Softcover • ISBN: 978-0-310-71534-4

Contains books 1–3: *The Society*, *The Deceived*, and *The Spell*

Invisible Terror Collection

Volume Two

Softcover • ISBN: 978-0-310-71535-1

Contains books 4–6: *The Haunting*, *The Guardian*, and *The Encounter*

Deadly Loyalty Collection

Volume Three

Softcover • ISBN: 978-0-310-71536-8

Contains books 7–9: *The Curse*, *The Undead*, and *The Scream*

Ancient Forces Collection

Volume Four

Softcover • ISBN: 978-0-310-71537-5

Contains books 10–12: *The Ancients*, *The Wiccan*, and *The Cards*

Shadowside

A New Trilogy by Robert Elmer!

Those who live in lush comfort on the bright side of the small planet Corista have plundered the water resources of Shadowside for centuries, ignoring the existence of Shadowside's inhabitants, who are nothing more than animals. Or so the Brightsiders have been taught. It will take a special young woman to expose the truth—and to help avert the war that is sure to follow—in the exciting Shadowside Trilogy, the latest sci-fi adventure from Robert Elmer.

The Owling
Book Two

Softcover • ISBN: 978-0-310-71422-4

Life is turned upside down on Corista for 15-year-old Oriannon and her friends. The planet's axis has shifted, bringing chaos to Brightside and Shadowside. And Jesmet, the music mentor who was executed for saving their lives, is alive and promises them a special power called the Wind—if they'll just wait.

Book 2 coming October 2008!

Pick up a copy today at your favorite bookstore!

Share Your Thoughts

With the Author: Your comments will be forwarded to the author when you send them to *zauthor@zondervan.com*.

With Zondervan: Submit your review of this book by writing to *zreview@zondervan.com*.

Free Online Resources at
www.zondervan.com/hello

 Zondervan AuthorTracker: Be notified whenever your favorite authors publish new books, go on tour, or post an update about what's happening in their lives.

 Daily Bible Verses and Devotions: Enrich your life with daily Bible verses or devotions that help you start every morning focused on God.

 Free Email Publications: Sign up for newsletters on fiction, Christian living, church ministry, parenting, and more.

 Zondervan Bible Search: Find and compare Bible passages in a variety of translations at www.zondervanbiblesearch.com.

 Other Benefits: Register yourself to receive online benefits like coupons and special offers, or to participate in research.